BOARDING PASS
NAME: SCARLETT SMITH
FROM:
TIME:
CLASS:
SEAT:
I0746583
President

AMERICA 100
AMERICA 100
TES OF AMERICA 1
WE TRUST
President

GREASED

THE THUNDERBIRDS SERIES

ALEXCIS MORRIS

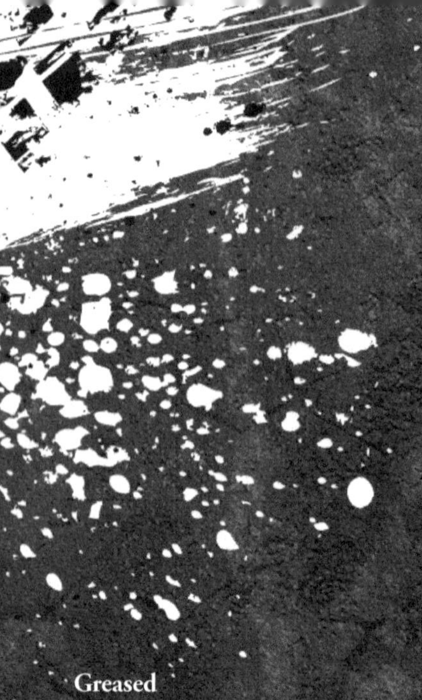

Greased
by Alexcis Morris

Copyright © 2024

Paperback ISBN: 978-1-7635204-4-8

Editing by CJ Editing
Cover Design by Artista Grafico
Formatting by Literary Fox

Dear anxiety and depression,

This book is a big fuck you to you.
You didn't win this time around.
I did and I finished a whole ass book while in the battle.
Suck a fat cock.

If you are struggling with mental health issues, please seek
help and know you aren't alone.
Don't be afraid to reach out if you are struggling.

CONTENT WARNING

You didn't think that this series was all summer lovin' did you?
I'm here to tell you that it gets dark from here on out.
Dark themes are both mentioned and present throughout.

These include, but are not limited to:

-MC/Gang

-Sex Trafficking

-Child Abuse

-Kidnapping

-Suicide/Self and Bodily Harm

-Mental health issues

-Drug and Underage Alcohol Use

-Gun Violence

-Rape and Sexual Assault (briefly mentioned)

-Graphic Sexual Scenes

-Double Penetration

-Group Sex Scenes

-Torture

-Fight Scenes

*If these themes aren't triggering to you,
welcome to the Dark side.*

BOARDING P
NAME: SCARLETT SMIT
FROM:
TIME:
CLA
SEAT:
President

chapter
ONE

scarlett

'm no stranger to heartbreak. It always seems to hit you in the moments that you already know are too good to be true.

Hearts are absolute traitors. Completely and utterly selfish. Zero consideration for any other part in the body other than its own. The heart almost resembles a toddler when they hone in on that bag of lollies at the shops; what they want is what they get. Tantrums are not below them.

We all seem to fall victim to the heart's recklessness from time to time. No matter how the brain believes it prepares itself for any incoming doom ensuring all sorts of walls are built, mine never seems to quite get it right. Even though my delusional self is convinced my walls are impenetrable. That I'm immune to red flags men seem to wave with zero shame. Yet here I am.

Once again.

Completely heartbroken after the most incredible summer of my life. Falling victim to five men who broke down those walls that I thought not even the nastiest of storms could break. The me who, a year ago, would have been ashamed of how quickly those walls fell for a few sets of piercing eyes and a couple of come fuck me smiles.

Come on, they were so fucking cliché it was ridiculous! Fuck boy was their collective persona. Right down to the tattoos that covered nearly their entire bodies. I still don't know why I thought getting caught up with five ridiculously hot American boys was ever going to do my heart any good.

We all knew this thing was going to have a deadline.

One very short but oh so sweet summer. To be honest, I don't think I ever stood a chance. My heart overruled my brain completely. Now I'm sure as fuck paying for it.

Nothing has ever quite hurt this bad.

Well as far as I can remember anyways. Which really isn't that far. At least my brain is the problem here, not my heart.

Of course, I would add the utter bullshit cliché of having fucking amnesia. Having no recollection before the age of 8 is for sure one of the most prominent causes of both mine and my mother's heartbreaks.

Another tick on the scoreboard of life completely fucking me up the ass.

My mother and I were involved in a car accident where my twin brother and father died. Not only did my Mum lose both of them in that accident, but she also lost a part of me. I think that was the worst bit. Waking up out of a 3-month long coma covered in newly healed scars with absolutely no recollection of who I was or who she was, was just the icing on the cake of her absolute devastation. She has to be the most incredible woman that I have ever come across. I've never admired anyone more than I have her.

Through the lengthy hospital stay, numerous doctor's trips and testings, that woman was an absolute force to be reckoned with. She held down her grief for me. I know a lot of other kids don't get the same treatment that I got.

There is a part of me that grieves the loss of my twin and Dad. Even though I have looked over albums upon albums of photos, I've never been able to remember a single detail about either of them. I'm sure my mum thought having them would help but it never did.

Every day I long for what could have been.

No number of stories, no matter how detailed, are ever enough.

Deep in my soul, I feel the loss of my brother. There's not a day that goes by that I don't think about him.

Stupid fucking brain. Stupid fucking heart.

I just wish I could remember a sliver of a detail about him. Mourning a person that you can't remember is just fucking cruel.

I absent-mindedly rub a hand over the tattoo of a dove that sits on my collarbone at the reminder of what I have lost. The heartbreak of waking up each day and grieving a loss that, no matter how much therapy and witchy woo woo I have tried, will ever bring back those memories that are forever lost to me now.

Even though it's been over ten years, the pain hasn't faded. I just know that my brother would have protected me from my current heartbreak. I can't help but daydream about that situation.

What would he have done? I'd like to think he'd act exactly as Noah has been: fucking furious.

Mum always boasts about how protective he was of me. No one stood a chance against Rhodes when it came to me. But would I have even listened to him if he was here?

I sure as fuck didn't listen to my own warning signs that rang out in my head that night at the beach when I first met them. They were like the male version of a siren. Fucking alluring and dangerous. They pulled me into their trap.

I feel dramatic over the fact that I'm heartbroken that they left. But fuck it, I am.

Those five boys changed everything for me.

Again with the cliches but I wasn't going to fuck around with just anyone. It's not like my virginity is sacred to me or anything, but it just felt wrong for me to lose it so some random bloke at a yardy while we were pissed.

I'm all for sexual positivity and if having a roster or sleeping with whichever person you find at the club is your thing, then go girl.

But for me, it just isn't. Which may seem weird because I'm pretty sure that I am in fact in love with five men.

They took my heart with them the day they left.

No amount of preparation could have equipped me for the day I said goodbye to Dawson, Nicky, Dacre, Sonny and Pike as they boarded their plane back to the States. My heart aches at the reminder of them and the utter devastation that followed in the days and weeks after. I don't think I've ever cried the way I did as I watched their plane leave.

Cue the violins.

Before they left, we had made so many plans.

Talks of my flying to them and them flying here so we can see each other. We exchanged every form of communication so that we could always talk. Yet, it's been nine months and I haven't heard a single peep. No phone calls, no facetimes, no texts, no dms, no snaps, no letters, no pigeon carriers. Nothing. It's like their plane just disappeared.

It didn't, mind you, because I checked. Multiple times.

They just did. Like they never existed.

Slowly starting to feel like my heartbreak is justified.

To dream of what could have been, to plan all of these

things you could have done, to fall in fucking love for God's sake to just be shattered in the end.

Fuck men.

BOARDING P
NAME: SCARLETT SMITH
FROM:
TIME:
CLA
SEAT:
President

chapter
TWO

scarlett

A cool nip of the fading winter's breeze bites at my skin, shaking me out of my self loathing. It's a welcome change to the sun's rays that were beating down on my skin, causing a light sheen of sweat to form.

I slowly get up and dust the sand off my ass. The beach has always been a place of peace for me. Whether it's to scream and cry after being overwhelmed thanks to one too many difficult doctor's sessions or just to simply think and reflect.

In the early days after I woke up from the coma, I would find myself sitting down at the beach, be that day or night, and just looking out over the ocean. Mum never seemed to mind my disappearing acts, at least not after the first time I went missing. I admit it probably wasn't a good idea to just up and leave in the way I did but I was an eight year old in need of an escape. The beach provided that for me. Mum understood that, as long as I had my location turned on my phone. It has now become a habit, one that never fails to dull down any unwanted feelings that seem to plague my mind.

It is my place of serenity. My escape from reality.

That, along with music.

Thankfully we live a few streets back from the beach, so my midnight beach escapades were never too much of a concern for Mum. It also helps that basically everyone knows everyone in our town. Trouble rarely finds its way to us. Not like any of that would stop her anxiety when it comes to me.

As I turn, I can't help but wish I could stay at the beach longer today but the near constant buzzing of my phone in my back pocket means Mum really must want me home. I don't bother checking it as I begin my slow walk home. I know exactly what it will say and I would give anything to prolong the quiet inside my mind. Even just for a moment longer.

The walk home from the beach goes way too quick as I look up at our house. My Jeep Wrangler sits in the driveway and I can't help but smile remembering the way Mum dressed it up for my 17th birthday. I swear it could have floated away with the number of balloons that were hanging off it, let alone the few she jammed inside the car. She knew that gifting me a car would be the perfect gift. The gift of an easy escape to my favourite beach, Five Rocks. Only accessible by four-wheel drive, it will forever be my happy place.

My gaze lingers on the unfamiliar blacked-out SUV that also sits in the driveway. I eye it with caution. Mum rarely has visitors over and the few she does definitely don't drive anything like that.

I slowly unlock the door trying to make as little noise as possible so as not to disturb her and whoever she's entertaining.

"Scar, is that you sweetie?"

I jolt, realising that my attempts to be quiet were unsuccessful.

"Yeah Mum." I call back, cringing at my not so subtle attempt of getting inside unseen.

"Can you come into the lounge room for a second? There's something we need to tell you."

We? Weird.

Her voice has a slight edge to it that instantly puts me on guard.

As I walk into the room, my attention is instantly drawn to the blonde man sitting on the couch next to a much older man. The two of them look almost identical. The man who I assume is the father, is quite literally built like a brick shithouse. His blonde hair that's slowly darkening in age is effortlessly styled on his head, like he just brushes his hands through it in the mornings. A beard of short stubbled greys, kept short on his face.

He's dressed casually, or from what I gather from the brand name I can see on his shirt, as casually as he can.

Blondie beside him is staring back at me with a shocked look on his face.

His hair is tousled effortlessly on his head, like he woke up, shook is head and said fuck it.

His face is cleanly shaved, unlike his fathers.

His eyes are a vibrant blue that tugs at something in my chest. My gaze darts back to his father's. The same icy orbs stare back at me.

The strangest feeling comes over me, sending a shiver down my spine. Kind of like déjà vu.

I feel a hint of recognition but I can't place it. Why do these men look so familiar?

I shake myself out of my stare down of these two blokes and look over at Mum. She has the strangest look on her face.

"What's up Mum?"

The entire room seems to stay silent for what feels like

forever but is most likely only moments. I can feel the gaze of the duo on the couch locked onto me but I keep mine on Mum who can't seem to decide where to look. I watch as she tries to find her words but each time she opens her mouth, they fail her. She exhales, rubbing her hands over her face and braces herself like she's going to, finally, begin speaking.

"Scarlett?" The rich American accent shocks me. My name rolls off his tongue like he has used it a million times before.

My head snaps over to Blondie who slowly starts rising out of his chair. Tears start to well in his eyes and in that moment it clicks. Those eyes are the exact same as mine. I eye him wearily, slowly taking a step back.

"W-who are you? Mum, what's happening right now?"

I stumble as I glance back over at Mum who now has noticeable tear tracks all over her face. I then finally take notice of the bodyguards standing either side of the door I just walked through. What the fuck is going on right now?

Blondie slowly makes his way over to stand in front of me. I have to tilt my head to look up at him. While I'm not short by any means, this guy is well over 6 feet.

"There is no way."

"My baby girl."

The deep husky voice makes me snap my head over to the other guy.

At this rate, I'm going to have fucking whiplash. Another man with an American accent. Fuck what is it with these blokes? And 'baby girl'? I don't know who this guy thinks I am, but I'm certainly not *his* anything. Both him and Mum make their way over to me. I take a further step back. I slowly feel my fight or flight start to ramp up.

My head darts around as I eye all the exits in the room, cursing under my breath as I realise the only one is the doorway behind me. Unless I wanted to jump out the window. I don't know if I'm that desperate yet.

"Scarlett, I'm sorry baby. Um, I, ah…"

She begins to stumble over her words as her eyes bounce between the three of us.

The man places his arm on my Mum's back and my eyes zone in on where his hand meets her. I then slowly take in their body language as Mum continues to stumble on her words as she tries to answer my 'what the fuck' question. Not once in the last ten years have I ever seen Mum remotely show any kind of intimacy with a man. Not once.

"I don't really know how to explain myself, Scar but ah…

Mum's gaze finally meets mine. Her eyes are bloodshot. The waterproof mascara that she put on this morning looks like it has put up a fight to stay on her lashes after being rubbed with a tissue.

"Rhodes."

Blondie chokes out. My gaze snaps to him as my eyes widen.

"Sorry, what did you just say?" I look at the guy in disbelief. Why the fuck is he mentioning my dead brother?

"My name is Rhodes."

My eyes remain locked on him for a moment as I try to process what he's saying. His name is Rhodes. Okay. A chuckle escapes me that slowly develops into a full on laugh. "If that's your version of a joke," I pause, trying to collect myself, "You aren't very funny mate."

"He's right Scar. This is your brother, Rhodes and your dad, Ren."

"Yeah, nice try Mum. It's not April Fools yet." I say, shaking my head.

"I'm not joking baby. They are here. They are alive."

I scoff and shake my head. She can't be fucking serious, can she? I feel like I stand there for hours as my gaze bounces around to the three faces staring back at mine.

My brain slowly starts to process what I've been told.

My brother and father are *alive* and they are standing in front of me right now.

What?

I shake my head before my eyes dart between the two men in front of me. Again.

My brain starts to throb at the information as it filters in amongst the mix of emotions that begin to plague me.

There is just no way.

For ten years I have been told these people were dead. How could they possibly be alive? How are they standing in front of me right now?

An intense feeling of betrayal pulses through my being.

Amongst my confusion, I know one thing for certain, I have been lied to.

Is anything I have come to believe real?

For years I had been convinced that I had lost two members of my family. Two people I had to re-learn were important to me, judging by the photos I was given.

Nothing knows persistence like a nine-year-old who has been told that she has a father and twin brother that died in an accident that she also should have. I remember carrying those photos around with me for months trying to re jog my memory. Like if I held onto them long enough it all would have just been some kind of nightmare.

"My sister. It's really you."

The guy apparently named Rhodes begins to step towards me as though to pull me in for a hug. My hand shoots out at the last minute to stop him and he quickly halts his advance. The smile on his face instantly dropping.

I take a further step back and begin shaking my head.

"No. No."

The tears that have begun creeping up on me, escape. Even if I wanted to stop them, there is no way that I could. Not now. Not when everything I had once believed has just come crashing down.

"I don't know what kind of sick game you are playing right now but my brother is dead. My Dad is dead. An-and I should be too." I shake my head, unable to hide the way my voice starts to shake.

"Fuck this."

I turn and bolt straight back out of the front door. They each call my name as I let flight takeover, but fuck them. Mum and I have never turned down a good opportunity to play a prank on each other, but they have always been light-hearted. Whoopee cushions and cling wrap over the toilet seat. Never something like this. What the fuck is she thinking? Pretending that those two yobbos are my family.

My *dead* family.

I don't even have to think of where I'm going. I eye my dirt bike that sits just outside the garage. I throw on my helmet, not even bothering to do up the buckle. It can wait. I kick up my stand and start the bike. Taking off down the driveway, I don't bother to look behind me. All I'll see is my mother's betrayal. The raw feeling of grief almost blinds me. It probably wasn't the smartest idea to get on my bike in the state I'm in, but I don't care.

The ride down the Farmborough beach is short. While I would have much preferred going up to Five Rocks, this late in the afternoon without a big group isn't a smart idea. I don't particularly feel like going head-to-head with a kangaroo that wants to play chicken.

BOARDING P
NAME: SCARLETT SMIT
FROM:
TIME:
CLAS
SEAT:
President

chapter
THREE

I collapse onto the soft sand as a scream of pain rips from my throat. I clench my hair in my hands as I pull my knees up to my chest just as another scream is torn from me.

How could they?

How could they do this to me?

Rip apart everything I knew.

My entire life has been a lie.

Everything I thought I knew is just pretend. None of it was real.

It feels like my life has been snatched from me yet again.

The one person that I have put all my trust into since the moment I woke up from the coma lied to me.

My brother isn't dead.

My father isn't dead.

Rhodes is alive.

My father is alive.

But I feel like I'm dead.

My heart clenches again as another wave of pain overcomes me.

It is all consuming in a way I have never felt before.

Nothing has ever compared to this.

Not when my life was explained to me ten years ago. Not when the five boys broke my heart and left the pieces to fall where they may.

How could they do this to me?

My parents lied to me. They allowed me to believe that two members of my family had been lost to me. Dead and gone like the remains of my soul.

They convinced me that I was just a normal girl that led a normal life.

What they didn't seem to realise is that I am smarter than what they believe I obviously am.

The kinds of clothes my father and brother were wearing don't point to a normal life.

I try to make sense of everything but it just seems to hurt more.

I allow myself to lift my head, wiping the tears and snot from my face.

Maybe later I will care about how disgusting it is but right now isn't the time for that.

All I am able to feel is betrayal.

Betrayal at my mother for feeding me these lies all of these years.

Anger at my father for allowing any of this.

Bitter at both of them for deceiving me for so long. Allowing me to finally start breaking out from the soul-crushing months that followed that fateful summer, all for it to just come crashing down again.

And my brother. I can't even begin to decipher just how I feel towards him.

While a part of me is angry and confused, another also feels relieved. Because amongst all of the hurt I felt in the moments of candour, I could see my feelings reflected in his.

Was he deceived like me?

Did he go all these years thinking I too was dead?

Is he angry at our parents?

God, my twin. The person I shared a womb with.

A person I never thought I would ever be able to know, left with only mentions of him. Memories told by second hand experiences.

How can I even believe them when they were told by the person who has spent so long lying to me?

Did she lie about them too?

Is truly everything I know a lie?

I curl even further on myself, allowing the pain to take over.

Maybe the waves will wash me away, taking my pain right along with them.

BOARDING P
NAME: SCARLETT SMIT
FROM:
TIME:
CLA
SEAT:
President

chapter FOUR

The sun has well and truly set by the time I hop back on my bike and begin the ride home. I feel drained after having cried more tears than I think I ever have before in my life. Nearing almost being sick because of the raw grief that tore me apart.

The last few hours feel like they are on repeat in my head.

My Mum's betrayal.

The return of my father and brother.

My accident.

Repeat.

And fuck while I'm at it, why not bring up the other five Americans that all but broke my heart.

Yep. Certainly not a stranger to heartbreak it seems.

The blacked-out SUV is still sitting in front of the house as I turn down my street. For some reason, I thought it may have been gone. Unfortunately, I'm not that lucky.

As I pull into the driveway, I notice my Mum's car is gone though.

I slowly take off my helmet and blow out a deep breath. I take my time hopping off my bike. As some kind of safety net that if they were to come barrelling out trying to ambush me, I can just take off again.

I'm sure Grace wouldn't mind a last minute sleepover.

The house is quiet as I make my way inside. Normally, Mum would have dinner on the table by now. The strict 6pm dinner every single night. It is used as our way to decompress and talk about our days. It's the one tradition that Mum likes to keep with the number of hours she works.

I make my way back into that same dreaded lounge room I stood in only hours earlier.

The room is empty except for Blondie, or should I say 'Rhodes', who has his head in his hands.

"Ahh, hey," I whisper quietly trying not to scare him.

Blondie-Rhodes shoots out of his chair, almost falling over in the process.

"S-s-Scar, hey. Ah, are you alright?'

"Nope," I reply, popping the P. There is no point in sugar coating it for this guy. I cringe at the thought of what I most likely look like.

"I'm sorry. When Dad told me that you were still alive, I had a similar reaction."

"Right." I draw out still not believing this guy's story. "Now let's say that you actually are my supposed dead twin brother that is actually alive and that I cannot remember whatsoever, how are you actually alive?"

Blondie-Rhodes breathes out a deep sigh, "It's a really long story."

"I'm sure we have plenty of time. Where is Mum and older blondie anyways?" I ask, remembering the missing car from the garage.

"They went out to get what Mum said it's, uhh, hot chook

rolls?" He laughs awkwardly as he brings his hand up to scratch the back of his head.

"Hot chook is a roast chicken. We normally have it on a burger bun with a bit of pasta salad." I confirm but can't help but cringe at the familiarity of teaching an American about Australian traditions. A month of doing so will do that to you. I can't even see a koala without having flashbacks.

"Oh yep, right." He nods in some kind of attempt to act casual but he fails. Epically.

We both then go silent as we look at each other. I take him in. Over the years, Mum has filled me in on all the details of the things the amnesia wiped which was quite literally my entire life before eight years old.

Mum said that Rhodes and I were identical twins, which for boy/girl twins is an extremely low chance. We did everything together. Had the same group of friends, insisted on sharing the same room up until our eighth birthday, and liked all of the same foods. We even sang together. While Mum said that Rhodes could sing, it was obvious that it was a natural talent for me.

The raw devastation I felt earlier seems to have slipped further back into my mind, leaving room for common sense to prevail. I really look at the guy. Take him in without bias and heartbreak clouding my thoughts. It's been ten years and a lot has changed in that time, but it's clear to me that this guy isn't lying to me.

Blondie is Rhodes.

Mum wasn't lying.

My mouth drops as I stare at him. Tears well in my eyes again. I swallow roughly, trying to gain control of my feelings but it's futile. My brother is alive. He didn't die.

It was one thing to come to terms with it when I was alone, on the beach. But now it is impossible to ignore.

A piece of me feels like it knits back together in that moment. Even amidst the betrayal I feel rooting itself deeper, I can't deny what's right in front of me.

After years of missing a part of me, of wanting so desperately to remember my brother, he is now looking directly at me. Waiting to gauge how I am going to react.

The similarities between Rhodes and I are obvious. From our hair, our face shape, nose and most obviously, our eyes.

"You really are Rhodes," I whisper. If he wasn't paying such close attention to me, he probably wouldn't have heard me.

"And you really are Scarlett. My sister."

Rhodes wastes no time in rushing towards me. I'm squished into his embrace as he picks me up and spins me around. I tighten my arms around his neck. My brother.

Even though the block in my brain holds strong, it's like my soul knows him. It's like some kind of weird twin thing. Probably not, but I grasp at straws trying to make sense of the entire situation.

The number one thing that rolls over in my mind is, my brother is alive.

New tears fall freely down my cheeks. But instead of being laced with grief, they are happy. So fucking happy.

"God Scar. I never thought I would see you again." Rhodes' voice is muffled by my hair that he has his face buried in.

I pull away from him slowly. While I feel fucking elated that he is alive, it still seems insane. A strange awkwardness settles in the air.

"This is weird," I blurt, unable to hold back the thought.

Rhodes laughs, "You're telling me."

"Glad I'm not the only one." I cringe remembering my reaction to him earlier, "I'm sorry about the way I reacted earlier. It's not every day your Mum tells you that your brother and father aren't actually dead."

Rhodes cringes as well, "Yeah, it isn't their finest moment that's for sure."

He scratches his head and blows out a breath.

We both stand there just looking at each other. Neither of us clearly know what to do or say. While it is clear we are both relieved that the other is actually here, ten years have passed. Neither of us know each other anymore.

I highly doubt his favourite superhero is still Spiderman.

"Um, so did Mum say how long she was going to be?" I say breaking the silence. I'm thankful no one else is around to witness our awkward interaction.

"I think she said ten minutes or so."

I nod my head.

We go silent again.

I try to think of something to say but I come up short.

What do I say to him? How's the weather?

"Did you want to sit down and talk?" Rhodes says, finally breaking the silence. I breathe a sigh of relief, nodding my head.

We walk over to the couches. I take one and he takes the other.

I twist my hands in my lap, anxiety slowly seeping into my system. I try to prepare myself for whatever Rhodes is about to tell me, not knowing the full extent of whatever this will be.

"There is a lot that both Dad and um.. Mum are better off explaining to you because they know the details better than I do. There's a lot of backstory." I nod, encouraging him to continue.

He takes a breath, "Long story short is, I was told that you and Mom had died. I never felt grief like that before in my life. I went insane. We did everything together, glued at the hip. A couple of other guys were part of our little group and while they loved you and you loved them back, I just wasn't as close with them as you were. You were my best friend, Scar. Knowing Mum had died hurt so bad, but losing you destroyed a part of my soul. After I came out of the haze, I vowed to myself that I would never let anyone feel the pain I did. I turned myself into a soldier. A weapon."

Rhodes pauses and shakes his head. He looks up at me slowly. A few tears escape his eyes and my heart clenches at the sight.

"Not a single day has gone by where I have not missed you. I've done a lot of stupid shit. My early teens were brutal. Me and one of our friends at the time couldn't handle it. Losing you was just too much. Drugs became our coping mechanism.

"While he was closer to losing his battles than I was, I just wanted to destroy shit. It took a long time for Dad to snap me out of it. So, when he came to me and told me that you were alive, all of that hurt that I had learnt to deal with all these years ago just came rushing back in full force. I completely smashed up my room and the majority of the house. I went on a three-day bender. I was a mess," He says with a grimace.

"To be honest, I still kind of am. It feels weird to see you sitting here in front of me only ten years older. It's like no time has passed yet a million years have.

"I will never let anything bad happen to you ever again, Scar. I may be the younger twin, but I refuse to let you go now that I have you back. The last ten years have been torture," He utters, almost like he is pleading his case with me.

In a way I can understand the way he is feeling. I went through my own kind of hell. I try to sympathise with him. To see it from his point of view. He remembers me. I'm not a stranger to him. Yet, he still is to me.

I shuffle towards him, grabbing his hands in my own. He looks down at them, like they are a lifeline.

"I know we are in this weird kind of middle phase, neither of us really knowing how to be or how to act. But one thing I know is, if you really are my brother, know that I'm not going anywhere. It's going to be a long journey. But I'm here," I say, trying my best to reassure him.

He nods his head as a sob escapes his chest. My hands tighten in his own automatically.

It's so easy to be blinded by your own grief at times. But seeing Rhodes be so vulnerable and pour his heart out to me, does something to me.

He can remember me. He lost his sister and his mum too.

He thought he lost me. That thought is staggering.

For years he has had to live with that fact. Waking up each and every day knowing the other half of him was gone. Because that's what we are. Two halves of a whole being.

While I knew I had lost him, it was different for me. While I felt as though a part of me had been severed from my being, I still had no memory. All I had to go off with was information from mum.

Yet, he remembers it all.

A part of my heart aches for him. It aches for the time we have lost. The utter betrayal that we have both faced in our parents' decisions. The fact that they allowed both of us to be devastated and expected to just keep on living. Until what? They just decided it was time to be a family again?

Yeah, fuck that.

Rhodes' breathing eventually calms enough that I'm able to pull my hands from his grip. He wipes the tears from his face and I watch as he collects himself before looking up at me.

"I want to know everything about what I have missed, Scar. How you were after you woke up. What your interests are now. If you still sing."

"I still sing." I smile up at him. The one I get in return is devastating.

"You do?" He asks.

"Yeah." I nod, "It's the one thing that Mum says refused to leave me even after the accident."

"You were always walking around belting out some song at the top of your lungs," he laughs.

"Honestly not much has changed."

We both laugh. A warm feeling settles over me. It feels strange to laugh with him like this but in another way, it feels so right.

We both turn our heads as we hear Mum's car pull up outside. Rhodes is the first to stand nodding towards the garage door.

"Come on, let's go give them a hand. If what you said is true, I'm sure they will need our assistance."

I nod my head and follow him towards the door.

I pause when I come face to face with my father. We stare at each other for a moment. Neither of us utter a single word.

"I'm sorry, Scarlett," he says, finally breaking his silence.

I nod at him. I can't say things like 'it's okay' because it's not. It's not okay. It's not okay that they lied to both Rhodes and I for ten years.

Led each other to believe we were alone in the world. Deceived us so greatly that I fear the mark will be buried too deep.

My father looks at me, like he's searching for something I don't know what he's hoping to find. Maybe the, now healed, wounds from my 'accident'.

Mum takes that opportunity to make herself known,

clearing her throat to get our attention.

Her arms are full of grocery bags as well as Rhodes' who resembles a pack horse.

My father runs over to her, collecting the bags from her arms.

I watch them both closely. It always stumped me on why my Mum hadn't moved on after ten years. No matter the amount of encouragement from me, she would flat out refuse to date other men. There was always an excuse.

But now, looking at the way she smiles up at him like the world begins and ends with him, it all starts to make sense. She never moved on because that wasn't an option for her.

My father was still hers and, hopefully, she is still his.

Mum looks over at me with a sad smile, "Why don't we go inside and make some dinner? Have a talk."

I nod my head and turn my back on the three of them. Anger still fuels my every move.

Seeing them out there trying to play happy family like my life hasn't completely imploded on me.

Like they didn't just take everything I know and crush it into pieces.

What even is real anymore?

Fuck, is my name even Scarlett Smith at this point?

BOARDING P
NAME: SCARLETT SMIT
FROM:
TIME:
CLA.
SEAT:
President

chapter
FIVE

scarlett

Turns out my name isn't Scarlett Smith. I should have seen it coming but fuck, I didn't expect them to stoop that low. To the point of changing my identity that greatly.

I push away the hot chook roll. The normally delicious meal now tastes like ash in my mouth. I force myself to swallow the mouthful I had just taken.

I sit there for a moment in complete disbelief. They aren't kidding are they? This isn't some bullshit episode of pranked? No this is real life.

I look up at them, raising an eyebrow, "Enlighten me then. What is my actual name? For God's sake let it not be some bullshit like Karen."

Knowing my luck today, that would be my name.

"The only thing we changed is your last name. Your name is Scarlett Crux."

I frown, damn. That's actually not that bad. Thank God. It's actually kind of cool.

"So why did my name have to be changed? I need a start to finish explanation. None of these half truths."

My father sighs as he sets down his roll. Clearly he isn't turned off his food like I am. Rhodes certainly isn't. The guy is on his third round.

I keep my eyes on my father as I wait for something. I watch as he collects himself. This cool kind of persona coming over him. He eventually looks up at me, resigned.

"My father – your grandfather – was the previous president of The Thunderbirds. Originally they started out as a motorcycle club. But my father wasn't happy with just rolling around on bikes and running the couple of small businesses he had. He wanted more."

My eyes widen and my mouth drops. What. The. Fuck.

He nods and continues, "At first it was things like selling drugs, weapons and laundering. But it was never enough. He was greedy. Eventually the opportunity fell into his lap to step into the prostitution game. Once he had a taste, he became hungrier.

"I wish I could say that's where he stopped but I can't." He looks up at me and a raw pain fills his gaze.

I know that whatever he is about to tell me will change the entire trajectory of my life. I can feel it in the air. This kind of live static. An omen for what's to come.

I hold my breath waiting for the inevitable bomb that is about to drop. My father looks to my mother. Her eyes are glazed over slightly, tears blur her irises as she looks back at him and nods in resignation.

He looks back at me, directly in my eyes as he delivers the brutal blow, "He sunk his teeth into the skin trade."

I gasp, sitting up straighter as I look between both my parents in complete disbelief. Anger floods my system, threatening to boil over. Nausea clenches my stomach as a million and one images float through my mind.

I shake my head, "No." I manage to gasp out but it's only a whisper.

Tears stream down my mother's face as she nods. If I had tears left to cry, I know they would be flooding down my face, but there's none left. Nothing but gut-wrenching grief.

"My twin brother, Clinton grew up to be exactly like my father. Nothing but a ruthless savage. He was in his element with the trafficking rings. He ran them like a fucking ring master at a circus."

I shiver at the image. My entire being fills with hatred for a man I don't know. Or alas don't remember.

"There was a standoff one day against us and a rival gang. We had already been climbing the ranks for years. We were involved with international organisations like the Bratva and the Cartels. Other gangs were envious and there was always someone who wanted to take down the big guys. My father was killed during this skirmish. I was next in line to take over. His heir.

"Clinton hated it. We had never gotten along, him and I. He was always jealous. The hatred only grew when I took over. The love my father and Clinton shared for the rings was never shared with me. I hate them. They make me sick."

Relief fills me hearing the clear animosity he has for them and their… activities.

"Together with the majority of the leadership, we stopped all activity with the skin trade. Clinton was furious. There was a situation and he left. We completely cleaned the club out. Anyone that wanted to be a part of that shit was removed."

I can't help but shiver at the word *removed*. Even though I agree wholeheartedly with whatever underlying meaning and actions that word has doesn't mean it doesnt give me the fucking heebie-jeebies.

"Things were good for a couple of months. We still kept our toes in drugs, weapons and other side businesses. One of the guys got word of a new club that had begun taking women off the street and selling them to high rollers. A couple of the guys and I began investigating them. At every turn just as we got a new lead, a road block came up. For months we tried tracking them until, eventually, we got an in."

My father shakes his head, the ghosts of his past haunting him to this day. He lifts his head up but instead of looking at me, he looks at Mum. They communicate something between each other.

"It's okay, Ren. They need to know. They deserve to know the full truth."

I look sharply between the both of them as if I can read their secrets off their face alone. I feel my heart as it starts to race.

My father stays silent as he fights with himself. It's my Mum that breaks the silence.

"I was taken off the streets one night when I was walking home from work. I had just moved to Los Angeles for a gap year. I thought I would do some travelling before coming home and working out what I wanted to do with my life. I didn't hear the car as it pulled up behind me. I barely felt the needle as it stabbed into the back of my neck."

I gasp, covering my mouth as I look at her in disbelief.

She swallows roughly as she looks between Rhodes and I. I don't turn my head to gauge his reaction to the revelation but I see his hands grip the table, his knuckles turning white in my periphery.

"I woke up in a cage. It wasn't even big enough for me to stretch out completely. I was stripped bare of all of my belongings. Left in just my underwear. Men would come around and occasionally give us stale bread and cups of water. Just enough to survive.

"Once a day we were taken to relieve ourselves. Then thrown straight back into the cage. They held me and twenty other women for months. Not once did any of us see the light of day.

"They made a sick game out of us; find the one who could scream the loudest."

A lone tear drops down my cheek. I didn't think I had anything left in me, but never in my wildest dreams could I have expected this.

Mum rubs a hand over a scar on her arm and my face pales. She always told me it was from a motorbike accident but it is clear that was just a lie. One I am actually grateful she hid from me.

"One day, we heard shots from outside. I was terrified. I closed my eyes and huddled in on myself just waiting for it to end. Waiting for it to be my turn. When a hand landed on my arm, I thought my day had finally come. But the same hand lifted my face up."

She turns to look at my father, grabbing his hand and squeezing it tight.

"It was your Dad."

My heart clenches as I look at the two of them. The grateful look on my Mum's face. The raw devastation but shared relief on my father's.

"I couldn't believe it when I unlocked the cage and found your mother. She was, and still is, the most beautiful woman I have ever seen in my life."

A tear drips down my father's face as they hold their gaze for a moment longer before looking at Rhodes and I.

"From that moment on, I knew my purpose in life. For twenty years we have been infiltrating sex trafficking rings all over the United States. We have saved hundreds of women."

I nod as I wipe the tears from my eyes. Even while feeling such anguish over the callous acts my parents have survived, I can't help but feel proud. Proud that they overcame something so horrendous. That still to this day, my father and his gang is able to fight against something so unbearable.

The realisation that my father is a part of a gang still hasn't left my mind though. Not just part of, but *runs*. As I look at the man, it makes sense though. The way he is dressed and that air of authority he seems to radiate gives it away.

The bodyguards are fairly obvious now too.

We all stay silent for a few minutes. Or has it been hours? I don't really know. Time feels weird as I slowly process everything. Trying to organise it in my brain somehow. To go through the motions of just how catastrophic the entire situation is.

"Do either of you have any questions?" My father finally says, breaking the silence.

I have hundreds of them. Thousands. But one comes to the forefront of my mind.

"How does all of this relate to me losing my memories?" I do my best to not try to take away the severity of my parents situation from them but it feels like I fail.

My father nods though in understanding.

"We were so excited when you and Rhodes were born. The entire club was. Not only were we blessed with a pregnancy but twins.

"You were both perfect. Scarlett, you came first." My father chuckles as he looks at me. "From the moment you took your first breath, you had this sheer determination. You were so strong. This light about you."

He looks over to Rhodes, "And my boy, from moment one, you adored your sister. You were fiercely protective of everything. You had this crease in between your eyes as you looked out at the world."

My Mum chuckles as she looks at Rhodes and I, "My light and my warrior."

"As you were first born Scarlett, it was always written that you would one day take over from me."

I blanch as my gaze snaps to my father. "Excuse me?"

He nods his head, "You are my heir Scarlett. Destined to take over The Thunderbirds when I retire."

I snort, "You are joking right? Please tell me you are joking."

The last bit comes out pleading. They can't be serious right now. From the look on both my parents' faces, they are deadly serious.

"It's true," my mother says with a nod.

I sit back in my chair as I process exactly what I'm saying. It feels like everything I had been told of my world flashes before my eyes. Here I was struggling with the fact that in only two months I would be graduating high school and would need to work out what the fuck my plan was. Did I want to go to university? Take a gap year and travel? Stay at my cafe job?

Taking on the roll as heir to a fucking gang certainly wasn't on the list. Shit, it didn't even enter my realm of possibilities.

But here we are.

Eventually I nod, "Okay. Yep. So what happened next?" I ask. My brain already feeling fried but if we are going to lay it all out, we might as well do it right now.

"From the moment you were ready, I began training both you and Rhodes. I never wanted either of you to be left in the dark or deceived when it came to what was expected of either of you."

I can't help but snort at the audacity but it doesn't phase or stop my father. He knows my feelings on the matter are justified.

"We had planned a massive party for your joint eighth birthday. The entire club was invited. I don't think I had ever seen either of you so happy before. Everything was going great until a bunch of vans pulled up."

My fathers fists tighten where they are held together on the table in front of him.

"We tried to collect all of you kids and hide you back in the clubhouse. But you never shied away from a fight, Scarlett. Other organisations were mad I had a female heir. Demanded that Rhodes take your spot but I disagreed. Just like me, the first born is the heir. We see it in royals so why couldn't you be mine?"

He demands, slamming his fist on the table. He collects himself quickly as he looks up at me in apology. I nod my head in understanding.

"They found you. The Scorpions. The club my fucking brother created."

My eyes widen and I feel my stomach clench. Words evade me completely.

"We tried for a week to find you. I couldn't sleep. I didn't stop trying to find you. On the seventh day of you being gone from us, we eventually got a lead."

He gulps, "When we found you, you were completely unrecognisable. You had been beaten beyond recognition. If you were left for another twenty four hours, it would have been too late."

I stay stock still as I look directly at my father. My brain swims, a heavy ache setting in right behind my eyes. Absently, I trail my hand over one of the scars on my side. A wound I was told was from the car accident I was in.

There was never a car accident.

I was taken as a child. Beaten by my uncle. Left for dead. My childhood was stolen from me. Everything I knew ripped from me.

I push myself up from my chair. I hear it crash down behind me but the time for caring is gone. Long fucking gone.

I turn from the table. I hear voices behind me but they are drowned out from the whooshing I hear.

I feel like I'm underwater. Drowning. Unable to breathe.

I eventually come to, starting as I look out over the now pitch black ocean. Waves only lightened by the full moon.

I don't know how long I've been out here.

I turn sharply as I hear the sand crunching behind me. My father walks towards me. His hair is messy, like he has spent the last however long running his hands through it.

"Your mum said I would be able to find you here."

I nod, unable to trust myself to speak right now. I don't know if I would even be able to form the words.

My father sits down beside me, bringing his knees up and laying his arms over them.

"I wish that I could make this all better for you. I never wanted this life for you. I didn't even want this life for myself. When I found your mother it was like the world finally made sense to me. That I was given a purpose, a reason to fight. That was made even more prominent when you and your brother arrived."

He shakes his head as he turns to look at me, "If I could have protected you both from this life, I would have. I should have packed us up the moment I found out your mother was pregnant. Escaped to here. Built a life far away from the darkness.

"It is something I will regret every day for the rest of my life."

I nod my head. Yet I can't help but feel like his regret is misplaced. Uncalled for.

"You didn't know all of this was going to happen. It's not your fault," I say, my voice rough and broken.

"It's every parent's first responsibility to protect their children. I failed you Scarlett. You were mine to protect and I allowed them to take you. Allowed them to destroy my little girl."

I shake my head, "It wasn't your fault. It's theirs. They saw me as some kind of bargaining chip."

He shakes his head. I know he disagrees with me but I can't help but see the otherside. I can see in his eyes just how hard this entire situation has been for him. I refuse to play the victim. Pull the 'poor me' card and allow myself to be walked over again and again.

That's not who I am. I refuse to be seen in that light. Be seen as weak.

I am a woman. I am strong.

"What happened after I was taken?" I ask. My voice is still meek but I don't bother to strengthen it just yet. Allowing myself to grieve a little bit more for that little girl.

My father sighs before rubbing his hands over his face.

"We rushed you to our doctor but we knew it would be too much for him to handle. Your mother knew a doctor back here in Australia, someone that we could trust. An old family friend who she knew would be able to save your life. The doctor was able to stabilise you enough for the flight. It was touch and go but you and your mother landed here safely."

"From the moment I watched the plane taxiing down the runway, I knew neither of you would be returning to us for a long time. I formulated a plan and ran it past your mother. It killed me to do so but the only thing I could see was your body, black and blue, huddled in a corner barely breathing. I had to protect you. It was the only way I could see to protect you."

He looks down at the ground like he is unable to look at me directly.

"I faked you and your mother's deaths."

I nod my head, having come to the same conclusion.

"The entire club was devastated. I was devastated. While I stayed in touch with your mother in regards to your condition, it felt like you had truly died. When you finally woke up and we found out you had lost all of your memories, we thought we had made the right decision in keeping you away. We didn't want to put the burden of this life back on your shoulders. But we also didn't want it to be forever. The end goal was to always bring our families back together when the time was right."

"And the time is right, now?" I question.

He nods his head, "Yes," he pauses and chuckles, "well I hope it is."

"What happens now?" I ask.

"No one except myself and your Mum know that you are actually alive. And now your brother. If it is okay with you, I want to bring you home."

"Home?" I ask.

"Los Angeles. Or more specifically, Rydell. We are in one of the smaller suburbs outside of the city."

I look at him curiously as my head spins at the thought of going to LA. A place I have wanted to visit for the longest time. Was it a part of my subconscious that was drawn there? Like a small part of me knew that is where I was from.

All along I thought I was Aussie through and through. Little did I know that I am actually American.

I instantly question my accent.

"Why don't I have an accent like you and Rhodes?"

My father chuckles, "I think that's one of the things that was lost along with your memories. Your mother said that you had a bit of trouble speaking the first few days after you woke up."

I nod.

"I don't really understand it but I think you just adapted to what was around you."

I nod again, his explanation making sense to me at least.

"What will be expected of me?"

"That is all up to you Scarlett. I would love for you to consider coming back into the fold. Your brother is my current heir but we both discussed what my wants are. I want you to retake your spot again as my heir."

I sigh having already come to the same realisation that that is what he had probably wanted. I sit for a moment as I think about it.

The idea doesn't turn me off as much as I thought it would. It terrifies me, sure. But the thought of helping women. Doing good in this world even while I still have to lead in sin, doesn't turn me off completely. It feels like the good might outweigh the bad.

Not only that but I'll get to be with my family. I'll get to know them again. Reform bonds that I have craved for the longest time. That I have grieved.

"You don't have to decide right away. This is a lot to take in. We have already bombarded you today. I want you to take this next couple of weeks to make your decision."

I nod my head, I can handle that.

My father stands up, dusting the sand off his pants. He holds out a hand and I take it, allowing him to help me up.

"Come on, I promised your mother I would find you and bring you home."

"I fought every single day to bring you home. For the last

10 years, that's all I've done. I knew I wouldn't be able to rest until I was able to bring you and your Mum home."

"Home." I confirm.

"It's time, Scar. This was always the plan, we just didn't know what that timeline would look like."

BOARDING P
NAME: SCARLETT SMIT
FROM:
TIME:
CLA
SEAT:
President

chapter
SIX

After a week of running over what I had been told, I knew my answer. Admittedly, I knew my answer from the moment I had been propositioned.

Packing up an entire house in two weeks is something I hope to never do again.

At least it has given me plenty of time to get to know Rhodes and my father better. It felt weird to call him Dad. He seemed resigned to fate when I first called him Ren. It's clear it hurts a part of him but a small part of me still holds the hurt of being betrayed.

Mum hasn't been shielded from my deep-seated anger. I've barely spoken to her.

Rhodes insists I forgive her but I can't seem to allow myself to. At least not yet.

A lot of damage has been done and I refuse to be the type that simply forgives and forgets.

The worst part about packing up and moving is saying goodbye to my friends. I know that it is only a 'see you soon' but it still fucking sucks.

My father has already granted me full use of the private jet for whenever I want to fly them over.

Yep. A private fucking jet.

My eyes widen at the damned thing on the tarmac. Yet another luxury I hadn't considered but one I'm certainly not mad about. Especially not considering how goddamned comfortable it is.

Did I mention it also has a bedroom in it?

We aren't in Kansas anymore Toto.

Rhodes and I talk the entire flight. I feel like I haven't laughed this hard in a very long time. He tells me about all of the crazy shit that we use to get up to. I fill him in on my life since the 'accident', as we are now referring to.

It's been refreshing getting to know him. We have become close very quickly.

He is just easy to be around. Isn't afraid to talk a bit of shit but also has been a massive support in being able to process everything.

In turn, I've also been there for him. A shoulder for him to lean on. Reassurance when he comes rushing into my room in a blind panic, not sure if I'm actually real.

Yeah, that sure as fuck hurt.

"I've got to admit Scar, I was nervous about seeing you again."

"Why's that?" I question, raising my eyebrow.

Rhodes lets out a deep breath as he looks down at his hands that are fidgeting in his lap.

"When Dad told me that you and Mum were both alive, I couldn't wrap my head around it. I didn't believe him. I know I've told you a bit about this already, but I really did lose my shit. I stormed out of the clubhouse and just drank myself into oblivion. Dad found me three days later at some run-down bar in a mess.”

He grimaces at that. I can see the disappointment written on his face. And so much heartache. It is raw and seems to utterly consume him.

“I thought the bastard was playing tricks on me or some shit. Trying to toughen me up,” he scoffs, like something similar has happened before.

“Losing you is one of the hardest things that I’ve ever gone through. Just because you are technically my big sister doesn’t mean that I didn’t or don’t feel protective over you. I can’t get the image of seeing you hurt out of my head. For ten years I’ve had nightmares.”

I grab both of his hands and hold them in mine. Like by my touch alone that can somehow reassure him that I’m okay.

“It still scares me. I don’t know what I would do if you were taken from me again.” Emotion catches in Rhodes’ voice.

“I don’t plan on being taken any time soon. Nor do I plan on letting these motherfuckers get the best of us. We’ve only just gotten our family back. While I don’t remember a single thing, I don’t plan on letting any of this go. No matter how wild all of this feels.”

“I’m just so fucking happy to have you back. Life was so lonely without you.”

“I feel the same way. I wish so much that I could remember what it was like back then. It might seem strange, but it was like something was missing from my life. Obviously, a big chunk of that was the fact I’m missing a whole eight years of my life but it was more than that. But now with you both being here, it’s like that hole is starting to mend.”

I smile up at my brother. It’s kind of strange to think that he is actually my baby brother. The man has stubble and is built like a brick shithouse. There is nothing child-like about him.

"I'm going to have to apologise in advance because I'm about to be a crazy overprotective brother. I've got ten years to make up for after all."

We laugh together at his declaration. Knowing what I have learnt both from him and our parents, I can't say that I'm surprised.

Rhodes has hardly left my side since we have come back into each other's lives. I would have thought it would have annoyed me, but I love his company. I'm more than happy to give him some leeway with the overprotective brother act because I can understand what it would have been like for him.

Yet another reason why I'm glad I don't have the memories. It has been hard enough just knowing I did have him. I don't know how I would have fared having remembered him. The thought makes me sick to my stomach at the thought of something happening to him now.

It's only a few weeks but I know I would burn down the world if something happened to my family.

As we touch down in the United States, it's hard to believe that I've actually been here before. That I was born here. You wouldn't be able to tell though. Both mine and mum's accents are borderline bogan, a fact that both Dad and Rhodes aren't shy about teasing us for. There have been plenty of light disagreements about how to pronounce certain words and what things are called. The look Rhodes gave me when I asked him if it would be good thong weather in California was priceless.

We all load into a blacked-out Chevrolet Suburban which I've been told is completely bomb-proof. Something that instantly had my eyebrows raising and questioning what the fuck I am doing here.

There are another two blacked out Suburbans both full of

heavily guarded members of the Thunderbirds. If I thought the private jet was an indication as to the seriousness of the gang and the level of protection that both Dad and Rhodes ensured us would be provided, it was nothing on seeing just how heavily guarded we are.

Coming from Australia where this type of lifestyle seems like something that you could only see in the movies is quite the reality check. Guards carrying around AK-47's and handguns on their hips like it's just a regular Tuesday. The sensible part of my brain is telling me that I should be shit scared of my new, or should I say old, life but the other part of my brain that doesn't give a fuck is telling me that this is family. This is home.

The obvious respect and power my father holds over his gang radiates off him. The men all bow their heads as they all welcome us home and help us to unload off the plane. Majority of our belongings had to be shipped over with only bare essentials brought onto the plane. I just wished some of those belongings had included my bike. Apparently it's something I couldn't bring with me. Noah was all too happy to take it off my hands. At least I can trust him with it. Unlike Grace. Last time I let her ride my bike, it spent a month needing to be repaired.

We landed on a private airfield not too far from the Thunderbirds' Clubhouse. Rhodes informed me that the airstrip is owned by the gang. Apparently, it makes it easier for shipments to come in.

I'm still waiting for the inner Karen to come out in me and demand that the drugs and guns stop. Yet I've seemed to just accept it. I'm still trying to work out if it's the part of me that is just accepting of this life or if one day it will all come crashing down on me.

Or if it's the fact that while the Thunderbirds do all this

illegal shit, they are at least trying to make it safe. Ensuring that the weapons aren't falling into children's hands to be used against their peers, drugs are made clean and safe, so users know what they are actually getting. The sex trade is heavily policed with consenting workers that are paid fairly and provided with the necessary protection.

While the sex work industry may seem taboo to some, I'm glad that my father took a stand and helped to provide these men and women with a space to perform their trade safely. Which is something I know he has repeatedly ensured us, I can tell just how proud he is of how much he is changing the underworld in America.

Not everyone can be a saint. At least while they are sinning, they are safe I guess.

As we begin our short trip to the clubhouse, Rhodes begins filling me in on some of the more legitimate ventures of the gang. The clubhouse is a massive building smack bang in the middle of the Thunderbirds' compound. He explains it to be more of a gated community with the majority of the members living in houses built by the gang. Not only do the members live there, but they also have the opportunity to work as well. Grocery stores, boutiques, bars, mechanics – you name it, they own and run it. For the Thunderbirds, having these more legitimate businesses in the community help to keep the Feds away according to my brother.

"The best part is the Pinks' Lounge."

"Pinks' Lounge?" I ask.

"Yeah, the ladies that were inducted into the Thunderbirds decided to make a club within a club I guess. They call themselves the Pink Ladies, hence the name Pinks' Lounge.

"It's an eighteen plus gentlemen's club but the majority of us just use it as our hang out space. They have live bands perform occasionally."

"You still sing right?" Our father jumps into our conversation.

I turn towards him, giving him a small smile, "Yeah I do."

"God, I miss hearing your voice, even if it used to be the bane of my existence," Rhodes laughs.

"You will have to get up on stage with some of the girls and play a couple of songs for us." My father smiles at me.

I sit with what he says for a moment. Normally, my singing has been completely restricted to the shower and the occasional round of car karaoke with my friends but I've never sang in front of a crowd. Or at least haven't in the last ten years. While the idea scares me slightly, I nod at him. It's time I start taking risks. Live my fucking life. Not let simple things like stage fright get in my way.

"Pinks' Lounge is also a front for our sex trade as well. The Pinks wanted to take ownership of their bodies and Dad allowed them to do just that. They now run the show, we just provide the muscle." He lifts his arm and flexes his muscles. After these past few weeks, it's been blatantly obvious that Rhodes loves himself sick.

Laughing, I smack him in the belly.

"God, you are so full of yourself."

He just chuckles like I didn't say anything at all, "Anyways, you will be the Pinks' new prey. They've also got a little initiation task that you will have to complete."

Rhodes rolls his eyes and scoffs as he mutters to himself under his breath

"What? What's the initiation?" No one said anything about an initiation. I'm instantly on guard.

"Every chick that joins the Thunderbirds automatically is initiated into the Pink Ladies no matter the status they hold within the Birds. I guess it's another part of them taking control of their bodies, but each woman is required to perform a strip dance in front of the entire club. In their lingerie."

Well shit. Not quite what I was expecting.

"Don't worry Scar, I'll introduce you to Brandy. She will be able to show you around the club and fill you in on everything."

I nod my head in answer. But I'm far away from the current conversation. While I am completely comfortable in my skin, the thought of stripping down to what I imagine will be barely enough fabric to cover anything in a room full of horny men is just a little bit intimidating.

Shit, who am I kidding? I'm already nervous and trying to think of ways I can get out of doing it.

For the rest of the drive, this initiation is the only thing that consumes my thoughts. My family talks around me but I can't hear them.

My hands fiddle in my lap. Why the fuck did my father not warn me about this? Isn't this something he should be concerned about? His daughter swinging around on a pole practically buck-ass naked.

I'm dragged out of my thoughts as we pull up to a set of gates. The fence stands at least ten feet high with rolled barbed wire around the tops. It's like a high-end prison. Bougie but secure. Just from what I can see, I notice six cameras each pointed in different directions as well as a handful of fully armed guards. I raise an eyebrow at them. Are they truly necessary? My father apparently thinks so.

The driver rolls down the window and nods at the guard walking over to us. He glances in the back of the car where the four of us are all sitting. Surprise lights in his eyes as he nods his head in respect. I don't know whether he realises just who Mum and I are, his facial expressions not giving much away as he schools his features again.

"Prez, Rhodes. Welcome back."

"Thanks Tom." My father nods to him.

As we drive through the gates into the compound, I can't help but hum in surprise. Rydell is nothing like I thought it would be. To be honest, I'm not even really sure what I envisioned the community to look like, but it certainly wasn't this.

When thinking of members of gangs, the last thing I could see them living in is beautiful two-storey all American houses with white picket fences. Children run around in front yards and play with their friends. Neighbours are leaning over fences and gossiping.

The scenery starts to change as we get further along. A range of different shops begin lining the streets. I notice a coffee shop that I commit to memory.

We turn down another street and a massive home appears in front of us. Another set of gates set at the beginning of the driveway. More heavily armed guards line the outside of the property.

"Welcome home Scarlett, Bonnie," My dad says.

Home.

My family.

The place I grew up.

The place where it all came crashing down around us.

I'm finally home.

BOARDING P
NAME: SCARLETT SMIT
FROM:
TIME:
CLAS
SEAT:
President

chapter
SEVEN

scarlett

After another greeting from the guards stood outside of the home, we pull up in front of what looks to be a six-car garage. I get out of the car and stare up at the house in awe. It's not a damned house. This is a fucking mansion.

"Rhodes, you take Scar inside and show her around. Your Mum and I need to have a quick meeting with the council."

He then looks at me and his eyes instantly soften. He places his hands on my arms.

"I've waited ten years for this moment. I am so happy to finally have you home, my beautiful girl. You are so precious to me and I'm so proud of you. I can't wait to see you become the woman I know you were yearning to be when you were taken from us. My little fighter."

I see the longing in him to wrap his arms around me. While his words pull at something deep inside of me, I'm not ready for that quite yet. He seems to be understanding of that fact, accepting the nod I give him as words fail me.

Since the massive bomb was dropped, I haven't had a better chance to sit down and talk with him properly. There have been a few conversations here and there but I need something more.

We mainly spoke about the kidnapping and injuries. He told me all about the training that we used to do and what I will have to relearn now that we are home. To be honest, I'm actually looking forward to all of it.

A few years after my 'accident', I took a few sessions of mixed martial arts classes. But I wasn't ready. Or my body wasn't at least. But as I stretch my limbs out, I feel like I might actually be ready. Either that or now I don't have much of a choice.

Rhodes takes me in through the massive garage and into the house. We come out into a beautiful big open planned kitchen and living area.

"Obviously this is the kitchen. There's a big butler's pantry through there with basically every kind of snack you could possibly want. One of the older Pink Ladies helps around here with meals and cleaning."

Rhodes takes me through the rest of the house. There is a massive movie room off the living area fit with recliners that look like literal clouds. He shows me what he calls a den, something I would just call a rumpus room.

Arcade games line one wall. A fully stocked bar, with alcohol I've never even heard of, sits full stocked in a corner of the room. A few bar tables are dotted around the front with a perfect view of the small stage off to the side. There's a drum kit, guitars, a piano and microphones already set up like a band just finished playing.

"Wow. This is insane," I murmur in awe at the space in front of me. I run my hand over the bar as I look around the room, seeming to find something new each time.

"We used to spend so much time down here when we were younger. A couple of the members' kids around the same age as us would come over and we would just play music all day long. Not like I got a lick of talent, but I played band manager," Rhodes replied with a laugh. His face starts to turn solemn as he looks around at all the gear.

"I guess it hasn't really been used since you left," he says, the mood turning sombre.

"Well, it will be now. I promise to play you live shows. Do those kids still play now?"

"Yeah, they do. They normally do a weekly show at Pinks' Lounge. Tonight, they actually have one of the girl groups playing. Some nights they do an open mic night where, instead of a jukebox playing a backing track, they have one of the live bands playing."

I nod my head as he continues, "They are actually the girls I was hoping you would get up and sing with. Rippy is currently their singer but it is obvious it's not her calling."

The thought of actually being able to get up on a stage and sing sends a spark of thrill through me now that I've had the chance to really mull it over. Being able to express myself through music is so freeing. After the chaos of these past few weeks, I feel like I have a fuck load to say and having a microphone in my hands might just be the perfect way to do that.

"Come on, I will show you upstairs and to your room."

We head up the stairs to the second floor. Rhodes points to a few different rooms explaining what they are but not bothering to show me inside.

He opens the last door though and walks inside, pausing at the entrance.

"This is your room. It stayed as you left it for a few years. Around the time we turned sixteen, I just lost it. The grief just got too much, when I went on the bender, I came in here and just started ripping your things off the walls and tearing things off the shelves."

Rhodes pauses as he looks around the room with a grimace. He turns back to look at me with so much sincerity in his eyes.

He turns away and walks over to one of the other doors in the room. He pulls out a small shoe box and hands it to me.

"What's this?" I ask.

"That's everything that I didn't destroy. I'm sorry Scarlett."

"It's okay Rhodes. I understand. You were angry and lost. In all honesty, it would have been a little weird coming back to eight-year-old me's bedroom. I feel like it would have been an explosion of pink and unicorns."

I laugh as a smile and reassurance begins to brighten Rhodes face back up.

"You would be pretty spot on there."

I look around and take in the re-designed room. There is a massive California king bed centred in the room. The sheets are a light grey with a few coloured pillows for decoration. One of the walls is practically all window letting in the beautifully Californian sun. A long seat stretches underneath with a few of the same coloured pillows from the bed scattered across it. The room is fairly bare leaving it for me to get creative with how I want to decorate. There is a second door that I assume leads to an ensuite.

"I love it, Rhodes. You guys did a good job." I smile up at my brother.

"Don't give me too much credit. A few of the old ladies came over and decorated it for you." I smile at that.

"I will give you a bit of time to settle in and unpack. Tonight, I want to take you out to Pinks' and I guess reintroduce you to everyone. I think Dad is planning on having a big meeting with everyone in the next couple of days, but I thought it would be good to give you a chance to warm up a bit before you are just thrown to the vultures."

With that he comes over and gives me a hug. I'm surprised at the gesture for a moment before I wrap my arms around him. "I don't think I'm ever going to stop saying it but I'm so glad you are home, Scar."

"I'm so happy to be home."

Rhodes eventually lets me go before he turns around and shuts the door to the room, leaving me to the silence. I let out a breath and start to unpack the boxes of stuff that flew over earlier in the week.

BOARDING P
NAME: SCARLETT SMIT
FROM:
TIME:
CLA
SEAT:
President

chapter
EIGHT

Rhodes eventually knocks on my door, startling me from my unpacking and gives me an hour's warning before we leave to go to Pinks'.

I jump in and give myself a quick shower and wash my hair. This bathroom is nearly as big as my entire room back in Australia. It's obvious that no expense was spared when building the house. I'm grateful but it's absolutely unnecessary. Although that's not going to stop me from absolutely spoiling myself to a little pamper session.

With no idea what kind of dress code Pinks' Lounge has, I opt for a pair of light wash Mum jeans, a long sleeve crop top and a pair of converse. Simple but as I look in the mirror I smile, happy with how cute I feel.

I give my hair a quick curl and decide to do a full face of makeup. I've never been able to successfully master the effortlessness that is a swish of mascara and lip gloss. Props to the girls that can. But me? It's a full face of makeup or nothing at all.

I meet Rhodes in the garage. He's standing beside a Harley with two helmets in his hands. The sight of the bike makes me miss my own even more. Would it be too far if I asked Noah for photos of my bike? Like some kind of fucked up divorced parent situation. Rhodes hands me a helmet and I chuck it on quickly and jump on behind him.

God only knows how he rides so I make sure to hold onto him tight. Last time I made the mistake of not holding on properly, I sailed off the end of my mate Locky's bike. Something I don't want to relive any time soon. I don't feel like adding more scars to my collection.

How appropriate, Scar who is covered in scars. Punny.

As we ride through the streets, I try to take note of where everything is. Thank God the little community is small, but I would at least prefer to not look like an absolute wanker and get lost.

I hear a rumble coming our way and look down the street. Five bikes drive in formation and I take them all in.

Two, of whom I assume are guys, are driving Harleys like Rhodes' bike. The third guy is riding an all-black Ducati Panigale with the fourth riding a Ducati Xdiavel.

Holy. Fucking. Drool.

But what really gets my attention is a brand-new Kawasaki KX450. The green of the bike stands out amongst the other blacked out bikes. My jaw drops. I'm sure a little bit of that previous drool would be swinging behind me in the breeze if it wasn't for my helmet. I've had my eye on that bike for such a long time and to finally see it in the flesh thrills me.

I try to take in as much as I can of the five guys riding the bikes, but the visors don't give anything away.

Shit, for all I know they could be wrinkly old dudes under those helmets. Normally, those three types of bikes would never ride along together. I don't know why, but I assume it's some kind of bike culture bullshit. But these guys are and, fuck me, it suits them.

As we pass each other, all the guys give Rhodes a nod of respect in which he returns. I swear I can feel their eyes burning into my skin as they try to work out who is on the back of his bike. My own visor hides my identity, only my clothes and hair blowing out under the helmet give away anything about me. I kind of like holding onto the anonymous illusion. At least for as long as I can.

My mind stays back on the five mysterious men on the bikes even as we pull up to Pinks' Lounge. I have to physically shake myself out of my daydream, like I'm still lost in the mystery of who they were. Rhodes gives me a funny look as we get off his bike and take off the helmets.

He laughs a little as I try to fix my hair that's now all over the place.

I give him a death stare watching as all it takes to sort his helmet hair is a little shake of his head and a comb through with his fingers.

Fucking men.

"Come on Scar, let's head in. Shelly will just be dying to see you."

We head into the club and I'm instantly overwhelmed. Being told that Pinks' is a gentlemen's club, I instantly thought of just a normal strip club like the ones back home. While there is nothing at all wrong with them and their vibe, Pinks' is completely different.

The lingerie the ladies are wearing is classy. Yes, it is essentially underwear but there's just something extra that gives it a level of elegance and pure sex appeal. Goddamn, these women are making me want to bend a little which is saying something considering dick is all it has ever been for

The mood lighting is set dim. There is a large stage at the back of the room. Band equipment is set up towards the side of the back of the stage, not to interfere too much with the runway that leads to a lone pole sitting in the middle of the room. A red head with the most beautiful curly hair is currently spinning around on the pole while *Pour it Up* plays in the background.

There are booths around the stage with small tables for drinks. Even though it is early afternoon, a few men occupy the seats throwing money at the girl. There are a few booths around the rest of the room with lounges surrounding small platforms with poles in the middle. A couple of them are occupied with a couple of younger guys and a stunning brunette who is currently shaking her ass in a guy's face. Poor lad looks like he is going to bust where he's sitting.

It takes everything in me to hold in a chuckle.

Rhodes directs me towards the bar that sits off to the right of the stage.

"Oh my god! My babies are back!" A voice yells out causing a few of the patrons to glance over at us with curious glances. It's obvious they all know who Rhodes is with the nods they give him, but their eyes stay locked onto me, curiosity filling their gaze. The newbie. Great.

I startle as I'm pulled into one of the tightest hugs I've ever had as the wailing lady embraces the both of us. It seems like she holds us there forever as she rubs my back non-stop repeating 'My babies are home'. I stiffen, not quite sure on what to do or how to react.

Eventually she pulls back, her gaze stays locked on mine.

"Oh my sweet Scarlett. I couldn't believe it when your father told me that you were alive. It broke my heart all of those years ago. Your Mum was one of my best friends." She rushes out but waves a hand in front of her face, like she shoos away the thought. She dabs at a few tears that leak down her cheek. "But enough of that. That's a story for another day," She says, grabbing my shoulders and holding me directly in front of her.

"God, you are just as beautiful as your mother. Look at that beautiful blonde hair. Oh my lord Jesus and those eyes. Just like your Dad and your brother."

Tears begin to well in her eyes again as her hands move to my cheeks. I feel like they are about to be squeezed but I don't care. I don't know what it is but I instantly love this woman. There is just something about her that makes me feel at home. Like she could be a second Mum to me. By the way she is acting, it seems like that may have almost been the case back before everything happened.

"Dakes is going to be so relieved when I can finally tell him you are home. He has been so lost all of these years without you, my girl. He should be back soon."

Dakes?

It occurs to me that no one has mentioned any of my previous friends I used to have. This 'Dakes' was obviously one of them. It makes me question just why none of them have ever been mentioned.

Who are they? How did they cope with my accident? Will they still want to be friends now that I'm back? The thought is pushed aside as Rhodes jumps in, swinging his arm around my shoulder.

"Jesus Shell, I'm sure feeling the love here."

"Oh, shut up you."

The woman in front of me says as she smacks Rhodes in the stomach causing the wind to knock out of him. For such a short lady she seems like she would be a pocket rocket.

"Come on you two, let's get a drink. Rules are a little bit more relaxed here. The whole twenty one drinking age thing doesn't apply. All you young kids are running around here doing much worse shit than drinking alcohol. What's your poison, my girl?" She asks me as she directs us over to the bar and calls over one of the bartenders.

"I'll just go, a Bundy and coke."

The dumbfounded look she gives me makes me question myself.

"Sweet girl, we aren't in Kansas anymore. What in the fuck is a Bundy?

"Ahh, like Bundaberg Rum?"

"Oh, my darling. We don't have that here. I'll order it in for you."

Shelly taps my hand in a motherly gesture.

"I'll just get you a Captain Morgan and coke."

I nod my head as she tells the bartender our orders. Soon three Jack and Cokes are sitting in front of us.

I can't help but let the feeling of displacement trickle through me. I never would have thought that something as simple as asking for a Bundy and coke would make me feel that way.

For the first time since we touched down, I feel homesick.

As I take in my surroundings, it really starts to set in that this is my reality. There's no Ashton Kutcher about to jump out and tell me I'm being Punk'd; this is all real.

I start to feel nervous. What if I'm not made out for this life? What if I can't live up to the expectations that have been set for me?

As the doubt filters in, so does the overwhelming feeling of knowing that I can in fact do this. That I can live up to the expectations I have set before me. That I can exceed in fulfilling them. There are people that will be counting on me. Lives that need to be saved.

I know deep within my soul that I was born to do this. That

while I may have moments of nervousness and moments where I will inevitably doubt myself, I know I can do this. That I will make a change. One for the better.

I take a deep breath and try to push the feeling away. I give Shelly a smile as she looks between Rhodes and I.

"Now Rhodes, while I absolutely adore you my boy, I'm going to steal your sister here and take her to introduce all the ladies out the back. Dakes mentioned they would be in soon."

Rhodes gives me a cautionary look. It's obvious he isn't too keen on leaving me alone. I give a small nod of my head to reassure him that I will be fine. He looks at me a little bit longer and eventually backs down not wanting to argue. He pulls me into a hug and whispers into my ear.

"I'll be over in one of the booths. I'm here if you need me."

He gives me an extra little squeeze.

"Go on, I'll be okay," I say as I watch him walk away after a slight hesitation in his step.

"The six of them were all so lost when we thought you were dead, my girl."

Shelly says as I turn to her. I notice not for the first time that she seems to have a nickname for me. It makes me wonder if it was what she used to call me... before everything.

"You were all thick as thieves. You did everything together. If there was one of you, the others wouldn't be too far behind," she sighs as we begin walking through the club. "The news hit us all hard. But your poor brother and my boy were destroyed. Over the years your brother learnt how to cope. But it's been a bit harder for my boy. I normally wouldn't tell others all his business but because it's you and I know how much he still loves you; I know I can trust you in this."

I give her a small nod. A strange sadness filling me over this person I cannot remember but clearly, I mean the world too.

"Dakes suffers from severe anxiety and depression. Even after all this time he still wakes up with horrific nightmares. He was right there with you when everything went down."

A few tears start to roll down her face. I struggle to hold mine back, swallowing a lump in my throat. Now isn't the time to cry.

A strange urgency to find this Dakes and make things right for him again overcomes me though. I've always been a bit of an empath but it's like I'm suddenly in overdrive. The thought of someone I used to care about hurting brings an ache to my chest that I can't ignore.

Shelly snaps out of the sombre thoughts and quickly wipes away her tears. "Enough of that, my girl. We can all cry later. Right now, I need to introduce you to the other girls. We also need to organise your induction. Unfortunately, there's no way around it. The rules are there for a reason. But don't worry, we will have you all trained up and dressed in whatever you feel most comfortable in."

My gut drops a little bit.

Fuck.

I almost forgot. Induction. The strip dance.

Rest in peace, Scarlett.

BOARDING PASS
NAME: SCARLETT SMITH
FROM:
TIME:
CLASS:
SEAT:
President

BOARDING P
NAME: SCARLETT SMIT
FROM:
TIME:
CLAS
SEAT:
President

chapter
NINE

scarlett

Shelly leads us out the back into a dressing room. A few girls come in from their stage sets while others walk out for theirs. She leads me through to a hallway lined with closed doors. A big door with an exit sign is at the end of the hallway. We come to the second door down and a sign saying *Pink Room* hangs down in the centre, near where Shelly knocks.

A female voice yells out to come in. Shelly turns the doorknob, smiling as she pulls me into the room.

I take in my new surroundings. They weren't kidding when they said it was a pink room. A couple of makeup mirrors line the back wall. Couches sit in the middle of the room with a beautiful white coffee table separating them. A kitchenette sits off to the side of the room, well stocked by the looks of things. There are four girls each in different stages of getting ready around the room.

A short girl with black hair and pixie cut is bent over at the mirrors applying a crimson shade of red to her lips. She looks like one of those pin-up girls just with a goth edge. It suits her.

There is another girl beside her sitting in her underwear looking at herself as she pins up her mousy brown hair on top of her head. She has a softer edge to her compared to the other chick. Kind of like a yin and yang. Two halves of a whole.

I glance over to the couches to where a chick is stuffing her face with the food in front of her. I hold back a chuckle as she looks up at us, smiling even though chocolate sits on her lip. I cannot relate to another human more than I do right now. She's in a pair of high waisted dark acid washed jeans and a bralette. Her hair sits in a short bob around her cheeks.

The last girl is in a black skater dress. Pink curled hair falls over her shoulders. Her face instantly lights up as she sees us.

"Shelly!" she squeals as she runs up and embraces her tightly.

"Hello, my darling. I've got a very important person to introduce you to. This is Scarlett."

The girl with the pink hair sucks in a deep breath and her head snaps in my direction. Her eyes are blown wide in disbelief.

The three other girls all pause what they are doing as they too snap their heads towards me. A mixture of emotions appear on their faces.

"It can't be." The pink haired girl finally chokes out.

"It sure is. Our girl is alive and she is home." The smile that Shelly gives me is bright. Like she is proud to show me off. I'm not going to lie though, with this many eyes on me, I kind of feel like a deer in headlights.

"Shit you are right, Shell. Looks exactly like Rhodes."

The brunette girl that was sitting down at the makeup

table says as she gets up and moves towards us. She puts her hand out for me to shake.

"I'm Maxie Maraschino, like the cherry."

She gives me a smile as she turns to the girl with the pink hair who is just standing there gobsmacked still looking at me. Maxie nudges her with her elbow, knocking her out of her trance.

"Oh my god. I'm so sorry. It's just we've heard so many stories about you from everyone that it's just surreal that you are actually standing in front of me right now. I'm Brandy."

Instead of shaking my hand like Maxie did, Brandy brings me into a tight embrace similar to the one she gave Shelly when we walked in.

"I can just tell we are going to be best friends."

I chuckle but I can't help but feel like she is right. Not for the first time today have I felt a sense of home and comfort in a person. It's obvious that I've never met Brandy before by the way she reacted to me. It's refreshing. Meeting so many people that knew you from before is daunting. I feel like I have some kind of expectation to live up to. One I'm worried I won't.

But Brandy has that air about her that makes it impossible for you to not want to be around her. She reminds me of Grace in a way.

The girl that was sitting on the couch quickly gets up while wiping her hands on a towel.

"Oop, sticky," she laughs, quickly finishing wiping her hands and throwing the towel back onto the table.

"I'm Jan." Jan extends her hand to shake mine but thinks better of it and gives me a quick hug.

The pin-up girl finally makes her way over to me. There's a hardness in her eyes. Like she has seen some shit.

She extends her hand to shake mine.

"Hi doll, I'm Rippy."

She squeezes my hand much tighter than the normal female handshake instantly reminding me of two males trying to assert dominance. I silently scoff at her alpha bullshit. Rippy eventually steps away and crosses her arms over her chest. I turn from her to not let her get under my skin like she clearly wants to.

"So, Scarlett, we've heard so many stories about your voice from Rhodes and it just so happens that we need a new singer. Think we could get a little sample?"

A deep chuckle sounds behind me. I turn and face Rippy who is just shy of pissing herself laughing at Brandy's question.

"I don't know Brandy. I think this Aussie Sandra Dee is a bit too *pure* to be a Pink. I don't really feel like playing some Taylor Swift bullshit."

"Hit me with a song then Rippy," I snark, crossing my arms over my chest. While I'm not a massive Taylor fan, the girl does have some bangers.

The sinister smirk I get in reply tells me all I need to know about her. She is way too comfortable being a grade A bitch.

"I will give you something easy. All I Wanted by Paramore."

My own lips turn up in a smirk.

Little do these girls know, the only thing that has stuck with me is my complete and utter obsession with Paramore. Some days I feel like their music was the only thing that kept me going through relentless therapy and doctor's visits.

Not bothering with any further conversation, I begin to quietly sing the verse leading up to the chorus. I close my eyes to help keep me in the zone. I give a slight pause right before the chorus. Slowly, I open my eyes again, looking directly at Rippy I suck in a deep breath and sing. Her eyes bug out of my head at her surprise at just how well I can hit the high notes.

Yeah, how's that for this little Aussie Sandra Dee. Fuckhead.

Once I finish the last note, I take a deep breath and look around the room.

All the girls have shocked but impressed expressions across their faces. Brandy starts jumping up and down clapping.

I'm brought into a big hug. Shelly holds me tight to her as she hiccups through low sobs.

"Oh, my girl. Your voice has just gotten more beautiful with age. You must get up on that stage and sing for us. I won't be letting such raw talent be wasted."

Her compliments bring the biggest smile to my face.

"Thank you, Shelly. There's no way I wouldn't get up on that stage," I say with determination. Any shred of nervous energy dissipated the moment I sang that first word in front of them.

"Well shit Australia. I'm impressed." Maxie stands up and pulls me over to the lounges to sit.

"What other songs do you know? You've got to come up on stage tonight with us. It would be the best welcome home you could have," Jan says right before she goes back to hooking into the food spread out on the table.

"I will leave you girls to it then. Scarlett, my girl, if you need me, I will be floating around the club somewhere, but I trust these girls. You're in good hands here. Remember ladies, show time is in 30 minutes." Shelly gives each of us a kiss on our cheeks. With one last look at me before she walks out the door she turns around and says, "It's so good to have you home, my girl."

The girls and I sit down and organise a small set of songs to play tonight. We decide on five songs. Starting with *Nobody's Home by Avril Lavigne, Gasoline by Halsey, U + Ur Hand by Pink, GAY 4 ME by G Flip and Lauren Sanderson* that both

Maxie and I will sing together. Rippy eyed me when I agreed to sing it with Maxie. It's clear the girl isn't my biggest fan, but fuck her.

We then decide to end with *Decode by Paramore*. Working out what songs to sing that we all know is fucking hard. We all promise to sit down before the next gig and organise a better setlist. Ideas of songs already start swirling around in my head.

"So, Scarlett, tell us the goss. Is there a man or woman in your life?" Brandy asks with a wiggle of her eyebrows.

"Well, I mean there were a few guys I met back home. Funnily enough they are from America too," I reply. A pang goes through my body at the memory of the boys and the absolute mess it's now in.

"Tell me more, tell me more." Brandy leans over and puts her head in her hands. Her face is eager as she looks up at me. I can't help but chuckle.

"So, there were these five guys. So goddamn cute." I reminisce, trying to ignore the pain in my chest.

"I was swimming down at the beach from my house on the night of my eighteenth birthday. Suddenly, these guys just come bounding into the water and lift me out and carry me back to the shore. Complete show-offs."

"Was it love at first sight?" Brandy asks with stars in her eyes.

"How much dough did they spend?" Jan asks with a wink.

"Ugh, they sound like a drag," Rippy says, rolling her eyes. I snort, shaking my head.

"It was honestly the best summer of my life. I mean things are a little bit different over in Australia with how our holidays all work, but it was magic. We hung out basically every day."

"So did you hit it?" Rippy asks as she imitates giving a

blow job.

I roll my eyes.

"I mean…" I pause, letting the innuendo catch. The girls all squeal and begin peppering me with more questions. "It wasn't just about that though. They genuinely wanted to get to know me."

"There ain't no such thing." Rippy shakes her head at me as she begins filing her nails.

"It was romantic. It was the best few months of my life." My mood turns sombre, remembering how it ended.

"Then I guess it started to turn cold and they had to come back home. They promised to keep in contact, but I still haven't heard from them. Guess it wasn't meant to be."

"True love and they barely laid a hand on you, sounds like a bunch of creeps to me."

"Well they weren't." I snark back. She can think what she wants but I know them. Well, I think I do. Or did.

"Well, tell us their names. Do you have any photos with them?" Maxie asks as they all lean in waiting for me to reply. Rippy even leans over slightly.

I pull out my phone, opening up my photo album and clicking on a folder full of our photos. I find the first photo we took together. I tilt my phone so they can all see.

"Dawson and Nicky Zelko, Dacre Miller, Sonny Martinez and Pike Taylor," I say, pointing at each of them.

Maxie, Jan and Rippy start laughing at me as Brandy just sits there with her mouth dropped.

"What? What's wrong?' I ask, confused at their reaction.

Rippy shushes Maxie and Jan to stop laughing and glares at them for a second before turning back to me and pasting a fake smile on her face.

"Well, they sound perfect and maybe if you believe in miracles, your prince charmings may show up again someday.

Someplace unexpected."

I frown at her words but she doesn't give me another moment's notice as she turns away and calls out, "Now come on girls, we've got a show to put on."

I shake myself out of the strange moment as Brandy grabs my hand and begins to pull me through the hallway to the back of the stage.

The lights are blinding on the stage as I walk up to the microphone. I guess it kind of helps with the bit of stage fright I began to get backstage. I learn that Jan plays the drums, Rippy plays the lead guitar, Maxie plays the bass guitar and Brandy is on the piano.

"Ladies and gentlemen. We have a little surprise for you tonight."

Rippy says into the microphone as she turns to look at me.

"All the way from Australia, please welcome Scarlett!"

The crowd that has slowly trickled in since we have been out the back, cheers for me.

That nervousness that I thought I brushed off earlier is back ten-fold. I consider making a run for it and vowing to the girls I will sing another night but I've already committed. The setlist is already sorted and the girls are waiting for me to take it away.

I suck in a breath and lift up the microphone to my lips. Here goes nothing.

"This first song is called *Nobody's Home*. Sing along if you know it."

There is a little shake to my voice as I introduce the first song. I quickly brush it off, not wanting it to transfer into the song. The less shit I can give Rippy to nag on me with, the better.

Before I know it, the first song is done and the second song begins. The nerves I started to feel are almost non-existent now. My confidence continues to grow the more I sing.

I allow myself to move around the stage, getting a feel for the song. More people begin to gather at the front of the stage. It helps even more as I see them swaying and singing the words back to me. As I begin to sing *U + Ur Hand*, I venture out onto the platform that runs down to the pole. I look out into the crowd and see Rhodes with a few younger guys around our age all singing along with me. I give him a massive smile that he returns.

I look over to the bar and spot Shelly up on the bar singing into an empty vodka bottle. I shake my head at her. Its obvious she is sober but her I don't give a fuck attitude helps fuel me.

As the song finishes, I give a little bow and return to the microphone stand.

"We are going to go a little different with this song. Maxie, come up here," I say into the microphone as I motion for her to come stand up next to me. I begin to sing the first line into the microphone. I instantly hear cheers coming from the crowd as they all get into the song.

Maxie and I sing to each other and dance around the stage. I feel like I haven't had this much fun in as long as I can remember.

I smile to myself. Something in my soul feels like it begins to heal. It may only be a fraction but it happens.

chapter
TEN

dawson

The boys and I pull up at the front of Pinks' Lounge after dropping off info at the clubhouse. Dacre's Mom has been non stop texting him for the last hour demanding we hurry up and finish up our shit and get our asses to the club. Apparently, it's some kind of urgent surprise. Fuck knows what that woman has in store for us.

As I pull off my helmet, noise from inside travels to us. I hear the sound of one of the most beautiful voices I've ever heard singing from inside. My interest instantly peaked. I know that the girls are playing tonight, and I love them but fuck, they could never sound like this chick does.

"Fucking hell, who is that?" My brother Nicky asks as he swings his legs over his Harley, putting his helmet on the handlebars. Nicky and I are what you call Irish twins. Born in the same year. Nicky in January and me in November. He never lets me forget that I'm the younger brother.

The other guys all get off their bikes and take their helmets off as they look up towards the club.

"Beats me but all I know is she can hum on my cock any fucking day of the week," Sonny says as he grabs himself through his jeans.

I roll my eyes at him, snarling my lip.

"You haven't even laid your eyes on the chick and you are already thinking with your dick," I say smacking Sonny over the head.

"With a voice like that, how could she not be hot as fuck?" Pike butts in nudging Sonny.

"Fucking aye." Sonny and Pike high-five. Fucking idiots.

We all turn our heads to the direction of Pinks' like we have some kind of fucking x-ray vision and can see through the walls to whoever that voice belongs to inside.

"I need a fucking drink," Dacre says as he storms into the club.

I sigh at Dacre's retreating back.

He was alright there for the few months that we were in Australia. Like some of the light came back into his eyes. A pang of hurt goes through my chest as I remember leaving the only light any of us have felt in fucking years.

Having to leave behind someone that I know the each of us had a soul level connection with has fucked us all up just that little bit more. Not like we needed any more encouragement.

Fuck, Dacre is basically a shell of a human now. Worse than what he was before. He wears his heart completely on his sleeve. In the span of a few weeks, it was clear he began to fall in love, if he wasn't already. I think we all were in some way.

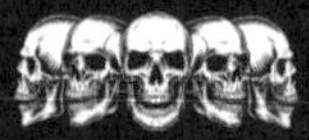

Pinks' is absolutely packed tonight full of members and non-members alike. Even though we live in a gated community, Pres wanted to make it a safe space for everyone. Not that any non-members can live in the community, but they can come in to get an education, shop and party. With plans to expand further, I have no doubt that in time, there will be a mix of members and non-members living and working here eventually.

With how many people are in here, it's near impossible to even see who is on the stage, so we head straight to the bar and each grab a beer.

We look around and find Dacre's Mom, Shelly up on the bar singing her heart out into an empty vodka bottle. She doesn't even notice us yet and by the looks of her, she isn't going to any time soon. It wouldn't be wise to disturb her while she's in the zone.

The current song the band is playing soon ends and the crowd absolutely erupts in cheers.

"Come on, let's head back to one of the booths to get a better view."

I nod towards a surprisingly empty booth. As we get to the table a familiar female voice sounds through the speakers. The five of us all snap and turn towards each other. There's no fucking way.

"Thank you everyone! For our last song, this is for all of you Twilight lovers out there. This one is called Decode."

We rush over to the booth, pushing each other to get there first. I need the highest vantage point. We are all well over six foot tall but there must be some giants in this room or something tonight. Visibility is shit house.

Each of our jaws drop as we finally get a glimpse of who's on the stage.

Scarlett.

What the fuck is she doing here?

How is she here?

Why is she here?

Holy fuck, that's our girl on that stage.

Holy fuck, how didn't we know that she could sing like that?

I turn to look at the other guys. I'm sure their shocked expressions mirror my own.

I glance around the room and spot Rhodes and a few of the other guys towards the front of the stage all singing back to Scarlett. It soon clicks that the girl we saw on the back of Rhodes' bike is Scarlett. Her clothes are exactly the same.

What the fuck is she doing with him? That motherfucker!

There has always been a bit of competition amongst all of us guys. Majority of the time it is just a bit of friendly banter, but sometimes it gets a bit messy. If that cocksucker thinks he can just slide in and steal my girl, he has got another thing coming for him.

"T-T-T-This s-s-song," Dacre stutters out. His eyes are blown wide and filled with tears.

"What about it?" I ask, bewildered as to why it would bring him tears.

"It was h-h-hers." His gaze never leaves Scarlett's as she dances around on stage.

God, she is fucking beautiful.

I give him a confused look that also sits on Nicky, Sonny and Pike's faces.

"Star." A single silent tear rolls down his face.

I instantly snap my head back towards Scarlett on the stage.

No.

No.

No.

I instantly start shaking my head and an unhinged laugh

escapes me.

"Fuck off dickhead," I retort. How the fuck could he think that this Scarlett is the same Scarlett from when we were kids?

No, that Scarlett died after to succumbing to her injuries after being fucking taken by those bottom feeding cunts.

No, I won't believe it. We met Scarlett Smith in Australia. Scarlett Crux was from right here in Rydell.

No.

No.

I guess the fact that they both had blonde hair could be classed a similarity.

No.

Nope.

I look back over towards where Rhodes is now right in front of the stage. Scarlett takes his hand and pulls him up onto the stage. Still facing the crowd, Rhodes puts his arm around her shoulders as they both sing into the microphone.

Fuck, his voice balances hers out.

How could I have forgotten that *Twilight* was little Scar's favourite movie. That no matter where we went, she would sing this song at the top of her lungs, enough that after she was taken, none of us could listen to it again. I remember watching her as she sang. She'd get this look in her eyes.

God, her eyes.

I suck in a breath as I squint, trying to see them closer even from the otherside of the room.

No.

No.

Her eyes.

His eyes.

Their eyes.

I've never felt utter fucking disbelief like I do in this very moment. I don't know whether to cry, scream or throw up. Maybe all three at the same time.

She's alive.

Our girl.

Dacre's Star.

Sonny's *mi estrella*.

Nicky's baby girl.

Pike's Princess.

My girl.

My Scar.

My first and only love.

Right here. On that stage. Singing with her fucking twin brother.

I can't stop the tears as they fall.

For over ten years, my heart has been shattered into a million pieces. Not a single day goes by where I haven't missed her. Even at eight years old, I knew just how much I loved her. She just had this air about her. It was intoxicating. To be around her was like standing next to the brightest star in the sky. No one has ever been able to even amount to her.

I guess until we met Scarlett Smith in Australia. It played with me every day just how much this new person started to worm her way into my heart. Not wanting to let anyone back in again. Trying to protect my heart against damnation. There was no fighting with it. I was doomed from the moment I stepped foot on that beach. Fuck, from the moment I stepped foot on Australian soil.

Little did any of us know, it was our Scarlett all along. It makes me question how the fuck we were so oblivious? Rhodes and Scarlett are quite literally identical twins. *God, we are dumbasses.*

I turn and look at the other guys. I don't see a single dry face. Their feelings are written all over them.

Devastation, disbelief, shock, relief, confusion.

"It's her," Sonny chokes out. "*Mi estrella.*" More tears fall down his cheeks as he turns back and looks at her.

"How? How the fuck did we miss that it was her back in Australia?"

Nicky turns to look at me. The look in his eyes breaks my heart just that bit more. If that was even possible.

I just shake my head. Not being able to find the words to answer him. I wouldn't have any even if I tried. I'm terrified to look at Dacre. Not sure if the tiny bit of hold I have over my emotions will be able to handle what I might see.

While Sonny, Pike, Nicky and I were absolutely shattered when Scarlett was taken and eventually pronounced dead, Dacre was on a whole other level of devastation. Not long after her death, Dacre was diagnosed with severe post-traumatic stress disorder, depression and anxiety. He turned completely into a shell of the person he used to be. Losing Scarlett destroyed him.

He was right there when she was taken.

They had just gotten off the bouncy castle and headed to get a drink when everything went down. Once the men were all disposed of, his Dad found him sobbing and rocking in the foetal position repeating over and over again, "She's gone. She's gone."

He was sedated for 3 days. Coming good for another few days until some dumb cunt told him of Scarlett's passing where he was then further sedated for another week.

After he finally was able to calm down, he completely retreated on himself.

He was ten when he first attempted suicide.

I've lost count of the number of times the boys and I have had to shove our fingers down his throat to get him to vomit up the concoction of pills he took. The number of times we've gone searching for him, fearing the worst. Watching him try to pull a gun on himself.

The only thing that eventually seemed to help along with a heavy dose of medication, was music.

Specifically beating the living shit out of a drum set. Music was a deep-seated love we all shared with Scarlett. From as young as six, we would all gather our parents and put on shows for them.

It was obvious even from back then that Scarlett was the centre of each of our universes. We became her ultimate protectors. Wherever she was, we were right behind her. After losing her, we all steeled our hearts and honed our skills to become the ultimate machines.

We couldn't lose anyone else the way we lost her. We wouldn't allow it. We failed once before. We will never make that mistake again.

I gain confidence from fuck knows where and turn to look at Dacre. Utter disbelief is plastered across his face even as tears stream down his cheeks. What shocks me the most, is the raw happiness in his eyes. Something that is so foreign to see on his face after all this time.

Each of us stand there, stiff as boards as we watch our girl own the stage.

A multitude of questions and *what the fuck's* run through my head. But all I can seem to do is just stand there admiring her.

She is fucking radiant.

Our girl.

She's alive.

She's home.

All of a sudden, the feeling of anger rushes over me as I come to my senses after the shock of her being home wears off.

I shake my head.

No.

She can't be here. Not when the club is in the fucked up state it is. When it's not fucking safe. She needs to leave. To go back home.

I settle on my decision at that moment.

I don't care about the relief I feel. I don't care how the other guys feel. I don't regret the thought as it comes to my head. I know it's the right choice.

Scarlett needs to leave.

I will make sure of it.

BOARDING P
NAME: SCARLETT SMIT
FROM:
TIME:
CLAS
SEAT:
President

chapter
ELEVEN

scarlett

There is no way to even remotely describe the way I feel right now as I sing my absolute fucking heart out. It became a running joke with Mum and I about how even after completely losing my memory, my love for *Twilight* quite literally fought through life or death to ensure its place as a forever obsession.

After the accident as a way to help bring me comfort, Mum and I would watch the movies on a continuous loop. Say what you will, but I will forever and always be Team Jacob. I wouldn't be mad if a sexy as sin werewolf shifter came into my life.

After Rippy's guitar solo, the song slows down a little. As I look out over the crowd that seems to get bigger and bigger the longer I am up here, Rhodes has moved closer to the stage with a few of the guys I saw him with earlier in the set.

Just like me, he is singing with all that he's got. I know from the many stories told over the last few weeks that Rhodes is quite the singer too. I also know he isn't big on performing;

singing around a campfire is more of his thing but I can't help myself. Once the song ramps up again, I reach my hand out to him and pull him up onto stage with me to finish off the song. I put the microphone between the both of us as we sing the last few lines.

Holy fuck. My brother has a set of pipes.

Cheers erupt as we finish our set. Sweat is pouring off me but it's obvious Rhodes doesn't care as he picks me up and swings me around. I erupt into laughter as he puts me down. I feel elated. Free. Like the weight of the world isn't currently sitting on my shoulders.

I know music has always been my salvation but this has just gone and proven it, to me and everyone else in this room.

Rhodes takes the microphone from me as he faces the crowd.

"My sister, ladies and gentlemen," He says while gesturing for me to bow to the room. I do so with a hint of caution so as whispers start up. Muffled questions sound around the room as the revelation of who I am is revealed.

"Birds, please ensure your attendance at Wednesday's meeting where we will go into further detail about what this all means. But for now, let's celebrate the return of my beautiful twin sister."

If I thought the cheer after our set ended was loud, it has nothing on the hoots and hollers the crowd yell out.

A rumbled war cry begins and slowly the entire room chimes in. Men and women alike begin stamping their feet and smacking tables. The noise almost becomes unbearable as everyone eventually erupts into celebration of my return home.

The DJ begins playing some track over the noise as it slowly drowns out. A few of the girls I saw out the back in the dressing room come out and begin spinning on the poles.

Rhodes turns to me and shouts over the noise.

"Come on Scar. There's a heap of people we need to re-introduce you to."

I hand my microphone off to Brandy who before Rhodes can drag me too far off the stage wraps up into a tight embrace. I hug her back just as tight even though we are sweaty messes.

"Thank you so much Scarlett. You were incredible," she says.

"No, thank you. That was one of the most insane things I've ever done."

The rest of the girls come over and we each give each other a hug in congratulations. Even Rippy, which comes at a surprise to me.

"Not too shabby Australia," she says with an approving nod of her head, "we will come find you once Rhodes is done making the rounds." There's a strange look on her face that I don't quite understand, but I just smile and nod in response, shrugging it off and turn back to Rhodes.

Rhodes takes me over to the two other guys he was with in the crowd.

"Boys, this is my sister Scarlett. Scarlett, the blonde is Wyatt and the big dickhead beside him is Jethro," he says with a smirk. Said dickhead, punches Rhodes in the arm and curses him out under his breath.

"They have been training with me as my right-hand men. Jethro was to be my Vice and Wyatt my enforcer. Now that you are stepping back into the role, you obviously have the right to choose who you want, but I would love for you to consider the boys."

He pauses briefly. There's a sadness and a pinch of anger in his face. I know how much it meant to him to one day become President of the Thunderbirds. He's been working hard for it. I already asked Dad if he was able to keep his position even if I was to come back, but unfortunately it just doesn't work like that.

"I'll definitely consider it." I give them all a big smile trying to reassure him. There's an obvious relief in Rhodes knowing I'm not going to instantly let them go as he sighs. He picks up a glass of brown liquor and throws it back.

"Come on, let's go introduce you to everyone else."

By the time we have done the rounds of nearly the entire room, I feel like I've met more people than I knew back home. Never have I felt as overwhelmed as I do right now. While everyone was kind and incredibly welcoming, I've felt inundated with new faces. People hugging me with tears in their eyes and telling me they are glad I'm home.

There was an expectation in the eyes of the people I had apparently known before. Like they expected me to just remember them instantly. The look of disappointment on their faces sent a sharp pain through my chest.

It hurts to not remember. Not for the first time have I tried to push the memory but the stabbing pain in the back of my mind reminds me just how bad of an idea it is. It won't work, no matter how determined I am. There's no thread to pull on. The memories don't exist inside me anymore.

We take a quick break from the introductions for a while and head to the bar. I'm glad for the break, needing five minutes just to sit down and breathe. I consider making an escape for the front door but with the way Rhodes is hovering, I don't think I will be escaping his clutches anytime soon.

"My girl, that was incredible!" Shelly yells out as she drops down two Captain Morgan in front of Rhodes and I. "I just saw Dakes and the boys over by one of the booths. Make sure you take her over there Rhodes." Shelly gives my brother a stern look.

He nods. "Yes ma'am."

She rolls her eyes at him before chuckling, "You little shit. Don't forget that I used to change your diapers young man."

"Thanks for the reminder, Shelly," he grumbles, throwing back the drink she sat down in front of us. I sip mine slowly, allowing the relief of the alcohol to take hold.

After we are done with our drinks, we slowly get up but come to a stop as we see Brandy, Jan, Rippy and Maxie headed our way.

"Hey girl, having fun?" Maxie laughs as Rhodes staggers slightly. I give him a questioning look. He must have had more to drink than I thought. He gives me a reassuring smile as he collects himself but I don't buy it for a moment.

"A little overwhelmed but that is to be expected," I laugh, answering the girls.

"Come on then, are you ready for your surprise?" Rippy says as she sticks her hands into her pink leather jacket, turning around nodding for us to follow. I'm left with little option as I follow behind them.

Brandy begins fixing my hair quickly as we walk through the crowd. I can't even begin to imagine the kind of state it is in after being on stage. Ignorance is bliss, I guess.

We eventually stop at one of the booths on the other side of the room. I don't stand a chance at even trying to hear the conversation the other girls are having with whoever they have stopped to talk to. The three of them are acting like a wall. That and Brandy is still busy fluffing around with my hair. She has also procured a compact powder from fuck knows where and begins patting it onto my face.

"Jesus Brandy, anyone would think I'm about to meet the

Hemsworth brothers," I laugh.

"Close enough," She says with a wink, a cheeky smile sits firm on her face. I begin to give her a suspicious look.

Before I can question what she means by that, a hand grabs me around the arm and I'm pulled through the girls.

I give a sharp glare at Rippy who grabbed me.

"What the fuck Rippy?"

Her smirk is sinister as she lets go of my arm and nods her head.

I turn my gaze from hers to face the people she was talking to and my heart all but falls through my ass.

Scarlett Smith has all but left the building.

Pike, Sonny, Dacre, Nicky and Dawson are standing in front of me.

In Pinks'.

In front of me.

In Pinks', in front of me.

It feels like the entire world shuts down. Even worse than a pandemic condemning the world.

The breath gets caught in my throat. I've completely forgotten how to breathe. I long for that break outside to gather myself. But the possibility for it now seems far away.

A feeling of anger washes over me. I have to hold myself back to not storm up to the men looking down at me dumbfounded and demand answers. To relieve me of my grief. To make me understand why I wasn't good enough. Why they broke my heart to pieces all those months ago. Shattered me beyond repair.

They built me up only to allow me to crumble back down.

A sob gets stuck in my throat. Tears threaten to spill from my eyes. I do my best to will them away but I don't think I'm that strong. I pretend I am. After these past weeks, my emotions are raw. The bad ass bitch persona I'm desperate to claim and hold onto is currently sitting in the corner crying.

While I feel so goddamn angry at them, so beyond betrayed as they stand in front of me, why do I feel relieved? Why do I feel the need to run into their arms? Would they even want that? Did they ghost me because they didn't want me anymore?

Why do I feel elated when they are the ones that have caused me so much pain?

A million questions run through my head. I'm a slave to them. A slave to my emotions as I feel my soul get dragged through the pits of hell. Tortured by Satan himself as we stand in front of each other in some kind of shoot-out.

How are they here right now? Why aren't they saying anything?

My question is immediately answered as Dacre's soft voice chokes out, "My Star."

The new nickname doesn't even register as he pushes through the other four boys who are standing in front of me looking like stunned mullets.

Smoking hot stunned mullets.

I curse the thought away just as it comes. Damn them. I will myself to not allow those kinds of thoughts through. Not until I get some kind of explanation.

Dacre reaches me before I can even blink, slamming into me and taking the last dregs of breath I had in my lungs.

The tears then come in full force as he holds onto me in such desperation. There is no hope in stopping them. Not when one of the men I fell desperately in love with is holding me.

My head and heart are at war with each other. Fighting over what I should be doing right now. How I should be reacting. But I shut them out. I allow myself to feel the relief, even if whatever will follow this embrace will crush me.

I need this. I've needed this more than I realised.

Even though months have passed with no contact, I can't help but love them. Love him. The things they made me feel. The way it felt like I had known them my entire life. How normal it felt to be with them. With Dacre, it's different. It was even back then. We just get each other. I see his demons and he see's mine. We had this instant connection, something that I haven't felt with anyone else before.

I feel Dacre's shoulders start to shake knowing like me, he has been reduced to tears.

"Shh, my sweet boy. I'm here," I whisper through the tears into his ear giving him a small kiss to the side of his head.

His hands tighten around my body. We are a mess of broken pieces as we grip each other, both desperate to know if the other is real.

"Scar. You're here. You're real." His voice is so quiet that if I wasn't this close to him, I wouldn't have heard him. I keep my voice low. This moment is for us.

"I'm here and I'm real. I'm never letting go, sweet boy."

We hold each other for a little bit longer before I pull back and hold his head in my hands slowly lifting so he is looking at me. To be honest, I don't think he plans on letting me go anytime soon.

God, those green eyes of his. They seem to be brighter even in the dim lighting of the club.

I wipe away the tears running down his cheeks with my thumb.

"No more crying Dacre," I say.

The absolute raw emotion in his eyes could bring even the strongest man to his knees.

"How are you here?"

"It's a really long story. But also, how are you here?" I throw his question back at him with a smirk.

A smile lights up his entire face. Back in Australia, his smiles never quite met his eyes no matter how hard he tried. But getting the real thing, fuck. This man is fucking devastating.

"It's a really long story," he says with a wink that sends us both into a fit of laughter. The light heartedness is exactly what I needed. It was feeling way too dark there for a moment.

I unwrap myself from Dacre as I remember the four other men standing behind him.

He reluctantly lets me go as he turns us both around.

Even though time seemed to slip away as Dacre and I reunited, it seems like it wasn't enough time for the boys to wrap their heads around the fact that I'm standing right in front of them.

Nicky eventually snaps out of his frozen state, a massive smile taking over his face. He rushes over to me and picks me up and spins me around in circles. He eventually stops and grabs my face to look at me in my eyes.

"Fuck baby girl. I never thought I'd see you again." Before I know it, his lips are on mine. It won't register until much later the double meaning behind what he said.

His kiss is intoxicating, stealing all reasonable thoughts from my brain. Nicky is the type of guy that I could easily get lost in. Nothing else matters when I'm in his arms.

His lips eventually pull away from mine.

Still in a daze, it takes me a second to realise Pike is standing in front of me. I could never understand why he wanted me. While all the boys are utter perfection, Pike could very well be a god. His eyes are a bright blue. His blonde hair sits in a perfect mess on his head, looking like he just came from a fucking photo shoot.

Like Dacre and Nicky, Pike's smile is fucking devastating. Butterflies tear up a storm in my belly as he aims his smile at me.

Fucking hell, I'm a goddamn simp for this man.

The months of heartbreak have done nothing to dim that feeling.

I curse myself internally. I shouldn't be allowing myself to be this excited with any of them but it can't stop. My brain is a muddle of mush.

"Pike!" I yell as I jump into his awaiting arms.

He laughs as he squeezes me tight.

"Fucking hell Princess. You have no idea how good it is to see you. Maybe those other fucking losers will get off my dick now that you are here."

"*Vete a la mierda pendejo.*"

The beautiful Spanish makes my head snap up off Pike's chest as I look at Sonny who is glaring daggers at Pike. As he turns to look at me, I'm hit with yet another heartbreaking smile.

Sonny doesn't bother with greetings as he rips me out of Pike's hold and engulfs me in his. A muttered 'never could share his fucking toys' comes from Pike, but Sonny either didn't hear him or he couldn't care as he holds me.

"*Mi estrella.*" Even though my Spanish lessons all but began and ended with the song Despactio, I gaze up to meet Sonny's eyes. I know whatever he said to me would be something sweet. Something that would for sure redden my cheeks even more.

"That performance was fucking incredible. I didn't know you could sing like that. Shit, I have been hard since I heard you out in the parking lot."

I slap his shoulder as I look down shyly, my cheeks flaming hot at his omission.

I cuddle deeper into his chest. Out of all the boys, Sonny is the comedian. Never failing to make a witty joke or send me into a blushing mess with his flirting. God, I've missed him. I've missed *them.*

I eventually pull away from Sonny with a smile and look over at the last owner of my heart. He is still standing near the booth. His arms are crossed over his chest and a look of nonchalance on his face. That grumpy look on his face never far away. It makes him hard to read but that never changed the way I felt about him.

"Hey Daws." I give him a wide smile as I walk over to him. As I reach him and go to embrace him, quicker than I can even blink, he side steps me leaving me confused and a little dazed.

What the fuck?

I turn to his new position. His arms are still crossed over his chest but a harsh smirk now sitting on his lips. The Dawson I met back home was gone, and a new and what seems to be cuntier version in his spot.

"Dawson?"

"That's my name baby, don't wear it out."

Snickers sound from a few of the other Thunderbirds standing around watching our reunion. My gut drops. I stand there staring at the man in front of me unable to form words. I don't even know what I would say right now. Don't wear his fucking name out? What kind of bullshit is that? Anger slowly begins to bloom in my chest.

"What the fuck Dawson?" Dacre pipes up from behind me but my attention stays fastened onto Dawson.

Before he can begin to explain his bullshit attitude, Rhodes pushes through the crowd.

"Hey Scar. I was just about to bring you over to these idiots, but it seems the girls beat me to it." He pauses with a chuckle.

"You wouldn't remember but we grew up with these boys."

Rhodes turns me to face the boys.

I feel as the colour drops completely from my face. I feel my heart as it begins to pick up its pace. We… We grew up with them? The boys I fell in love with are the same boys I was friends with when I was younger?

"Scarlett, this is Pike, Sonny, Nicky, Dacre and over here…" He turns me back around to Dawson. I feel like a ragdoll. It's also obvious that Rhodes completely missed our little reunion.

"…and this is Dawson. I had planned your reunion to be a little bit different but here we are."

"I know who they are, Rhodes." My voice feels empty as I speak the words out loud.

"Wait," he says as he yet again spins me around and puts both of his hands on my arms to hold me in place. "What do you mean you know who they are? Do you remember them from before?"

"Those boys I told you about." I pause as he nods for me to continue, "They are those boys."

Realisation dawns over his face. A look I've never seen on him before embraces him as he turns around sharply.

"Yo, what the fuck," Rhodes says, his face reddening in anger. "Why the fuck didn't you lot tell me earlier that my sister was fucking alive?"

His voice deepens and gets louder until he is almost yelling. If I had any sense I would probably have stepped away from him. The last thing I need to get in right now is a bar fight.

"We didn't know that Scar was actually *our* Scarlett man," Nicky says calmly to Rhodes.

"We thought she was dead, Rhodes. You know that if we even thought it was possible, we would have called you straight away."

"Be that as it may, you lot have been fucking around with

my fucking sister. Left her fucking heartbroken with not even any kind of communication," he says, swinging his arm back around my shoulders and pulling me into his body. I go, unable to resist as I stare at yet another person who has betrayed me. Five more people who shoved a red hot iron through my chest, piercing the last pieces of myself I had.

"We…" Pike pauses like he is trying to find the words.

"Come on Rhodes man. It's not that deep," Dawson says as he walks over to stand with the other four boys. "It was just a summer fling. Not like it meant anything." He shrugs. A look of disinterest still on his face.

"A summer fling? Is that fucking right?" I stare at him in utter disbelief. Fuck this. I'm angry now. How dare this asshole dismiss the best few months of my life!

His only reply is a shrug as he takes a drink of whatever bullshit juice is in his cup.

"Fuck you Dawson."

I refuse to stay for a moment longer. Any previous feelings of happiness or love completely dissipate. I refuse to allow myself to be broken again by men that don't deserve my heart. I cannot allow myself to fall apart.

I turn to Rhodes and without asking, snatch the keys out of his pocket and storm out of the club, completely ignoring the other boys and Brandy's calls for me to stop and wait. I feel like I am walking away from a part of my soul. A vital part of what has made me who I am today. That Scarlett from all those months ago is gone. She doesn't exist anymore. How can one survive after so much heartbreak? How can you pick up the pieces when time and time again they get destroyed by people you trust. People that you love.

Shelly goes to stop me, but my face must give enough emotion away that she thinks better and steps aside to let me through.

The club quickly fades away and I allow it, giving myself over to my base needs.

Flee. Run.

Normally I would stand up for myself but right now, there's no way I could even begin to. Not without breaking down and falling apart at the seams.

They don't deserve my tears. They never did and they never will again.

Once outside, I swing my leg over Rhodes' bike. I'm used to riding dirt bikes, but I don't hesitate at all as I start the bike and shoot away from Pinks' leaving behind Scarlett Smith and everything she was.

BOARDING PASS
NAME: SCARLETT SMITH
FROM:
TIME:
CLASS:
SEAT:
President

chapter
TWELVE

dacre

I stand rooted in place as I watch one of my best friends be a complete dick to my Star. Heartbreak and confusion are written all over her face. It breaks an integral part of me seeing him like that. I don't know what the fuck is wrong with him.

Even though I was in a state of shock after realising the Scarlett we met in Australia is the same Scarlett who has owned my heart my entire life, it was impossible to not notice the impact she has had on each of us. I don't know what the fuck Dawson's deal is but it's clear that this isn't the same person that stood beside me not even half an hour ago. The man I thought I knew.

After Star's performance ended, we all sat down at the table we accompanied and remained in silence. All of us are too stunned to speak.

Shit, my tears had barely dried when Rippy came over explaining she had a surprise for us. It wasn't half obvious just who that surprise was. I don't think I have ever moved as quickly as I did when she came over. The anticipation of seeing my girl again.

After connecting the dots, I felt like a complete fucking idiot that I didn't realise just who Scarlett was to me, back in Australia. It was near written on her fucking forehead in flashing lights. She told us all about her amnesia. Explained the scars covering her body. Fucking disgustingly ironic that her nickname is Scar. Yet, when she explained the accident to us, it was a car crash where she lost her brother and Dad. Our hearts all ached for her.

Clearly, it was a fabricated lie to ensure she never found out the truth. I understand their desperation in wanting to protect her better than anyone.

Losing Scarlett destroyed me. She was my light. My shining Star.

Even knee-high to a grasshopper, I followed her everywhere. She was my best friend. Sure, I had the guys but with Scarlett it was different. She saw me. Understood me. Supported me in a way that no one else ever has before. I was always the sensitive kid. She never held it against me. She cherished it, wise beyond her years.

I loved her before I knew what love really was. No one was ever able to amount to her. When the other guys started to show interest in other girls, I thought there was something wrong with me. I wasn't interested in guys either. It was my imagination of a grown-up Scarlett that I imagined every time I thought about what I wanted.

What would she have looked like grown up?

What would her voice have sounded like?

Would she still be just as obsessed with Twilight as she was when she was younger? Would she still sing?

Her voice is like a fucking angel.

A part of me knew it was her the minute we pulled up out

the front of Pinks'. Yet it only made sense when I finally saw her and heard that Paramore song spilling from her lips.

Life finally seemed to begin to make sense when I finally saw her again.

It always stunned me that she had the kind of power in her voice that she did when she was so young. Over the years, it's clear she was able to fine-tune it and control it even better.

The last ten years have been fucking hard. Nightmares have haunted me every single night since that day. The day I lost her.

I can hear myself screaming. Repeating 'she's gone.' Over and over like a fucking broken record. The feeling of my heart being ripped out of my chest.

Being diagnosed with severe post-traumatic stress disorder at the young age of eight is no joke. Add that to also being diagnosed with depression and anxiety, it's been a fucking hoot. Depression has ruled my life for a long time. The black dog just never could fuck off.

My heart aches remembering the number of times when it all got a bit too much and the only thing stopping me from meeting my maker was the guys. If it wasn't for them, I know I wouldn't be here. I owe them my life.

The thing with depression and anxiety is it never just magically disappears. You learn coping mechanisms to help deal with the mess in your head. Medication dampens the feelings. Makes them just that little bit easier to survive. But they are never truly gone. Healing takes time and patience.

Music was a part of that healing for me. It was a language both Star and I understood and communicated through. When I found it again, I was able to slowly pull myself out of the pit that threatened to consume me. Don't get me wrong, I still have bad days. But now, they are much less frequent. The boys and Mom aren't terrified that they will wake up each day and find me overdosed on pills or swinging from a fucking tree. That's the one thing I regret the most. Even though it was mostly out of my control, the hurt I caused the people I love the most consumes me. While they were grieving the loss of Scarlett and Bonnie, they were also terrified for me.

I'm shaken out of my thoughts as Scarlett rips Rhodes' keys out of his pocket and storms out of Pinks' without a single care that she sat one of the bigger Bird's members on his ass with her determination at getting the fuck out of here.

"Scarlett!" I yell as I take off after her. Before I get too far, a hand wraps around my wrist and pulls me back. I yank my arm out of their grasp and turn to the fuck wit trying to keep me from my girl.

"Dakes, just let her go. She's not worth it."

I see fucking red.

"Not fucking worth it?" I bellow at Dawson. By the look on his face, he knows he just fucked up. But he is one stubborn motherfucker.

"I don't know if you were hit on the fucking head or drank a dose of fuckwit in the last few hours but you are kidding yourself if you think that girl isn't worth it!"

I get angrier and angrier as I get up in his face. Over the years, we've gotten into our fair share of bullshit fights, but this is different. She is different.

"Did you miss the last ten fucking years of our lives? Did you miss that trip to Australia? I'm not fucking blind, Dawson. I know what she means to you. To all of us." I gesture to the other guys who are just standing back not expecting my outrage. To be honest, I'm not either. But when it comes to her, I would go to war without question.

"For you to go and treat her the way you just did is unforgivable. To belittle her feelings. To make her think she isn't the fucking air I breathe. The literal light in the dark that is my life. You can lie to yourself all you like, but don't you dare speak for me. Not when it comes to her."

I shove Dawson as I step past him, making him stumble away. He's a big dude on a good day but with the amount of anger coursing through my body right now, he doesn't stand a chance.

"I'm going to get my girl. Try to fucking stop me."

I tear out of the club just as quickly as Star did. As I come out of the club, I see the taillights of Rhodes' bike off in the distance, her gorgeous blonde hair floating out behind her.

I race over to my KX450 and jump on it, starting it as quickly as I can before taking off after her. There is nothing in this world that could even begin to stop me from being with my girl. Not heaven or hell and sure as fuck not Dawson.

I follow after her as quickly as I can, pushing the limits of my bike. I know that she can ride. She proved that back in Australia on the day we took the bikes to that beach spot she loves so much. I don't think there is anything sexier than my Scarlett sitting on the back of her bike, the wind in her hair and the look of bliss on her face. The image is imprinted in my mind.

It's obvious that Scarlett hasn't been back here for very long. It wouldn't surprise me if she had only just got here. She turns up the street that leads up to the Crux house. Sailing through the gates, she doesn't bother to slow for the guards. I slow down as I reach the gates and give the boys a nod as they usher me through.

I pull up at the front of the house, I find Scarlett still sitting on Rhodes' bike with her head in her hands. Her shoulders are shaking slightly as she cries. My heartbreaks for her.

Dawson is so far out of line and seeing her heartbreak firsthand just makes me wild. A part of me wants to turn back around and rip his stupid fucking head off. To break him as badly as she is. Instead, I shove it down. Star needs me. My want to be here for her is more than my anger for Dawson. I kick down the stand on my bike and make my way over to Scarlett. Soft whimpers escape her chest, slowly getting louder the closer I get.

"Star," I say quietly, my heart shattering knowing the cause of her tears.

She startles as she snaps her head towards mine. In her state, it's like she didn't hear my bike pull up beside hers. I don't blame her. I've felt this kind of all consuming hurt. A pain that just takes over. It's blinding.

I grab her off her bike and pull her into my arms. She fights me for a minute. I can't blame her. I wouldn't want to see me either right now. Not when I am a part of this hurt she feels. Not when I broke her. Rhodes said as much. Fuck, if that didnt break me. Knowing that I did that to her. That I was so selfish in my want for her to be protected, to be safe, that I destroyed the only woman I have ever loved.

Eventually she gives in to the fight, her body sagging against mine. I lift her into my arms, supporting her like I know she so desperately needs right now. She can yell and scream at me later. Lord knows I deserve it. But right now she gives in. Allows me to comfort her. I don't deserve this privilege that she has granted me but I take it anyway. I'll take whatever scraps she feeds me. The anger that has been building up inside of me slowly fades to the back of my mind and is replaced with contentment and love for this girl even while she breaks. Her sobs get louder as I make my way over to the steps on the front porch and sit down, still holding her tight in my arms.

"It's okay baby. I'm here and I'm never letting you go. Fucking ever."

"H-How can he be so f-fucking cruel?" Her sobs make her hiccup over her soft words.

"I don't know, Star. But he is a fool. You are the best thing about this punishing world and if he is too stupid to see that, it's not you that is missing out. It's him."

"It hurts." I pull back and bring my hands up to hold her face in my hands, mimicking the way she held mine in hers back at Pinks'. I lean in and kiss away the salty tears that are streaming down her beautiful face. Her eyes are puffy and red but she is a masterpiece. A perfectly broken sculpture.

"I know. But if it helps, I'm here. He will wake up to himself sooner or later. He is probably just shocked. Fuck Star, the last person I ever thought I would see in Pinks' was you."

I don't know why I bother even trying to defend Dawson's actions towards Scarlett. He doesn't deserve it. But I can't help but see reason amongst my anger.

"The last person I thought I would find here would be you too. After you guys left…" She trails off as she looks down at her hands that fidget in her lap. A small tear escapes her eye again.

"That has been one of the biggest regrets of my life, Scarlett. Ghosting you like that. You didn't deserve it. When we got home, the club was in complete fucking chaos. We had to instantly jump in and fight. We had to protect you. These people that we are up against are fucked up. They will do anything to hurt the people that we love. Fuck…" I breathe out. "…they already hurt the one person that I love," I say as I look at her. It takes a few seconds, but she eventually catches onto what I'm trying to say. Her eyes widen into massive saucers as tears still drip from them.

"Love?" She questions as she looks right into my eyes. I nod my head.

"I love you, Scarlett. I have loved you for a long time. I loved you as a beautiful little seven-year-old girl with pigtails that brightened any room she walked into. I love you now as the most beautiful woman I have ever laid my eyes on. I loved you before your accident and I love you now."

"No," she says, shaking her head but I give her a sad smile, nodding.

"I do, Star. Desperately, I do. If you let me, I will treat you right. I will make you happy. I fucked up with the way I handled things after leaving you back in Yeppoon. I will regret that every day of my life. But I will make it up to you. You are it for me baby. You are the only woman I have ever seen. My whipper snapper self even knew it." Her lips quirk and I take it as a win, needing to see that smile on her face. God, that beautiful smile. The one that is still the same even ten years later that seems to light up her face.

"Dacre, I…" She begins but I interrupt her before she can continue.

"No, Star," I say, shaking my head, "I don't deserve a single thing from you right now. Not with the way I have hurt you. I have a long way to go in earning your forgiveness." I chuckle and pull my hand that isn't wrapped around Scarlett through my hair, "This is irrevocably the worst time to confess my feelings for you but I never claimed to be smart. I just had to be honest with you. I need you to forget even for a moment the pain you have been through because that's what you deserve."

I move my hand to her face, caressing her cheek, "You deserve a love that consumes you. When you are ready; when I have proven myself to you, I hope that you will allow me to give that to you."

"You are too good for me, Dacre," she whispers. I can tell a part of her fights with that revelation. Like it hurts to admit it in the state she is in.

"No baby, I'm really not," I say. How can she not see what I see? She is fucking perfection. There and then I vow to make sure she knows just how perfect she is for me every day for the rest of our lives. Call it what you will but she is end game.

She rolls her eyes at me, making me laugh.

"Come on. You should head inside and get an early night. We've got school tomorrow."

"Ugh. I forgot about that," she groans, running her hands through her hair. She slowly composes herself. I watch, feeling immense pride as she pulls herself together. This woman is stronger than I ever gave her credit for.

"Come on, you will love it. You will have the best study buddy in me," I say as I wiggle my eyebrows at her, earning a little chuckle.

"I don't know. I think you will be more of a distraction than anything." She raises one eyebrow, that defiance slipping through slowly.

"No chance, Star. That would be the other pain in the ass, Sonny."

"Oh god, I'm already behind and I haven't even started," she groans, rubbing her hands over her face.

"Don't stress. I'll be here to pick you up at 8 tomorrow morning. I won't let you go in there alone."

"Okay," she sighs in relief.

I stand up and let her legs fall down off my waist. I don't let her go too far as I capture her soft lips in mine, even only for a moment. I know I'm stealing this from her. I'm unable to not be selfish. I want to take everything she has to offer me. I'm not too proud to get down on my knees for it either when the timing is right.

The Captain Morgan I taste on her lips might have been

her choice of poison for the night but she is mine. And god, is it sweet. Exactly as I remember. There's a slight saltiness too from her tears but it just adds to her appeal. I force myself back before I get too carried away. She is way too easy to get lost in.

"See you tomorrow," I say quietly.

"See you tomorrow, Dacre."

BOARDING P
NAME: SCARLETT SMIT
FROM:
TIME:
CLAS
SEAT:
President

chapter
THIRTEEN

The sound of the alarm on my phone wakes me up from a deep sleep. I groan as I smack at my phone trying to turn off the ear piercing noise.

After going inside having said goodnight to Dacre last night, the overwhelming fatigue finally set in and I crashed the minute my head hit the pillow.

Going through a tidal wave of emotions and realisations these past few weeks has made me incredibly tired. Normally I can survive on an easy six hours sleep, but I'm now exhausted from the moment I wake.

I blink my eyes open begrudgingly. The memories of last night filter in painstakingly. I allow myself a moment to process them, something I haven't done whatsoever; but this is something I need to do.

Each interaction I look back on makes me furious. Those memories of our time at the beach, wandering hands across sweaty skin and whispered promises, all shattered. I shake myself at how naive I was. How could I possibly believe they were everything I had hoped for? Why am I allowing myself to be broken by men that didn't give me a second thought. Dacre believes there is a good reason for what they did? What could be worth it? A moment of remembrance flickers in my mind of Dacre telling me that the club was in a mess when they got home but my brain doesn't allow myself to focus on it. At least not right now. There's too much pain and heartache to focus on anything at all. Why turn your back on someone all just to be ecstatic when you see them again? Well, apart from Dawson that is. It makes me question what is real and what's fake? Who do I believe?

Was our time together all just a lie?

Banging from the other side of the door startles me out of my thoughts. The noise rattles my brain. Groaning, I roll over and bury my head into my pillow wishing for just a moment of peace.

"Go away." My voice is muffled but I don't care.

"Up and at 'em sunshine. It's a new day, the sun is shining and it's time to get ready for school."

"Ugh, why did I ever think a twin brother would be a good idea."

Nothing would have prepared me for the weight of Rhodes jumping onto me and squishing me. I don't know when he managed to slip through the door when I'm sure I locked it last night.

"What was that? You like being annoyed by your baby brother?"

Rhodes launches straight into a tickle attack. A laugh is ripped straight from me as he keeps me pinned to the bed. His attack is relentless. I feel like I can't breathe. No amount of kicking around and pleas to stop make him quit.

"Stop. Stop, please." I beg in between spouts of laughter.

"Say 'Rhodes is the greatest and best brother in the world

and I love him so much'."

"Rhodes… is the….greatest….. and omg… RHODES!" I stutter.

"Keep going. I can't stop until you say it all."

"Best brother… in the world and… I love him… so much." I finish. "Now get off me, I can't breathe." Rhodes finally ceases his tickle attack and gets up off the bed, giving me the chance to breathe.

I roll over, finding Rhodes staring back down at me grinning like a Cheshire cat.

"How can you be so energetic at this time of the morning?"

"Come on Scar, it's your first day at school. You are finally back home. What is there to not be excited about?"

"I don't know. Maybe it's the whole school part?" I grimace. "I wasn't too far off graduating back in Australia, now I have to start senior year all over again. Kill. Me. Now." I think that has been the worst part about moving over here. I will almost be twenty by the time I graduate. What the fuck is that?

"Come on, you are going to love it," he says, nudging me so he is able to flop down on the bed beside me. He rolls onto his side and rests his head on his hand like he's ready to gossip, "Remember what I explained to you. The Birds run the school. You will be fine. Plus you have the inevitable training sessions to look forward to."

I roll my eyes, slamming my head back into my pillow again.

No matter how in depth Dad and Rhodes explain all of this stuff to me, it almost feels like a movie. Like someone sitting behind a computer screen is just thinking up the most insane and impractical shit and just writing a story about it. What twists and turns are going to happen next? Which of your favourite characters will be the one that gets killed? You will betray who? Authors are fucking sick and twisted. But God, do they write some entertaining shit. Not to mention some of the smut that Grace has forced upon me. Ten out of ten.

"I know you might not be ready to talk about it, but I need to ask." Rhodes trails off and sighs. I can already tell where this conversation is going to go and he is right, I don't want to talk about it. But there is no time like the present, I guess. "What the fuck happened last night?"

I take a deep breath before I begin to answer, knowing I need as much time as possible to process it all myself.

"To be honest, I don't actually know," I sigh before sitting up and brushing the stray hair around my face away with my hands. Rhodes sits up beside me and crosses his legs, waiting for me to continue.

"You obviously remember what I told you about those guys from America that I met back in Australia?" I wait for him to nod, when he does, I keep going, "Well, things started off really great. I met them on the night of my, well our eighteenth birthday. From the first moment, we had this connection. It was electric. It felt like it moved fast but it also felt right. Like we were meant to meet when and how we did. To form this kind of soul connection. I showed them around a bit and we just hung out. Got to know each other on a deep level. Feelings started to form from my side but I always knew that their time with me had an expiry date.

"It may have seemed strange and greedy to a lot of people to have five people that you are romantically interested in, but for me at least, nothing had ever felt more right."

"So, what happened then?" Rhodes asks, his hands twitch in his lap like he doesn't know what to do with them. Trying to prepare himself to be royally pissed off like I know he would be. I've told him snippets of what happened but could never go into detail. Until now, I suppose.

"We all promised to stay in contact just before they left. Promises of facetime calls, me potentially coming over, them even potentially coming back over. But I never heard from them once they landed. It's like they never existed. All of my calls and texts went unanswered. I couldn't find them on social media. I was completely ghosted."

"Fucking assholes," he seethes. I hum in response.

"Then last night," I blow out a breath, "Fuck, I don't even know what that was. They never spoke much about what their home life was like and I never questioned them obviously."

I go quiet, allowing my head to fall back and look at the ceiling.

"I never expected to be lied to and betrayed as much as I have."

Rhodes grunts in response. When I look up at him, stone cold fury radiates off him in waves.

"It's okay, Rhodes. I'm fine." I'm not fine and it's not okay but it's not like it wouldn't be the first lie told.

"No fuck that Scarlett! I refuse to sit around like some incapable idiot while those assholes are just getting away with breaking your heart," he says launching up from my bed. He proceeds to wear lines in my carpet as he walks back and forwards like he's trying to come up with a plan.

I groan, "Let me handle it please, Rhodes."

He halts as he turns to me, fury dark on his face.

"I don't think I can do that, Scar. I just got you back. I thought I lost you forever. It's my job to protect you." His hands fist in his hair, "I can't allow you to be hurt. Not in any form."

"Heartbreak happens Rhodes. It's not something that you can necessarily protect me from. But, you can be here for me. Have my back. Be a shoulder when I need you to be."

He nods his head as he processes my words.

"Okay, I can do that." He smiles down at me as his anger slowly dissipates. "Right, well now that's settled, get up," he says, grabbing my arms and trying to pull me up. He lets me go and I flop back down onto my bed. "You now have 20 minutes before we need to leave."

"You could have started with that, you know," I retort, throwing a pillow at his retreating back.

I rush around my room quickly throwing on what according to my father is required by Rydell Prep to wear. The vision of the American high school with lockers, a cafeteria and the freedom to wear what you like quickly diminishes before my eyes. Instead of ripped jeans and a band tee, I have to settle for a white collared blouse and a black and white tartan pleated skirt, then finishing off the look with a black blazer; the school's emblem on the left pocket.

I think the provided shoes might just be the bane of my existence: chunky *heeled* Mary Janes. I don't know what kind of misogynistic fuck decided heels were appropriate for school girls but I would gladly shove the heel up their ass. Give me flats any day of the week. At least the school got one thing right with the colours. None of that horrendous green some of those poor kids are forced into wearing.

I part my hair down the middle and braid both sides, really embracing that school girl look. Throwing on a quick but simple amount of makeup, I grab my bag and race down the stairs.

Mum, Dad and Rhodes are all sitting in the kitchen when I wander in.

"I need coffee. Pronto," I grunt.

"Here you go madame. One full strength cappuccino, two sugars just the way you like," Rhodes says, passing me a cup of liquid gold. I smirk at his ridiculous attempt at a posh English accent.

"I knew I loved you for a reason." I say, thanking him anyways.

"Are you ready for your first day, Scar?" My father queries while looking nothing like the president of the Thunderbirds that he is meant to be. He looks like he just rolled out of bed with his hair in a mess on his head. A pair of glasses sit low on his nose while he holds a newspaper in his hands. He is still wearing his pyjamas, something I wish I could be doing instead of wearing my uniform. His trackies are a navy blue while his shirt makes me snort. It's old and looks like it's been worn a million times but reads, 'I keep all of my Dad jokes in a Dad-a-base.'

Over the last few weeks, I've come to learn that the seemingly scary president of the Thunderbirds is actually just a typical Dad at heart. I have heard enough ridiculous Dad jokes to last me a last time. It seems his version of humour isn't limited to just verbal. While I am slowly warming up to the idea of him, it's hard to just let go of the grudge I'm holding so tightly to my chest.

"I think so. Dacre said he would be picking me up this morning for my first day."

My father just grunts in reply.

"What?" I question as I take a sip of my coffee.

"I'm not fucking happy with those boys, Scar."

"You and me both," I grunt. No matter how excited I feel that I don't have to put out a missing person's report or do some wicked social media stalking just to find them, what the boys did just can't be forgotten that easily. No matter how much I wish it could. How much easier it would be. But that anger? It won't dissipate. Nor will I let it. I need an explanation, a good one at that.

"Rhodes gave me the long story short as well as a couple of the senior members that were hanging around Pinks'. No one on this fucking planet will dare hurt my baby girl again and those little fucking boys are going to learn that the hard way."

I sigh a breath, lifting up my cup of coffee before draining a bit more of it, "I understand that, and I agree. I won't be forgiving them quickly. But in saying that, Dacre at least made an effort to explain a little. There are still a lot of gaps missing and they will be getting their balls busted. I won't just forgive and forget."

He chuckles, putting down his newspaper and taking his glasses off. He looks up at me with a massive smile on his face. "That's my girl."

A knock sounds at the door and as Rhodes goes to answer it. I quickly down my coffee and grab a granola bar from the pantry knowing I will need some form of sustenance. Thanks to my darling brother and his need to gossip so early in the morning, anything more than a grab and go just isn't achievable.

"Well, when you speak of the devil, he shall appear," Rhodes snarls, walking in with a Dacre that has a slightly concerned look on his face.

He looks straight at my father, greeting him first. "Morning Prez."

It's obvious just how much respect Dacre has for him. He gives him a small nod in greeting but stays silent. There's a deadly look in his eyes and for the first time, the stories that Rhodes has told me finally make sense. If a lesser man was on the end of that glare, I am sure they would piss themselves.

The saying 'If looks could kill' is somewhat accurate in this instance. Because that is exactly what he looks like now. Ready to kill someone. *Lord give me strength.*

Dacre quickly turns his head towards Mum.

"Mrs Crux. It's so good to see you again."

"Thank you, Dear. You've grown into such a handsome young man. How is Shelly?" Mum asks.

"She is great. She is over the moon that you and Scarlett are alive and here. She couldn't shut up last night when I got home." He smiles that devastating smile of his. Fuck, it's going to be hard to stay mad at them but I know my resolve won't fail.

"I'll go down to Pinks' and see her. It's been hard not having her all of these years." Mum turns to me as she nods towards Dacre, a smile on her face. "Dacre's Mum, Shelly, and I were inseparable from the day we met each other." Her smile drops and a haunted look overcomes her face as she takes a deep breath. "We were caged side by side. If it wasn't for her strength, I wouldn't have gotten through it."

Dacre nods, looking solemn.

"She would really love that, Mrs Crux."

"Please Dacre, it's Bonnie," Mum says as the smile returns to her face.

Dacre then turns to me. His face completely lights up as he takes in my uniform. He doesn't hesitate from closing the distance between us and pulling me into his arms. My arms hang beside me for a moment. I can feel Dacre deflate in disappointment. I don't push him away though and I don't really know why. I know I probably should but I can't. Just not yet. Maybe in a moment.

"Morning Star," he whispers in my ear. A chill runs over my body. *Yeah, fucking fuck.* This is going to be so much harder than I thought.

"Morning," I reply, unable to use my normal nickname for him. I notice again the new nickname he has for me. That same shiver that went through my body also replicates in his. He lets a breath go, like he has been holding it all night. Knowing that I affect him just as much as he does me, sends a strange ping straight to my heart.

He eventually pulls away from me but doesn't step back too far.

"Are you ready for your first day?" Dacre asks. I give him a small, sharp nod in reply. I attempt to put on a confident front when in reality, as the morning has gotten on, I've become increasingly nervous. These people all know the old me, yet I don't. The old me would already know who to stay away from, who is an ally and who is the enemy. The new me has no fucking idea and just has to trust in everyone else around me.

"Come on then, let's go."

I quickly say goodbye to both Mum and my father. Mum gives me wishes of good luck with the latter giving me a proud look and whispering, "Give them hell baby girl."

I turn to Rhodes who gives me a quick hug.

"I'll meet you there, Scar." He turns and steps right into Dacre's face. My brother's features turn cold and the threat of 'fuck around and find out' radiates from him, mirroring our dad's look from before. He shoves his finger into Dacre's chest. I go to step forward but Dacre puts up a hand stopping me. "If my sister gets hurt while in your care, I will fucking gut you," Rhodes snarls in his face.

"I'll let you."

"That goes for those other little fuckwits too."

"I'll make sure they are aware." That same respectful demeanour from earlier when faced with Dad is back and firmly in place. When Rhodes said he would be an overprotective brother, he really wasn't kidding. Not that I'm complaining one bit. I may be tolerating Dacre right now but that sure as shit doesn't mean that he is even close to being forgiven.

Dacre and I head out the side door and, instead of a car, I see the same green Kawasaki that I saw in the group yesterday.

"Holy fuck Dacre! Is she yours?" I ask rushing over to the bike and begin looking it over. My hand trails over the seat of the bike, rubbing it like it's a precious gem.

"Yeah it is. I was going to bring my car but I remembered how much fun we had riding those bikes on the beach and thought you'd prefer to take the bike instead."

"You would be right. God, I'm obsessed," I replied with hearts in my eyes. Seeing this bike up close is even better than I originally expected.

During my thorough examination of the bike, I swear I hear Dacre mumble under his breath.

"I'm obsessed with you."

"Huh?" I ask. There is a slight blush to his cheeks as he combs his fingers through his hair.

He clears his throat quickly. "Ahh. Nothing. We should get going. We don't want to be late and I'm not too keen on seeing what your Dad and brother would do if you are."

I laugh, "You are probably right."

Dacre eyes me for a moment longer but quickly shakes himself out of it and jumps on the back of the bike, handing me the second helmet.

I swing my leg over the back of the bike, excitement filling me even if I'm just on the back as a passenger. I slide my hands around Dacre's waist. I don't fail to miss the little shiver he gives as I tighten my grip.

The rumble of the bike starting gives me an all too familiar giddy feeling. I didn't get to enjoy my hasty getaway from

Pinks' yesterday, too caught up in my thoughts.

But as the bike launches down the driveway, I allow myself to soak up the freedom that comes with being on the back of a bike.

BOARDING PASS
NAME: SCARLETT SMITH
FROM:
TIME:
CLASS:
SEAT:
President

BOARDING P
NAME: SCARLETT SMIT
FROM:
TIME:
CLAS
SEAT:
President

chapter
FOURTEEN

scarlett

The drive to Rydell Prep is less than five minutes. It helps that Rydell itself is pretty small considering it's an outer suburb of Los Angeles. I've been told a decent amount about the history of Rydell and the Thunderbirds during the last few weeks.

Apparently, the prep school was originally built back in the early 1900s and has been passed down through the Crux family. When Great Grandpa Crux handed it down to Grandpa Crux, The Thunderbirds had already established the building as their headquarters. Once my father became president and completely transformed the Birds, he turned the former headquarters into a school for the children of the Thunderbirds and the outer community.

As we head into the school car park, Dacre pulls up beside a couple of familiar men also getting off their bikes. I cock my head as I try to place them.

Are these the same guys from last night?

When they take off their helmets, I find myself looking at

Pike, Nicky, Sonny and that other fucktard who shall not be named. Gone are the dark jeans and leather jackets and in their place is black slacks, white button up shirts, black coats and a black tie with thin white stripes, identical to the ones Dacre is wearing. They seem to take a double look when they look over at Dacre and I as if they didn't realise I would be coming to school with him this morning.

They rush over the minute I swing my leg off the bike. I am barely able to straighten my skirt before Nicky is picking me up and swinging me around. I try not to soak up the familiar feeling of how he used to greet me back in Australia.

"Morning baby girl," he whispers in my ear causing a shiver to run down my body.

"Morning Nicky," I whisper back to him, cursing myself as a lump forms in my throat. Nope, not today. I will myself to be strong, refusing to allow my resolve to crumble over a few whispered words.

I wiggle and he puts me down, giving me a small smile as he cups my cheek. Before he can say anything else, Sonny barrels him out of the road and swiftly picks me up and throws me over his shoulder. I let out a shriek.

"See you later, *idiotas,*" he yells out over his shoulder at the guys standing around their bikes with dumbfounded looks on their faces.

"Sonny, put me down you bastard. Everyone is going to see up my skirt."

"No one would dare to look up your skirt, *mi estrella.* They would all have their eyeballs removed quicker than they could say purple elephants."

I hit his back with my fists but he is completely unfazed.

"Sonny, I swear to god! Put. Me. Down!"

"Ugh, you are no fun." Begrudgingly, he finally puts me down. I grab his shoulders allowing the blood to retreat from my head.

"You're an ass, Sonny."

"A sexy ass," he says with a cheeky smile and a wink.

The boys all finally catch up to Sonny and I. Pike whacks Sonny over the back of the head.

"Don't worry Princess, I'll save you," Pike says as he sweeps me up in his arms. As I go to wrap my arms around his neck, I hesitate in just how easy it is to fall back into old habits with them. It would be too easy to allow myself to be sucked back up by their presence again. To let bygones be bygones. Yet as my arms snake around his neck, I allow myself to be caught in the moment. Why? Maybe I'm just a sucker for pain.

"Finally, my Prince Charming is here to save me from the big bad villain. We can finally live happily ever after," I sigh dramatically, but there is an edge of sarcasm to it. Something I don't think Pike gets the hint of.

Pike chuckles as he puts me down.

"I'll always save my Princess." There is a strange look in his eye that he quickly blinks away before he continues on, as If it was never there in the first place.

"Looking forward to your first day?" He asks.

"Having to restart my senior year at the end of what was already my senior year wasn't really on my bingo card." Not only is the time difference and lifestyle completely different in the States, so is the school running year.

That's the one thing I wasn't entirely thrilled about when moving here. An almost nineteen year old still in high school? I still can't help but wonder if I begged enough Ren would let me drop out early? I feel like shadowing him is a perfect excuse to drop out. I could even take a course on the side.

I make a mental note to ask him.

"You will be ok, Scar. You will have us to help you adjust," Nicky says.

Dawson scoffs and I snap towards him.

"Got something to say? Or are you lost?" I ask in the most sweetly sarcastic voice I can muster up.

He scoffs again. "You won't last a day here. Run back to Australia before you get yourself hurt. You aren't made for this lifestyle, Scarlett."

"I don't know why you think anything you have to say even deserves any merit, Dawson," I take a step toward him, "You seem to have forgotten just who my father is and what my role will therefore be. So, before you go running your fucking mouth, you should mind it."

Dawson can't seem to find the words to reply to me. He just stands there silent and stares at me. There is a slow clap behind us. Nicky, Pike, Sonny and Dacre are all standing there with looks of bemusement on their faces. Nicky stops clapping and a big smile lights his face.

"Thank fuck! I was just about ready to lose the plot after the shit this douche was carrying on with last night." Nicky comes up to stand beside me and puts his arm around my shoulder. "Come on, baby brother. We have lost Scarlett one too many times. She is back now. Stop being a fucking asshole."

"That exact carefree attitude will be the same thing that allows Scarlett to be hurt again. She shouldn't be here." His teeth clench. The anger deepening in his expression. "She. Will. Fucking. Die."

I jolt at his tone. Before any of us can reply, he turns around and storms off. His anger in regards to me is actually surprising. My head feels like a mess as I watch his retreating form. Why is he so angry when last night he didn't seem to care?

"Don't worry about him, Scar. It must be shark week," Sonny jokes, attempting to lighten the mood. Yet, Dawson's bullshit has seemed to shake me out of the haze that seems to come over me when I am in the presence of these men. I shake Nicky's hand off my shoulder as I find myself again.

"What the fuck was that last night?" I demand, looking between the four men standing in front of me.

"I don't have any kind of explanation for what that was last night, Scarlett. But as for my – our – actions, you more than deserve an explanation. Just name a time and place and we will tell you everything," Pike says as he steps closer to me. "But until then, we are going to be hanging around like bad smells. The way we handled shit was wrong and while I can't speak for the other guys, I won't let you down again."

A shred of me wants to break down in front of Pike. But a bigger part of me is wild with anger. Wild at how they have treated me. Beside myself with resentment towards the men in front of me. No matter how pretty their faces are, they can't expect me to fall to my knees.

Not today Satan.

I nod, "Unfortunately Pike, you already have. I'm not a stranger to heartbreak but it's going to take a bit more than that to butter me up." I watch his face falls. I pull up the straps of my bag and sigh. "Right, well I need to go to admin." I nod towards the building feeling slightly awkward all of a sudden. Pike, Nicky, Dacre and Sonny all rush forward to usher me there. Their enthusiasm to get back into my good books fills me with way too many ideas on ways to fuck with them and more importantly, make them grovel.

No, I'm going to make these motherfuckers get on their knees and beg to be forgiven.

I take a look at the timetable handed to me by the adorable lady at administration.

First up, Maths. Ugh.

"Fuck, Maths first thing on a Monday morning is brutal," I groan.

Nicky takes my timetable from me and looks it over.

"It looks like we have almost all of the same classes together," Nicky hands me back my timetable. "We've got training Monday, Wednesday and Thursdays as well."

"What do we actually do in training?" I question.

"Rhodes or your Dad hasn't explained it to you yet?" Sonny queries, his brow frowning slightly.

I shake my head. "No they haven't. A lot of the conversations since they came back into my life have been more about catching up on lost time. There have been a few things mentioned about the Birds but I am still pretty clueless, really." I grimace, realising just how much I am going to have to learn. The weight of it feels like it might consume me. The pressure to live up to the expectation my father has in place for me.

"Ok, that gives me a good idea on what to go off then. Once we hit our junior year, we are required to start attending training. While those of us that will inherit the leadership roles and have been training for years," Dacre begins, "The rest of the greenies only start then. Think, learning how to infiltrate high profile companies, setting up legitimate businesses to filtrate profits from our illegal businesses, weapons, and combat. Some of us go into the tech side of the gang. Others go into the dealing side. Basically, we learn the ins and outs of every activity in the 'Underworld'. When the Pres took over, he didn't want a bunch of unreliable gang bangers controlling the masses. He wanted people with their heads screwed on and this was the outcome."

I nod taking in the information. It makes sense that he would feel that way and by the success I can see that they have achieved, it's a no brainer. The idea of infiltrating a business though seems unimaginable to me. For some reason, the weapons and combat seem more tame, if that is even a possibility.

We continue the hallway and take a couple of different turns until we reach a classroom with a few stragglers filtering through the door.

Taking in my surroundings as we walk down the hallways, I feel like I'm in one of those American high school movies. Lockers line the walls with couples unable to keep their hands off each other. In Australia, lockers are a rare commodity. Only a select few schools have them. The majority of us have to carry all of our textbooks around on our backs. Surely the government should provide some kind of compensation for chiropractor appointments.

Not only that, but the fact that American schools seem to be one massive building with all the classrooms inside, versus Australian schools that have a heap of scattered buildings normally dedicated to a single subject.

I didn't fail to notice the number of stares the guys and I seemed to get. Seems my return is hot gossip amongst the masses. I wonder just how many of these people I used to know before. Were they any of my friends? My enemies?

Every time I even attempt to bring up the conversation on who my old friends were with Rhodes, he becomes cagey and steers the conversation in a different direction.

Almost like he wanted to keep me all to himself.

Weird.

Speak of the devil and he shall appear. Rhodes comes up the hallway flanked by the two burley guys I met last night, Jethro and Wyatt.

They have this presence about them that demands respect. Either that or they have a 'don't fuck with me' sign on their foreheads. Students hurry out of their way, clearing the hallway almost immediately.

"Hey, Scar," Rhodes says as he embraces me.

"Hey, baby bro."

Rhodes groans as he releases me. "Not around the guys, big sister," Rhodes jokes, making the guys around us chuckle.

"Morning Scarlett. Looking forward to your first day?" The blonde one, Wyatt says as he steps closer. I catch the small flirty smile straight away. While it doesn't give me butterflies like the men behind me do, I see it as an opportunity. The perfect one to get some of my own back. Remind certain individuals of who I am. Who I belong to.

I take a step closer and place my hand on his forearm. Wyatt's smile broadens at the touch and I feel his eyes heat where they are locked on me.

I feel the guys all stiffen the moment I touch him.

Fuck with me and I'll fuck with you right back boys.

"I'm a little nervous but more so worried about the workload." Lowering my eyes slightly and returning the flirty little smile.

Wyatt looks shell shocked for a moment that I actually flirted with him back but sobers quickly, that cocky bravado back firmly in place. His body relaxes into my touch.

"Don't worry baby. If you ever need a tutor, I don't mind helping out. I'm sure there's a lot I can teach you." He winks as his eyes roam my body, completely unfazed by the fact that my brother and the guys are watching us.

"I'm sure you can, big boy."

His eyes heat as he takes a step closer.

"Come on Scar, we are going to be late," Nicky grunts, taking my hand and dragging me into the classroom.

Rhodes, Wyatt and Jethro all chuckle. I have to do my best to hold mine in too.

Hook, line and fucking sinker.

My eyes scan the classroom.

The blood drains from my face and I freeze where I am.

Dawson and some bimbo give everyone a show in the middle of the walkway.

Motherfucker.

What is his problem?

He actually had some bitch and doesn't want me to get in the way? Thinking he can have a girl at home while he goes around fucking around with bitches in different countries?

Game on motherfucker.

I reach back and grab Wyatt's hand and drag him along with me. He doesn't hesitate to follow me.

I slam my shoulder into the whore's back as we walk through the desks. She stumbles and instantly turns around with fire in her eyes.

"Do you mind you fucking bitch?" Her cheap red lipstick is smeared across her face. Her pash rash making her look like a cheap hooker.

"I do actually. Get a fucking room."

"You better watch yourself," she snarls but instead of it being threatening, she looks more like an aggressive little puppy.

"Aww that's cute. Are you threatening me?" I plaster a smile on my face. I'm not to sure where this cocky confidence is coming from but, fuck me, do I embrace it. I have never been a fighter. It's almost like a part of my brain recognizes this place and is filtering in what I need to step up into my role. I take every little bit of it that I can right now.

This new Scarlett is fucking bad ass.

She steps up closer to me, getting right in my face. I can

see Dawson out of the corner of my eye. His arms are crossed over his chest. The same lipstick smeared across his face. His eyes are drawn tight. I can't hide a giggle.

"What's so funny?" The bitch sneers at me.

"The circus called. They want their star clowns back," I snigger, gesturing at my mouth sending the entire room into howls of laughter.

Her cheeks redden out of what I'm sure is both anger and embarrassment before she takes off out of the room, stomping off like a child. Meanwhile, Dawson clearly couldn't care less and just wipes the lipstick off his face. Without even a second glance my way. He turns around, sits down in his seat and opens his textbook.

Offering him the same courtesy he offered me, I turn my back on him and take a seat right behind him with Wyatt following close behind me. The other guys all filter in around us looking at me like kicked puppies.

Scarlett, one, Boys, zero.

Maths is the same as back home. Boring as all fuck. Wyatt flirts with me the entire lesson and I sure as fuck go along with it. If anything, I go completely over the top. He loves it too by the heated look in his eye. Unfortunately, it still does nothing for me. It sucks because he seems like a really nice guy. The kind of guy that maybe I should have fallen for. Instead it had to be the five knuckleheads that demanded it.

I can't even blame it all on them. I did this to myself as well. Stupid heart.

Not only do I have Wyatt's attention, I have the other guys as well. And a few other men looking at me like I'm a snack.

Dawson would never admit it, but I have him by the balls too. His shoulders are tight the entire lesson and each time I laugh, he clenches his desk. It makes me want to be even more abrasive.

Fuck him.

"So Scarlett," Wyatt begins. I turn to him and instantly notice the confident flirting demeanour is gone and in its place is a nervousness I didn't think Wyatt would be capable of. He runs his fingers through his hair before taking a deep breath.

"I don't want to overwhelm you seeing how you've just gotten back but I feel like if I don't jump at the chance now, I will miss out." He gives a nod towards the guys.

"You seem like a really cool chick and only an idiot wouldn't be able to see how gorgeous you are." He coughs and rubs his hand behind his neck.

"Come on Wy, don't choke on me now." I tease making him laugh, some of that nervousness fading.

"I was just ah… wondering, if maybe, you might want to go out for a couple of drinks at Pinks' tonight with me? I mean it's completely fine if you aren't inter-"

I stop him before he continues rambling, "I would love to." I give him a big smile.

He turns to me shocked, like he thought I was going to reject him "Wait really?"

"Yeah of course. I mean I have to head to Pinks' anyways to meet up with Shelly to talk about initiation and I know for a fact that I will need a stiff drink after today." I laugh expecting the worst for what's to come this afternoon.

"Initiation?" Wyatt questions. "You mean you still have too…" He trails off waiting for me to confirm.

"Yeah." I blow out a breath, "Rhodes was hoping that there would be a way around having to see his sister shaking her ass on stage but neither of us are that lucky unfortunately.

The cocky flirting is back in his expression. He licks his lips like he is already imagining me on stage in a thong and heels, "I'll be making sure I have front row seats."

I laugh, thankful for his relentless flirting. I didn't know I needed it until now. It helps to make me feel not so awkward about the fact I will quite literally have my entire ass out in front of a club packed full of men. Absolutely not daunting whatsoever.

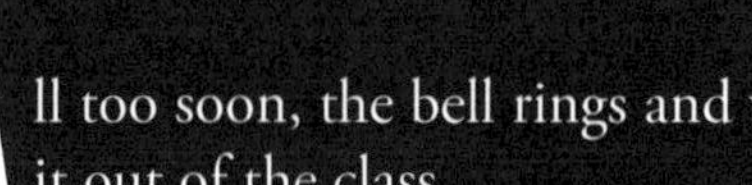

All too soon, the bell rings and we pack up and high tail it out of the class.

"What class do you have now, Scarlett?" Wyatt asks as the other guys all filter in around us, Dawson included. Fuck knows why, nor do I care to find out.

"Ah, I think I have History now."

"Damn. Well, make sure you save me a seat at lunch." He winks before turning around and walking off in the opposite direction.

I take a look at my schedule and confirm that I do in fact have History and I wasn't just taking a stab in the dark.

"We have got History too, Star. We can walk you there if you like?" Dacre asks meekly. That beautiful, soft person I began to fall in love with back home showing through. I have to work hard and keep by my mantra as he unknowingly chips away at it. Damn him. Damn him for softening me. I take a moment before I answer, needing to add a few more bricks to my wall. The devil on my shoulder refuses to bow down to them.

"That would be good." I nod, now confident in myself not to fall to pieces.

We take a couple of different turns, down hallways and up a staircase, ending up at yet another door. The stares and whispers follow us but we all stay silent. I don't allow the questions that hit my ears affect me. I don't need their opinions of how and why I'm here and why these five guys are following me around to throw me off course.

Dawson is still brooding behind us, but I just choose to ignore him and brush him off just like he did to me last night. That same unrelenting anger I feel towards him helping to fortify the walls around my heart I have been trying to keep built.

I need the strength. It would be too easy to let them fall. To let them back in. Each time I feel them droop, I remember just how broken I felt. The touch of abandonment never really goes away and right now, it helps to fuel my resolve.

History goes relatively the same as Maths; a teacher that makes me wish I could be sticking pins in my eyes then listen to him droning on about some wrinkly old bloke that died a million years ago and did something of mild significance to my life. While each of us is completely uninterested in a single word he is saying, I'm surprised to see everyone is at least being respectful of the guy. I spend the lesson doodling in my book, revenge on my mind. That inner cunt I keep tucked away making an appearance. She fits in right beside Betty, my drunk alter ego.

I slowly come up with a plan on just how much I can fuck with Pike, Nicky, Sonny and Dacre. The latter makes it hard to stick to my guns but, for the thousandth time today, I push it down.

My thoughts sway to Dawson for a moment, but it's clear he wants nothing at all to do with me. The feeling is mutual though, it doesn't hurt any less. If anything, it tastes bitter.

Just by how willing and interested Wyatt is in me and further, just how much the guys hate the way I flirt with him and in turn, him me, using him to my advantage just might work. While I feel a slight bit of remorse for using the poor guy, it doesn't stop me from running with the idea. He's a big boy, he will be fine.

The bell eventually rings and I shake myself out of my revenge fuelled day dream. I slowly pack my things away, the teacher is up the front going on about some test, or assignment or something. I don't know to be honest. I checked out a good five minutes into the lesson.

"You ready, baby girl?" I don't even have to look up to know it's Nicky.

"Yeah," I say, shortly. *Remember Scar, revenge.*

If Nicky was bothered with the tone of my voice, he doesn't show it. I look up at him. That massive smile is still all for me. Not for long I'm sure when he realises just what's in store for him if he wants to earn my forgiveness.

Without another word, he nods towards the door. I sigh, before falling into step with him. The guys all fall in around us just like they did earlier.

The hallways are all hustle and bustle as everyone begins to make their way down to the cafeteria.

Another difference between America and Australia. Our tuck shops are like the school's takeaway shop. Rhodes explained to me just how different Rydell Prep is. Really, it shouldn't surprise me considering the types of uniforms we are required to wear.

The cafeteria resembles more of an all you can eat restaurant. You name it, it's on offer. I watch some kid stack his plate with steak. Just steak and nothing else. I mean one look at the guy and it explains it all. He looks like he could break bones without breaking a sweat. Wouldn't put it past him.

He has to be a Thunderbird for sure.

I grab myself a plate and quickly fill it with some chicken, pasta and salad. Grabbing a drink out of the fridges at the end of the bain-marie, I look around the room and try to find Rhodes and hopefully along with him: Wyatt. It doesn't take me long to spot my twin who is also looking around the room for me.

I head over to him without sparing a second glance back at the boys knowing that they are most likely going to follow me anyways.

Rhodes finally notices me and jumps up out of his seat. He takes my tray before picking me up and twirling me around. I laugh and smack his shoulder, amused by his playfulness.

"Missed me, did you baby brother?"

"Always, big sister."

We both laugh together as he quickly sets me down. I feel the boys right behind us. Perfect timing.

I make my way over to Wyatt who is currently stuffing his face full of food. I lean down and slowly brush a kiss over his cheek. Wyatt jumps in surprise, not expecting me at all. His food must go down the wrong hole because he begins to choke.

"Hey babe, missed me?" I say loud enough for the boys that I'm sure are standing right behind me to hear.

Wyatt tries his best to clear his throat and starts banging on his chest. "Ahh, yeah. Shit." He swallows his food before giving another small cough. "I sure did." He smiles before turning to the guy next to him. "Move dweeb." The kid beside him pales and quickly moves tables completely. I take his seat and turn a sugary sweet smile to him.

Sitting down in the now vacant spot, I watch out of the corner of my eye as the guys all filter in around us trying to find a seat. For some strange reason, Dawson is still hanging around. His glare feels like daggers where it is currently locked on me.

Rhodes tucks himself in close beside me. His plate is stacked with nothing but protein and carbs. I give him a funny look. "Are you allergic to salad or something?"

"Come on Scar. How else did you think I was able to get these muscles and keep them?" He wiggles his eyebrows at me, chuckling.

"God, you are so full of yourself. Remind me to never compliment you. That head of yours might just explode," I laugh.

"Tell us about it. I think his ego grows daily at this rate. Those girls." Wyatt nods his head towards a group of girls sitting at a table across from us, glaring daggers at my head. I spot the same chick from Maths. Pash rash gone, "Really don't help. It's constantly 'Oh Rhodes baby, your muscles have gotten so big' and 'Meet me behind the staircase, Daddy.'" Wyatt's imitation of the girls sends the entire table into laughter, causing the rest of the room to all look over at us.

"While your imitation of those voices is one of the greatest things I've ever heard, the last thing I need to know is just how much of a man whore my little brother is," I say, clutching my stomach as my laughter fizzles and I shudder.

"Ouch, Scar." Rhodes clutches his chest like my man whore comment hit him like a bullet but we both know that I'm right as I watch him cringe slightly.

His extracurricular activities have already been exposed. That being a dirty message coming through on his phone while he was showing me photos one night.

Things got awkward real fast.

"Moving on," I break the now awkward silence.

I think that's enough talk of my brother and his conquests

to last a lifetime.

to last a lifetime.

chapter
FIFTEEN

nicky

can't help but stare at Scarlett the entire lunch break. I still haven't been able to wrap my head around the fact that she is actually here. In front of me. *Alive.*

The fact that none of the guys or I were able to piece together the clues back in Australia is fucking embarrassing. Come on, both of their names are Scarlett, both had blonde hair and those stunning blue eyes that I could just dive into; not to mention a brother.

I feel like that guy from *A Cinderella Story,* who had no idea who his girl was when her face was barely concealed by a mask. For fuck's sake, the guy interacted with her multiple times after they met in person and still couldn't see what was right in front of him.

It's obvious Scarlett was right when she told us about her memory loss. She can't remember us. I try to not let that fact affect me as much as it should. Especially when I can remember every detail about her. The cheeky smile that would adore her face as we planned mischief together. The way she had this carefree attitude about her. Her voice that penetrated your soul. She was a fucking powerhouse. Still is.

I'd never tell the other guys but I have listened to an old recording one of the Mom's took back when we were about seven. Scarlett is up on stage with nothing but a backing track keeping her in time. Her hair in braids, a butterfly shirt and matching skirt belting *Creep by Radiohead.* I remember that day as if it were yesterday. We had been rounded up by Scarlett as per usual. It wasn't hard for her to get our attention. It was her first performance in front of the club. It wasn't unusual to hear her singing. That's all she ever did. We all pretended it annoyed us, but we were enamoured by her. We had sat and watched her practice for weeks. Rhodes was always a little jealous of how close we were with Scarlett. I mean we did follow her around like lost puppies, but they were a package deal. Where one went, so did the other.

I knew that I was going to marry Scarlett even from a kid. Losing her was the most painful thing I have ever experienced in my life. Nothing has ever been able to compare. No matter what the trainers have put us through during training, I'd prefer to go through all of that ten times over than have her taken from me again.

Now that she is back, I refuse to let her go.

It feels surreal to see her just sitting there laughing along to whatever Rhodes and Wyatt are talking to her about. The fact that she was alive all this time. That she was right under our noses and we still didn't know that it was her. I instantly caught onto her plans. It doesn't stop the raging jealousy inside of me every time she pins him with one of those breathtaking smiles of hers that I wish were only for me.

I don't mind Wyatt. I haven't had much to do with him since he became friends with Rhodes. He didn't grow up in the club, instead transferring here in freshman year after being found in one of the trafficking rings the Birds were able to infiltrate.

While I know she is only flirting with him to get back at us, I hate every second of her attention that isn't directed at us. Her laughter is ours. Her touches are ours and I will be fucked if he gets anymore.

I'm a possessive fucker. I always have been when it comes to her. We all are. Except when it comes to each other.

We've just never had that jealousy when it comes to her. If she was hanging out with one of us, we would be happy. It was the same in Australia. I don't know if it's just the fact that even a tiny piece of her is enough or what exactly.

I'll allow her to play her games for now. But she better make no mistake, she is mine. I will get on my knees, crawl through glass, do whatever she needs to know just how sorry I am that I hurt her. The reminder of the way we just dropped her like nothing eats at me and has done daily since we got back from Australia.

We meant what we said to her before we left. None of us had any intentions of stopping communication. Pretty sure we all fell in love with her. I know I did.

Finding a, drunk off her ass, girl on the beach was not on the cards when we went down for a walk that night. Seeing her face once we finally caught up to her and Pike, I could have fallen to my knees in front of her right there and then. She had us hanging onto every single word she said. I felt like I was drunk off her that entire trip. Fate pulled us to her for a reason. Like it was waving her in our face but we were too busy being fucking *Austin Ames.*

Yet, unlike him, I refuse to lose the girl and be a complete Chad about it. I will suffer through whatever she determines is necessary. Even if it tastes like shit in the process. She will forgive me and my mistakes. Even if I have to force the point.

I never claimed to be a good guy.

Lunch seems to drag on forever. Dawson sits beside me, grouching and broody the entire time. After the way he has been speaking to Scar lately, I don't even understand why he's here. Unbeknownst to me, he wants her gone. I still haven't been able to work his issue out.

He hated having to ghost Scarlett. Was constantly going back through the photos of her we took over the break. I'm sure all of us did. But coming home to the club in absolute pandemonium, we had no choice. We each refused to drag an innocent civilian into our mess. No matter how much she meant to us.

The whole aim of the club is quite literally to protect innocent people. After already losing one person, we couldn't lose another. It was better for her to stay safe. Although, that plan well and truly blew up in our faces. Now that she is here and won't be leaving, it's our job to keep her safe. History won't repeat itself.

The bell rings and I groan remembering we have English, then perk up when I realise Scarlett's schedule is almost identical to mine.

Thank fuck Wyatt doesn't have English with us.

Getting into class, I push past the guys throwing back a smirk at their grumbles and protests. I sneak up behind Scar as she tries to find a seat, throwing my arm around her shoulder and whispering into her ear, "You can sit with me, baby girl."

She jumps slightly, not expecting me to have snuck up behind her. She turns and attempts to pierce me with a stern gaze but I don't miss the way the corner of her mouth turns up slightly.

"It's your lucky day."

"Baby, it's always my lucky day whenever it's spent with you."

"Damn Nicky, that was smooth. I didn't think you had it in you. I would have expected something like that from Sonny," she retorts, rolling her eyes.

"I'll have to work harder than won't I?" Scar doesn't reply but her little smile she attempts to hide before she heads in the direction of a few seats up the back is enough for me.

I rush to grab the seat beside her. The other guys grumbling in my direction, but I don't care. I have my girl for the time being, even if it's only for just over an hour.

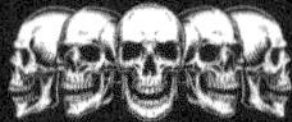

English goes better than I expected. The seats we currently sit in are the ones we keep for the rest of the year. That also means we are partnered up for assignments together. I revel in the fact that I at least get this piece of her every lesson. Although, I can already see how she is going to make me work for it. She doesn't give me an inch the entire lesson. While she may still swing an occasional smile my way from time to time, that wall is still firmly up.

The teacher has given us some book to read and an assignment where we have to completely dissect it and give our thoughts. Seems pretty basic to me. I see the dread on Scarlett's face. Thankfully it's a group assignment this time around.

Do I dare say this is a win?

BOARDING P
NAME: SCARLETT SMIT
FROM:
TIME:
CLAS
SEAT:
President

chapter SIXTEEN

The rest of the school day goes surprisingly smoothly. The boys do their best to stick close by my side. I watch them as they glare at random guys that attempt to come up and introduce themselves to me and watch as the poor things walk away, disappointed and pissed off glares aimed straight for the five of them. What surprises me though is the fact that Dawson joins in. I have never been more confused in my life when it comes to a person.

He had been fucking amazing back home in Australia. Even though we only had a month to spend together, it felt longer. I felt like I was able to learn so much about them. That we were able to get to know each other well enough that labelling ourselves 'off the market' wasn't a reach.

I let the months of heartbreak and tears build up my wall throughout the day. I have been way too soft on them. They hurt me beyond what I could have ever imagined possible. Watching the way Noah rampaged after I called him bawling my eyes out after days of not hearing from them. It took everything in me to stop him from doing something stupid like jumping on a plane and finding them. He was very descriptive about the way he planned on and I quote, "Bash those stupid jacked up, steroid sinking fucking cane toads heads in". I have no doubt that he would have given it a red hot crack too.

My phone buzzes in my hand and I flip it over from where it sits in my gym bag. As the screen lights up, I smile seeing who the message is from.

NOAH

> SCARLETT BABY!!!! I fucking miss your face! How is the US? Have you settled in properly?

> What is it like there? Is everyone being nice? Do I need to come over there and bash anyone yet?

> Because I fucking will!

I laugh, not realising how loud I actually was. I give those few glaring at me an apologetic smile before turning back to my phone and sending a quick reply.

ME

> HAHAHAHA! And this is why I love you Noah.

> It has been really good here so far. I have so much that I need to tell you though!

Noah's reply is almost instant.

"Well, you moved on pretty quickly didn't you Scarlett? I knew something was fishy between you and the football player. You just can't fake those kinds of longing looks. I'm sure the boys are going to be pretty fucking devastated when they find out you actually have someone back in Australia. And then all that flirting with Wyatt today? I think there is a name out there people call women like you? What was it again? Something rhyming with door?"

Anger thumps through my veins at the ballsy motherfucker standing behind me. I crack my head from side to side. If this motherfucker thought meeting Betty at the beach back home was eventful, he's seen nothing yet.

I slowly start clapping as I turn to face Dawson. It seems to gain the attention of the entire class. I don't focus on them or the way the guys start inching closer with confused looks on their faces. My focus remains entirely on the man that insists on carrying on with his bullshit. A sadistic smile creeps onto my face as I now completely face him. I give a few more claps of my hands before completely stopping. The silence in the gym is deafening as everyone watches

"Wow Dawson, look at you. Using your big boy words in an attempt to what?" I question him, quirking my eyebrow, "Get me to leave? Are you trying to slut shame me into getting back on a plane to Australia? Because if that was your grand plan, I'd hate to tell you but I'm not fucking taking the bait. Because this is my fucking life. A life that was ripped away from me and I refuse to stand down just because *you* have your knickers in a twist. So from the bottom of my heart Dawson, shut the ever living fuck up." I didn't realise that the entire time I was telling Dawson where to shove his postering bullshit, I had edged closer and closer to him until we were both chest to chest and I was right in his face.

The entire gym is silent as we stare off against each other. Neither of us backing down. I can hear whoops and cheers, mainly coming from Dacre, Sonny, Pike and Nicky but I pay them no mind.

"You are making a big fucking mistake staying here, Scarlett."

"And you are making a big fucking mistake by thinking my whereabouts have anything to do with you. You think that this is a position I can just turn down?"

The anger in his eyes seems to heat then as he closes the distance between us. If we weren't so pissed off at each other, our lips would be close enough to touch.

"You can. Give it to Rhodes. It's what he has spent the last ten years training for!"

"What, you think I can't handle it?" I ask, crossing my arms over my chest.

He chuffs, a cruel smile overcoming his features. "No, I don't think you can. Maybe the old Scarlett could have, but this new one?" He shakes his head before taking a small step back and looking up and down my body. "No, this new Scarlett is weak. The first sight of blood and she will be running back home to Daddy crying."

"That's where you are wrong, *sweetie*. When the day comes that I draw my first blood, you just better hope that it's not yours."

His face darkens as he steps further away. I see a flicker of what looks like heartbreak but it's gone before I can be certain. He doesn't say anything else. Just nods before turning and walking away. I give his back the finger. Even though he can't see the action, it satisfies the beast inside of me. The one desperate for a win.

"What was that all about?" Pike questions as he makes his way over to me followed closely by Sonny, Nicky and Dacre.

I shrug my shoulders, "Seems like your brother is determined to run me out of town," I say, looking from Pike to Nicky. He frowns but I know his issue isn't with me, it's with his brother.

"What the fuck is his problem?" His question isn't directed at anyone in particular. I couldn't answer him even if his question was aimed at me. I watch as he looks over in the direction Dawson strolled off into. "It doesn't make sense. He was just as conflicted in what we did to you as any of us were. Jesus, he hasn't stopped talking about you since we left."

I quirk my eyebrow at that but remain silent. I could rack my brain all day wondering what Dawson's problem is with me. I could make up charts researching it, but I still don't think I would come to a final conclusion. The man is an enigma. One I have zero interest in figuring out any more.

The doors to the gym slam open then and a smile lifts the corners of my mouth as I watch Brandy, Jen, Maxie and Rippy walk through. Brandy instantly spots me and an honest to god squeal escapes her lips.

"Scarlett!" She yells, causing the attention again to be diverted towards me, yet again. She practically sprints to get across to me. Brandy nearly knocks me over as she engulfs me into a hug.

"Hey babe! Ugh, I am so excited to have you here. Last night was epic! We have to meet up again before our next gig and organise some songs. I have been bursting with ideas, I've barely been able to sleep." I just stand staring at the woman in front of me as I watch as she talks a million miles a minute. "I know, I know, I know! We can have a sleepover this weekend to start planning. Now that I know you can hit those high notes there is no stopping us from doing some *Evanescence.* I have been dying to do covers of their songs. I mean, we did try it but Maxie couldn't quite hit those notes like I know that you will be able to. No offence Max baby."

Brandy turns an apologetic look Maxie's way. She is unfazed by it though as she stands there with a lollipop in her mouth, which makes a popping noise as she pulls it past her lips.

"Brandy, and I say this with so much love pumpkin pie, but shut the fuck up. You are talking a million miles a minute and poor Scarlett can't understand a single thing you are saying." I notice what I am guessing from my limited knowledge of America, is a slight southern twang to Maxie's voice. It mustn't have gotten my attention after the absolute chaos that was last night, but I definitely notice it today.

Maxie walks over towards me, throwing an arm around my shoulders. "Come on hon, let's go finish getting ready for this bullshit class. Once we are done, we will talk, 'kay?" She turns and smiles at me, before shooting a look at everyone else.

I notice the guys each have a scowl on their faces as they look at where Maxie's arm sits on my shoulder. Rippy also has the same look on her face. Why would she be jealous? I know why the boys would be, but Rippy has no reason to be. Surely she isn't one of those possessive friends. A shudder runs at me at the thought, eugh.

I still can't wrap my head around Rippy. If a person could be a black cat, it would be her. A constant resting bitch face has adorned her face from the moment I have met her. It briefly lifted last night while we played at Pinks' and again momentarily when she indirectly complimented me but it is firmly back in place.

It actually makes me think that her and Dawson would actually make a good couple. Both cranky motherfuckers living happily ever after. Why does that stupid thought send a pang of hurt through me?

Dawson has been nothing but an asshole since the moment he saw me again. Dawson has always been a bit of a closed book. Even when he eventually opened up to me back in Australia, it still never felt like I never got all of him. I knew I would have to take a pickaxe to his walls to finally see the guy underneath but now, I know that will never happen.

He has completely shut himself off. With the way he is going, it wouldn't surprise me in the slightest if he does the same thing to Dacre, Nicky, Pike and Sonny. It also wouldn't surprise me if they shut him out themselves. If they are being honest in their determination to get back into my good books, with what I know, they aren't going to take his shit for much longer.

Then again, I also didn't think them to be the kinds of guys that would have ghosted me after practically confessing their love for me. So really, what do I actually know?

The gym teacher finally makes an appearance, much to my relief which must be saying something because something tells me I'm not going to love this class.

"Right, gather around everyone," He calls out to the class before looking at me. "If you losers hadn't taken a second to look up from your book faces and tok tiks or whatever bullshit application you have wasted your precious teen years on, we have a new student. Don't be assholes and make Miss Scarlett Crux welcome. I'm Mr Green. If you have any questions, don't ask me," he says but his tone remains completely uninterested.

He quickly turns his attention back to the class. It shocks me as I hear the way he speaks to the class. It's also kind of refreshing. But what shocks me more is the verbalisation of my name. I vaguely remember Rhodes using it last night but hearing it from someone else jars me. The stark reality of my situation sets in. I have to reinforce myself so I don't break down right here in the middle of the gym.

Sonny leans over to me, snapping me out of my resolve and whispers in my ear, "Mr Green is also one of the trainers. He mainly teaches weapons. I did once see him break some guy's finger from a single touch. Nice guy though."

I snort, which has Mr Green snapping his head in my direction. I wince as his gaze narrows one me. I mouth a 'sorry' before giving him my full attention again. Fucking Sonny. Not even the first day and he has already directed the attention of one of the teachers at me, and not in a positive way either.

Mr Green's attention lingers on me for a few more seconds before he looks back down at the clipboard in his hands.

"Right, give me 15 laps to start with. Scarlett, come see me." He quickly turns away, heading towards some equipment against a wall. My stomach drops. I turn a heated look Sonny's way who just holds his hands up in surrender. He looks panicked, knowing he fucked up. He tries to mouth an apology but I am already heading in the direction of the pissed off teacher, not wanting him to have any more excuses as to why he doesn't like me.

Fuck. Me. Dead.

BOARDING PASS
NAME: SCARLETT SMITH
FROM:
TIME:
CLASS
SEAT:
President

chapter
SEVENTEEN

scarlett

"**N**ow, Miss Crux, while I know good and well what your standing in our organisation is very well, I will not accept disruption from anyone," he says, giving me a pointed stare, "and that includes you."

"Yes, sir." I nod. Fucking Sonny. I'm going to kill him.

"I don't want us starting off on the wrong foot, so I will let this one instance slide. You weren't aware of the rules or my expectations before. Now that you do, ensure you adhere to them." Mr Green doesn't waver. He's a commanding force even though he seems unthreatening standing in front of me with his arms crossed over his chest. He seems fitting to not only be our gym teacher but also be a trainer for the Thunderbirds.

He gives me one final glance. This time though it feels like he's assessing me. Finding all of my strengths and in particular weaknesses which I am sure he could find an abundance of compared to half the school population. I stand a little bit taller and try not to bulk at the weight of his gaze. It's like a switch has flipped in my brain.

The moment it knew there was something bigger out there for me, it's been unwavering in everything I have had thrown at me so far. I'm not delusional enough to believe that this is even a smidge into what I will have to go through, much to Dawson's disappointment. Or rather, his enjoyment. I'm sure that asshole would celebrate seeing me fail. But I'm not a quitter. That's one thing he never got to learn about me.

In the last nine months, I've come to grow a lot. That girl he thinks he fell in love with at the beach is gone. After what feels like a lifetime, Mr Green finally gives me a small nod. "Fifteen laps. Make sure you're done when everyone else is, I'm not waiting."

Thinking that I would get away from this exchange without some form of punishment is foolish. Honestly, I was prepared for hell to be rained on me but at least this is somewhat manageable. I thank whoever is watching over me that he let this one slide, slightly. I know that next time I won't be so lucky. By now, I'm sure the majority of the class is at least five laps in.

I don't bother wasting any time sticking around. I instantly take off in a run, following the direction of the class. I catch up to the guys fairly quickly, considering I'm at a full on sprint.

Dacre turns, gracing me with a gentle smile. I don't react, instead keep my gaze firmly on the track in front of me. I see the hurt on Dacre's face from the corner of my eye as I pass. I know it's unfair to be so harsh towards him considering he has been nothing but kind and considerate from the moment he saw me at Pinks' but in the same breath, he also knowingly ghosted me, even after all we shared. Giving him a part of my soul in the way I did and having it ripped apart, and then again four times over has turned the thumping organ a shade of black. At this point, it would probably resemble whatever scraps are still left beating in Dawson's chest. If they are even capable of doing that anymore.

By the time my fifteen laps are done, I'm near collapsing in exhaustion. While everyone else around me looks like they went on a nice little leisurely jog through the park, I felt like Makybe Diva at Flemington except I don't have the Melbourne Cup to greet me at the finishing line. In its place, I have a stone face Mr Green who looks like he ate something sour.

"Right slackers, this morning we are going to be playing volleyball." I hear a few groans from around the class. I watch as Mr Green's face turns red in anger. I hold back a giggle as I watch a few students straighten under his gaze, knowing they fucked up.

"You four, set up the nets. You two, go grab the balls," He says pointing at a few different students I haven't had the chance to meet yet.

I'm thankful that Mr Green's attention is at least redirected for the moment while I catch my breath. I take it as the pity that it is.

Out of the corner of my eye, I catch Nicky, Pike, Dacre and Sonny watch me. The latter looks like a wounded puppy.

It doesn't take them long to make their way over to me. I keep my gaze firmly ahead, still bent over attempting to catch my breath, watching some guys as they set up the volleyball net.

"Did he give you a lashing?" Nicky asks, nodding his head towards Mr Green who currently has his back towards us.

I shrug my shoulders, feigning nonchalance

"He can be pretty brutal when he wants to be." Dacre steps closer to me and I straighten, praying a cramp doesn't bend me in half again, "I've been on the receiving end one too many times." He looks sheepish at the confession. His eyes slowly dart between mine as he tries to gauge my feelings towards our teacher. I give him nothing though, allowing a cold resolve to slide into place

If I'm going to follow through with making these boys grovel, they are going to do just that.

"He could have been worse," I begin, keeping my tone even, "could have been better if Sonny learned to shut his fucking mouth." I aim a glare at my target who lowers his head.

He doesn't even look up as he starts to apologise. "I'm sorry, Scarlett. I was just trying to make you laugh. I didn't think he was going to single you out like that. I would promise I won't do it again but I can't do that." I still, my body stiffening, as he finally lifts his head, his eyes meeting mine, "All I want to do is make you laugh. If I could set the sound as my ringtone, I would. Your happiness is the most important thing to me in the world."

I scoff, crossing my arms across my chest, "Yeah, my happiness was so important to you when you ghosted me, Sonny. No explanation. Just a whole lot of empty promises." I can't keep the anger from my tone. I just seem to get more worked up the longer I stand there looking at them. "You know what? Fuck this. I'm not going to pretend I'm even remotely okay with anything that happened all those months ago. I had the most incredible month of my life with you guys. I have never laughed more in my entire existence." I step closer to Sonny, Dacre, Nicky and Pike. "I fucking fell. In. Love. With you assholes." I punch out each word knowing that the words hit their marks just by the sheer heartbreak on each of their faces.

"I was vulnerable with a man for the first time in my life.

I shared shit with the five of you that not a single person has ever gotten before." I look directly at Dacre then, watching the way his heart breaks even further. I let my eyes move over to Pike. Then Nicky. And finally Sonny.

"I trusted you. I gave you my heart. My love. And you fucking betrayed me." They each at least have the audacity to flinch at my words.

"Scar, I…" Pike steps up, but I cut him off before he can continue any further. I don't have it in me to listen to them anymore.

I shake my head, holding my hand up to stop him. "No, Pike. None of your excuses will ever be enough. You say you stopped messaging me to protect me? Yet all you did was break my heart beyond repair and I don't know how you will ever be able to fix it."

I step away, turning from four of the loves of my life. It almost feels like there is a weight lifted off my shoulders until I come face to face with Dawson. His expression is emotionless but I know him better than that. He thinks I don't, but that's where he is wrong.

I know almost everything there is to know about these men. They let me into their hearts after all. How could I not have devoured every piece of them I could have? Retained even the smallest details of them.

Like the way Dawson fights a smile everytime one of the guys does something ridiculous. Or the way Nicky occasionally rubs at the scar on his face, like he's tracing it. Remembering why and how he got it. Or how Sonny looks at each of the guys for approval after making a joke. Needing validation he shouldn't need to seek because no matter how fucking mad I am at him right now, god I love him desperately.

Then there is how Pike is constantly running his fingers

through his hair. Even more when he is nervous. And Dacre, who gets a far away look in his eyes every time he flicks open and close his switchblade, a habit that should have been a massive red flag for me but it's not.

"Fuck off Dawson." There's no hesitation where there would have been before. He wants to hate me? He wants me to leave? Fine, I will make his life just as hard in return.

I watch as his eyes heat in anger. He should be intimidating right now but my care factor well and truly flew out the window the moment I laid out my soul for the entire class to hear.

I don't bother to wait for a reply as I storm off, collecting his shoulder as I pass. Before I get too far, I'm yanked back into a hard body.

"Watch it, you are skating on thin ice, Scarlett." His voice is a low growl directly in my ear. Where this sound would have sent shivers through my body a few months ago, all it does is fuel my anger. I snatch my arm from his tight grip, which I'm sure by the throbbing pain I feel would have left finger shape marks, if not bruises.

"No you listen here you pig-headed motherfucker. You aren't in charge. You don't get a fucking say or an opinion in anything when it comes to me. I am in charge. I am the next fucking President and if you don't cut your male postering bullshit and pull your head from where it is so far shoved up your asshole, I," I snarl, pointing my finger to the centre of my chest, "will fucking make you regret ever stepping foot onto that beach that night."

His eyes are wide but he quickly shoves his surprise down, that signature resting cunt face where it belongs. He scoffs, "I'd like to see you try."

A sinister smile spreads across my cheeks, "Watch me."

I turn my back on Dawson, keeping my head high as

I walk over to Brandy, Maxie, Jen and Rippy who are all looking at me with proud looks on their faces. It's strange to see that kind of expression on Rippy's face, especially when it's directed at me but I'm in no state to dive into that one right now.

Brandy meets me halfway, throwing one of her arms over my shoulders, giving a little squeal in the process. "Fuck yes, Scar! That was badass! If you weren't a Pink before, you sure are now!"

I can't help but laugh. Her utter acceptance of me from the beginning warming a place inside of me. No one could ever replace Grace or Noah, but Brandy is going to worm her way into a spot on that top shelf very quickly.

We walk over to the group of students all standing near the volleyball net, waiting for Mr Green's instruction. I prepare for a lashing, his warning earlier still at the forefront of my mind. I brace as his eyes catch mine. Where I thought I would see disapproval or the promise of some bullshit punishment, I see pride. He nods his head at me, a gesture I quickly return.

I don't have to turn my back to feel Nicky, Dacre, Sonny, Pike and Dawson's presence but even if I was unsure, the look Mr Green gives them is utterly terrifying.

"Boys, seeing how you enjoy laying out your personal lives and wasting my time, detention this afternoon."

It takes everything in me not to let out the laugh that threatens to escape me. But I swallow it down.

Suck shit, fuckers.

AMERICA 100
AMERICA 100
SOFAMERICA 100

chapter
EIGHTEEN

pike

We fucked up. I fucked up. I destroyed the single most important thing in my life and I didn't even know it. I broke her just like she said, beyond repair. I shattered her fucking heart like it never mattered in the first place. The shame I feel in myself is immeasurable.

I'm mad at the boys. I'm mad at our situation. Our parents. At Scarlett for making me fall so incredibly in love with her. For her leaving me in the first place. Then even more mad that I was the one to leave her once I finally had her back in my hold, even if I didn't know it.

The shock of our little Scarlett and Australian Scarlett being the same person still hasn't sunk in, even though she is standing right in front of me. Seeing her on that stage last night was the most indescribable feeling. She looked beautiful up there.

A true goddess.

Sonny had the right idea, bowing at her altar; a sentiment

I vow to do everyday for the rest of my life. I'm not ashamed to put her up on a pedestal like that. She deserves nothing but that. My undying loyalty to her.

My gaze doesn't stray far from her as Mr Green organises teams and runs through the rules of the game. I don't even pretend to listen to anything he has to say. My focus stays purely on my girl even after she gave me the most brutal lashing I have ever received. I deserved it. If anything, I don't think she was tough enough on us.

I watch her as I run through ways I can make it up to her. Now that I think about it all, our reasonings for ghosting her weren't even worth it. We were just scared. Scared that we had fallen in love. Scared to lose someone that we cared deeply about. All of it was for nothing anyways. We could have had her back in our lives sooner if we had just pulled our heads out of our asses and didn't act out in fear.

Her place is here, even if that thought terrifies me. Anxiety courses through my veins. The scenarios of what can happen to her, of the things she will see. Will it trigger her memory?

As far as any of us know, she doesn't have a lick of memory from her life before the accident. In a way, it's a relief. In another, it fills me with nothing but devastation. She doesn't remember who we are to her. What she is to us. All she has to go off is our short time in Australia and our major fuck up.

I know that I won't back down in this fight to get her back. To rewin her heart. To make her fall in love with me again.

I want her. I crave her.

I've never felt this kind of obsession for a person before. Even though Scarlett believes we completely ghosted her, it didn't keep me from following her on every social platform I could.

Yeah, 'Harry Tomlinson' was probably not the most inconspicuous name out there but alas I was able to keep a close eye on her. I could see the pain we caused on her face from the first selfie she posted almost a month after we left. It killed me waiting around for some kind of indication on what she was doing. Her friends' social media accounts were also incredibly bare too. I had to refrain daily from getting the first plane back to Australia just to make sure she was okay.

The relief I felt when she finally posted was instantaneous. Knowing that she was somewhat okay. The sad look in her eyes still broke through, breaking a piece of me even through the screen. It didn't seem to fade either. Post after post, her haunted eyes broke me.

I had done that to her. We did that to her. We took her light away.

I count my blessings that I am placed on Scarlett's team along with Dacre. Nicky, Dawson and Sonny are all on the opposite team, a displeasure Sonny made sure we all knew about.

I stand as close as I can to Scarlett. She doesn't look at me but my attention will stay firmly on her. I've already noticed the way Coco has been watching her.

I've got no idea why Dawson is even entertaining her. He thinks he is fooling everyone with his act, but he can't fool me. Being best friends with someone since you were in diapers makes hiding your true emotions near impossible, even for someone like Dawson who hides his emotions like someone was paying him to do it. All he is going to do though is push her away until she has had enough and completely wipes him off.

I wouldn't blame her either. I can understand wanting to

protect her, but pushing her away? Treating her like she is worthless? She's not the kind of woman to stand for that.

Our volleyball game is fairly uneventful. Our team won. I smile watching as Scarlett celebrates with Brandy, Jen and Maxie who were also on our team. It's the first genuine smile I have seen since she's been here and I can't help but smile right alongside her. Some of the light comes back into her eyes, but once the celebration is over, it dims again. It causes mine to drop as well.

Mr Green calls our attention and we all turn, walking over to stand in front of him. "Well done blue team. You can all hit the showers. Nicky, Dawson, Sonny, Dacre and Pike," he says, catching our eyes, "see me once you are done." Without another word, he turns and makes off towards his office.

"Fuck. We are royally fucked, aren't we?" Sonny groans, throwing his head back.

"Yep." My reply is short. I watch Scarlett as she follows the girls into the locker rooms. I feel a tinge of disappointment as I watch her disappear amongst the throngs of people.

I turn my head back around, focusing on where I'm walking instead of watching my girl. Nicky catches my eye and gives me a knowing sad smile. "We will get her back."

I give a sharp nod. There's nothing I can say.

"I refuse to give up on her. She was in the palm of our hands and we let her slip." Dacre's voice hitches. He clutches his hair in his hands as he stops walking. "Fuck!" He shouts, the sound echoing around the locker room we just walked into causing the guys to all dart their heads towards us. His back straightens as he whirls around to look at us. Fear deep in his eyes. And heartbreak. Something I can feel mirrored on my own.

"We just fucking abandoned her! We broke our girl's heart. Did you see her out there?" He shouts, pointing back out the door. "That was a mask she was wearing with us all day. She had to put on a fucking mask just to deal with us. Then she finally snapped." His fingers return to his hair and he pulls to the point of pain. I honestly don't think he is even focused on the feeling of it right now.

He is too consumed with self loathing in what he has done. In what we have done.

He starts shaking his head, muttering quietly to himself. I step closer to him and I'm finally able to hear his pleas. "I can't lose her again. I can't lose her again." He repeats over and over.

I grab his shoulders in an attempt to snap him out of it, but he fights me for a moment, like he is lost and doesn't know where he is.

"Dacre," I say, firmly but quietly. He doesn't hear me. "Dacre." My voice gets louder. Still no response.

I turn a pleading eye at Nicky. We don't have to say words, he just knows. He needs Scarlett. If I can't calm him down, none of us will be able to. It'll only be her.

Nicky takes off out of the room in a dash to find Scarlett. I pray that she will hear him out. That there is a part of her that loves us, or Dacre, enough to help him.

Mental health is a fucking demon. It's plagued Dacre for fucking years. Yet, it went quiet the moment we met Scarlett and again now that she is back. But it's the threat of losing her that has sent him back into that pit.

The door to the boy's locker room swings open and Nicky rushes back through it. I look at him as if waiting for an answer but I don't need it.

It's like the entire room stops moving, everyone frozen in place as Scarlett darts through the door. A towel is all that is wrapped around her body. The ends of her hair are wet from where it looks like she has tied it up halfway through her shower.

Her eyes widen when she sees the state Dacre is in before she rushes towards him. I step away to give her enough room but decide to stay close. I trust Dacre completely but I know that his episodes can be unpredictable. I know he would hate himself if he did something to hurt her and I refuse to let that happen.

"Sweet boy." She coaxes, her voice whisper-quiet. I note the slight shake to her voice. She is scared.

My eyes stay glued on them. I watch as Scarlett tucks the towel tighter around her chest so she is able to use both of her hands.

Slowly, she brings them up to cradle his face. He jumps the moment her skin touches him. Like a jolt of electricity through his system.

"Sweet boy, you aren't going to lose me. I'm right here." His head shoots up. Tear tracks line his cheeks from where the emotions were just too much for him.

"But, we broke you." His voice is so quiet I can barely hear it. It's loud enough for Scarlett though. She shakes her head, sighing.

"I'm not going to lie to you Dacre, you did break me. You broke my heart. But that doesn't mean you are going to lose me. You know that right?"

He nods but I can tell he doesn't believe her. It's obvious she can too, as she straightens back to full height. Dacre does too, imitating her movements like she is a conduit keeping him grounded.

"I'm mad at you. Really fucking mad. But I'm not going anywhere."

"Promise?" he whispers, desperation laced in his voice. A deep seated need for her, one we share.

"I promise." Her voice is firm and I can see the moment

the reassurance settles the demon inside of him.

"But," he stiffens again, as if bracing for impact, "that doesn't mean you are just let off the hook. I need an explanation from you."

He starts nodding straight away. "You have it. Time and place. I'll hold nothing back."

She gives him an assessing look, "You are going to work for it. Just because you have a soft spot in my heart doesn't mean I'm going to be any less firm with you. You will be in the trenches with those assholes." Her head nods back towards where Nicky, Sonny and Dawson are all standing.

A small smile creeps onto his face. While there is still a whisper of the episode still lingering in his eyes, it's mostly gone. I let out a sigh in relief. Never before has anyone of us been able to settle him as quickly as Scarlett was able to. She is a fucking miracle. We don't deserve her. None of us do. But God, if I won't do everything in my power to keep her.

Scarlett steps away then, "Okay, well if you are all good, I better head back to the shower," she says awkwardly. We seem to then all clue into the fact that the only thing covering her wet naked body is the thin towel she has clutched around her body.

Dacre's eyes drop and instantly widen, a blush spreading across his cheeks. He gulps and goes to talk but his mouth just gapes like a fish. I share the sentiment too. It shouldn't feel this raunchy to see someone in a towel, especially considering the circumstances but goddamn, Scarlett could make a potato sack look sexy.

"Okay. Bye," she squeaks, turning quickly but before she gets too far, I grab her arm, halting her escape. She turns to look at me and I have to name the President in my head to regain control of myself. To stop myself from fucking this up even more.

"Once training is done, can we talk?" I ask, hopeful that we will get the chance to explain everything to her sooner rather than later.

My hope is crushed as she shakes her head no. "I'm sorry. I've got to meet Shelly to go over the induction stuff."

I nod, remembering she had mentioned it to us at lunch. "Tomorrow?" I ask, yet again hopeful.

She shakes her head again in a no. "Sorry, the girls have organised band practice." I'm just about to ask about Wednesday but she beats me to it. "Wednesday I've got a meeting with Dad and the leadership. Thursday, I've got band practice again. Friday, I'm going to Pinks' with the girls."

"Saturday?" I ask.

She nods her head and relief fills me, "Saturday."

"Okay," I say, a smile brightening my face.

She returns a smile for a moment before realising she is still standing in a boy's locker room in only a towel. Her eyes widen as she looks around the room, noticing all the guys with their hungry gazes on her.

"Yep. Catch ya."

I chuckle, watching as our girl takes off out of the room like her ass is on fire.

BOARDING P.
NAME: SCARLETT SMIT
FROM:
TIME:
CLAS
SEAT:
President

chapter
NINETEEN

It doesn't take long for me to finish off showering and get dressed back into our school uniform. There is a grim tint to everything though. I knew that Dacre has struggled with mental health but seeing him in person in that state was harrowing. Then the way he looked at me after I was able to bring him out of it was nothing short of devastating.

He looked at me like I am the air that he breathes. The only thing that was able to bring him back to himself.

It's making me rethink everything. About not being so harsh on him. While he still needs to explain, in depth, to me what actually went on and make it up to me, I don't think I can shut him out.

Under all of this newfound feminine rage that has been marinating for months now, there is still a beating heart. A heart that cracked the moment it saw Dacre so raw and vulnerable.

I vow to listen. To hear them all, but especially Dacre out.

It's clear he needs me. That fact warms my soul. I don't have it in me to be a cold, relentless bitch. It would destroy me if something happened to Dacre just because I was mad at them for what they did. It may seem like I am bending, like I'm not strong enough, but that's not the case. Under everything, I can't forget the way I fell so incredibly in love with them. The way it felt like I had known them in another life.

It's clear that I had.

This life.

The before.

Before I was taken by a rival gang and abused.

My hands absently run over one of the scars that is still raised on my stomach. All along I had thought it was from a car crash that stole my memories and half of my family.

But that was just a lie. Instead, reality is a much harder pill to swallow.

Some motherfuckers saw an innocent fucking child and, due to their fragile masculinity, decided to kidnap and torture her out of some kind of petty revenge against my father.

It fuels the rage inside of me that has been growing since the moment they laid everything out on the table for me. Don't get me wrong, I was, and still am, pissed at them for keeping me in the dark. It made me feel like a fool. Also completely unprepared for the role in which I am to take over from.

A part of me is utterly terrified at the path that lies ahead for me. Going from a barista in a small town in Central Queensland to the next president of a gang? Yeah, I don't think there is much that could have prepared me for that. In another way though, this feels right. It feels like I am meant to be here. It helps to ease some of the lingering anxiety I was feeling.

It's been hard to keep all of this from my friends back home. Especially Noah and Grace. The thought of keeping something like this from them seems like a betrayal of our friendship. We have always told each other everything. No matter how small or massive. They were the first people I went to when I had finally got my period. Noah told us before his parents that he had gotten into the Brumbies Academy. Grace couldn't wait to boast to us about finally losing her virginity. Noah is a patient man for being able to deal with Grace and I this long.

God, I miss them.

I send them both a quick text letting them know just that too. I get a message back from both of them almost instantly. He clearly didn't get the earlier hint to go to bed.

NOAH

I miss you more Scar. I hope you are having fun over there with all the stars. Don't forget us when you are famous.

I chuckle before I send a reply.

ME

If there is anyone that should be concerned about remembering their friends when they are famous, it's you hot shot. Why aren't you asleep?

Instead of a message in reply, my phone lights up with a call. A photo of Noah's goofy face brightens my screen and I can't help but chuckle.

"Ugh, why are my fans so obsessed with me? I swear my

manager redirected my calls through to an assistant. That's it, she's fired." I put on the most ridiculous posh accent I can manage.

I hear an eruption of laughter from the other end of the line and I can't help the laugh that escapes me either.

"God, I miss you Scar," Noah says once he finally stops laughing, "It's not that same with you not here. Can I come visit yet?"

I can't help the wave of sadness that overcomes me. I sigh, fighting back the tears that threaten to spill down my cheeks.

"I miss you more than you could ever know, Noah. Don't you worry, the moment you can, I will be buying plane tickets for you to come over."

"I wouldn't be too concerned about needing to buy me tickets, Scar," Noah says trailing off. Just by the tone of his voice, I know he has a surprise in store for me.

"Spill." Is all I need to say. Noah chuckles.

"Well, Coach Winters called me into his office yesterday. My manager was there as well, and a couple other head figures."

I could instantly tell that Noah was just trying to torture me with the extended version so before he could continue, I but in. "Hurry up and spit it out Noah. You know I don't have the patience for this shit."

"I'm making my debut for the North Magpies next year. They want me apart of the thirty."

The scream that leaves my lips has the entire girls bathroom startling, trying to look for what I'm guessing they think is a snake or spider or whatever creature they are terrified of but I ignore their stares.

Noah chuckles down the line. "Holy fuck!" I shout. "Please don't tell me this is some kind of sick joke, Noah," I say with an edge of caution. It wouldn't be the first time he has pranked me and I know it won't be the last.

"I'm not joking. I wouldn't joke about this." He promises, his tone serious.

"I'm so fucking proud of you. You are almost there!" I gush. I'm sure I look like an absolute nutcase to the girls still lingering in the bathroom but I refuse to hide my pride for my best friend.

"You are the first to know outside my manager and the team obviously. I'm planning on telling my family and everyone when I go back home once the seasons over."

"Wait, I am?" I say in disbelief.

"Of course, Scar. I have been waiting until I could finally talk to you and tell you. You have been one of my biggest supporters and I knew you would be just as excited as I am."

That does it. The tears I have been fighting finally break and I let out a choked sob.

"Shh Scar, please don't cry. You will make me cry," Emotion overcoming his voice.

"I can't help it. I'm so fucking proud of you. I don't think I have said it enough, but I am. You are there, Noah. After all the bad shit, you are living your dream. Being selected to debut for the Brumbies now is a real possibility!"

"Thanks, Scar," he whispers.

"Now I guess it's you who still needs to remember us measly peasants when your face is posted on billboards around the country," I laugh, recalling our earlier conversation.

Noah chuckles too, the heavy mood instantly lifting. "I could never forget you. You are my best friend. My ride or die. I still hold you to the pact we made when we were ten," he says and I snort, instantly recalling what he is talking about.

"Noah, I love you but I'm not marrying your ass."

"Come on, future wifey. I know you have secretly always

wanted to be a WAG," he laughs.

"Maybe when I was ten," I chuckle, then since knowing what I'm about to tell him isn't going to go down too well. "There's also been a little bit of change in events."

There is a slight hesitation to his reply, "...okay."

"Um, so Rhodes took me to this club the night we got here. It's kind of like a gentlemen's club but super classy. It's also kind of a main hangout spot for everyone. Long story short, I ended up getting up on stage with these girls and singing which was incredible." I hear Noah laugh but I don't stop. "Afterwards, Rhodes introduced me to a couple of people. The girls from the band then dragged me over to this other group of people." I pause, taking a breath. I feel like everything is coming out in one jumbled mess but I can't seem to explain it any better, needing to just word vomit, "You will never guess who they introduced me to."

I wait for a reply for a long time. Long enough that I have to check if we are still connected.

"No." Is all Noah replies with.

"Yes," I sigh.

"Those motherfucking cunts!" Just as I expected Noah begins yelling obscenities through the phone. There is one thing us Aussies are good at and that's hurling the most obscure abuse at people. Noah is creative, I'll give him that.

"So what, I guess those ass sucking toads are begging for forgiveness now?" He finally says once he finally exhausts his creative name calling skills.

I groan, rubbing a hand down my face before collapsing onto one of the benches that lines the locker room. "Well Dacre, Nicky, Pike and Sonny are."

"What about Dawson?" Noah asks with a grunt. I can just imagine the scowl on his face. It's not often that grumpy Noah comes out to play. That is normally saved for the footy field and whenever someone wrongs his mates. If Noah is one thing, he's fiercely protective of the people he loves, which makes what he went through in his childhood so incredibly traumatic for him.

"He believes I don't belong here. Says I need to catch the first plane back to Australia."

Noah snorts, "Yeah, and that fuck face can take the next train to Cuntsville."

I can't contain my laughter. "He would be the fucking mayor too." Noah adds in which does nothing but heighten my laughter. We sound like a cackle of hyenas.

"Stick to your guns, Scar. Don't let him get one up on you. This is your chance to get to know your family and make something of yourself." There's an edge of pride in Noah's voice as we finally collect ourselves. My stomach drops knowing what I still have left to tell him.

"Ah, there's also something else that I didn't get a chance to tell you or Grace before I left." I hesitate slightly. My best friends deserve to know the truth. They shouldn't be blind sighted. Especially if something was to happen to me. Which is a real risk. Apparently.

"Go on."

I begin telling Noah the shortened version of my Dad's involvement in the Thunderbirds and who they are. I then go on to explain the ambush and that I was the one that was kidnapped. I hear a sharp inhale of his breath and shuffling down the end of the line, like he's gotten up out of bed to pace his room.

"Jesus fucking christ, Scarlett!" His voice sounds panicked. "I.. I can't…" He trails off as if trying to find the words for what I just told him.

I let out a breath that I had been holding. "I know. It's fucking hectic to say the least."

"The very least." I note the disbelief in his voice. I can relate. I felt the same way when I was told.

"Yeah. I guess it helps to explain why I can't remember my childhood and why my father did what he did to protect me."

Noah just replies with a hum. I can imagine just how raw some of this information is for him. His story isn't a pretty one but it's not mine to tell. I will leave that to him and when he is ready.

"That's not all though." I wince.

"Fucking hell. What next?"

"Um, well. Obviously, Dad is the President of the Thunderbirds. There's a hierarchy that sees the first born child claiming their parents position once they become of age. If there isn't an heir I guess it all goes to a vote within the club."

I let my words settle for a moment. Waiting for Noah to fully process what I am trying to say on his own.

He lets out a brash laugh, "Nah."

"Yeah," I whisper in reply.

"There's no fucking way," he chuckles. "My little Scarlett Smith. A motherfucking President of a gang," he says in absolute disbelief. "Do they know that you have a hint of crazy?"

"I think that's what they are wanting from me," I laugh.

"Shit, Scar. I knew you didn't know what you planned on doing after school, but becoming a gang member wasn't in my top ten picks."

"Top one hundred at least?" I question. I can't help the way a giggle escapes as I say it or the way it turns into a full blown laugh as he replies.

"Top twenty for sure. Although, I would have pegged Grace to be up there. That girl is a full fledged psycho."

He is so true. Ever since she learned of Nicky, Pike, Dacre, Sonny and Dawson; she has been planning at building a harem of her own. Much to her disappointment, the guys she has been talking to aren't really in the 'sharing' scene.

"Surprised?" I ask once the laughter has settled.

"That's a good way of putting it," he says.

"You aren't mad?"

He pauses for a moment. I can't help the anxiety that fills my chest. Noah and I don't fight. Sure we will bicker here and there, but the thought of having an actual fight with him makes me feel physically sick.

"I could never be angry at you for something like this, Scar." I let out a breath of relief as he continues, "I just want you to be safe. If things get too much, you jump on the first plane home. I know I'm not much but I will lay down my life to protect you. Do you hear me?" His voice is firm and there is no room for joking around. Noah has been a fierce protector from the moment I met him. If he wasn't firmly in the friend zone, I would have stayed true to our childhood pact and married him right then and there.

I nod, even though he can't see it. "Okay."

"Promise me, Scarlett."

"I promise," I say with all the sincerity I can. It settles something in my chest knowing I have some form of escape plan. I didn't realise I even needed one, but now that I have it, I will keep it close to my chest.

"Right, well this is heavy as fuck," he laughs after a moment.

I laugh too as I pick up my bag and begin heading out of the locker room. It's completely empty now. The girls all left after hearing me cackling.

I open the door and begin to step out but as I do, I hit a brick wall. Or what, in that moment, feels like one. I let out a yelp in surprise. Hands grab my waist to help steady me and as I look up, instead of it being a wall, it's Nicky looking down at me with just as much surprise on his face.

I clutch the hand that doesn't have my phone in it to my chest as I try to calm my racing heart. "Jesus, Nicky. You scared the fuck out of me."

"I'm sorry, baby girl. We were just getting worried since you hadn't come out yet. Just wanted to check and make sure you were okay," he says, as he slowly steps back and his hands drop from their place on my waist.

He looks over my entire body, like he is checking for injuries before coming back to my face. He then sees the phone and gives me a questioning look. Before I can say anything to Nicky, what sounds like a growl comes from down the line.

"Put that motherfucking dog cunt on the phone, Scarlett. I have a few choice words to say to him." I giggle, shaking my head before pulling the phone away from my ear.

I look at Nicky, letting my features become as sweet as I can muster. "It's for you."

He looks at me with a questioning look but I just hold my phone out to him, letting my features give nothing away. He grabs the phone out of my hand and slowly lifts it to his ear.

"Hello?" Nicky says, slowly. That gruff voice of his unsure at who's on the end of the line.

For a moment there is nothing. Noah must say something and knowing him, its fucking creative. The colour drops from Nicky's face as he locks eyes with me. I just give him an innocently sweet smile.

He listens still for a while longer, humming his agreement every so often. His eyes are still blown wide at the abuse I'm sure he is copping from my best friend.

Checkmate.

BOARDING PASS
NAME: SCARLETT SMITH
FROM:
TIME:
CLASS:
SEAT:
President

BOARDING P
NAME: SCARLETT SMIT
FROM:
TIME:
CLAS
SEAT:
President

chapter
TWENTY

scarlett

Nicky's face is comical during the entire exchange. He remains silent during the entire call but every so often, his face twitches or he shivers during what I am sure is an absolute beat down. I know that even if Nicky wanted to reply to whatever he was being told, he would haven't even been given a chance. When Noah gets into these rants of his, there is no stopping him.

His words cut Nicky deep. I watch as his face contorts. At first it's in shame, knowing just how deeply he has hurt me. Then it's in horror. I chuckle to myself as I watch the way his eyes blow wide. Nicky and the guys might be big and tough but when it comes to fiercely protecting people they love, Noah is unstoppable. After a while, Nicky eventually nods.

"Yeah man, I hear you loud and clear. I know my promises may seem empty to you right now and I'm not trying to butter you up. I know just how badly I fucked up. I will forever regret the choices I made that day," he lets out a sigh, "I broke my girl's heart. I will regret that everyday for the rest of my life. But nothing will stop me from making it up to her. I will win her back. I will protect her with my life. I will be there no matter what, even if she doesn't want me anymore."

Nicky then listens intently, nodding every so often before saying a short goodbye to Noah. He hands me back the phone. I pull it up to my ear, already chuckling.

"I would love nothing more than a word count on how many times you said the words 'cunt' in that exchange."

"There's a reason it's my favourite word," Noah sniggers. "I set that fucker straight though, Scar," I go to butt in but he doesn't give me a chance, "and before you go saying that you already had it under control, I would be the world's shittest best friend if I didn't tell at least one of those fuckers exactly what I thought." I roll my eyes but I can't help but feel grateful to have someone like Noah in my life. There is a reason he is my best friend and this is one of them.

"I love your face."

"I love your face even more. Now that I'm done abusing men for the night, I'm going to head to bed. I've got training first thing in the morning."

"Ok. Good night."

"Night, Scar."

I end the call and quickly tuck my phone away in my back pocket. Nicky hasn't moved from his position in front of me. I look up at him and note the expression on his face. I remain silent as we stare into each other's eyes.

It's not some kind of alpha versus alpha pissing contest, but more of a communication between injured souls. Souls that refuse to fight the distance the bodies continue to put between them. We both know where our path will lead us. Our fate has been set from the moment our journeys collided. We are both equal in our inability to fight it. He has always been mine and I have always been his.

At that moment, as we remain locked on each other, I am able to see it clearly.

For god's sake, I even lost all memories of where our childhoods were so deeply intertwined. No matter how far we are apart, whether that be different cities or on opposite ends of the planet, we will always find our way back to each other.

Not a single part of me rebels at that fact. If anything, I hold it closer to me. It might not be okay right now, but it will be.

Nicky eventually smiles bringing us both out of stupor. "Noah was fucking brutal," he chuckles quietly, his voice low.

I nod. "He's fierce when he is in protection mode. I've never been on the receiving end of his wrath but I can imagine how your ego might be feeling right about now."

He laughs, nodding. "Yeah, you can say that again. His choice of abuse is quite…" he pauses, trying to find the word, "colourful."

I snort, "That's an understatement. I've heard some of the things he has thrown around at dickheads down at the pub. They don't quite make sense but they are effective."

"Lets just say I've never been called a 'douchemonging koala fucker' before."

I can't help the full belly laugh that escapes me then. I eventually calm myself down enough to look up at Nicky. His smile is wide as he looks down at me as I catch my breath.

"So your ego took quite a hit then I guess?" I ask.

He nods but his stare is still locked on my face, "Yeah, it did. That along with the dressing down Mr Green just gave us too. But it's healing with the way you are looking at me right now."

I will the smile off my face but it won't fade. I feel a light blush slowly tinge my cheek. I look away, trying my best to cover it. Nicky brings his hand and lifts my chin back up to his gaze.

"Don't shy away from me, baby girl. I want all of your emotions. No matter what they are, I can handle them."

I smile ruefully at him, an eyebrow lifting, "Be careful what you wish for."

He shakes his head at me. I watch as his expression changes to one of seriousness. "I don't think you understand, Scarlett. I know just how desperately I fucked up. I can't speak for the guys but I can speak for myself. I never should have ghosted you in the way I did. I see the pain that I caused written all over your face and it kills me." Pain seeps through his tone, vulnerability pouring from every word he says, "I will never be able to take that back but I know that I can work every day to prove I'm not that person. That I deserve a position in your life no matter how big or small you decide it to be."

Words fail me as I stare up into his eyes. I dissect every single word he says along with every single emotion I see in his eyes as I try to find a lie or hint of deception, but I find neither. I see nothing but the truth in his hazel eyes. The eyes that have taunted me for the last nine months.

I nod again as I force myself to swallow the sob that threatens to bubble from my throat. I can't help the way my eyes water though. Nicky instantly notices and gives me a sad smile. He brings his hand up to caress my cheek before he wipes away one of the tears that involuntarily falls down my cheek. I lean into his touch, soaking up the strength from him that I need right now.

I don't know how these men do it so easily but they break down each wall I erect around myself almost instantly.

"I know that all of these pretty words are just that. I want you to know that I plan on backing them up with action.

You are my soul, Scarlett."

More tears leak from my eyes at his admission. Three words threaten to burst from me but I force them away. He knows exactly how I feel. He doesn't need them right now. There is another time for that.

"I will grovel at your feet every day for the rest of my life to make it up to you, baby girl. You need someone, I want to be the first person you call. You've had a shit day and need someone to rant to about it, I'm there. You need a cheerleader, I'm there. A shoulder to cry on, I'm there. Someone to love every single inch of the incredible human being you are. To love all of your flaws. To stick it out during the bad and celebrate in the good. I am there."

I launch myself at Nicky, wrapping my arms around his waist and holding him tight. He reciprocates instantly. His embrace tight, even if there were gale force winds, it wouldn't be able to separate us. I hold onto him like he is my lifeline, just like he said he would be. After his proclamation, it feels like he is. He stripped me raw only to slowly begin putting back the pieces. I know we still have a long road ahead of us. But this is a good start.

This right here is what I needed. This is what I have been aching for. A declaration. A dedication.

The tears fall freely now and the sob I tried to fight slips free. Nicky brings his face down to the top of my head.

"Shh, baby girl," he whispers, "I've got you."

"Promise?" My voice is weak and trembles slightly.

"Promise." His declaration is final. A weight lifts off my chest albeit slightly. A part of me is rejoicing at his vow but the other part is reminding me that he once promised something similar. Something that within hours he destroyed. I do my best to keep myself in the present. Second chances should always be given to those that deserve it; and every part of me wants to give it to Nicky.

I take in a deep breath as I slowly collect myself. I bring my hands up to my face through where our bodies are so closely bound. I wipe the tears that had yet to soak into Nicky's t-shirt. His arms loosen from around me and I take a slow step back from him.

He gives me a questioning look, checking in with me without using words. I give him a curt nod letting him know I'm okay.

"Come on then, Scar. Coach will murder us if we are late for training. You think he is brutal during class? That's got nothing on the hell he rains down on you if you fuck around during weapons and combat."

Sonny, Dacre and Pike walk over to us, knowing smiles on their faces.

"Nicky is right Scar, he is brutal. I was late once and he made me clean the entire armoury with a toothbrush. It took me three days. I can still feel the calluses on my hands." Pike shivers.

My eyes widen, and I instantly quicken my pace. "That settles it. Hurry up fuckers, I don't plan on being late." I walk past Dawson who is standing within earshot of us. I shoulder check him as I steam past, "Except for you. You can get lost off a cliff."

Dawson just grunts, not bothering to retort any of the bullshit he has come to spew since I got here. A stab of pain shoots through me at the way our relationship has failed. While things ended exactly the same as the Nicky, Pike, Dacre and Sonny, they didn't spew absolute venom at me and partially demand my head. I'm just thankful my earlier tantrum has seemed to take the wind out of his sails. I don't know how much more I could have taken before eventually snapping.

Training is held at the Thunderbirds' headquarters. The building looks way too modern to belong to a gang. Initially, I expected some kind of beaten down bar with motorcycles out the front. While the image of the bikes runs true, the building is really what surprises me.

My eyes widen even further as we walk through the front doors. A wall of alcohol in every single flavour covers the entirety of the back wall. A bar just as long takes up the space in front. I spot a few gruff men I haven't met yet sitting at stools with neat glasses of amber liquids. When they notice me, their eyes spark with recognition. One guy stands up from the bar, a mix of emotions dazzling his face. Disbelief, surprise, and relief are all prominent. He reaches us at lightning speed. I am instantly engulfed in an embrace so tight, my lungs feel like they are crushed. I stiffen in shock.

"Oh, Scarlett, my sweet girl. Shelly told me you were back, I couldn't believe it. Then Dakes came home and confirmed it. But, seeing you with my own eyes." The man pulls back, his hands stay gripped at my shoulders as he looks at me, "God, you have become the most beautiful young woman. I never thought I'd see the day our Star was brought back to us." His eyes well with tears and my heart clenches at the sheer emotion on the strangers face. Dacre slides up beside us, wrapping an arm around my back in what I think to be reassurance.

"Scarlett, this is my Dad, Grant." My shoulders relax at the confirmation of who the man is. I look at him then and on closer inspection, I instantly see the family resemblance. Dacre looks exactly like his Dad. Where Dacre keeps his hair styled, Grant's mousey brown hair is kept short, almost in a buzzcut.

"Nice to meet you, Sir," I nod, before offering my hand.

Grant looks at my hand before scoffing. He doesn't hesitate as he steps forward and engulfs me in another hug. I pause but return the hug.

"Don't you dare call me Sir. I have known you since you were in diapers and it's always been Grant. Except for that period of time where you called me Ant." Grant laughs as he pulls back from me. I can't help but chuckle.

"Your mother and Shelly always got a good laugh out of it too. It was near impossible to separate those two. Then that gene was passed down onto the both of you. Dacre here used to follow you around like a little lost puppy dog," he laughs, his voice turning babyish as he ruffles Dacre's hair.

I laugh as I watch Dacre's cheeks turn crimson as he looks away shyly. When he looks up I give him a reassuring smile. "I can't wait to learn more."

BOARDING PASS
NAME: SCARLETT SMITH
FROM:
TIME:
CLASS:
SEAT:
President

BOARDING P
NAME: SCARLETT SMIT
FROM:
TIME:
CLA.
SEAT:
President

chapter
TWENTY-ONE

scarlett

The front doors bang open and everyone snaps their heads around to see Rhodes, Wyatt and Jethro walk in with a couple of other guys. I roll my eyes, watching the way Rhodes struts through the doors like he is king shit.

"The king has arrived," I say, my voice laced in sarcasm. Rhodes gives me a sly wink as he heads over to our group.

"King of the castle. King of the castle," he chants in the most ridiculous Borat accent I've ever heard. I can't control the snort that escapes me.

"You're ridiculous, Rhodes," I say once my laughter subsides. Rhodes just chuckles before pulling me into a hug.

"How was your first day?" He asks before letting me go. My face drops slightly before I can stop it and he doesn't miss it. He quirks a questioning brow at me. I let out a sigh before tempting a smile that falls flat. "It was like any first day, I guess."

He gives me an understanding nod but he doesn't pressure

me for any more information. I know that he hasn't completely dropped it though, there will be an interrogation later that I'm already dreading.

Rhodes turns and aims a murderous glare at someone behind me. I follow his gaze, turning my head and finding Dawson. His expression is completely blank. Like there is nothing behind his eyes. All emotion is void. Honestly, it is absolutely fucking psychopathic. A smarter woman would run for cover. Yet I don't shy away.

After the stare down match of the century, with no real winner declared, Rhodes leads us to one of the doors leading off the main bar. We step into a near identical gym to the one at Rydell Prep. Instead of volleyball nets, rings have been spaced out around the room. As I look around the room, I notice a room toward the back of the training area with a sign saying '*Warning. Live Fire Range*' on the door and a small viewing window showing the gun range beyond. A few ear muffs hang next to the door.

I look further around the room watching as the last few recruits filter in through the door we just came through. Mr Green stands at the centre eyeing everyone that comes in. His demeanour is the complete opposite of what it was at school. The hard-ass warrior in its place. He is exactly as I expected him to be. The trainer of the Thunderbirds' newest recruits. It makes sense for someone hardened to be leading a bunch of rowdy teenagers. Someone that has the ability to break them down just to build them up into a soldier.

I watch as Mr Green brings two fingers up to his mouth and lets out a shrill whistle, all but piercing our eardrums.

"Alright recruits, gather around," he shouts. "Today, we will be sparing. Considering we have a greenie in our presence, we need to virtually start from scratch." I don't hear any groans compared to the ones that would have sounded if we were standing at the gym at Rydell Prep but I can feel the stares aimed at me. I hold my head high, not letting their judgement bother me. What they think of me is the least of my concern.

"I will be pairing you each off, testing what level you are at and areas we need to focus on." Mr Green looks down at his clipboard before listing off pairs. Dacre is paired off with Rhodes, Sonny off with Jethro; something he looks way too excited for. Nicky and Pike pair off and I can see the excitement in their eyes at being able to roll around on the mat together. Thoughts of them both in compromising positions give me way too many ideas and I need to shake my head of those thoughts before I start spiralling. I do put a mental pin in it though. For future reference, obviously.

A couple of other recruits are paired off with each other. The group begins to drastically thin out until there is just myself, Dawson and two other guys. "Cody and Blake. Lastly, Dawson and Scarlett."

For fuck's sake. Of course I couldn't have been paired off with a stranger. Instead I get paired off with a guy that has had a sneer on his face the entire day. You could almost assume the wind had changed direction and his face was permanently stuck that way.

I take a deep breath, needing to steel myself for what I am sure is going to be a fucking shit-show. Not only do I have absolutely no idea of what I am doing, but from the look on his face; Dawson isn't in the business of giving me any graces. From what I can tell, which really isn't much to go off considering how emotionless he is, I am going to have my work cut out for me.

We silently walk over to the last available sparring mat. Dawson doesn't say anything as he takes a fighting position. His eyes stay locked on mine but I don't let his judgement sway me. I was born for this whether he likes it or not. I am made for this. Being here feels right and I am going to do everything in my power to show assholes like him what I am made of.

I mimic Dawson's stance on the mat, something he clearly finds amusing as finally he shows a slither of emotion. The corner of his mouth tilts up slightly. It feels like he is mocking me or trying to rattle me. I won't let him slip under my defences. I refuse to allow him to.

I hold his gaze and wait for him to strike.

He moves like lightning. The moment I blink, he is already on me. I hit the mat instantly. I am so out of it, I dont realise the wind has been completely knocked out of me until Dawson's face pops up directly in front of me.

"Fuck's sake Scarlett, breath!" he shouts. He gives me the jolt I need as I rasp in a breath. My lungs burn as I keep sucking air in.

"Like I said: this world isn't for you. I've tried to warn you but you just won't fucking listen. Do you have a death wish?" He snarls at me. The only noise that escapes me are rasps as I greedily suck in breaths trying to slowly calm myself down.

Dawson scoffs, shaking his head as he looks back over towards the other sparring matches. It gives me the perfect in though. Wrapping my arms around his neck, I smash my knee into his balls.

His reaction is instant. He goes to curl into himself but my reaction time is quicker. I bring my legs up, wrapping them around his neck. With as much force as I can muster, I flip him onto his back and pull the closest hand towards me, keeping my hold firm on him. He doesn't say anything. The shock of being brought down stunning him for a moment.

"Yield." My voice doesn't even sound like my own. If it wasn't so imperative that I make him surrender, the shock of how quick I moved would have me in an absolute state.

Dawson is silent for a moment. "Yield," he eventually says, his voice a low rumble.

I instantly release him and scoot back a few paces as the reality of my ability sets in. I don't notice the way Nicky, Pike, Dacre and Sonny all stop their fights obviously having witnessed what I did. I don't notice the way Dawson sits up and stares at me.

All I can focus on is the fact that I was able to overpower all six foot three of sheer muscle and ego that is Dawson Zelko. My hands shake. I can't help the panic that slowly seeps into my system. The way my breath quickens. I know all the signs of a panic attack, having had them regularly after the accident. But the shock to the system is intense after not having one for years. Tears slowly begin streaming down my face.

Hands grip my shoulders and I jolt. I beg for the touch to pull me from the panic slowly setting in but it's no use.

"Breath Scarlett. Come on, with me, pretty girl. Deep breath in." The voice is almost a whisper but hypnotic. I follow the instructions instantly, sucking in a deep breath and holding it. "Now, out." The husky voice stays silent until I fully release my breath.

"Good girl. One more time." The voice coaches; I follow instantly pulling in another breath before releasing it. The panic still lingers on the edges but I am self aware enough to do the exercise again.

"Are you alright?" My head snaps up in shock. Dawson's face is ridiculously close to mine. His arms still linger on my shoulders but I'm thankful for it. Right now he is the only thing still holding me to this earth; even though a part of me holds resentment to the way he has treated me today. The part that hates him for the way he has treated me, is holding onto him just as tightly as he is me.

I notice the way his brow is furrowed but where it would normally, since last night, be in disinterest or in anger, it's concern. His eyes are gentle as they run over my face waiting for a reply.

I don't know whether to be surprised that he is capable of an emotion other than broody or of the fact that he was the one to pull me out of my panicked state. I give him a curt nod but he doesn't move away until he does one last check over my face, trying to find the lie. He stands up straight from his crouched position; almost instantly offering me a hand up. I take it without question. My limbs feel strange, like they aren't my own. Nicky, Dacre, Pike and Sonny eventually walk over to where Dawson and I are staring at each other.

"Are you okay *mi hermosa*?" Sonny asks, his voice gentle. I don't look over at him though as I rasp out a quiet, "Yes."

I see him out of the corner of my vision give a questioning look towards Pike who just shakes his head. The four of them just stand there waiting for me to say something.

"I don't know how I did that." My voice is meek. Any strength I showed during our spar completely evaporated like it was never there in the first place.

"Muscle memory." Is all Dawson says. I quirk a brow at him to continue. "While your brain completely forgot everything that you learned as a child, your body still remembered what to do. So when in a fight or flight situation, your body completely took over and you were able to take me down." All concern for me completely drains from Dawson and in its place is something I struggle to decipher. Too many emotions mix into one. Maybe if he wasn't so closed off all the time I would be able to work him out, but for once I am stumped.

Pike walks over and stands next to Dawson, "He's right,

Princess. You were a weapon when we were younger. You were never left behind from us in training. You were so determined even from a young age. I remember watching you take down one of the recruits when we were seven." Pike's eyes gloss over as he recounts the memory, "He was talking smack about your Dad during one of the training sessions. You saw red. Any disrespect towards Pres and it was like someone had lit a fire under your ass." The five of them all laugh at that, "You took him down instantly. From that day on he never spoke shit again. It was impressive. You looked like this sweet little songbird, but you were really a little hellcat."

I laugh at Pike's description of me at that age. It does send a ping of pain through my chest. I'd do anything to have those memories back. To remember what I was like before. To who I was before. But being here is the best place I can be to reclaim some of my old life.

Even if I never get my memories back.

chapter
TWENTY-TWO

watch Scarlett intently as the panic slowly ebbs away from her features. To say I was shocked at the way she so quickly overpowered me is an understatement. My balls still throb from her cheap shot but in all honesty, I can't blame her. My shot at her was just as cheap.

When you see an opening, you've got to take it.

Didn't make taking her down the way I did feel even more of an asshole than I already do. The amount of self-loathing I feel for myself after the way I have treated Scarlett today is deserved. She doesn't deserve an ounce of my anger but I can't help it.

Doesn't she know just how fucking terrified we all were after what went down when we were kids? How the events that unfolded changed our genetic makeup?

That there hasn't been a day that has gone by in the last ten years that I haven't thought about that day. Replayed it over and over in my head. Berated myself for being a scared little boy. Regretted the fact that I didn't grab one of the guns from the bloodied bodies that were scattered at the party and shoot one of those motherfuckers.

That day is the reason I train as hard as I do. It's the reason why I am so dedicated to our cause.

Its the exact fucking reason Scarlett needs to go home.

It would destroy us if something happened to her again. But I know that this time, we won't get lucky. She has no idea what she is doing. At least back then she had actual training behind her. Admittedly, she was only a kid but at least she had an awareness about her. Now, she has no idea.

Scarlett takes a breath and I feel as though I take one with her. Even though the fight has been drained from her body I still see a determined look in her eye. One I know all too well.

"Ready to keep sparing then?" She tries to brush off her panic attack like it's nothing but I can tell how tired she is by the way her shoulders have completely sunken. Even though I only spent a month with this new Scarlett, I have memorised her tells almost instantly. Just an inkling to how fucking obsessed I am.

Because underneath all of the bravado, is a man that is irrevocably in love with the woman standing in front of him.

I don't know why I am fighting it so hard. I could have my girl in my arms. Safe. Where she should be. I long for the feeling of her against me again. I fucking ache for it. Having her so close to me while we were sparring felt right.

I don't bother with a verbal reply, instead just giving her a brisk nod. I feel a bit of satisfaction as I watch as she rolls her eyes. There's still a hint of a spark in my girl. I don't think anything could dull it. Except maybe me, if I keep on this track I'm heading down. But the will to care just isn't there. The need to keep her safe is. It fuels me. I know it's not something I can do while my soul focus needs to be on taking down the rings. It's easier to push her away. It's better that I treat her like she never mattered. If her hating me is the only thing that will keep her safe, so be it.

Pike, Sonny, Dacre and Nicky all go back to their mats after having rushed over to Scarlett. I can't help being pissed off. Coddling her isn't going to make her stronger if this is where both Pres and Rhodes seem determined for her to be. She needs to be able to stand on her own two feet.

I don't miss the way Nicky eyes me for a moment longer. I have felt his eyes on Scarlett and I the entire time we have been over here. He's waiting for me to hurt her. While it's obvious I'm stupid enough to break her heart, I could never physically hurt her.

As we step onto the mat, Scarlett mimics my previous fighting stance. I decide against a proper sparring session. I want to push her limits but even I know when to call time. I turn my back without a word and grab a set of punch mitts and hand wraps. I throw the wraps at her which she catches.

"Wrap your hands," I say, fitting the mitts onto my hands. I watch as she slowly starts wrapping her hands. It's obvious she has no idea of what she is doing but I commend her for the effort. I made a note to teach her how to wrap them properly. I'm not interested in dealing with broken hands.

I wait for her to finish, taking in my fill as I wait. Scarlett's entire focus remains on her hands. Her brow is furrowed slightly in frustration and concentration. She seems smaller than she was back in Australia. It hits me then; has she not been eating properly?

I can't stop the way my emotions riot. I feel the colour slowly drain from my face at the realisation of what we had done. What I did.

We did that to her. We hurt her so fucking deeply that she hasn't been eating properly. That her body has suffered because we couldn't send a single fucking message letting her know that we were done.

If I could hate myself anymore in a single moment, it would be then. My eyes remained glued to her collarbone. Like I am storing the image away for when I need a reminder of why I don't fucking deserve her but why I will always want her.

I'm shaken out of my stupor when Scarlett throws the tape off to the side of the mat.

"What do I do?" she asks, waiting for my instruction. My eyes travel down her body, looking at the way she holds herself. Almost like she is bracing in case I rush her again, which I don't plan to do this time around. My eyes slowly travel back up her body as I eventually meet her gaze again.

She gives me a knowing look, a hint of a smile turns her lips that I devour, while giving nothing away. On the outside, I am completely unaffected by her but on the inside: I'm drowning in her.

"Hit the pads. There's no real technique needed right now. Just keep your face guarded."

She gives me a nod before bringing her hands up to her face just like I told her. I watch as the rest of her body follows, just like I thought. Her muscles know what to do.

She has done this before. She and I have done this before. It was always one of our warm up routines. The guys would all grouch because Scarlett and I would automatically team up.

I used to revel in it. My crush on her was ridiculous even back then. From the moment I noticed girls, my sights were set on Scarlett. Even after she was gone, no one ever amounted to her. There were just spot fillers. Not like the way she has always filled a spot in my soul. Just like she was so easily able to do from the moment I saw her on that beach, sopping wet and fucking delectable.

Scarlett's first hit on the mitt is weak, barely even making my arm jolt back.

"Come on, you can do better than that," I tease. It lights a fire in her eyes, just like I was wanting. Her next hit is slightly harder than the next.

"Harder," I encourage.

Her next two hits come in quick succession, both with more power behind them than the last.

"Harder!" I yell. *One punch, another punch.* "Harder!" *Another punch.* "Is that all you've got?"

She lets out a yell, a determination I once saw in her coming alive again. Her eyes darken and her stance strengthens. Her punches this time finally come with the force I was looking for from her, knowing she just needed it coaxed out of her. That fight that was so rich in her just dying to come alive again after being suppressed inside of her.

"Again, Scarlett!" I yell, pulling out every ounce of fight I can from her. Coaxing her inner demon to come and play.

"Fuck you, Dawson!" she yells as she returns two punches.

I can't help the psychotic laugh that escapes me. "Time and place, baby doll."

"I wouldn't touch you with a ten foot fucking pole," she retorts.

I can't help the smile that takes over my face. "Oh, Scarlett, I didn't know you liked my brand of foreplay."

"Ugh, disgusting," she grunts, but her fight doesn't relent. She still continues to give me all she has got. I slowly start to notice the fatigue setting in though. The earlier panic attack having well and truly exhausted her. A shrill whistle sounds and I watch as Scarlett blows out a breath in relief. Her shoulders slump and her hands drop to her sides as she turns to face Mr Green.

"That's enough for today. Thursday I expect you to bring your A game. No more fucking around. Understand?"

"Yes, Sir," we all say in unison.

He then gives us all one last assessing glance over, determining our worth to the Birds just like he does every session. Something seems to soften in his eyes as he looks at Scarlett, but it's gone as his gaze swings to mine. I give him a respectful nod, one he returns.

Over the years I have grown a lot of respect for Mr Green. I watched in awe of him that day back when Scarlett was taken. He was able to snap me out of a full blown meltdown.

I'll never forget his words, *'Face them all like a warrior. Whether you are one or not.'* Pretty sure he just found that quote from a book, but it did its job that day.

I stood up from my cowered position behind a knocked over picnic table. I couldn't remember how I had gotten there or where my parents, brother or friends were. All I could see was the .22 pistol Mr Green handed me. It wasn't the first time I had been handed a gun of a similar calibre.

From the moment we could comfortably hold a gun in our hands and not fall on our asses from the recoil, we had been trained to use them. Which at the time I didn't realise was for situations like the one I was thrown into.

It was the same day I looked a six foot man in the eyes and shot him in between his.

An innocent eight year old turned killer in the blink of an eye.

I didn't hesitate for a single second. Because as his gun slowly began to raise, I knew that he would have no qualms shooting me dead. From that day on, nothing has ever been able to penetrate the walls I built up around myself.

I became the perfect warrior.

The soldier I was needed to be. I built my body to become

a weapon.

Mr Green saw the fight in me. Every session I attended without fail. Sitting in and listening in on the older training classes. Memorising every bit of information I could. Eventually he pulled me aside and offered me private lessons.

For years now, I have been ready to be inducted in the Thunderbirds. I can't help the bitterness I feel from being constantly held back. My Dad says I'm not ready. Pres says I'm not ready. Yet, Mr Green is the only one that believes that I am.

"Dismissed." Mr Green turns his back on us and walks out of the building. I've always been fond of his assertiveness. I've never seen the point in banging around the bush. While others find it rude, I find it refreshing.

I decide to make my escape too, needing to put as much distance as I can between me and my girl, even if every inch kills me.

BOARDING P
NAME: SCARLETT SMIT
FROM:
TIME:
CLA
SEAT:
President

chapter
TWENTY-THREE

I watch as Dawson turns his back to me without a single glance my way and makes his way out of the training room. Really, I don't know what I should expect. While he seemed to be attentive and caring whilst he brought me out of my panic attack. It shouldn't surprise me that he is already turning his back on me, yet again, like he didnt save me from myself.

Like he wasn't that man that I fell desperately in love with all those months ago that shined through, just for a moment. It sparks something within me, some kind of determination. That if I can see even a fraction of the person he used to be, that maybe not everything is lost between us.

I don't bother saying goodbyes to the guys, instead I race out of the swinging doors Dawson just disappeared behind. I almost tumble out of them but instantly right myself as I snap my head in both directions, watching as Dawson disappears around a corner.

"Dawson, wait!" I yell in the hopes of him stopping but

after a moment and still no sign of him, I groan. "Oh for fuck's sake."

I take off running down the now deserted hallway. As I turn the corner he went around, I get my hopes up in catching up to him but I meet another quiet hallway leading to God knows where.

"Fucking Farlap motherfucker. Needs to clear his goddamn ears out," I grumble as I come to a stop. I'm just about to turn around and head back to the training rooms when a strong grip grabs onto my arm. I'm pulled into a dark room and slammed up against a wall. I attempt to fight the figure but it's useless. The grip on my wiggling arms is firm and the weight against my body sees me going nowhere anytime soon.

"Fucking Farlap is a new insult. I think I like that one better than asshole."

Dawson. That fucking dick.

His grip on my arms loosens but only slightly.

"Oh, fuck you!" I snarl, "Did you also hear the part about where I told you to clean out your ears?"

"What was that? I didn't hear you." His tone is laced with sarcasm but I don't find him remotely funny.

I stay silent for a moment and so does he. None of us saying anything. He doesn't step away from me and I don't attempt to escape his hold. I feel my heart race, like it tries to fill the silence between us.

"Why did you help me?" My voice is a whisper but it's loud enough for him to hear. I know he does by the way his grip on my arms tighten again and the way his breath hitches, like he wasn't expecting me to say anything. Especially not this.

He is silent for a moment but I wait him out.

His voice is hoarse as he eventually replies, "I don't know."

"I saw *you*."

He scoffs and I can imagine the eye roll that would have followed. He goes to step away but my hands shoot up, pulling him back into me.

"Don't deny it Dawson. I saw you. That man I met that night on the beach. The man that I fell in love with so irrevocably that I've seem to have lost all sense of self-preservation. Because that man has me running after him trying to pick up any pieces of what we lost." I hear Dawson suck in a sharp breath as his body goes rigid underneath my hold. I don't let it deter me as I continue to pour all the scraps of my broken heart out for him.

"You might be hell-bent on seeing the tail end of me. You might have only seen me as a summer fling, as someone to pass time with but it was never that for me. You stole a piece of my heart the day you left. The day you promised me it wasn't the end. A piece that will forever belong to you no matter how fucking awful you are to me." I pause, shaking my head, knowing just how ridiculous I probably look. But the hold he has on me is unrelenting.

"You were never just a fling, Scarlett." My head snaps up as I try to look at him through the darkness of the room. I don't expect the soft lips that crash down on mine and for a moment I'm stunned as Dawson's lips glide over mine; but it's only for a second before I'm returning his kiss.

Our lips move together desperately. I can feel just how hungry he is for me and I return the sentiment ten-fold. Dawson's hands slide down my body, causing goosebumps to pebble over my skin at the descent.

He caresses the globes of my ass and I can't control the groan that escapes me. I press my body into his, trying to find any reprieve for my aching core. I yelp in surprise as Dawson lifts me into his arms. My legs swing around his body automatically as I throw my hands around his neck, threading my fingers into his hair.

I roll my body into his, my inner vixen coming alive at his touch. Dawson groans and I swallow it with a kiss, barely able to contain one of my own. Our tongues move together in unison. Like we had been dying for thirst all this time, and are finally quenching that thirst with each other.

Dawson pushes me further into the wall at my back, holding me with nothing but the weight of his body against mine as his hands moved to my waistband.

Breaking our kiss, he tilts his head back. I can feel his stare on my face through the shadows compromising our vision.

"Tell me you don't want this. Tell me to stop." Under his gravelly tone, I note the seriousness of what he is trying to convey. He wants me just as desperately as I want him. That his hunger for me is just as strong as mine is for him. That he will only stop if I tell him too.

But over nine months of separation from him has made me desperate, if not completely lost of all self respect for any ground rules I had set for myself. All the anger and resentment I feel for him completely faded. All I can see is the man in front of me. The man that promised me we would never be done.

"Don't stop." My voice is a pathetic groan.

"Fuck, baby." Dawson's voice cracks as he pushes my legs down from his waist. His hands instantly find their place at my wist band again, immediately stripping me of my shorts and underwear. I gasp as the cool air, of what I assume is some kind of closet, hits my flesh.

I feel Dawson crouch in front of me, his hands tapping my ankles as I step from my clothes. I jump when I feel his nose connect with the mound of my pussy. I hear him take in a deep breath and I can't help but feel self-conscious, knowing just how much I was sweating during our sparring session.

There's a deep groan straight from Dawson's chest as I try to turn from his hold on me.

"Fuck, you smell delicious." I snort, my cheeks reddening in embarrassment. Dawson moves his hands from my ankles and I go to step away.

His hands grip my waist and push me back to the wall. "Where do you think you are going, Vixen?" His voice is a deep rumble, turning me into mush.

I stumble on my words as I feel his face return to the spot between my legs. His stubble scratches my sensitive skin as I hear him take another inhale. "You aren't going anywhere until your legs are shaking and my cum is running down your legs. I am going to fucking destroy you for anyone else, do you hear me?"

I scoff, unable to stop baiting him. I must be a masochist. "I'd like to see you try. What was your name again? Declan?"

Dawson's hands tighten to the point of pain on my waist, a deep growl escapes him and I know then, I've really gone and done it.

"Such a naughty little slut aren't you, Vixen? You will be eating your words soon enough. The only name you will know is fucking mine." He doesn't give me a moment to hit him with another word as he swings one of my legs over his shoulder and dives into my pussy, immediately finding my clit and sucking it into his mouth.

"Fuck, Fuck. Oh my god." Dawson's attack on my pussy almost brings me to my knees, the only thing keeping me up right is his hold on me. His tongue attacks me with a hunger I didn't know one could possess. One of his hands moves from its spot on my hip to my centre where he instantly finds my entrance.

His fingers don't hesitate as they sink to the hilt inside me.

I suck in a sharp breath at the invasion. He instantly adds a second finger and my body stiffens at the slight twinge of pain.

"Relax, Scar." His voice purrs but it does the job. I feel my body relax at his instruction. He must feel it too as he chuckles. "So fucking obedient for me. You like to act so fucking tough, but really you are just begging for me to tell you what to do, aren't you?"

I can't help but moan at his words. That independent woman I thought I had built myself up to be seeming to melt away completely.

"Such a good fucking girl. Milk my fingers baby."

His tongue returns to my clit as he slowly flicks it. His fingers fuck in and out of my cunt and if it wasn't for him holding me up, my legs would have collapsed from under me.

I feel my body tighten up, the beginnings of an orgasm tightening my lower stomach. I gasp as Dawson pulls away, his fingers slipping from me.

"What the fuck, Dawson?" I yell at the man who just chuckles in reply. My leg drops from his place on my shoulder as he stands back to full height.

"If you are going to cum on anything, it's going to be my cock." Dawson's hands wrap around my thighs as he lifts me back up into his hold. I scream as his cock sinks to the hilt. Tears spring in my eyes at the burn.

"Jesus fucking christ, you are so tight," he groans, dropping his head into the crook of my neck. I expect him to instantly start moving but he gives me a few moments, seeming to also catch his own breath. Eventually, the burn fades away. It's almost as though he can read my mind as he pulls his head back.

"Move," I whimper, needing the orgasm he denied me.

His chuckle is dark, sending a shiver over my skin. "You aren't in charge here, Vixen."

I instantly nod, unable to be disobedient. "Sorry, Daddy." My voice is a meek whimper but I know he hears me.

Dawson inhales a deep breath as his hands tighten on their place at my hips.

"That's right, baby. I'm your fucking Daddy."

I gasp as he pulls out right to the tip and slams back inside me. My eyes roll into the back of my head as he begins fucking in and out of me relentlessly.

My nails dig into his shoulders.

Dawson groans, "Mark me, baby."

"Fuck, Dawson," I breathe. Dawson instantly stops mid trust. His hands seem to grip my thighs tighter and I'm sure I'll have bruises there from his grip.

"What did you say?" he growls.

I instantly realise the error of my ways, my eyes going wide. "Daddy. I mean Daddy."

"I thought you were my good girl?" he rumbles and I can almost imagine the expression on his face. "I don't have to punish you do I?"

"No, Daddy. I'm sorry," I apologise, slightly shocked at my instant submission.

It seems to do the trick though as he follows through on the thrust he was halfway through.

"Holy shit, Daddy!" I yell, tightening my legs around his body.

"Fuck yes," Dawson moans as his pace speeds up. He fucks me into the wall behind me as I feel an orgasm tighten my stomach again. My pussy clenches around Dawson's thick length. All inhibitions leave me as the most intense orgasm takes over me. I can't help the scream that escapes my throat. I feel a rush of liquid flow from my cunt as Dawson's pace stutters. He follows me over the edge with a roar.

As each of our orgasms slowly start to fade, we stay holding each other tight. The only sound in the dark room comes from our heavy breathing. Eventually Dawson's cock softens enough that it slips out of me along with what feels like a stream of fluid. I cringe at the unfamiliar feeling. I then also thank myself for taking the pill consistently, at the reminder of Dawson not wearing a condom.

I let my legs drop from Dawson's waist. He doesn't step away from me just yet and I'm thankful for it because I know my legs still feel wobbly from the most intense orgasm of my life.

Dawson mumbles something that I can't quite hear.

"Huh?" I question him but he just chuckles,

"Told you that you'd be eating your words."

"Shut up," I grumble but there is no heat to it. I straighten my legs and cringe again as I feel our combined juices fall down my legs.

"Is there anything I can use to clean myself up with? I can feel it all running down my legs." Dawson finally lets me go but only takes one step away from me. I hear him fumbling around with something, eventually taking a step back into me as he hands me some paper towel.

"That doesn't surprise me," That familiar dark chuckle escaping his lips, "you squirted."

I pause my attempt at cleaning my legs. "What?"

"You squirted. It was hot as fuck."

I stand there speechless as I squint at him through the darkness of the room. Squirted? I think back to all of the times with my faithful satisfyer and not once did I ever cum the way Dawson was able to make me.

I finish wiping my legs down, eventually finding my discarded underwear and shorts. I feel Dawson's eyes on me the entire time as I pull them back on. He stays quiet and so do I. Once I fasten the button on my shorts, Dawson steps away from me and opens the door. I follow him out but come to a quick stand still as I meet the eyes of four very pissed off men. I suck in a gasp at the realisation of what just happened and what they heard.

My cheeks redden as I look around at Nicky, Sonny, Pike and Dacre. None of them are looking at me though. They're all glaring at Dawson who stands strong with a shit-eating grin on his face.

"So what, you think you can just be an asshole all day then get your dick wet and expect everything to be fine?" I jolt at the tone of Dacre's voice. My head snaps towards him in shock. My normally sweet boy's face is incensed.

Dawson just responds with something between a grunt and a scoff. He is about to retort something that I know won't help his case whatsoever, so I butt in instead.

"Dacre," I say, stepping towards him. His eyes shoot to mine and they instantly soften, "it's okay. Dawson and I have a lot to talk about but he knows I'm not going anywhere."

I hear a scoff from behind me. I turn and take in the expression on Dawson's face. "If you think you aren't leaving Scarlett, you've got another thing coming."

My jaw drops as I stare at him. His eyes bore into me with intensity and I know that he won't budge from this bullshit ideology that I need to leave.

"You're fucking kidding me right?" I say in complete disbelief. The audacity of the man standing in front of me stuns me.

Dawson stands his ground, crossing his arms over his chest.

"Do I look like I'm kidding, Scarlett?

I scoff, "You're delusional, Dawson. What makes you think I can just walk away from this life? I was forced out of it ten years ago, and dragged right back into it. This is my path. Just because you don't like it doesn't mean you can control me." I shake my head, feeling disgusted in him, "I have been a mess for ten fucking years Dawson. For ten years I was under the assumption that my father and brother were dead. That it was just my Mum and I. Little did I realise that I had a whole other life just waiting for me. And this life feels right.

"You may not understand that. You can stand up and yell at me until you are blue in the face that you don't want this for me but I am finally seeing my true calling. A path that I can slip straight into and be successful. I can make a difference in this world, Dawson."

It's almost as though he can't hear a single thing I'm saying. I watch his body tense as he shakes his head.

His anger overcomes him as his stormy eyes darken, "No, Scarlett. You almost fucking died once!" he yells, his body shaking with anger, "I'm not going to stand by and allow you to drag us back in just to watch them take you again. Because this time, I know you won't come back."

Dawson doesn't give me a chance to bite back as he storms away, leaving the five of us staring after him.

BOARDING PASS
NAME: SCARLETT SMITH
FROM:
TIME:
CLASS:
SEAT:
President

BOARDING P
NAME: SCARLETT SMIT
FROM:
TIME:
CLAS
SEAT:
President

chapter
TWENTY-FOUR

I blow out a breath as I watch Dawson walk around the corner leaving the five of us stunned. My heart skinks. I thought we had come to some kind of agreement. An understanding of sorts.

My place in the Thunderbirds isn't optional. I thought he was coming to understand that, even if he doesn't like it, but I was wrong. I know Dacre, Sonny, Nicky and Pike don't like it; but unlike their idiotic friend, they would prefer to stand beside me and win me back.

I berate myself for letting Dawson have his way with me, especially after preaching to myself all day about how I wouldn't let him, or any of them for that matter, back in. I build back up the fallen wall around my heart slowly after yet again, allowing him to break me.

Fool me once, shame on you. Fool me twice, shame on me.

I look at Pike who is looking at me with a solemn expression, like he already knows exactly what I'm feeling. He walks over to me and collects me in his embrace.

I take a deep breath in of his cologne. That manly scent of his filling my nostrils. I don't even mind that he has been sweating. I need his comfort right now. I should refuse it, push him away. I haven't forgotten the way he hurt me too but if he stands by his words, I will be selfish and take what he is giving.

I know that I can't stay mad at Pike forever. The first of my men.

That day on the beach lives in my head rent free. I'll never forget the feeling of seeing his face for the first time. The concern that was etched into his features that seems to be perfectly replicated on his face right now as he takes a step back to look at me. He keeps a hold of my shoulders as he looks at me intently.

"Are you okay, Princess?" His voice is soft as his hands run over my shoulders in a comforting way.

I give him a small nod, "I will be. I don't know why I expected anything better from him. He is never going to be okay with me being here. I can't just leave. I have my brother back…" I swallow, fighting the tears that threaten to fall. Pike brings his hand up and cups my cheek. I know he means to be supportive but it makes fighting the emotion even more difficult.

I look up at Pike, "I have my Dad back. I have you back." I then look at Sonny, Nicky and Dacre, "I have you all back. How could I let that go now just because he's scared?"

Pike steps closer to me, our bodies touching in so many places that I can't help the hitch in my breathing. His hand stays firmly on my cheek. His thumb slowly caresses me.

"He is a fucking fool. I have regretted every single day of the last nine months. I have tortured myself day in and day out looking at the photos of us. You have consumed my every waking thought." I watch as he swallows, he gives a slight shake of his head, "I fucked up, Princess. We fucked up. Walking away from you was–is–my biggest regret. It has always been you."

The tears that have been threatening me finally fall. Pike catches them with his thumb, instantly rubbing them away.

"I've got a lot to make up for. I hurt the most precious thing to ever walk into my life. I promise you I will crawl to the ends of the earth to make it up to you. You are my life. You are every breath I take. My salvation. My bright light in the darkness."

He looks at me intently for a moment. I return the stare. Looking into the eyes of a man who with a precious few words has all but brought me to my knees. Screw sticking it to The Man. At this point I wouldn't even be able to see The Man if I bumped into him in the street.

"I know you aren't going to make it easy on us," Pike chuckles, and I hear Sonny, Dacre and Nicky all chime in with chuckles of their own, "I don't expect you to either. We deserve to bow at your feet. To accept whatever scraps you give us. You deserve the world, Scarlett."

Words evade me as I stare up into Pike's eyes. Those bright blue orbs suck me into their depths. I don't bother to give a verbal reply. I know he deserves one after the way he spilled his heart out to me but I know if I tried, it would just be a sob.

I bring my hands up, gripping his face and bring his lips to mine. I communicate everything I'm unable to say through words into our kiss. How much I appreciate him seeing me. His understanding of how I feel and not just pushing me away like Dawson. By vowing to fix the hurt he caused.

I let him know just how much he means to me in return. Just how much I have missed his golden smile. Missed his soul which now feels so intertwined with mine, it's hard to find where I end and he starts.

We eventually break away from each other but Pike doesn't stray far. Bringing his forehead to fine. He takes a deep breath, one I follow.

"I won't leave you ever again, Princess."

"Promise?" I whisper, not trusting my voice.

"I promise." Pike lays another gentle kiss on my lips before pulling away.

I take a step away from him reluctantly, needing space to pull myself together. I turn to look at Nicky who takes a step towards me. I open my mouth to speak but he beats me to it.

"Saturday," he says, taking the words out of my mouth.

I nod, making him smile.

"Come on, we don't want to keep Shelly waiting. She may have missed you but she will still give you hell if you're late," he says with a grimace. My eyes widen, realising just how much time has passed.

"Shit," I say, looking around at the guys who just nod. Sonny grabs my hand, pulling me down the hallway back towards the now empty training room.

"I'll drop you off if you like, *mi estrella?*"

A shiver runs down my body at the sound of the nickname rolling off his tongue. He notices my reaction but doesn't comment on it as I mindlessly follow him out of the clubhouse.

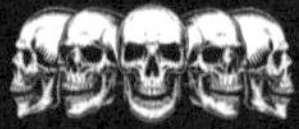

Sonny and I fly through the streets of Rydell. He was adamant that I take the helmet instead of him. He muttered something about not wanting to be scrapped off the side of the road from Dacre blasting his brains out. An image that made me cringe at the thought.

He drops me off at Pinks'. When he offers to walk me in I decline, knowing I need a little bit of space to collect myself. I still feel vulnerable and it makes my skin feel itchy. That barrier I spent months reinforcing seems to fracture around these men. While I know I will eventually let them back in, it makes me feel anxious at the thought of just willingly giving them my heart again, or whatever pieces are still left of it. Even the bits and pieces I seem to be giving them even sparingly, set me on edge. I know I shouldn't. I know it's just giving them more of me they could break but I'm apparently a sucker for pain.

He lets out a breath in disappointment, but he nods his head as I hand him back his helmet.

"I'll see you tomorrow, at school?" he asks, an almost hopeful look in his eye.

I lean down, kissing his cheek slowly before pulling away. Before I even go to answer, a bright smile takes over Sonny's face.

"Okay, perfect. I'll see you tomorrow."

I watch as Sonny carelessly throws his helmet on. He revs his bike a few times, watching me before giving me a sly wink and taking off. I shake my head, watching the tail end of him turn a corner.

Pinks' is dead quiet this time of the afternoon. The only inhabitants are the few bartenders who rush around getting everything ready for opening time and the dancers currently practising on the stage.

It gives me a chance to really take in the establishment. The tables are all clean of glasses and bottles. The entire place is completely lit up from the house lights. If I wasn't so familiar with the setup from last night, I would feel lost. Compared to the clubs back home, this place is immaculate.

As I take a few steps towards the centre stage, I notice the absence of sticky residue on the ground. Yet another difference between this club and the ones back home. Or is this home now?

Can they both be my home?

Shelly instantly spots me, "Scarlett, baby!" she yells, taking the steps one at a time until she is engulfing me in her embrace.

"Hi, Shelly." Her arms are locked tight around me so it's nothing more than a wheeze. Eventually she steps back from me but barely as she takes me in.

"My girl, you're even more beautiful in the daylight. Dacre was nearly senseless when he came home last night. Since he came home from Australia, he has non-stop spoken about this girl he met." She rolls her eyes as she folds her arms over her chest.

"That little shit was way too ominous about the details too, but last night, it was like this light had come back on in his life," she chuckles as she looks at me intently, "This whole time, it was you. I know this is forward of me and I shouldn't be sticking my nose in your business but I wouldn't be his Momma bear if I didn't tell you this," My heart skips a beat as Shelly grabs my hands, her eyes feel like they pierce my soul.

"That boy is in love with you. His world was all but destroyed when he thought you had died. My story is for another day but I have been through it. My demons haunt me everyday. But I've been able to handle them. But Dakes?" She blows out a breath and I watch the tears slowly begin to well in her eyes. I can't help the way my own eyes start to blur.

"That boy of mine wears his heart on his sleeve. His soul has been lost for ten years. I can't count the amount of times I dreaded coming home at night. The thought of my boy not being here still makes me sick. But now that you are home," she sighs, letting go of one of my hands as she wipes away a lone tear, "It's like all of that is gone now. That light is back in his eyes and I know it's all because of you. You have been the star in his dark sky."

A tear slips out of my eye as I stand there stunned. I knew the depth of Dacre's love for me. It has been clear to me from the moment he told me he was all in with me. But hearing this from his mother, it feels somehow deeper. I just nod, unable to give a verbal answer. Shelly gives me a sad smile as she reaches up and wipes my face.

"I know what those boys did to you. Dacre was very forthcoming with the details last night." She gives me a serious look that pulls a chuckle from me. "Give them hell." She smiles before we both burst out in laughter.

I shake my head, "I didn't think you would ever tell me to bust your son's ass for the way he treated me."

"Are you kidding? I raised that boy better than to ghost women just because of some fragile masculinity bullshit. If he doesn't treat you like the queen you are, you tell me." She gives me a pointed look, letting me know just how serious she is.

I nod, before looking over at the stage as a few of the dancers swing around on the poles. My eyes bug out as I watch one of them hang upside down and slowly spin.

"Impressive aren't they?" Shelly says and I note the hint of pride in her voice.

I nod my head before turning a worried look to the woman standing next to me, "You don't expect me to dance like that for my initiation?"

Shelly turns to me and laughs at the expression on my face, "God no! Your feet will be staying firmly on the ground."

I let out a breath I had been holding in. The nerves that had slowly started to creep in diminishing.

"Basically, I want you to pick a song that you feel comfortable dancing to. We will go to the dressing room and you can pick out one of the costumes we have. I'll let you have a play around with the music and some dance moves over the next couple of days. If you need help to coordinate it, call me or one of the dancers can give you some pointers."

I nod, songs already coming to me, "How long do I have to prepare?"

I notice Shelly wince as she looks at me, sympathy in her eyes. "Your father called me this morning. He wants your initiation set for Friday night."

My eyes bug. Three days? Jesus christ. "Um, okay."

Shelly gives me a reassuring smile, "It will be fine. You should have seen your Mum dance around the stage during her initiation. She looked like a drunk giraffe. Your father still had stars in his eyes though." We both laugh as Shelly leads us out the back.

※

Shelly brings me to one of the rooms that I didn't get a chance to see last night. The walls are lined with different props and costumes. I stare in wonder as I take in the sight in front of me. It's like a woman's playground here. Every form of lace and leather in a variety of colours and designs is here.

My eyes instantly meet a black lingerie set on one of the mannequins. The bra is mostly sheer lace with a leather buckle going over the nipples with the thong in the same style. A leather garter adorns the waist of the mannequin leading to sheer stockings. A pair of eight inch studded heels sit just underneath.

I don't even have to bother looking at any of the other sets. This one is mine.

I walk over to the mannequin, letting my fingers explore the scraps of leather and lace before I turn back to Shelly.

"This one." I smile.

Shelly chuckles as she walks over to where I'm still admiring the piece. "Those boys are going to regret ever messing with you."

A sinister smile takes over my lips. "That was my plan."

After Shelly and I undress the mannequin, I get dressed in the set. My eyes bug out as I take in my reflection in the mirror of the dressing room. I quickly pull the shoes onto my feet, wobbling slightly as I slowly get used to the height difference. Taking one last look at myself, I grab my phone out of my bag, snapping a few selfies and sending them to the girls back in Australia. They instantly blow up my phone with fire emojis and engagement proposals. I giggle as I tuck my phone away safely. Taking one last look in the mirror, I try to steel myself. Build up the confidence I need to pull back the curtain and do what I need to do.

A month ago I was just a normal girl in a small beachside town in Australia. Now I am standing in front of a mirror, covered in leather in lace in a club in America, ready to learn my initiation dance so I can inch one step closer to taking on my role as the next president of the Thunderbirds.

Straight out of a goddamn movie.

I stand there for a moment longer as I allow my eyes to

travel over my body once more. After a moment, I let out a breath before swinging back the curtain and making my way back to Shelly who is waiting for me. Her mouth drops as she takes me in.

She eventually meets my eyes after she has looked over the entire outfit, "Your father is going to kill me," she laughs, "Let's get started."

BOARDING PASS
NAME: SCARLETT SMITH
FROM:
TIME:
CLASS:
SEAT:
President

BOARDING P
NAME: SCARLETT SMIT
FROM:
TIME:
CLAS
SEAT:
President

chapter
TWENTY-FIVE

scarlett

I wobble down the carpeted hallway as Shelly leads me back out into the main stage. The other girls smile at me as they make their way back into the dressing room. Their nods of appreciation and comments help boost my ego and give me the pep in my step I need to learn this routine.

The club is still thankfully empty. The only few people that are left are the bartenders that are busy still tidying behind the bar. They don't give me their attention and I'm thankful for it, not sure if I'm ready yet for that many eyes to be on me just yet.

Shelly leads me over to the DJ booth where she instructs me to pick a song. I scroll through the list until my eyes settle on one of my favourites. Grace and I have danced to this song many times in the past few months so I know my body will find the rhythm easily.

"For the first run through, I want you to just get a feel of the music. Dance along if you want to. Remember, you want to seduce the crowd. Pull them in. Make them want more."

I nod as she starts the music. The beat slowly builds through my body, taking over as I slowly sway.

As the lyrics start, I move my body with a little more purpose. Eventually the music completely takes over as I continue moving to the beat. Each step gives me confidence as I become bolder with my moves, allowing myself to crawl along the floor and shake my ass like I've seen the other dancers do.

I snap my head up as the song ends, turning around to Shelly who is beaming at me, a bright smile on her face.

"Fucking hell, Scarlett! That was incredible! Are you sure you haven't got any dance experience since being down under?" She questions, her eyes shining with pride.

"Other than dancing at the club with my mates, none." I shrug my shoulders.

"I'm impressed. Usually girls come in here with not a single clue of how to move their bodies but you are a natural."

A smile brightens my face at her compliment. "Okay, what do I need to work on?" I ask.

Shelly just shakes her head, that proud look still shining in her eyes, "Darling girl, you do that same routine Friday night and you will have every single patron drooling."

I quirk my brow, "Are you sure?"

Shelly just nods, coming over to place her hands on my shoulders, "If I knew that your parents wouldn't have my head, I'd be writing your name down on my roster."

"Really?" I stare at her in disbelief. I never would have thought dancing would have been something I was considered natural at. My only real experience has come from nights out.

I'm not going to lie and say that I haven't lost myself countless times over the past few months since the boys left me. Finding the bottom of the bottle in some dingy ass club seemed to just take the pain away, even if it was only until the morning when I would wake with a raging hangover and regret all the choices that I had made the night before.

But it didn't stop me. Everyone could see that it was a nasty downhill slope to nowhere, but it was better than any other vice I could have partaken in.

Yet, it has given me something I can actually use today.

Shelly nods before pulling me back towards the dressing rooms, "I wouldn't lie to you about something like this. Now, go backstage and get dressed before the horny old Birds come strolling in and getting an eyeful of you. If I'm only going to have you for one night, you bet your ass I'm going to make a spectacle about it." she laughs as she pushes me towards the dressing rooms.

I quickly get dressed, carefully storing the lingerie set in the locker set aside for me for when I want to come here and practice. I decide to bring the shoes home with me. While Shelly may have said I looked like a natural, I could feel myself wobbling and throwing caution to the wind, I know I will need to practice in them.

I walk out of the club with my heels in my hand surprised to see Pike leaning next to a blacked out Harley. I slowly take him in while he is busy scrolling through his phone.

He's out of his school uniform from today, dressed in black jeans and a dark grey henley. His blonde hair is a perfectly tumbled mess on his head. His face is pulled down in a scowl as if whatever he is reading on his phone is bothering him.

Even looking pissed off, he's still perfect. It pisses me off a little bit about how effortless he is and yet is able to look like he just stepped off a Calvin Klein photoshoot.

He snaps his head up when he hears me walking his way, "Hey Princess," he smiles bright, the earlier frown completely forgotten.

"Hey. What are you doing here?" I give him a questioning look.

"I remembered that you said you had to see Shelly this afternoon and I just thought I'd give you a lift home," he replies, an almost bashful look on his face.

I raise an eyebrow, immediately seeing through his attempt at being nonchalant. He grimaces as he reads the expression on my face. He lets out a sigh before kicking some of the loose gravel on the road before meeting my eyes.

"I know that you said we had to give you until Saturday but I just thought I could squeeze in a little bit of time with you, even if it's just taking you home." Pike shrugs, dropping his eyes back down to the road.

It's strange seeing this kind of defeat on someone like Pike. Someone that always seems so sure of himself. Not in a cocky way, but in the kind of way that he has confidence in himself, even if at times he makes mistakes.

But seeing him like this, eyes full of regret, his shoulders slouched low as he absently draws shapes with his boot; I curse myself for feeling broken for him. I shouldn't, but alas, I do.

The man before me is not the man I feel so deeply in love with, that still months later, he is able to crumble my resolve.

I close the distance before us, coming to stand in between his spread legs. He doesn't look up for a moment, instead taking a few breaths, almost as if he is bracing himself for whatever he thinks I'm about to say. Preparing for the worst.

I reach up, grabbing his chin in my hand before slowly tilting his head up to face me. His eyes glisten as they finally reach my own and I feel my heart crack slightly at the sight.

"Take me home?" I whisper. His eyes search my own. Like he needs to be certain I'm not just playing with him.

He eventually nods as I take a step back, giving him room to swing his leg over his Harley. He grabs his helmet off the handle bars and instead of fixing it on his head, he places it on mine, fiddling with the chin strap.

He looks at me, his eyes serious, "I don't particularly feel like being murdered by Dacre."

I can't help the laugh that escapes me. That man is deathly serious about helmet safety. My laughter seems to snap Pike out of his self deprecating thoughts as a small smile graces his face. I absently bring a hand up and cup his face, slowly tracing my thumb over his clean shaven face.

"We will be okay, Pike. You hurt me…" I trail off, watching as his face falls. I continue on, knowing my next words will put him out of his misery. "But, I hope to God that you will be there to fix it."

His eyes instantly brighten. The hope that was lost returns to his eyes as he stares into my eyes. He straightens, cupping one of my cheeks in his hand, replicating the current hold I have on him.

"I swear to whatever higher power is out there, I will fix what I broke. You deserve the fucking world, Scarlett. If it takes until the day I die for you to forgive me, I will be on my knees everyday grovelling. Reminding you just how important you are to me. Telling you every day just how fucking lost I am for you. I meant what I said. There is no me without you."

Unable to find the words after Pike's declaration, I nod. He holds me steady for a moment as he takes me in. From anyone else this kind of moment would be uncomfortable but it's not with him.

With him, it's like the world just fades away. It is just him and I amongst the chaos. Two souls so drawn together that even if the world was fading away around us, we would still be lost in each other. Just like we are in this exact moment. Because while he believes there is no him without me; there is no me without him.

BOARDING PASS
NAME: SCARLETT SMITH
FROM:
TIME:
CLASS:
SEAT:
President

chapter
TWENTY-SIX

pike

Scarlett swings her leg over my bike, settling in behind me. Her body moulds perfectly to mine as she runs her hands around my body. I can't help the way my body shivers at her touch.

I have ached for her these past nine months. Dawson tried to convince us to just move on and forget her. Tried to fill our heads with the notion that if we just forgot about her that she would be safe.

At first I was onboard when we came back to the kind of club we did. The panic I felt rattled me. I knew I couldn't infect her life with it. She didn't sign up for that. She just thought we belonged to a regular MC. While that may have been what we started out as, it isn't anymore.

If only we knew then what we know now.

If only we knew that she was our Scarlett all along.

That no matter how hard we tried, she was always going to lead this life. None of us could have stopped it.

I can appreciate how Dawson feels. It's obvious he's scared.

Terrified that Scar will be taken again. That this time it won't be just her mind that is lost, it'll be her life.

That fear lives deep inside of me too.

But I know that I would much rather have Scarlett beside me than have her halfway across the world, completely out of reach.

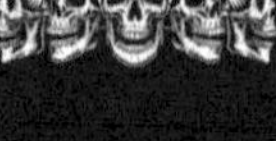

The drive to Scarlett's house takes only minutes. I long for her body the moment she pulls away, swinging her leg off my bike and handing me back my helmet. Having her that close to me, even if it was only for moments, felt like heaven.

I kick down the stand before swinging my leg off my bike. I instantly reach for Scarlett and she willingly comes. I hold her close, savouring each moment with her that I can before I have to let her go again.

I've seen the indecision in Scarlett with how to be around us. One minute I can see her completely distanced from us. Her walls are utterly impenetrable. Not that I can blame her. What we did has eaten away at me for months.

Sometimes I see her forcing herself to not give in though. I hold onto that glint that I can see in her eyes. The small glimmer of hope that it gives me.

I could comfortably keep Scarlett in my arms forever. There's this completion I feel each time I hold her close. Her body fits perfectly against mine. I don't think I'll ever be able to get the feeling of her wrapped around me as we rode on the back of my bike out of my head anytime soon. Everything with her just feels right.

Eventually she pulls away from me. She graces me a small smile and I swear my brain takes a mental photograph.

"Come up stairs with me?" she asks, her voice just louder than a whisper but it's like she said it into a megaphone.

I look at her in disbelief. I have no doubt in mind that I look ridiculous right now. My eyes are blown wide and my jaw hangs open.

I gain some kind of composure to muster up a reply, "Ah… are you sure?"

She gives me a nod, "Yeah, come on."

She doesn't have to tell me twice. I follow her as close behind her as I can.

Her house is surprisingly quiet this time of the night. I haven't been inside the Crux's house in years. We used to be close with Rhodes even after we thought Scarlett had died. Dacre more so than the rest of us.

Day by day we saw both of them slowly drift further and further away from reality. Drowning their feelings in substances. Anything to numb the pain.

Nicky, Dawson, Sonny and I could all see just how much damage it had caused to an already fragile Dacre. He became a shell of the person he once was.

It was hard to not blame Rhodes for leading Dacre down the path he did. The relief we all felt once Dacre finally broke away from Rhodes' influence was palpable.

Even all of these years later, I still hold an ounce of resentment towards him. He's just seemed to get worse as time has gone on. Losing Scarlett changed all of us. But it affected Rhodes differently.

Just before we reach the same room Scarlett had when she was younger, Rhodes' door opens and out walks him and Wyatt. They freeze in place as they see us. Wyatt looks disappointed as he looks at where Scarlett's hand is held in mine.

Rhodes frowns as he steps closer to us, "I thought you were

going to call me when you needed to be picked up from Pinks'?"

Scarlett just shrugs her shoulders, "Pike was already waiting out the front for me. I didn't see the point in calling and annoying you when he could just as easily bring me home."

She turns her head looking back at me, a cheeky smirk on her face, "Plus, Pike and I need to have a little... conversation." She winks and my knees nearly collapse from under me. Fucking hell, this woman will be the death of me.

Rhodes scoffs, both of our attentions snapping to him. "Going to forgive him already? Heard you've already forgiven one of those fucktards."

I stand up straighter, instantly becoming on guard. Rhodes' words seem to affect Scar in the same way as I feel her bristle beside me. Her hand drops from mine and I let it go.

"What the fuck is that supposed to mean?" she snaps, a sharp edge to her voice.

Rhodes just rolls his eyes, clearly not seeing the dangerous edge that Scarlett is holding tight to.

"Don't think we didn't hear you and Dawson earlier at the clubhouse. I'm disappointed, Scarlett. You harped on to me for weeks about how these five guys hurt you as bad as they did. Yet you fold the moment someone offers you a good time in a supply closet. There's names for people like that," he snides, looking Scarlett up and down.

Anger bubbles through my system. Where does this motherfucker get the hide to call Scarlett a slut? His own fucking sister, who we all thought for the last then years had been dead!

I go to step closer to Rhodes but Scarlett beats me to it. She instantly closes the distance between her and her brother. With strength I'm sure that both she and I didn't know she possessed, she slams him up against the wall. Their faces are only inches apart. The fury on her face burns like a wildfire. I see a hint of fear in Rhodes' eyes as he looks down at his sister.

"How fucking dare you insinuate that I'm a slut! What I do in my own time and who I decide to share that time with is none of your fucking business. If I decide to bang the entire senior class at Rydell Prep, you best fucking believe I will do exactly that."

Scarlett inches even closer towards Rhodes. I see the regret in his eyes the moment he realises he has fucked up.

"I don't give a fuck who you are to me. If you say shit like that again to me, you will see exactly what I think of slut shamers."

With Scarlett's promise thick in the air, she turns away from her brother, storms towards me before grabbing my hand and all but dragging me into her bedroom. The door slams behind her. I don't get the chance to take in her room before she's slamming me up against the wall behind her. I don't feel the pain in my head as it smacks against the door.

I suck in a breath as her body presses against mine. My brain only seems to register pleasure. The feeling of her being up against me is like my own personal kryptonite. She steps up onto her tiptoes, her body moulding further into mine.

"This doesn't mean I forgive you."

I instantly nod. She still raises an eyebrow at me, as if doubting me.

"I plan on apologising to you every day for the rest of our lives, Princess. I don't deserve your forgiveness. Not a single fucking ounce of it. But I'm going to beg for it anyway." I grab her head in my hands, leaning down so our lips are almost touching. I feel her breath coming out in short puffs and I long to feel her lips on mine again. I'm desperate for it at this point.

"If you weren't already aware, I'm obsessed with you. I want you in any way that you will allow me."

A smile slowly creeps over her lips. I watch intently as she licks her lips. I swear I can almost feel a wisp of her tongue. My knees almost collapse from beneath me in utter desperation.

"I look forward to seeing you on your knees in front of me," she chuckles.

Fuck, I'm so gone for this woman.

Scarlett closes the gap between us before I can move. Her lips are soft as they glide across mine. I swipe my tongue across her lips, begging for entry. She instantly opens her mouth, welcoming me in. Our tongues glide together in unison.

After a while I begin to lose all notion of where she ends and I begin. She has always been it for me. The other piece to my soul. Fated in the cursed stars.

I finally allow my hands to roam her body. I run my hands up the side of her hips. Grabbing her waist, I pull her into me. She rolls her body into mine slowly. My dick painfully presses into the zipper of my jeans at the feeling.

If I'm being honest with myself, it's been hard since the moment I saw her up on that stage last night.

She was like an angel sent from the pits of hell. Come to wreak havoc on our souls. But what she doesn't know is my soul is already hers.

She has owned me since she was knee high to a grasshopper. Then to that night on the beach when we thought we met her for the first time, she regained control over every single facet of me. I am hers. Hers to do with as she wishes.

Scarlett's hands move down my torso. I suck in a gasp as her fingers linger at the waistband of my pants. A shiver runs over my body at her touch. I feel her pull back as she grips the bottom of my shirt, slowly pulling it up my body and over my head. I don't pay attention to where she throws it. Not when her hands return to my waistband again. They slowly start undoing the button. I don't waste any time, helping to kick them off; discarding them like they are on fire.

Scarlett chuckles at my eagerness. I quirk my lips at her as I grip the hem of her shirt, chuckling when she sucks in a gasp of her own. "Your turn, Princess."

I pull off her top, throwing the fabric in a similar direction to where I'm sure my jeans landed.

My eyes travel down her body. It's like my hands have a mind of their own as they explore her. Just like she did to me, I painstakingly begin to remove her pants. She hastily kicks them off once they get to her knees.

For a moment we just stand their taking in every inch of each other. For once, I keep my hands to myself. But the need is there. The need to hold her. The need to caress her perfect body. A body that I plan on claiming every fucking inch of.

I don't know who breaks first but within seconds we are on each other. Our mouths glide over the other with such unrestrained hunger.

Now that the gates have been broken, there's no way either of us could stop at this point.

My hands roam around her back and with a flick of my fingers, her bra comes loose. She chuckles as she shakes it off. "Handy little trick."

I wink at her, "That's not the only handy thing I can do with my fingers."

She laughs, throwing her head back. My eyes can't help but stare at her throat and the desperate feeling inside me that calls to mark her there so everyone including that fuckwit Wyatt knows that she's mine.

"Smooth, baby," Scarlett whispers as her laughter fades. She wraps her arms around my neck. I feel my knees falter at the feeling of her unclothed skin pressed against my chest.

I grip either side of her face as I bring her lips back to mine. The hunger has slowly faded but it's obvious neither of us are able to stop. Her hands stay wrapped around my neck.

I allow mine to travel down her body yet again. This time without the interruption of fabric, I'm able to take in every inch of her body. My fingers graze the sides of her breasts. She moans into my mouth at the touch and it's like the sound reignites the hunger in me.

I grip her ass in my hands and haul her up into my body. Her legs instantly wrap around my body.

I slowly begin to walk towards the vague memory of where her bed is, praying I don't trip on anything. Her hands dislodge from around my neck as I throw her own on her rumpled bed.

While so much has changed in Scarlett from the person she was before her accident to who she is now, her aversion for a made bed has clearly stuck.

I'm finally able to take my fill in of her. Her tits sit rounded on her chest. Just by look alone, I know that they will be the perfect handful. My brain starts to run with ideas on just how many filthy things I can do to defile them. My eyes continue their trek down her body. I can sense her nervousness as she begins to close her legs. My hands snap out, startling her as I stop them from closing.

"Don't you dare hide from me, Princess," I growl.

"Pike…" she whimpers as the fight begins to leave her body. Little does she know it but she's slowly giving herself over to me. Something that I have been desperate for for a long time.

I chuckle as I slowly lower myself to my knees. My face

coming at a perfect height to take in her lace covered pussy.

"I'll take good care of you." I know she notices the double meaning behind my words. I don't shelter them for a single moment. She deserves them. She deserves the fucking world.

I grab the lace at her hips and slowly start pulling them down her legs. Once they are off, I begin my ascent back up her thighs. I take my time, peppering kisses as I go.

She begins to squirm, obviously becoming frustrated at how long I'm taking. But I savour it. Anytime spent between her legs is a fucking blessing. One I refuse to rush through.

I finally reach the apex of her thighs. Her pussy fucking glistens. My mouth waters as I take her in.

"Pike, please…" she moans, the desperation in her becoming unbearable as she begs for me.

"That's right, Princess. Fucking beg for me. Beg me and I'll do whatever you want."

"Pike, I need…" She cuts off as my hot breath blows over her pussy. She grips the sheets as her back arches.

"Tell me, Scar."

"Pike, I need you to lick me," she finally says, lifting her head to look down at my position in between her legs. I quirk my eyebrow at her waiting for the word I know she knows I need.

"Please, Pike," she begs and I crack. Before she can utter another word, I swipe my tongue from up her cunt. Her taste explodes on my tongue and I groan. I go back in for another swipe and chuckle at the guttural moan she releases as I continue eating my new favourite meal.

It doesn't take long before I feel Scarlett's orgasm begin to build. I bring my fingers up and slide two digits into her. She screams out her release at the first thrust of my fingers and I continue slowly fucking them in and out of her as her orgasm retreats.

I stand, grinning like a Cheshire cat.

"Pike, if you don't fuck me right now, I might explode." She looks at me wide eyed. The aftershocks of her orgasm are still bright in her eyes.

I hesitate. Fuck.

"What? What's wrong?" she asks, noticing the look on my face.

"Fuck. I don't have a condom. When I came to pick you up I wasn't expecting this," I murmur, tipping my head back and needing a moment to collect myself. I startle when I feel fingers begin to wrap around my legs.

In my moment of disappointment, I hadn't even realised Scarlett had moved. I look down at my girl. My dick twitching as I take her in. The look in her eyes as she looks up at me. The fact that even through my boxers, I can feel her warm breath blowing against my dick.

I feel like I'm about to lose my virginity again for the first time. I get now why Sonny said she didn't even have to touch his dick for him to cum. I also internally cringe at the thought of Sonny while I'm this painfully hard.

"You don't need one," she says. I frown down at her as I take in her words. But I thought she said…

I suck in a breath as she slowly starts pulling my boxers down. My cock springs free and I feel an edge of relief at not being confined by them. Scarlett sits kneeling at the end of her bed. I stand stock still, not moving a single inch. I see the hunger in her eyes as she stares me down. A bead of precum seeps out of my dick. She lifts her head to look me directly in the eyes.

All I see is lust, hunger and desire. She doesn't give me a moment before she leans in, her tongue licking up the mess I made. I don't know how my legs don't collapse from under me as Scar keeps eye contact with me before taking me in her mouth completely. She gags as she reaches as far down as she can take me. She slowly sucks me as she withdraws. A string of spit comes away as my dick slips free of her mouth.

"Fuck me…" I mutter at the sight of my girl in front of me. She has permanently destroyed me for anyone else.

"That's kind of what I'm hoping that's what you will do," she snickers, still holding eye contact with me.

I feel the disappointment all over again but before I can utter a word, she starts shaking her head. "You don't need a condom, Pike. I want to feel you. Every single, raw inch."

I groan at the filth that pours so easily from her mouth.

My hands grip under her arms, pulling her up off her position on her knees. This time when I throw her down on the bed I follow her down, covering her body with mine.

My cock lines up at her entrance. With one final look at her face to gauge if she still wants this as badly as I do, I slowly start pushing inside of her.

Her pussy clamps around my cock like a vice grip as I keep pushing each inch inside of her. Once I'm completely bottomed out, I look back up at my girl.

Heaven doesn't even begin to describe the feeling of her around me like this.

I pull out slowly until only the tip is left in her dripping cunt. She clenches around the head and I throw back my head cursing.

Scarlett giggles at my reaction. I don't give her a second before I slam myself back hard inside her. Her back arches as she squeals at the intrusion.

Each thrust earns me either a moan, whimper or another inhumanly sound and I soak it in. Pleasure is written across every inch of her features and I long to pour as much as I can from her.

I feel her wall squeeze me again and without any warning,

an orgasm comes crashing down over her. Just at the sight of
her head thrown back in the throes of pleasure, my orgasm
creeps up on me and I cum with a shout, emptying myself
inside her. My arms collapse as my orgasm subsides and I roll
before I can crush Scarlett.

We lie side by side for what feels like forever but must only
be minutes trying to catch our breath.

Another giggle comes from Scarlett and I turn to face her.
She's looking directly at the roof and I watch as a smile slowly
starts to creep over her lips. Little bursts of laughter escaping
her swollen lips.

It seems that her laughter is contagious as a chuckle escapes
my lips. At the sound, she turns her head to look at me. Her
smile gets broader if that was even possible and the next time
noise escapes her, she is unable to stop the laughter. I join
alongside her.

If someone was to see us now, they would surely think we
had just escaped a mental asylum.

Eventually the laughter calms down until we are both
laying down facing each other. Only inches separate us. I
reach up and push back a lock of her that had fallen over
her face.

"You are fucking perfect, Scarlett."

She smiles almost shyly at me. "Says you," she mutters just
loud enough for me to hear.

"Prepare to be sick of me, Princess. Now that I've had you,
I will never let you go." The smile drops from her face but I
don't back down, not for a second.

"At this point, I probably sound like a broken record. But I
need you to know just how fucking sorry I am, Scar. I fucked
up. Nothing that I do will ever be enough to make it up to
you, but I want to try. I want to be that man that you met
in Australia. The one who made promises that he wanted so

desperately to keep. You deserve the world and I want to be the one that gives it to you."

I watch as tears glisten her eyes. I watch her internal fight. The push and pull of the angel and devil on her shoulder as they war over my words.

I don't bother with waiting for her to reply. I pull her into my arms. Our naked bodies mould together. She instantly relaxes her body into mine, her arms wrapping around my waist as she settles in.

"Saturday," I murmur.

"Saturday," she whispers in reply.

It's only minutes before her body starts to get heavy. I kiss the top of her head but don't move as I suck in the faint scent of her shampoo.

Home.

She feels like home.

"My girl," I whisper before sleep pulls me under along with her.

BOARDING P
NAME: SCARLETT SMIT
FROM:
TIME:
CLAS
SEAT:
President

chapter
TWENTY-SEVEN

scarlett

The blaring sound of my alarm wakes me from my slumber. I attempt to roll over to smash the fucking thing but a heavy arm draped around my middle stops me. I startle, my tired brain not having caught up to last night's events just yet.

I turn my head and come face to face with a sleeping god.

Pike.

The memories of last night come rushing back in.

The way he owned my body. The way he began to slowly pick up the fragile pieces of my broken heart and slowly mend them with his words.

God, does he know how to use his words.

Typically, it's hard to find a man that is actually comfortable to air his feelings. It took years for me to weasel my way under Noah's defences and get him to finally talk to me. To be fair, that was for a good reason.

But the way Pike was able to slowly fix the damage he caused all those months ago has changed something in me.

I hold onto his promises like they are a life raft. Everything has been chaotic these past few months. When I had finally thought I could move on and heal after months of heartache, yet another load gets thrown on my shoulders. Clinging onto something that feels right is what I need right now.

I should know better than to trust Pike. After all, his words could very well be empty again. But something tells me that won't be the case this time.

I can see it in his eyes.

That heartbreak that is all but reflected in mine.

I need him. I need him like I need air to breathe. And after his confession last night, I know that he needs me just as desperately.

I try to wiggle myself around so that I can face Pike without waking him but his eyes pop open just as I finally roll over. His hold tightens on me slightly as he ensures there's not a single centimetre of space between us.

"Morning," he smiles as he blinks his eyes a few times to adjust to the morning light. His voice is a hoarse rumble still laced with sleep.

My insides tighten at the sound. God, he sounds like one of those spicy audiobook narrators Grace has forced me to listen to. Not that I am complaining for a single moment. The sound is fucking music to my ears.

I finally shake myself out of my stupor, thankful that Pike is still half asleep and none the wiser to my near meltdown over the sound of his voice in the morning.

"Morning," I whisper.

"Sorry that I stayed over. I could say that I was scared to walk out and face the music again with your brother but honestly, there was nothing that was going to make me walk out of here and leave you looking like that."

I chuckle, moving my hands up to rest on his naked chest.

"I'm glad you didn't go. Last night was everything." I admit without a single ounce of hesitation.

I know it wouldn't have been easy for him to be so open and honest with me so I give him a little piece of myself in return.

His smile brightens the room, "I'm so glad, Scar. I meant every single thing I said last night. You are my girl. I want you in any capacity that you will have me. I know it's soon. I know that you have only just returned home and had this whole part of your life thrown back at you but I want to be here every step of the way. For the good, the bad and the ugly."

I nod attempting to fight a smile but failing as it slowly spreads across my lips, "Baby steps?"

"Baby steps." Pike smiles as he brings his lips down on mine.

I hesitate pushing him back slightly, "Morning breath," I murmur, covering my mouth to stop him from being able to get any closer.

Pike pulls me closer towards him pulling my hands away from my mouth, he closes the distance between us leaving only a gap between our mouths. I force myself to not breathe, feeling self-conscious at how close he is and the fact that at this distance, he will be able to smell my morning breath.

"I don't give a fuck about morning breath, Scarlett. Every fucking inch of you is perfect," he says before his lips latch onto mine. I melt into his kiss as he licks my lips. I open, allowing our tongues to explore each other. My body takes control of the moment and I roll into him feeling every inch of his nakedness. I moan as I feel his hard length press into my stomach.

He groans in return as he slides his hands lower, grabbing my ass in his hands.

"Goddamn, you are going to make us late," he murmurs.

I chuckle, moving away slightly from his lips, "You don't seem to be complaining."

I feel his dick twitch against me. I clench my thighs together needing some kind of friction.

"Not at all. I think inability to get out of bed is an excellent excuse for a late pass."

I whimper as Pike's kisses travel down my throat. He slowly begins making his way down my chest, dotting kisses over my taunt nipples. My stomach clenches with anticipation.

My legs spread welcoming him in as he reaches the apex of my thighs. Pike takes away any care I have for being late to my second day of school.

Pike and I run through the doors of Rydell Prep like our asses are on fire. Thankfully, we only missed home room so we run straight for biology.

I'm thankful that I have Pike by my side because the chances of me not being even more late without his guidance are slim. We burst through the doors of the lab and as I look up, every eye is on us. The biology teacher whose name I can't remember gives us a disapproving look.

"Mr Taylor and Miss Crux, thirty seconds later and you would have been late. See to it that this doesn't become a regular occurrence," she snides, directing us with her eyes to the two empty seats at the back of the classroom.

We collapse down in our seats, breathing heavy in an attempt to catch our breath. Pike turns a shit-eating grin my way and I can't help but return it.

I finally look around the classroom and my eyes land directly on dark blue orbs that suck me in.

Dacre.

He mouths a *good morning* to me before dazzling me with a smile that I have missed these past nine months before turning back around to face the front.

The next set of eyes I meet are furious.

Dawson.

How fucking typical.

I don't give him another second of my attention. I stop short when I meet Rhodes' stare. Similar to Dawson, he seems to have not quite gotten the message.

Fury from his bullshit last night comes roaring back inside of me.

Who the fuck does he think he is calling me a slut? By the looks of the attention he gets from the female population, he's the last person that should be judging me.

I'm disappointed that the one person who I didn't think would judge me has been one of my harshest critics.

While I expect that kind of shit from Dawson, I didn't expect it from my brother.

He must see the blinding rage I feel towards him reflected in my eyes as he quickly turns, giving me his back. It doesn't stop me from glaring daggers into the back of his head.

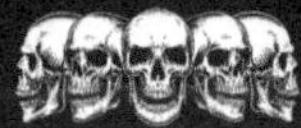

iology goes quickly. I don't retain a single lick of information during the entire class. My thoughts are a mix of flashes of last night. The feeling of Pike still covers me and sitting this close to him, it's taking everything in me not to rip his clothes off and ride him in the middle of class.

The other part of the lesson is filled with making up scenarios in my head of how I plan on confronting Rhodes.

He needs to know his place. He either stands beside me or not at all.

The bell rings signalling the end of class. I'm quick to pack away the books that were left unopened on my desk, shoving them in my bag as quickly as possible.

Rhodes must be able to sense the direction of my thoughts, like some kind of twin telepathy as he legs it out of the room.

I grunt as I watch his retreating back.

"Come on Princess, I'm lucky enough to have you to myself all day," Pike whispers in my ear but it's loud enough that Nicky hears.

Nicky body-checks Pike, sending him into one of the tables.

Swinging an arm around my shoulder, Nicky turns to a frowning Pike. "Not for long, Pikey boy. Scarlett is mine even if it's just for English." His voice is triumphant as he walks us both out of the room. I turn back and give an apologetic look to Pike who just smiles and shrugs his shoulders.

"Morning, baby girl," Nicky whispers in my ear, sending shivers down my spine as he kisses the top of my head.

I slam my elbow into his stomach but grown as pain shoots up my arm, "Fuck you, you over overgrown oaf. Is your stomach plated with fucking iron or something?" I growl, clutching my elbow in my hand.

Nicky chuckles lifting his shirt up, exposing his chiselled mid section. He lifts an eyebrow at me as I hear a wolf whistle from one of the groups of girls in the hallway. His eyes don't stray from mine as he looks at me. That shit-eating grin firmly on his face. I slap the exposed skin with my uninjured hand. He grunts, dropping his shirt as I take a step away from him. Before I can get any further, one of his hands snakes around my stomach and he spins me so I'm facing him. Cradling my face in his hands, he closes the distance between us.

"I hope he treated you right last night. Not like that bullshit with my brother. You don't deserve that kind of treatment, Scar. I don't know if he was dropped on his head or what as a child but I won't stand by him and his bullshit. Don't think for a second any of us do."

Nicky's expression is completely serious as he reprimands the actions of his brother. I hate that Dawson seems to be involved in every conversation I have with them lately.

"Fuck him," I say with resolve.

Nicky's lip quirks, "Fuck him."

"He doesn't get to treat me like shit just because he is running scared. This is my life. I was built for this."

Nicky's features give away everything he feels.

Pride. Admiration. Lust. I also note a hint of fear.

I don't understand fully why that is but I don't bother trying to decipher it.

Nicky nods, "Come on, we don't want to make you late again for class."

I chuckle, rolling my eyes.

It's not until lunch that I finally catch up with Rhodes. Slamming my hand on his shoulder, he jumps as he turns around, his eyes wide as he stares up at me.

"Scarlett," he chokes as he places his burger down on his tray.

"Baby brother," I smile at him but it's all malice. I feed every pissed off emotion since he spewed his bullshit to me last night into my glare.

Rhodes sighs knowing he's already lost the battle. He nods at the seat next to him. I don't take a seat nor do I let my eyes move from him.

"I don't give a flying fuck who you are to me, Rhodes. If you spew any of that bullshit to me that you did last night, I won't be so forgiving. You have no right. If you can't stand by my side through my choices than you don't deserve to be there at all"

Rhodes at least has the decency to look sheepish, "I'm sorry, Scar. It just infuriates me. They fucking hurt you. You didn't see the way they've acted these past few months. I can't just stand by and let them hurt you. You are my sister. A sister that I have missed with every faucet of my being. I can't let anything hurt you again. I don't know if I could survive it another time."

I war with myself as the fight completely drains out of me as I see the broken expression on Rhodes' face. I sigh as I take a seat next to him.

"Rhodes…" I trail off as I take in his haunted expression.

"I can't lose you again. I can't. If pissing you off is the only way that I can protect you, then so be it. No one fucking deserves you. Not them. No one will ever be good enough."

I sniffle as his words crack through my heart. I engulf my brother in a hug. "You make it hard to stay mad at you."

He chuckles as he wraps his arms around my middle, "That's always been the way with us." I lean back, letting my arms drop as I look at him. He smiles as memories of the past drift back in.

"You would get so mad your face would turn beet red. I'd cower because you were fierce, even back then. But then you would come back to me, snide at me for whatever bullshit I pulled but you always gave me this look," he smiles as he looks at me, "Just like the one you are giving me now."

We laugh together. It doesn't stop the stab of pain that goes through me. Even though I love listening to these memories from my past, I have to admit that it hurts. It hurts to not have a memory of someone that was such a critical part of my childhood.

Once our laughter settles in our chests, I look at Rhodes, "Please trust that I have this aspect of my life under control. If I need someone to kick some guy's ass, you will be the first person I call."

Rhodes laughs, "Something tells me that the thing you would be calling me for would be a clean up crew."

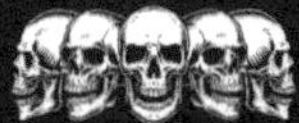

Sonny insists on walking me to Music. He hits me with those puppy dog eyes of his and it's all over for me. The smirk he gives me as I relent tells me everything I need to know. He knows that that look is a weakness of mine.

The teacher pairs us off. I internally groan as I'm placed with Dawson. And to find out we will be paired off until the end of the year?

Kill. Me. Now.

Dawson must see the look written all over my face, "Come on Vixen, it won't be that bad. You certainly weren't complaining when you rode me yesterday."

"If I knew you were a fucking coward, I would have left you high and dry," I snap, watching as all of Dawson's bravado falls from his face.

He doesn't bother with a reply, just grumbles and leaves me to pick a song for our duet. That's right. Our first assignment, a duet to be performed in front of the school.

Like I said, fucking kill me now.

The only thing that I feel works in my favour is the fact that I know Dawson can actually sing. A memory of us belting songs on the way to the airport brings a smile to the face. But then the hours, days and months that followed my last happy memory of the asshole dissipates any happy feeling that memory brings me.

I scroll through Spotify in an attempt to find a song suited to us. Each suggestion comes with a grumble or a grunt. Some don't even get awarded a response apart from a sharp glare.

One song out of the list finally stands out to me. A song that feels right. *One Day The Only Butterflies Left Will Be In Your Chest As You March Towards Your Death* comes over my speakers as I hit play.

I don't bother looking towards Dawson. Instead, I allow the haunting lyrics to flow from me. I take a breath as the chorus ends, just as the next verse is about to start Dawson's voice over-powers mine.

My words fall short as my head snaps in his direction. His eyes remain on me, captivating me as the lyrics pour from him. I nearly melt as he screams some of the lyrics. Tears well in my eyes as I watch him. I join in, my voice following alongside his as the chorus starts. His eyes heat as our voices melt together in perfect symphony.

We remain locked in some kind of heartbreaking staring contest. Emotions pour from our chests as if these lyrics were written specifically for us.

The song fades but we don't drop eye contact. His eyes tell me everything. His emotions are raw and right now I can see the man I fell in love with all those months ago. The man that promised me the world. I know that he was right. It was only just the beginning. Our story won't end yet. There is still so much left untold. But I don't know if I can wait for it. I don't know if I can continue to sit by as each of his words pierce my soul.

The room around us erupts in a cheer. I look around, catching the eyes of Sonny, Dacre, Nicky and Pike who are each looking at me with wonder. My sight blurs as tears slowly flood my vision. I feel like I have been flayed open yet again. My emotions are ripe for the picking.

I can't be here. Panic seeps into my chest as I shoot up out of my seat, grabbing my bag, rushing out of the room.

I don't stop until the gates of my house come into my view.

I don't leave my bedroom until the next morning.

BOARDING P.
NAME: SCARLETT SMIT
FROM:
TIME:
CLAS
SEAT:
President

chapter
TWENTY-EIGHT

I grumble through the entire next day. It's almost as though the events of the last few weeks have finally caught up with me. It's like a constant war that I'm fighting internally. When will I get a break? Just five fucking minutes of reprieve.

It felt like yesterday just broke the dam of my emotions.

I couldn't bring myself to answer a single message from Pike, Dacre, Sonny and Nicky. Rhodes knocked on my door a few times but after a while, I guess he finally got the hint.

I knew it was pointless to expect anything from Dawson. To wait on something even remotely close to an apology or even a ceasefire from him is fucking pointless.

Even opening myself up to him so completely wouldn't be enough. Giving him my body wasn't enough.

It feels like nothing will ever be enough.

It's like I just moved through the entire day completely numb. The boys hung around like bad smells but I couldn't bring myself to even grunt at them. Yet, they stuck by me the entire day. Became a barricade between me and the rest of the world. I didn't realise how much I needed them there until they were. True to their word they are standing by me even when I'm doing my best at pushing them away.

I still hear everything they say to me. Their promises and reassurances don't fall upon deaf ears. I take in everything they give me.

But nothing was able to pull me out of myself. Not until I walked back into my bedroom as the tears were finally able to fall free, if only just for a moment.

My father knocks on my door just before five. I yell out, telling him to come in.

He smiles at me as he watches me tie my shoes.

"Ready to face the vultures?"

I stand up grimacing at the prospect of being put under a microscope by these men. He must see my reaction as he laughs, coming over to place his hands on my shoulders.

"Oh my girl. You will be fine. You are made for this life. Rhodes told me about the other day during training," he says, raising an eyebrow. I can't stop the cringe before it escapes.

"Did Rhodes also tell you about my panic attack?"

He gives me a look of sympathy. It looks strange to see that look on his face. To be honest it seems weird to see any kind of look on his face, let alone see him in the flesh at all. It still doesn't seem real some days. Like I will wake up one day and all of this will have just been some fucked up dream.

"It will be common for you to have those kinds of flashbacks, Scar. Your body was trained for years to harness those muscles. When put into a situation where you need to use them, they will make themselves known," he sighs seeing the look on my face. I watch as he gets a far away look on his face. A smile creases his face as he turns back to look at me.

"You had this insanely raw talent. From the moment you stepped into the training room, it was like it lit a fire inside of you. You took to training like a fish to water. I see that spark in your eye even still." He puts a hand on my shoulder, "You were made for this life. You are a Crux. It's in your bones."

I nod but I'm filled with doubts. It helps to reassure me that he has faith in me and my skills but that life still seems so far away. Panic fills my chest at the thought of the way I took Dawson down on the mat the other day. The way my body just took over.

I take a deep breath as I stand up, allowing a false bravado of confidence to fill me. Maybe if I tell myself that I can actually do this enough times, maybe I might be able to.

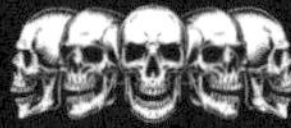

The drive to the clubhouse feels like it goes by within a blink of an eye. The clubhouse is full tonight. I instantly spot Nicky, Pike, Dacre, Sonny and Dawson. The latter completely ignores me. Which doesn't surprise me at this point.

Sonny gives me a wave, smiling from ear to ear, his face completely lit up the moment he sees me. Pike shakes his head at his giddy behaviour, elbowing him in the ribs before giving me a slight wink. My lips twitch back at him allowing myself to react towards them for the first time today.

Dacre's smile is shy as he sees me. Nicky doesn't bother with a smile, instead coming straight over to us and engulfing me in a hug. It honestly surprises me that he refrains from spinning me around like he normally does.

I take in a breath of him. I needed this. I needed him.

After doing my best at ignoring them today which was near impossible, I didn't realise that this would have actually helped.

He steps away from me after a moment. His face is serious as he looks down at me. "Are you okay, baby girl?"

I nod, not being able to find the words for anything else.

He shakes his head, "No, that's not good enough. I need words, Scarlett."

I draw in a breath as I look down to where my hands are clenched. He brings a finger under my chin, lifting it with a softness I forgot he possessed.

"I take that as a no," he smiles sadly at me.

"I just feel really overwhelmed. There's so much happening right now and I feel like I haven't had a chance to really breathe yet."

Nicky nods his head in understanding, "When you need to breathe, I'm here."

I nod my head knowing I will take him up on his offer. He finally takes a step away from me before turning his head to my father who's giving us a curious look.

"Pres." He nods, my father instantly returning a nod. He looks between us a few times, both Nicky and I waiting with baited breath. For approval? A scolding? I'm not sure, but the hum he finally gives us certainly wasn't it.

After one last look at Nicky, he turns to me wrapping an arm around my shoulders, almost as if dislodging me from Nicky's hold as he ushers me to the room known as Church. I don't know why I expect a full alter and pew setting but the large conference table seems to surprise me.

At the front of the room, a table large enough to seat the leadership members looks out over the chairs scattered around. A couple of members lounge around but quickly shoot to their feet as we walk through the door. Mumbled acknowledgements are heard as we walk to the front of the room. It feels as though we attract more curious looks. Each person desperate to get a look at me after all these years.

My father pulls out a chair for me at the table, gesturing me to sit. It feels as though the moment my ass hits the chair, I'm finally able to let go of the breath I had been holding.

Slowly, the room starts to fill with more people. I watch as a man who seems to draw the attention of the entire room to him walks through the doors.

I can instantly tell he is Nicky and Dawson's father, seeing how he is a spitting image of the former, if not just a good twenty years older.

The moment he sees me, a smile lights his face. Making a beeline straight for me, he rounds the table before coming to a stop right beside me.

"My God, I never thought I would get to see that beautiful face ever again," he says, looking at me with a mixture of awe and disbelief, "I'd say you don't remember me but I'm Rick, Dawson and Nicky's Dad."

I stand up, "Hi, it's so nice to meet you." I grimace, "Or see you again I guess." I chuckle, feeling awkward at my blunder. What do I say to these people? It's not like there's a handbook available for this kind of thing.

Rick instantly puts me at ease though as he laughs, putting a hand on my arm. From any other male, this kind of familiarity would be uncomfortable but there is something about Rick that puts me at ease. Whether it's some part of my brain remembering him from all those years ago or if it's just his aura that is able to set people at ease, I'm not too sure.

"Sit." He nods at the chair I just vacated, "We've got plenty of time to catch up. Your father here," he grumbles, slapping said man on the back hard enough to make him groan, "loves keeping us all in the dark apparently. I expect a cook up at your place this weekend." He shoots a pointed look towards my dad..

My father chuckles at the quirked eye Rick is giving him. He rubs his back before he replies, "Don't worry, Ricky. I've got a Bud in the fridge with your name on it."

"There better be more than one in there after this shit show."

He rolls his eyes, "And a bottle of whisky?"

Rick nods, "That'll do it."

Both men laugh at each other with such an ease of familiarity. It's clear how well these two work together just by watching this one interaction. My father told me that Rick, Valen (Pike's dad), and Grant (Dacre's father), have all been friends for years. Much like how the guys, Rhodes and I were all friends when we were younger, the four of them were incredibly close.

My father loved reminiscing, back in Australia, at the early days of the takeover of The Thunderbirds. Stories of missions they went on while having guns bigger than they were while still being freshed faced men.

Seeing that friendship now, especially as both Valen and Grant walk in the room, it's obvious to me that these four were unstoppable in their day. It makes me want to know more of their story. To dive into their lives even further, like an autobiography of sorts.

We eventually all take our seats as Valen and Grant both take seats at the table. I watch as they notice me, bright smiles on their faces as they take their seats.

The doors to Church swing open and my eyebrows lift as in walks a man who looks like he would fit better as some mafia don. His olive skin peeks out from underneath his fitted suit. Although it's hard to see as the majority of it is covered in coloured tattoos that crawl up his neck. Even though he looks young, it's obvious this man has seen a lot; the age visible behind his eyes. Movement from behind him catches my eye.

Sonny.

My gaze shoots between the two of them.

This man must be Sonny's father, Rafael.

I watch as both men walk side by side. A stern look seems to sit comfortably on Rafael's face until Sonny whispers something in his ear. It's like his whole face completely transforms. Lines around his mouth and eyes crease as he turns to his son, nudging him with his elbow as they laugh.

Rafael takes a seat at the table before he looks down at each member, nodding as he makes eye contact. Once he gets to me, his eyes brighten in curiosity, his mouth tugs at the corner. He gives me a nod before continuing down the table.

A hand lands on my shoulder shocking me out of my stupor. I turn to see a smiling Rhodes staring down at me, I return but it fades as I notice a strange look in his eye.

"What's wrong?" I ask.

Rhodes just gives me a tight smile, shaking his head, "Nothing," he says, trying to reassure me. I can see straight through him though, something is bothering him.

I let it drop for now.

As I go to turn my head back around, I notice that Rhodes isn't the only one standing behind everyone seated at the table. It seems each heir is standing behind their current head.

The doors swing open as the last person walks in.

My eyes widen slightly. This man is the definition of built like a brick shithouse. There is nothing nice about this man. His face is a permanent scowl. His eyes are hard as he glances around the room. He doesn't bother returning nods but it's obvious no one is expecting them in return.

As he reaches the table, he finally turns his head towards my father, gracing him with a short nod. He doesn't bother acknowledging anyone else, instead leaning back in his chair, spread out without a care in the world as he inspects each member in front of us.

Eventually my father smacks the table as he stands, commanding every eye in the room turning towards him.

"Welcome." His voice echoes throughout the room, "Thank you for all for turning up on such short notice." He pauses for a moment before turning an eye towards me.

I notice how different he is at this moment. Gone is my father. In his place is Ren, the President of The Thunderbirds. His face is stern as he looks down at me but the glimmer in his eye shows me that he is still in there, just hidden behind the man he needs to be.

He turns his head back towards the rest of the room, "As you may have heard through the rumours or if you were at Pinks' on Sunday night, my daughter Scarlett is, in fact, alive."

My eyebrow quirks at the deathly silence that fills the room as each eye turns to look at me. Their eyes feel like daggers piercing my skin.

Anxiety starts to rush in at the magnitude of their stares. I jump as a hand lands on my shoulder. I scold myself, knowing I should have prepared myself better for their appraisal of me. But having their eyes on you, assessing you like you are some kind of a meal ticket is daunting to say the least.

I turn my head following my gaze up the tattooed arm, coming face to face with Nicky. He doesn't say anything but his eyes plead to know everything.

Am I okay? No. Hard no.

Do I need to get out of here? Fuck yes. But I can't.

Even though my father hasn't said anything, I know this is a test. He needs to see if I can handle this life and what better way to find out than quite literally put me on display for the entire club to hold judgement towards me.

Instead I suck in a sharp breath, as I blink up at Nicky. He gives me a nod, barely viable to the eye.

I turn back around, smiling as I do. Feigning a confidence I don't have. Building myself up to be someone I know I'm not but someone these people need me to be. Someone that I want to be for them.

"As the majority of you may remember the devastating events that occurred that fateful day in November ten years ago. The day of my children's eighth birthday, we were ambushed by an enemy that didn't care who was caught in the crossfire. My own daughter was taken that day. The tragedies she suffered haunt me to this day. Thankfully, we were able to find her. But the damage was already done." He pauses, leaning against the table as he takes a breath.

I shuffle over in my seat, wrapping an arm around him knowing he needs support at this moment. He's only human and no matter the hurt I feel towards what he and Mum had to do, the decisions I don't necessarily agree with, I can't help but at least give him this. He lifts his head from where it was hanging between his shoulders. His smile is tight as he wraps his arms around me, bringing me tight to his chest.

"My daughter had been tortured. Beaten beyond recognition. When we got her to the hospital, she was placed in a coma. The damage to her body was unfathomable." I can feel him shake his head as he places it on top of my own. I hear him suck in a breath as he tries to compose himself.

Eventually, he continues, "It didn't look good for a really long time. Things got worse on the streets. The last thing

Bonnie or I wanted was for Scarlett to be caught in the crossfire again. We made the decision for Bonnie to take Scarlett over to Australia where she would be able to receive the best medical care she needed.

"She wasn't meant to stay there for long. Just until she got better. But when she woke, she had no memories. She didn't remember Bonnie. She didn't even remember her own name. We both knew we couldn't drag her back into this life again. Not until she was old enough.

"We also didn't know if and when her memories would return. They have not, unfortunately. Once she turned eighteen and with the influence of a few individuals," Dad turns his head. I lift my head from his chest and follow his gaze towards the boys. I frown. What does he mean by that?

The guys seem sheepish as they look down at their feet as Dad continues, "We knew our girl had to return home. It was time for her to claim her position. To train and become the next president of The Thunderbirds."

I look up at my father as he looks down at me. Pride shines over his face. He looks back at the rest of the room then down the table, "It was also time for Bonnie to come home. Ten years was too long."

The men all seem to chuckle as his lip quirks at my visible cringe.

He instantly turns back to the stone cold president within the blink of an eye, only allowing a little snippet of my father to shine through.

"I expect you all to ensure that you welcomed Scarlett appropriately. She will be undergoing training with the other prospects and, from my understanding, is ready for her initiation on Friday night."

This time, it's my father's turn to cringe at the thought of what I need to do for my initiation as a few of the men hoot and holler. I chuckle at the disgusted look on his face. Payback's a bitch.

BOARDING P
NAME: SCARLETT SMITH
FROM:
TIME:
CLAS
SEAT:
President

chapter
TWENTY-NINE

scarlett

I drown out the majority of the rest of the meeting. Every now and then I tune back in to make sure I grasp some of what they are talking about but for the most part, nothing is retained. The exhaustion has slowly been creeping up on me over the last few days and I know that if I don't focus on staying awake, I will fall asleep sitting up. The thought of anyone hearing me chop down an entire forest gives me enough incentive to keep my eyes open.

"Any more questions?" My father's voice booms through the room as he looks around at each member before down the table. After a couple of seconds of silence, he slaps his hand down on the table, making me sit up taller.

"Alright. That concludes tonight. I expect to see you all at Pinks' on Friday night. Initiation attendance is mandatory."

I let out a sigh, slumping back down in my seat as the room slowly begins to empty. Relief fills me as they retreat. I know I should feel kinder towards the people I'm meant to lead one day but I swear their looks were starting to give me hives.

The only people that don't leave the room are members of the leadership. Sonny leads the guys standing behind us around to the front of the table, lining up almost like soldiers.

"Thank you for staying behind," Dad says, finally breaking the silence, "I wanted to confirm with each of you just how important Scarlett's training is. I know just how capable she is but having to relearn everything, I want her to know she has a panel of men standing behind her in support."

Each of the guys nods.

"Dawson, Nicky and Jethro. I want the three of you to rotate Scarlett's combat training. Dacre and Wyatt, I want you to assist in her weapons training."

Dad then moved onto Pike, "Pike, I want you to sit down with Scarlett and go through the ins and outs of our businesses and the workings of what we do both legitimate and not so much," he laughs, making the guys all chuckle.

Leaving Sonny for last, he finally turns towards him, "Sonny, I'd like you to run Scarlett through our policies and laws. She needs to know *everything*."

Sonny nods before turning his head towards me and smiling. His smile is soft and so very unlike him that I can't help but return it.

"Even though I don't mind stepping in and helping Scarlett to train, can I ask why we are the ones tasked with doing it?" My head snaps to Jethro. His brows are drawn in a frown which from what I can tell seems to be his normal facial expression. His arms are crossed over his chest as he leans against one of the tables. His eyes are locked on me.

I arch my eyebrow at him. He looks at me as if assessing me, like he is working out all my weaknesses. I hold eye contact with him. With the way he is looking at me, I know that he's trying to intimidate me and I already know that our training sessions will go much the same.

I don't let it show that he's bothered me, because he hasn't. I can see right through him. I can read just from his expression alone just what he thinks of me being my Dad's successor.

Women clearly aren't valued, like they should be, in his eyes. It makes me wonder just why Rhodes is friends with this guy. I make sure to make a mental note. Seems like it'll be vital information one day.

Eventually the douche canoe averts his eyes and looks at my father. It clearly didn't skip his notice the way Jethro was eyeballing me. He arches an eyebrow at him too and I give a questioning look at Grant who snorts, not bothering to mask the sound in the quiet of the room.

It takes him a moment to respond to Jethro as he gives him an assessing look.

"I want you all to train her because, when it's time for her to take over, you lot will be the ones at her side. If things were different, you would have developed these relationships years ago." He blows out a breath as his mask slips a little, "I want to leave my legacy in the hands of someone who has people around her that she can trust. She's being thrown into a dangerous world and I want her to know that the men standing with her now are men she can trust." He then turns to each of the guys and gives them assessing looks, "Can I trust you *men*," he says putting emphasis on the word, "to stand beside Scarlett and help her lead The Thunderbirds to be successful?"

I watch as each of the guys nod without hesitation. Jethro is yet to nod though. His eyes remain on my father for a moment before he looks back towards me. His eyes give away nothing. It's like they are empty pits in his head. Eventually he turns back to my father and gives him a nod.

He nods before looking back at the rest of us. "Right. I expect each of you to be at Pinks' Friday night. No excuses," he says, voice stern as he looks directly at Rafael who chuckles and at least has it in him to look sheepish.

"It was one time," his thick Spanish accent draws.

"You were late to your own initiation," My father grumbles.

Valen, Grant and Rick all laugh. "You haven't let him forget it either, Ren," Valen says as he leans back in his chair.

He attempts to shake his head as if dismissing Valen but I notice the way the corner of his mouth quirks before it drops again, like it was never there.

"Right, does anyone have anything else they need to add?" He asks the room, waiting for a beat while everyone stays silent. When nobody speaks up, my father nods. The guys' dads all rise from their seats and so do they; I follow suit.

A tap on my shoulder turns me around and I find the older Sonny smiling down at me, "*Hola, Princesa.*"

I smile at the endearment. After Sonny's use of Spanish back in Australia, I began to slowly learn Spanish.

"*Hola, señor,*" I say but cringe at the spin my accent gives on the words. Rafael doesn't seem to mind though as he beams brightly.

"Not only are you beautiful but you are smart as well. Maybe it was a good thing your Papa kept you away all this time. You would have given us all a run for our money," he says, making us both laugh.

"My name is Rafael but everyone calls me Rafe," he says with a smile, "I'm so glad that you are home. Sonny told me all about the girl he met down on the beach in Australia. I have fond memories of you as well when you were a bèbe."

Before I can reply Sonny waltzes over and swings his arm around his father's shoulders and chuckles.

"I heard my name and you know I couldn't resist coming over straight away." He raises an eyebrow at his father in question. "I hope it was only nice things you were saying about me?”

I note the hint of unease in his voice.

Rafe chuckles as he pats Sonny on the back, “Actually, I was just about to tell Scarlett about that time you got your head stuck in the staircase railing. No-one knows just how long you were there as you refused to ask for help. Only indication of how long you had been was you had soiled yourself at some point.”

Sonny stares wide eyed at his father for a moment, a variety of looks flashing across his face. His arm drops from where it was hanging around Rafe's back.

“Fuck Papa, now Scarlett will never agree to go on a date with me,” he mutters, as he turns towards me. I watch as he swallows sharply and tries to regain some kind of dignity.

I can't help but roll my lips together in an attempt to keep a laugh from escaping, but it's useless as a snort escapes me. A chuckle soon follows until I can't take it anymore and I burst out into a full belly laugh. It doesn't take Rafe long until he is laughing right alongside me.

Sonny stares at us both in disbelief, “Wow, both my Papa and *mi Corazón* laughing at my expense.” He shakes his head as he looks between the two of us.

Rafe's laughter dies down instantly as he looks at his son, eyes wide and a shocked look on his face.

“¿Estás seguro hijo? Ella es tu corazón?”

“Si Papá. Ella es mi todo. Le rompí el corazón una vez pero seré yo quien lo arregle.” Sonny replies in his native tongue.

“Asegúrate de que lo hagas.”

Sonny nods before he turns back to me and gives me a small smile. “I hope my Papa didn't totally ruin my chances with you before I even got the chance to repair what I broke?”

I look over Sonny's face, not replying for a moment as I take him in. Seeing him like this, so vulnerable and open, his walls completely down for me to see the real him, just makes him even that more desirable. There's something about a man that isn't afraid to show his feelings and be so transparent with them that is just so insanely attractive.

The anxiety of my silence seems to affect him more than I realised. I watch as the hopeful look drops from his face to one of regret and understanding. His shoulders drop as his eyes find a spot on the ground to stare at.

He takes in a breath, "Scar," he begins but I don't let him continue.

"I expect there will be more of those embarrassing stories when you take me on this supposed date?" I say.

Sonny's head snaps up as he looks at me wide eyed.

"Really?" he gasps before shaking his head, "Babe, you can have every single photo album Mama has of me when I was a kid."

I chuckle at his reaction. If he was a dog, he would absolutely be wagging his tail. "I look forward to it."

True to his word Sonny messaged me the moment I got home with details about our date. I chuckle as I look at his message.

I instantly copy and paste his Spanish into google translate. I can't help the way my heart stutters as I see the translation. My love.

With the opportunity in front of me, I can't help but play

with him, if even only a little. He always makes it way too easy for me. I change the translation from Spanish to English and type in my reply before copying the translation and sending it to Sonny. It doesn't take long before I get back a reply.

ME

No te preocupes, papi. Prometo que seré una buena chica para ti ;)

SONNY

Fóllame nena muerta. Te mereces un azotaina

ME

No me amenaces con pasar un buen rato

SONNY

Si tu papá no me asesinara, estaría allí mostrándote a quién perteneces.

My mouth hangs agape as I read the translation for Sonny's message. I bite the corner of my lip as I read his message over and over again. Why the fuck do these men turn me into an absolute nympho?

With my phone still tightly in my hand I roll over on my bed, reaching over as I dig around in my bedside drawers. My fingers find my satisfyer and I pull it out. My old and faithful has never let me down and after the teasing from

Sonny, I can feel my body desperately needs this release more than ever.

I quickly roll my sleep shorts and panties down my legs, not giving them any mind as to where they land. I turn the satisfyer on and place it straight on my clit.

I jolt at the sensation, my back bowing as pleasure rolls through me.

"Fucking hell," I moan as I turn it up a notch.

I clutch my phone tighter in my hand as I inch closer and closer towards my orgasm.

The pulsing of the toy seems to vibrate through my entire body as my lower stomach clenches.

I can't help but think of the exact scenes Sonny all but threatening me with. Sonny crawling through my window in the middle of the night. Him placing his hand over my mouth so I don't make any sounds as he wakes me from my slumber. The feel of his hands on my body as he pulls me up off my bed, only to bend me over the mattress. The feeling of the cool air hitting my bare ass as he pulls down my panties. The sting of the slap as he fulfils his promise in spanking me; followed by the whisper of '*You've been such a bad girl*' in my ear.

The thought immediately sends me over the edge, the most intense orgasm rolling through my body.

"Sonny, fuck, fuck, fuck!" I shout at the height of my orgasm. My back bows off the bed and for a moment I swear I black out for a moment.

I pant as I come down from the high. I lie still for a moment as I try to catch my breath. I hear a sound come from the side of my head. I frown, confused as I look at my phone that's still clutched in my hand.

The screen lights up and I feel my gut drop out of my ass. I stare at the screen for a moment before I bring my phone to my ear.

"Hello," I say quietly.

"You are trying to kill me aren't you, *mami?*"

I feel my cheeks burn as embarrassment pulses through my system. I can't believe I just gave him front row seats to one of the best orgasms of my life and over a phone call? One I accidentally dialled.

"I'm so fucking embarrassed right now. I can't believe you heard that," I say covering my face in some kind of fruitful attempt to hide my shame.

"That was single handedly the hottest thing I have ever heard in my life. The way you screamed my name," Sonny groans, "I will never be able to unhear that. You are the most delectable creature, Scarlett."

"Really?" I ask, uncovering a portion of my face as I stare at the ceiling wishing it would collapse on me.

"Absolutely. You have me wrapped right around your little finger." He begins in a voice that sounds almost resigned to his fate.

"There's not a thing on this earth that you could possibly do that would turn me in the other direction. Want to put a collar on me and walk me like a dog? You can bet that I would be on my hands and knees crawling through the toughest of terrains for you. And that's not just because of the way you sound when you scream my name." I can hear him smirk through the phone, and if my cheeks could burn any hotter, they would be the gates to hell.

"Sonny," I start but he cuts me off.

"No, *mi corazón.* I already know where I stand and fuck, do I deserve it. I deserve to be put through the ringer for what I did to you. You didn't deserve that. If we had just pulled our head out of our asses, things would be so much different right now." I hear him sigh.

"I'm sorry, Sonny."

"Me too, *Princesa.*"

I sigh as I return my gaze to the ceiling. Sonny remains quiet and I know he's giving me a chance to collect myself.

"It feels surreal being here," I finally say.

"In what way?"

"Like this is exactly where I need to be. Sometimes it feels like it's just a dream that I will wake up from. Or like I'm still waiting for the ball to drop. Shit, maybe I'm just waiting for Ashton Kutcher to jump out and say I'm being punked."

Sonny laughs, "It sometimes feels like that for me too."

"In what way for you?" I question.

Sonny pauses for a moment and I give him the same opportunity to collect his thoughts. "I've never told you or anyone really about this but I know if I want to get back in your good books, I need to start by being completely honest with you."

"You don't have to tell me anything if you aren't comfortable with it, Sonny," I say in a gentle voice. Opening up to people can be hard and I don't want to force him to, especially not if he's not yet ready.

"No, I want to talk to you about it," he reassures me, "It's just it's not necessarily my story to tell; it's my parents story."

I nod my head even though he can't see me.

"My Mama and Papa's families are rivals. They were destined to grow up to despise each other. According to them they did for years. Now the details aren't too clear but there was some kind of situation that went down between the two families and a supplier or something and Papa ended up running into Mama." I hear Sonny chuckle, the sound bringing a smile to my face.

"Papa said that Mama was this absolute light. He called her his *tesoro.*"

"What does that mean?" I ask.

"It means treasure. He said that she was the diamond in the rough. The shining light amongst all of the darkness of his life."

I can't help but smile. Their love sounds radiant.

"What happened after that?"

"In all honesty, I checked out for the majority of the stories," he chuckles, "Those two can get a little... much sometimes."

We both laugh and I nod. If it's anything like the PDA I have been seeing between my parents the last couple of weeks, I totally get it.

"But basically, they began meeting up in secret, which was hard to do considering nothing much stays secret when you are heirs to the biggest cartel families in the northern hemisphere."

My eyes widen. "Cartel?"

Sonny chuckles, "Yeah. The Martinez family and the Ladrón families have been the most prominent families in the drug business since the downfall of Escobar."

"Holy fuck! How did they get out? Your Dad seems so nice, I don't see how he could even be remotely associated with people like them. I have so many questions!" I exclaim, already thinking of other questions I need answers to.

Sonny laughs, "Don't worry *mi amor*, I'm sure Mama would love to sit down with you and tell you her story. Honestly, you probably won't have much of a choice."

"Done," I say, already excited to meet or remeet his mother.

"Anyways," Sonny says, directing back to his original story, "Sometimes I get nervous. Even though my parents were able to detach themselves from their families and escape the life, the threat still looms over their heads. Being the eldest son from both of them, it would be a shit fight if they found out about me."

I hear the anxiety in Sonny's voice and it immediately sparks my own. "That can happen? That's an actual threat?"

Sonny blows out a breath, "Yeah, *mi estrella.* It's a real threat. But being a part of the club definitely has its protections and, with how well I've been trained, I don't plan on letting them take me."

I sigh in relief, releasing the breath I was holding. It still doesn't relax the anxiety I feel. The thought of losing Sonny or any of my guys at this point is unthinkable. Even Dawson.

"Don't worry Scar, none of us plan on disappearing anytime soon." I hear the smile in his voice. He gives me the reassurance that I need.

"I'm glad. I haven't finished making you lot grovel."

Sonny laughs, "I haven't either. I know you plan on seeing me on my knees more often."

"You bet."

Eventually we hang up the phone. It doesn't take me long to fall asleep and like an absolute simp, my dreams are filled with Sonny and every single devilish thing I pray he does to my body.

BOARDING PASS
NAME: SCARLETT SMITH
FROM:
TIME:
CLASS:
SEAT:
President

BOARDING P
NAME: SCARLETT SMIT
FROM:
TIME:
CLAS
SEAT:
President

chapter
THIRTY

scarlett

I wake up feeling refreshed. Maybe all I need is body shaking orgasms in order to actually get some good rest.

I pull on my school uniform and apply some basic make-up. Originally, I wasn't too thrilled with having to wear such a formal uniform to school. Back in Australia, our uniforms were much more laid back. A fairly simple polo with an emblem on the chest and plain coloured shorts. The skirt has absolutely been a bit of an adjustment but it's starting to grow on me.

The kitchen is empty as I make my way down to get some breakfast. I grab an iced coffee from the fridge and smile when I see a wrapped up breakfast muffin with my name on it.

Sorry that we aren't there this morning for breakfast. Your Dad had business to attend to and Shelly demanded I meet her for brekky. Love you, Mum.

I smile as I throw the note in the bin. I groan as I take my first bite. Mum has always made the best breakfast muffins. I don't know what she does to the eggs but they are cooked to perfection.

A ding from my phone has me looking down mid chew.

NICKY

Fuck, I never thought watching you eat breakfast would be so fucking hot

I freeze and slowly turn around to where Nicky is standing in the doorway with a shit eating grin on his face. I watch as his eyes trail down my body, appreciating everything he sees.

After a moment, his eyes trail back to mine. I raise my eyebrows in challenge before letting my eyes roam his body and damn do they appreciate what they see.

When you think of hot biker guys, the last thing you would think is seeing them in a prep school uniform, but goddamn does it suit Nicky. His slacks seem to hug his legs in just the right areas and I know the view from the back is just as mouth-watering, it's just too good to miss. It's made adjusting to school much more pleasurable.

After perusing his body, my eyes finally return to his. They heat as he finally makes eye contact with me again.

"Do you like what you see?" he says, voice so low it's almost a growl.

I smile sweetly at him, feigning an innocence I don't possess, "Hmm, I don't know what you are talking about."

Nicky takes a step towards me and I take one back but instantly hit the counter, stopping my escape. Nicky's eyes darken as he closes the distance between us, bringing our bodies together. My breath catches at the contact and I see the moment Nicky catches my reaction.

"See that's where I think you are wrong, baby girl," he says in a low voice. He bends down close to my ear, his hot breath against my neck causing a shiver to roll over my body, "I see the appreciation in your eyes when you look at me."

"Don't let that big ego get in the way of the truth now, Nicky." I chastise him but it holds no heat. He knows he is right.

Nicky chuckles and I don't know if it's the proximity, the after affects of last night still in my veins or simply the hold that this man holds on me but I can almost swear my pussy tingles at the sound.

"Never," he whispers in my ear. He moves his head away from my ear but doesn't dare to take a step away. If anything, he pushes me further into the counter. I wet my lips with my tongue and his eyes capture the movement. They don't move as he slowly edges closer to them. His own mouth dropping slightly. My hands snake up his arms as I grip him tightly, needing to hold onto something. Just as our lips are about to meet, a groan sounds from behind us, startling us away from each other.

"Fuck's sake, could you keep the PDA out of the kitchen. Some of us don't feel like watching their sister being mauled while they are trying to eat," Rhodes says with disgust as he enters the kitchen with Dawson and Jethro in tow. The former frowning at the both of us while the latter just gives us a blank look.

"That sounds like a you problem, baby brother." I snide as I push Nicky away before walking away from the counter, grabbing my forgotten muffin and taking a bite.

"Gross," Rhodes shivers and I can't help but laugh at the disgusted expression on his face.

"As much as I love being judged this early in the morning, what are you guys doing here?" I question looking at Nicky,

Dawson and Jethro.

"The guys came over because we needed to sit down and work out a schedule of sorts for your training," Rhodes says and I nod before he continues. "Seeing how I have been next in line all these years, Dad suggested that I also assist in helping you get up to scratch with everything you need to know."

I nod, agreeing with Rhodes. He smiles at me but I swear I could hear an undertone of bitterness in his voice. I shake my head at the doubt. He would tell me if he wasn't happy. Wouldn't he?

"I'll train you Monday, Jethro will train you Tuesday, Dawson will train you Wednesday and as far as I know Dacre will tap in after him?" Rhodes confirms with Dawson who nods, still not bothering to look at me since he stared daggers at me after he entered the room.

"Nicky will train you on Thursday. You will just have to double check with Pike, Sonny and Wyatt what days they will be training you."

I nod, trying to commit each of the days to memory but know that I have no hope. Rhodes must sense my internal struggle as he comes over, wrapping his arm around my shoulders, "Don't worry, I've already sent the schedule to you in an email that you can add to your calendar.

I smile at him, "Thanks Rhodes."

He nods at me before taking a step away and grabbing the muffin with his name on it from the fridge, he groans in appreciation as he takes a bite.

"Your brother doesn't share the same appeal you do when you eat," Nicky whispers in my ear. I choke on my mouthful of food. Forced to spit it in the bin, I glare at Nicky as I take a sip of my coffee. He at least has the decency to look sheepish.

"Sorry, baby girl," he says with a wince.

"You owe me." I frown, pointing a finger at him.

"Add it to my tab," he chuckles, making me laugh.

The school day seems to fly and I'm thankful for it. First period was Spanish. Sonny was insistent on sitting next to me during the class, much to Dacre's dismay. The only reason Sonny got away with it is because he reminded Dacre that he is fluent and the best person to teach me. With a frown, Dacre took a seat next to a guy that I haven't yet met.

Poor guy can't catch a break.

Sonny took every single opportunity to wind me up through the lesson. The way his voice sounds when he whispers Spanish in my ear nearly broke my resolve.

He could call me a horse's ass and I would be a mess on the floor at this point.

Nicky grabs my hand, stopping me before I can rush out of Maths at the end of the day. Maths has never been my strong suit but I swear there was something about this lesson that dragged.

"You are all mine this afternoon, baby girl," he says in my ear, my body shivers at the underlying innuendo in his voice.

I follow him outside to his bike. I step back as I wait for him to pass me his helmet. Being a dirt bike girl, I've never given much thought into road bikes or Harleys for the matter but there is something about seeing Nicky on his bike that is doing something for me.

His smile is devilish as he hands me his helmet and I chastise myself for allowing my attraction to be so clear. I'm doing fucking terrible at making these guys grovel. But, god, it's hard. Especially when they look just as fucking delectable as Nicky does right now. I'm insatiable.

Eventually I snap myself out of my daze and hop onto the back of Nicky's bike. I can't help but tease him just as much as he does me. My hands snake up his torso, gripping the bottom of his dress shirt and lifting it up. His stomach clenches as my hands meet his bare flesh.

"You are a fucking tease, Scarlett," he groans as his hands grab the outside of my thighs and squeeze, making them clench tighter around his body.

"Focus," I say, rubbing the hard planes of his stomach. I hear Nicky moan as he starts the bike, the grumble of the engine drowning out his sound.

He doesn't give me any warning as we shoot off out of the parking lot. Nicky keeps one hand on my thigh the entire drive. Rubbing small circles on my lower thigh, each pass over seeming to edge higher and higher.

By the time we are pulling up to the clubhouse, I'm panting in desperate need of a release. I launch myself off the bike in an attempt to get away from him and the growing need inside of me. Nicky doesn't let me get far as he grabs my wrist before pulling me right back into his body.

"Be a good girl for me today and I'll give you that release you are so desperate for."

I can't help the moan that escapes me. The submissive side of me is already nodding, knowing she will do absolutely anything to get the release she needs.

Nicky's smile is triumphant as he looks down at me.

"Come on, I don't want to see any of these old fuckers looking at you the way you are right now."

That seems to be just the thing I need to get some of myself under control as I slowly start to calm my breathing.

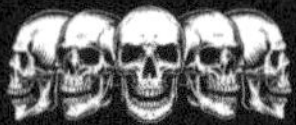

We enter the same training room as Monday. The room is clear apart from two pairs of soldiers currently in the midst of sparring. I watch their technique closely. The placement of their hands, their feet and when those movements change. My eyes stay locked on one of the guys in particular. He isn't much bigger than me but it's obvious that even up against his opponent, who is at least a foot taller than him and a good fifty kilos heavier, he is still the one with the upper hand.

"When it comes to combat, it doesn't matter who is bigger than who. Obviously size does have a lot of benefits, but if you don't have skill, you aren't worth anything," Nicky says, jolting me out of my trance as he comes up beside me.

"Take Blake as an example. The guy isn't big and he knows that. He's one of our best soldiers. Every single recruit in his year doubted him. He was teased for it relentlessly. But he trained day in and day out. Now, he is one of the Thunderbirds' best. Almost every single mission, you can bet he is in on it in some form."

I nod, impressed as I watch as he finally takes down his opponent. He lifts his head as he notices us standing on the sidelines watching him.

"Scarlett, Nicky," he smiles as he looks at me before Nicky. His voice is southern, I raise my eyebrows not expecting it. Blake sounds like he's straight off the farm. Looks are certainly deceiving.

I return the nod.

"Blake," Nicky says with a nod. "Scarlett and I are going to be in here training this afternoon. Don't worry about locking up when you leave."

"No problem," he says as he gives his sparring partner a hand up. He gives us a nod in greeting as well.

"Scarlett, it's nice to meet you. My name's Grover." I smile at his outreached hand as I step forward and shake it.

I step back from him, and he gives me one last smile before turning to Nicky who he nods to. It doesn't pass my notice at just how respectful he was to me. Majority of the people I met with Rhodes at Pinks' were respectful, but it was obvious they had doubts. I clocked it up to just being because they were surprised but now it makes me think that it might have to do with a being female thing.

Nicky eventually pulls me away from Blake and Grover who return to sparring. He brings me to an area of the training room away from everyone else.

Nicky grabs tape and starts wrapping my hands. He's gentle as he wraps them and my heart clenches at the treatment.

"While I go and grab the pads, I want you to stretch for a bit."

I nod and start stretching as I wait for him to come back.

I stretch out the top half of my body quickly. Starting with my lower half, I stand with my legs spread and keeping my back straight, I bend down and touch my toes.

A wolf whistle sounds behind me and I snap up, bristling instantly. I turn around prepared to give whoever it is a dressing down but come up short when I see Nicky giving me an appreciative look.

"Damn, baby girl. You make stretching look way too appealing."

A blush heats my face at the words as I feel the burn of his eyes work down my body. In an attempt to keep a cool façade which, I know I entirely bomb, I roll my eyes before turning my back on him and continue stretching. Now he's back in my vicinity, I'm way too distracted to make the stretching I need to do worth my while.

I shake out my limbs as I watch Nicky finish setting up. Eventually he turns around to me with a smile.

"We are going to start with light warm ups. There's no point going straight into a sparring session if you don't know your basics. That kind of bullshit will just set you up for failure."

I grimace knowing he's right.

"I know you have muscle memory but if we want you to actually remember, we need to start from the basics."

I nod, watching as Nicky turns around and grabs punching pads, similar ones that Dawson and I used the other day. Putting them on, he nods towards the sparring ring. Nicky stands with his hands out ready and I shake my limbs out making sure they are loose.

"Right, I want you to punch the pads. Don't focus too much on putting much force behind it. Just get in the rhythm of punching one at a time."

I nod my head as I clench my fists, making sure to keep my thumbs out. I bring my arms up into a fighting stance, something I caught from watching Blake and Grover. I know I've at least done one thing right as Nicky gives me an approving smile.

I snap my hand out, punching one of the pads. I instantly look at Nicky for the approval I feel I need from him right now. His smile settles the raw anxiety I feel in my chest. The unease I feel is palpable.

I take a breath before I snap my other fist out, punching the other pad. I know I put a little more force behind that one when Nicky steps back slightly.

As I catch the sight, it feels as though some kind of veil comes over my vision. Like something within me awakens at the spot of weakness.

My next punches snap out with more force causing Nicky to put more strength in his defence.

After a few more hits, I snap myself out of my advance, feeling those slivers of resolve wanting to snap. I'm thankful that this time I seem to still hold the majority of the pieces of myself intact. Not wanting a repeat of the other day with Dawson, I pull myself up short.

I pant for breath, knowing I exerted myself more than Nicky intended for our first session.

Eventually I look up at him and catching him smiling down at me, a proud sheen in his eyes.

"You did good, baby girl. You are ready for this."

I blow out a breath, "Sometimes it doesn't feel like I am."

It's all too easy for my insecurities to make themselves known.

"Why do you say that?" Nicky questions as he slides the pads off his hands, not giving any mind to where he throws them behind him.

"This world seems completely unrealistic sometimes. Like how is this life mine? It seems so far from the little beach-side Aussie girl who worked in a café for a living. Yet here I am set to take over from my father. To be the person that an entire gang turns towards for guidance. To lead jobs to stop trafficking rings. To potentially kill people?" I shake my head as I blow out a breath, willing myself to not get worked up yet again. I've cried way too many tears, I don't need to let anymore fall but fuck if they don't threaten their presence.

"I don't want to let anyone down. Because even though it can feel so far-fetched, it feels so right. Like every single awful thing that has happened was always meant to lead me back here. That I needed to lose everything to become the person I need to be to be able to do this."

After a beat of silence, Nicky takes a step towards me,

"Scarlett. You are made for this life. I see it in you every day. I saw it in you back in Australia even when both of us didn't know what it was or what any of this meant. You have the most admirable resilience I've ever seen in a person. The way you keep hitting back at my cockhead of a brother even when he is relentless in trying to tear you down," he laughs, helping to break some of the tension seeping into the air. "He is digging himself an impossible grave when it comes to you."

I shrug my shoulders, "Sounds like a him problem."

Nicky laughs, "Too right, baby."

chapter
THIRTY-ONE

nicky

I pick up the punching pads back up again as I read Scarlett's demeanour. Even though she tried to act nonchalant at the mention of Dawson, I can see at just how much even a whisper of his name gets her riled up. The tension slowly starts to simmer under her skin. Her fists clench and I hold up the pads, ready for the onslaught she is about to hit me with. Her face slowly shuts down and the cool killer she is destined to be takes over.

Her features are sharp and she hones in on the pads like they are her greatest enemy. Her first punch is quick and full of impact. I step one of my feet back to help balance myself.

Her next few punches come out in quick succession, each with more force than the last. Before I know it, she is snapping both fists out, hitting the pads with a strength I don't think either of us knew she possessed.

To say I'm surprised is an understatement. It's been hard trying to connect the two Scarlett's together even though they are the same person. The Scarlett from Australia seems so far from the Scarlett in front of me who is all but raining down hell on me.

The person in front of me is exactly who the Thunderbirds need to lead them. She isn't the meek little girl that Dawson is making her out to be.

She is anything but.

She is a fucking warrior. Full of sheer determination and feminine rage, something I'm glad she hasn't aimed directly at me too harshly.

Doubting her would be your downfall.

I let her go until she is exhausted. When she finally stops her fight, she steps back as a sheen of sweat rolls down her face. The inner killer slowly melts away as my baby girl slowly comes back to me.

I don't move. Instead I just watch her as she slowly gets her breath. Allowing her to come back to herself.

Eventually she meets my eye. Neither of us move as I watch her pant, still fighting to control her breath.

I have never seen a single person look more beautiful than Scarlett does right now. Not even when she only had scraps of fabric covering her body at the beach. But here, right now; her work out clothes wet with sweat. Her long blonde hair messy in the bun she threw it up in before we started. Her face red as sweat slowly drips down her brow. She is fucking magnificent. She will be my downfall. I know that for certain. But do I care? No. She could ruin me, and I would still say thank you.

"How did I do?" she whispers.

I take a slow step as to not startle her, knowing she might only just be holding on to that edge of control.

"You did incredible. You are born for this baby girl. Our enemies don't know just the kind of weapon you are going to amount to," I say as I take another step.

I watch as Scarlett takes each of my words in slowly. Her hidden predator is still silently protecting her. There must have been something in my words that did it for her as her eyes heat and that sly smile I am infatuated with adorns her face.

I catch her as she launches herself at me, having to take a few steps back at the force of which she hits me. My back slams into the brick wall behind me and I feel a jolt of pain as my head connects but I don't pay it any mind. Not when my girl's lips descend on mine, and I'm sucked into her orbit.

Our lips move together in perfect harmony. My tongue invades her mouth and we both groan at the intrusion. Her body grinds against mine and I pull her into me, squeezing her ass as I do. I feel Scarlett jolt as a second body presses up against her. I already knew he was here, having heard the doors swing open when he walked in and the small conversation he had with Blake and Grover as they left the training room.

"Fucking hell Princess, you sure know how to put on a show for us don't you?" Pike whispers in Scarlett's ear. She relaxes back into him as he pushes into her further.

"You saw that?" Scarlett breath in is almost a gasp as Pike trails kisses up her neck. My eyes fixate on the spot where they connect.

I haven't shared a girl with anyone like this before. Tag team, yes but nothing like this. But the idea of not only being watched but fucking my girl with one of the other guys makes me insanely hard.

Pike chuckles in her ear, "I sure did. You were glorious. I've never seen anything like it before."

"A true goddess," I murmur as I close in on the other side of Scarlett's neck, peppering kisses on each bit of skin I can get to. Her body rolls between Pike and I, a guttural moan escaping her lips.

"I need more," she breathes.

"Anything for you baby girl," I whisper in her ear as I feel a shiver roll through her body. I can't help but chuckle at the reaction, but I need more. I'm fucking desperate for her.

I let her legs drop from around my waist. Dragging my hands up her body, I tease her as Pike's hands tease at her waistband. He slowly starts pulling her pants down until they fall at her feet leaving her completely bare from the waist down.

"I think this needs to go, don't you think Pike?" I say playing with the bottom of Scarlett's shirt.

She moans and nods in desperation as I slowly start pulling her shirt up her torso. Pike lifts Scarlett's arms over her head, making her shiver as he trails his fingers back down her body.

By the time I drop her shirt to the ground, Pike already has her bra unclipped and is pulling it off her body. I push her back just enough to get my fill of her. I can't help my groan at the sight of her.

"She's fucking stunning isn't she, brother?" Pike says, his eyes heating as they travel over Scarlett's naked body.

"Breathtaking," I say, capturing the moment Scar's breath hitches.

"She's fucking saturated too," Pike chuckles. My eyebrow raises as my hand dips between her thighs feeling the wetness saturating her.

"Are you ready for us baby?"

Scarlett comes back to herself as she looks down at my chest, "Hmm, almost. It seems you have too many clothes on though."

I chuckle and make quick work of shedding my clothes in utter desperation of needing my girl in any way I can have her.

I hear Pike shedding his clothes too from behind Scarlett. I watch as she nibbles at her lip, just as impatient as we both are.

Something hits my chest just as I'm about to pull Scarlett back into me. I look down finding the foiled packet containing a condom and thank the stars that Pike at least has enough sense still to think of protection because if it was left up to me, in the current state I'm in, I would have fucked her raw. Not that I would complain one bit. Just the thought of what unprotected sex could mean with her gets me even harder.

Hello, breeding kink.

I slide the condom on my cock, grinning over Scarletts shoulder at Pike who returns the sentiment.

I turn back to my girl, pulling her against me. "Are you ready?"

Her nod is enthusiastic, the need radiating off her and I eat it up. There's something about seeing your partner's enthusiasm that just turns you on even more and seeing it in Scarlett is like my own kryptonite.

I lift Scarlett up into my arms just as Pike steps into her back but leaves a little space. My cock nestles against the opening of her pussy. Her breath hitches as she digs her nails into my shoulders.

I slowly start sliding my cock into her heat, groaning at the feel.

"Fuck, you are so tight baby girl."

Scarlett's response is nothing but a moan and I can't blame her. It's hard to make any kind of sense when it feels this good.

She clenches tight once I seat myself inside her fully. I take a few moments just to breathe, clenching my jaw so I don't make an embarrassment of myself.

Pike chuckles and I shoot him daggers, "Don't worry man, I felt exactly the same way. She feels incredible doesn't she? So wet and tight."

"Like heaven," I murmur as I slowly pull out of her, just to the tip before slamming back inside of her.

"Fuck, Nicky," Scarlett moans, throwing her head back to rest on Pike's shoulder.

I fuck in and out of her a few more times, each of us unable to control the dribble of explicits that all but fall out of our mouths. Pike's hand snakes between mine and Scarlett's bodies, travelling right down to her clit. The moment he touches her, her moans seem to get louder.

I take her in as she tightens around me, watching as her orgasm hits her. I soak in the look on her face, the sounds of her cries and the way she feels around me. It's hard not to take in every moment I spend around her.

"Beautiful," I mumble, smiling as her orgasm slowly ebbs away, leaving her sated but I'm not done and I know Pike is far from. I hear him spit in his hand before I feel him press himself as Scarlett's opening.

Her body tenses as she sits up straight in my arms, eyes wide as she looks at me, a mix of emotions on her face, "Pike, I can't…"

"Yes you can Princess. You are such a good girl, I know you can take both of us." Pike praises her and I know it does the trick the moment I feel her relax in my arms.

"That's it baby, we are going to take such good care of you." I continue as Pike adds more spit to his dick.

I feel as he slowly starts to push himself alongside my cock that's still seated in Scarletts pussy. Her nails dig even further into my skin, at the point of drawing blood but I don't care. Let her scar me up. I want her mark on my skin.

Scarlett starts shaking her head, "I don't think I can do

this, it's too much."

"Yes you can baby," I whisper in her ear, "You were made to take the both of us. I can feel how wet you are for us. You are such a dirty little slut, I know just how much you want this. Now relax, and let Pike slide in alongside me so we can fuck that greedy little cunt."

She nods as Pike keeps pushing in, taking his time to allow her to stretch around the both of us. It's a tight fit but Scarlett eventually relaxes enough. Once Pike is fully seated, he moves his hand still between Scarlett and I, gripping her thighs like I have.

We give each other a look, silently communicating just how we plan on pleasuring our girl. Slowly, we both pull out until just our tips remain inside her before nodding to each other and thrusting back inside her at the same time.

Scarlett's answering scream echoes throughout the room and I can't help the satisfied chuckle at hearing it.

Pike and I are relentless as we fuck in and out of Scar's pussy. Between us, Scarlett is a mess. Her words are incomplete as they fall from her mouth, moans overriding anything she tries to say.

"Fuck me, you are so goddamn tight. I won't last much longer," Pike whispers in her ear.

"Me either. Fuck baby, don't squeeze," I groan as Scarlett answers us with her pussy. Affective form of communication if I don't say so myself.

I feel the moment Scarlett's next orgasm starts to crest.

"Come on baby girl, come on our cocks. I want to see you let go again," I mutter.

My words seem to be her undoing as she falls over the edge. Both Pike and I follow her over.

It's a delicious mess and it takes me a moment to come back to myself as I finally look up and see an angel grinning back down at me.

Scarlett chuckles at the look on my face but I don't care. Not after just receiving the best orgasm of my life. Scarlett seems to know it too as she looks down at me before turning her head and looking back at Pike who looks just like I imagine I do.

"Thank you," she says.

"No, thank you *mi cielo.* I thought someone was being murdered in here but it just seems like it was Scarlett's pussy."

We both snap our heads to the door of the training room, finding a smug Sonny standing there with a phone in his hands.

"Recorded what I saw too. If I wasn't possessive as fuck over you Scar, I'd say that shit needs to uploaded on *Only Fans* or some shit because damn," Sonny whistles as he tucks his phone away, "that shit was *caliente como la mierda.*" he says, smacking his lips together in a chef's kiss motion.

Pike groans as he pulls out of Scarlett, "Fuck man, shut up."

Sonny chuckles, "Aw, don't be like that Pikey boy. I was a good friend and made sure I sent you all a copy because sharing is caring, obviously," he says with that shit eating grin as he looks between Pike and I before his eyes land on Scarlett just as I pull out of her, allowing her to get her bearings before letting her go.

"And you *mi hermosa diosa,* I'm a little hurt you didn't consider me for this sharing exercise. You know that I share my toys really well."

Scarlett rolls her eyes as she picks up her clothes from where we threw them in our rush to get her undressed.

"Maybe if you're good, you will get a turn next time," she says as she pulls her panties on.

Sonny looks like he has had all of his Christmases come

at once.

"You promise?" he says, not bothering to hide his desperation.

"Sure," Scarlett replies, shrugging her shoulders. Sonny doesn't wait to rush over to a half dressed Scarlett. He grabs her from around the waist, spinning her around before placing her back on the ground. His attitude doesn't seem to annoy Scarlett. She glances up at him, that same smile given to the three of us bright on her face as she stands on her toes, placing a light kiss on his mouth.

Sonny goes to deepen the kiss but Scarlett puts up a hand to his chest, "Be a good boy, Sonny."

Sonny takes a step back before raising a hand, "Yes ma'am!"

BOARDING P.
NAME: SCARLETT SMITH
FROM:
TIME:
CLAS
SEAT:
President

chapter
THIRTY-TWO

scarlett

wake up riddled with anxiety. Initiation day is finally here. After training and the activities that followed after, Sonny insisted on taking me home. But instead of going back there, I got him to drop me off at Pinks'.

Insisting, with a heavy threat or two, that I would be okay with Shelly, he refused to leave until I was done practising to drop me home. He muttered something about it being his job to fulfil his duties. I didn't bother to try to decipher what he meant as I took full advantage of my practice time.

Shelly directed me to one of the back rooms. It was obvious it's used for more of the discreet private parties. A bed that seems to be the size of two kings pushed together took up one wall. It looked out over a couch that sits in front of a pole in the corner of the room. An open bathroom was set in the other corner of the room and I made a note to ask Shelly to rent the room for a night just so I can take a shower in here.

I set up my music in the Bluetooth speakers connected to the room and my song choice belted out. I couldn't help but smile as I walked over to the pole. It didn't take me long before I was rehearsing the routine that came naturally to me. I did throw in a couple of pole tricks this time that I eyed a couple of the girls doing out in the main room. It shocked me at just how hard the moves are. I take my hat off to them. The strength that is required to dance pole is no joke.

By the time I was done, I was utterly exhausted. My bones felt like they were made of jelly as I walked out of the room to where Sonny was waiting at the bar. I took him in at that moment, watching as he talked animatedly to one of the servers. It's obvious they have been stuck with him for a while now by the impatient look they had on their faces and the way they keep trying to excuse themselves.

I walked over towards Sonny, tapping him on the shoulder to take his attention away from the bloke. He looked at me with relief as he sauntered away.

I chuckle at the memory from last night. Sonny isn't for everyone. His quirks are definitely a required taste that's for sure.

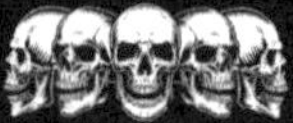

I spend the entire day filled with the same anxious feeling I woke up with. It only seems to get worse as the day goes on.

"Hey baby cakes, what's got you so gloomy?" Maxie asks as she slides in beside me at the lunch table.

I groan, smacking my face into my hands, "The initiation tonight."

"Nerves got you babe?" she asks as she takes a bite of her

mac and cheese. I don't bother to even look at the plate Dacre forced me to grab. He didn't care that I didn't have an appetite for food. While I appreciate his concern for my health, the thought of anything being in my mouth makes me want to chuck.

"They do. I just can't believe I have to walk out onto that stage in lace and fucking dance for the whole club." I shake my head.

"It's a right of passage for us, Australia," Rippy snips. I look up and blink back at the glare she is giving me. Mainly at the spot where Maxie's arm is touching mine. It hasn't escaped my notice the way Rippy looks at her. She couldn't be any more obvious but it seems Maxie is none the wiser. Shit, even blind Freddy could see the heat in Rippy's eyes every time she looks in Maxie's direction.

"Rippy's right. The older girls were never accepted in the Thunderbirds until your Dad took over. Shelly told us that even just to be an old lady they had to be sexed in." Brandy shivers and Jen who sits next to her follows the sentiment.

"Sexed in? What does that mean?"

Brandy looks at each of the girls for a moment, taking a deep breath before she looks back at me. Dread instantly fills me and I know whatever she's about to tell me is going to make me even more sick than I already feel.

"The women were required to be passed around each member of the Thunderbirds. The President and leadership team was always left for last."

"Oh god," I murmur, looking at each of the girls in horror.

Jan nods, "We were told stories from those days. The women were never the same. They say the leadership was especially brutal with their… practices."

"When your Dad took over and saved a heap of women, it was one of the first things they sought to change. They needed a way to take control of their sexuality again."

I nod my head as Maxie tries to reassure me but it doesn't do much. The thought of this being something I was born into fills me with dread. Women were seen as nothing but a hole to fill to these vile creatures. My heart aches as I think of them. Of how they are now. Of how they survived it.

"The women came together and decided if they were going to be initiated in, they wanted something that suited them. None of them were interested in the initiation the males go through so they came up with doing an initiation dance. It was a way to take back control of their bodies. A way to control their fate," Brandy says with a smile.

"That, and Shelly was a dancer before she was trafficked," Maxie adds, holding up her fork.

"A fucking good one at that," Rippy says as she bites into her apple. The four of us laugh, helping to brighten the doom of our conversation. Just when I seem to think I have gotten to the depths of the depravity of the Thunderbirds' history, I seem to get caught at each turn. It does do something to settle my wandering thoughts at knowing my father has changed a lot of the said history.

Anxiety is a killer though and I can't help but think that maybe we haven't escaped these issues entirely.

I take a sigh of breath the moment the last bell of the day rings. I throw my stuff into my bag, not giving a single fuck about any bent pages. I know Grace would kill me at my mistreatment of books but these are for knowledge, not smut.

Nicky calls out after me as I rush out of the room. I don't look back. The clock already feels like a ticking time bomb over my head.

Rhodes is already waiting for me as I burst out of the front doors. I roll my eyes at the hoard of girls already flocked around his black mustang. I scoffed my eyes at him the moment I saw the car. It may be pretty but it's got nothing on the R8 Mike has back home. Give me that car any day of the week.

My brother finally looks up at me, instantly dismissing the now very disappointed women as Jethro growls making them all scatter.

I don't bother acknowledging either Wyatt or Jethro as I throw my bag in the footwell of the passenger side. Or what I thought was the passenger side, groaning and blurting every single explicit word that comes to mind as I see the pedals and steering wheel. I throw my bag into the passenger side, flipping off Rhodes, Jethro and Wyatt who are all laughing at my expense as I storm around the other side of the car.

I fall into the car, slamming the door before taking a deep breath to centre myself.

Rhodes doesn't say anything as he finally gets in the car after saying goodbye to his fan club.

It's either he is able to tell by the expression on my face that I'm not in the mood for any of his bullshit or he is smarter than I pegged him for, but he stays silent for the entire drive.

He pulls up at the house but I don't get out of the car. The moment I do, I know the rest of the night will be chaos and I need a moment to breathe.

"Are you alright Scar?" Rhodes asks quietly.

"No," I say honestly, "but I will be. I just need this night done."

Rhodes nods as I turn to look at him, "To be honest, I'm not looking forward to it either. I love you but the thought of you wearing lingerie dancing on a stage gives me hives. I might also vomit, to be frank."

I chuckle at the honestly but I'm thankful for it. It also helps to take some of the pressure off my shoulders knowing I'm not the only one not looking forward to it.

"I think Dad has already researched therapists for himself," he says with a chuckle.

My mouth drops, "Fuck, I forgot that he is going to be there."

Nope. Nup. There is no way I'm getting on that stage if he is in the crowd.

"He's going to have to turn his back and stand in a corner or something." I shiver.

"Don't you worry, I will be there right beside him."

We pull up to Pinks' and it's already packed. I thank my lucky stars that we are with my father, as the crowd parts to make way for him and Mum who are holding hands. It still feels so weird to see her with a man, let alone the man who is my dad. I had always just thought she wasn't ready to move on but really, she was always just waiting to return to him. Feels like some kind of tragic love story.

I smile even as I pass the mildly familiar faces in the crowd, only spotting a few I remember from Church the other night.

I feel relieved as I spot Shelly who is already making a beeline for me. The excitement is palpable on her face.

"Hello, my darling, we don't have much time. You need to get backstage and get ready." Shelly grabs both mine and my Mum's hands and pulls us through the crowd. She doesn't bother acknowledging my father or Rhodes as she pushes her way through the masses.

The dressing room is just as packed as when we walked in. I swear each direction I look I spot another naked female body part, some only partially covered by scraps of lace.

Shelly rushes me over to a vacant chair at the vanity that spans the entirety of the wall,

"You sit here my darling," she says forcing me into the chair as she frantically looks around the room, "Brandy! Brandy! Well, wherever Brandy is…" Shelly says before she is interrupted by a frazzled Brandy.

"I'm here, don't get your panties in a twist," she says as she dumps the bags she was carrying on the table in front of me. My eyes widen as makeup pallets and hair tools fall from the bags. Good god, what have I gotten myself into?

Shelly takes a sigh of relief as she steps behind me and puts her hands on my shoulders, "Brandy is going to take care of your hair and make up. Is customary that the last girl initiated helps the next girl get ready."

I nod at her words as I turn to look at Brandy who is smiling at me with a cheeky look on her face, "Don't you worry sweet pea, those stupid boys won't know what hit them once I'm done with you."

After what feels like every single product known to man applied to my face and hair, Brandy finally steps away from me. If I don't see another can of hairspray for the rest of my life, it will still be too soon.

"You look beautiful, Scar," Brandy says as she pulls her hands up to her chin. A proud look donning her face as she admires me.

I finally turn my head and look in the mirror. Brandy refused when I asked to watch, something about wanting it to be a surprise. My hair hangs in perfect curls down my back. The different blonde shades seem to pop through each twist.

My eyes are dark and smoky but not overdone with my lips in a similar dark colour. I can't help the smile that overcomes me.

Brandy comes to stand behind me, patiently waiting for a response.

"I think it's time to ruin some men's lives." The entire room erupts with cat calls and whoops, each sound helping fuel my ego.

I pull the zipper of the boots up, taking a breath as I stand to my full height. Even though I have been practising in them every night, I still feel like a newborn foal walking for the first time as I get used to being this high again.

My eyes widen in surprise as I take in my appearance. The last time I was in my costume, I had my hair in a messy top knot, but now that my hair and make-up is done, I'm generally shocked at my appearance. I'm not normally one to toot my own horn but god fucking damn, I look hot as fuck.

I grab my phone out of the pocket of my discarded jeans and take a couple of selfies, instantly sending them to both Noah and Grace. I go to set down my phone but pings make me pick it back up again.

GRACE

THAT'S MY FUCKING BITCH

If I wasn't straight, I would be wifing you up.

NOAH

Nope. Get a fucking robe or something.

Absolutely not. Grace, do you have one of those douchebags' numbers? There's no fucking way you are going on stage in that.

ME

Calm down, Dad. You should have seen some of the other options I was given. This was the safest. Not only that but I know just how much it will piss those boys off.

NOAH

Now that you have said that, please go and destroy their lives. Maybe collect their balls on those heels and wear them as a lucky charm.

ME

Blood thirsty, I love it

GRACE

I sometimes question why I'm friends with you two some days.

NOAH

Aw you love us. You know your life would be boring without us.

GRACE

True. Knock 'em dead Scar. I want full reports tomorrow.

Or whenever the fuck our time zones aren't being cunts. I miss you.

NOAH

I miss you too. It's not the same without you.

ME

Don't make me cry. Brandy spent an hour on this face and I don't intend on spending a second longer in that god forbidden chair.

But I miss you both more than you can imagine xo

Maxie is the first to spot me as I walk out of the dressing room. Her eyebrows raise and she lets out a low wolf whistle.

"Yes, mama! That's what I'm talking about. I knew there was a baddie under all that goody two shoes exterior."

Rippy grunts as she crosses her arms over her chest, not bothering to comment.

Jen twirls her finger around in circles so I follow suit, giving a very unsteady spin before facing the girls again.

Jen nods her head, "I can't wait to see the way those boys' brains melt when they see you."

Brandy chuckles, "Come on, let's go knock them dead."

I stand behind the curtain that leads out to the stage. If I thought I was nervous before, it has nothing on the jitters I feel now. I grab my hand to stop it from shaking but it's no use. I will myself to take a few deep breaths before opening my eyes again.

I peek my head out far enough that I'm still hidden but enough that I can see the crowd. I instantly find Rhodes, Wyatt and Jethro. It's obvious by just how uncomfortable Rhodes is as he looks around the rooms in an attempt to escape. When I find my father, he looks very much the same. I watch him throw back two shots of brown liquor, swallowing hard as he looks up at the stage and grimaces.

It doesn't take me long before I find Nicky, Sonny, Pike, Dacre and, to my disgust, Dawson. They are sitting on the couch right at the end of the stage. I couldn't have asked for a better spot for them to be sitting, especially with what I have in store for them.

Dawson sits beside them but the distance is obvious between them. Dawson's arms are crossed over his chest and it looks like he would rather be anywhere but here.

Something the both of us can actually agree on right now. Sonny looks like a kid at a candy store and all his dreams are about to come true.

Pike and Nicky are deep in conversation by the serious looks on their faces. Lastly, my eyes fall on Dacre and to my surprise, he's looking right back at me. I can feel the heat in his eyes as he looks up and down my body. He catches his lip between his teeth and I instantly clench my thighs together.

Damn him for looking so goddamn delicious. He leans back on the couch, spreading his thighs apart and I have to reinforce my knees so they don't collapse from under me. He looks like a complete fuckboy right now and I'm utterly at his mercy.

His finger turns in the slightest of motion and just like a string puppet, I turn giving him a full 360 view. His eyes darken as ours meet again.

'*Fucking perfection,*' he mouths and my cheeks heat. I've never seen Dacre this bold before. My sweet boy seems to have turned devilish but, shit, am I here for it!

"Ladies and Gentlemen, do we have a surprise in store for you tonight," the DJ says as the current song gets drowned out, "it's time for one of our own to initiate. Now I want you to give a Thunderbirds welcome to our one and only Scarlett Crux!"

The entire club erupts in applause and hoots, the sounds of feet thumping deafening before my song starts to play and the chaos dies down.

Sugar by Sleep Token rings out over the speakers. The smooth and sultry sounds give me the perfect entrance as I slowly walk out onto the stage. The crowd cheers around me but I keep my eyes locked in on Dacre as I slowly walk down the runway. I eventually start letting my hands roam my body, teasing the audience as I go.

I stop half way down before dropping to my knees. I slide my hands down the stage, arching my back before sliding back into a kneeling position.

My eyes leave Dacre's whose stare feels like molten lava and find Pike. His posture is stiff and I can't help the quirk of my lips as I catch the slight tent to his jeans.

I let my hands trail up my body, grazing my lace covered

cunt which causes the crowd to holler but I drown them out. Pike's eyes zone in on every inch of my body.

It's almost as though I can feel each spot they zone in on. I let my head drop back as I reach my tits cupping them and biting my lip. I hear moans and a muffled "for fuck's sake" but I pay it no mind.

I eventually let my hands drop back to the stage until I'm on all fours and zeroing on my next target, Dawson.

His eyes are wide, and I swear there's a spot of drool in the corner of his mouth.

Slowly I begin crawling to him, letting my hips sway. As I reach the end of the stage, I sit back on my legs and let a devious smile turn my lips. I swing my legs around before slowly lowering myself off the stage. I thank the pleasers I'm wearing for the additional height to do it with an ounce of grace.

I take the two steps towards Dawson, forcing him back into his seat before crawling into his lap. His hands instantly go to my hips, his grip tightening to the point of pain as I slowly roll my body against him.

I see the fight leave his body. The desperation for me to stay exactly where I am prevalent in his eyes but after his asshole tendencies this past week, he doesn't stand a chance. I give him a quirk of my lips before pushing off him and turning around. I grip the stage before shaking my ass in his face. The guys all laugh at his expense. I turn around for one last look and blow him a teasing kiss before swinging my legs back up on stage.

I walk quicker towards the pole just as the beat starts to ramp up and right at the crest, I launch at the pole, swinging my body around before hooking my knee in and allowing my body to spin.

My body takes complete control, like I become one with

the music as it sounds through the club. Every other noise drowns out until it's just me and the pole. I dance until the final moment, slowing down as I face towards the front of the room again. I drop back down onto my knees and let my head fall back just as the final tones ring out. My breath comes out in pants as I allow the adrenaline to seep from my body.

I lift my head when the crowd erupts in a cheer. I can't help the smile and the following giggle that escapes me. Brandy, Maxie and Jen are standing on a nearby chair hooting and screaming my name.

Rhodes looks like he's going to be sick but grimaces as he claps. Wyatt and Jethro are both standing and cheering and I can't help but chuckle at the look on Wyatt's face. The guy is way too excited.

I finally look down at Pike, Nicky, Dacre, Sonny and Dawson. The former four are all standing cheering and calling my name but the latter sits stock still in his seat. A mix of emotions running over his face. Desire, disbelief and fear all mixed together in a face that looks both constipated and turned on. I send him a wink which he frowns at before I stand and bow to the crowd before turning and exiting the stage.

BOARDING PASS
NAME: SCARLETT SMITH
FROM:
TIME:
CLASS:
SEAT:
President

chapter
THIRTY-THREE

sonny

My eyes stay glued on Scarlett's retreating form. I memorise the way her hips sway with each step she takes. The curve of her ass and how fucking delectable it looks in a thong. My cock presses impossibly hard against the zipper of my jeans but I take the pain and embrace it. I deserve it because I know just how unworthy I am of being in the presence of an absolute goddess. I groan as she retreats behind the curtain. But I don't plan on letting her out of my sight for much longer.

I've never seen a female body move the way Scarlett's did. I felt envious of the stage as she rolled her body against it and I swear I almost came in my pants watching as she spun on the pole. Then came the jealousy that tore through me as I watched Scarlett crawl into Dawson's lap and give the smug fuck a lap dance, one he definitely didn't deserve.

But I know *mi estrella*, it was all in her plan to fuck with him and damn if he wasn't absolute putty in her hands.

His mouth still hangs open as he looks at the stage in disbelief. Dawson may have his doubts about Scarlett but since she has been back, she has done nothing but prove to me just how ready she is for this life and just how desperately I need her in mine. I need her like she is the only fucking air I can breath. Life feels empty without her. It's like she has this power to make every day better just by being in it and I refuse to waste anymore time sitting around with my dick in my hand. I would much rather Scarlett sitting on it.

I launch out of my chair startling the guys out of their stupor, "Where the fuck are you going?" Nicky questions, throwing back what was Jack on the rocks but is now just watered down whisky.

"Ah, to get my fucking girl and show her exactly what I thought of that dance," I say with a questioning frown. What the fuck else would I be doing? Going to shoot my load in the bathroom? I mean… it's probably not a bad idea seeing how close I am to embarrassing myself but my dick can wait.

I don't bother wasting anymore time explaining myself to the boys as I make my way through the crowd.

I barge through the dressing room doors and instantly start looking for Scarlett. Some of the girls squeal and tell me to get the fuck out. I pay them no mind. I don't give a fuck about them or what little they have on.

I spot my girl in the back laughing at something Brandy says to her.

I instantly make a beeline for her. Brandy eventually sees me coming, her eyes blowing wide before she nudges Scarlett.

I stand right behind *mi amor* just waiting for her to acknowledge me. Ever so slowly she turns, allowing me to take her in up close again. My breath hitches at just how breathtaking she looks this close up.

"Scarlett, you were… I…" I stutter, trying to find the

words but find nothing comes to the forefront. I feel like a blubbering fool and maybe I am.

Maxie, Rippy, Brandy and Jen all giggle at my expense, but a sultry smile curves Scar's lips, "Tell me about it, *Stud*."

I groan, knees at buckling point as her words nearly bring me to my bitter end. But instead of bowing at her altar like any other mere mortal would, I pull her close to my body, bring my lips close enough to her ear and whisper, "I have no words right now. Instead, let me show you."

A shiver runs over Scarlett's body and I know I already have my answer without having to hear her verbalise it. I bend down, sliding my arms around her legs before throwing Scarlett over my shoulder, eliciting a squeal from her lips as I turn tail and make my way out of the room.

Shelly gives me a disapproving look as I spot her walk through the door and I know there's no way I'm getting out of this without being punished but it's going to be so worth it.

"Sorry Shelly, but I have a woman I need to worship," I say. She shakes her head as if in disapproval but I catch the slight quirk of her lip.

"You look after my girl Sonny Martinez or I'll have you scrubbing the floors with a toothbrush every Saturday morning," she says, crossing her arms over her body.

"I would scrub the floors every day of the week if that gave me even a moment in *mi amor's* presence," I reply with nothing but the truth.

"Don't tempt me boy. Room five," she says with a nod and I smile thanking the sex gods that someone is watching over me tonight.

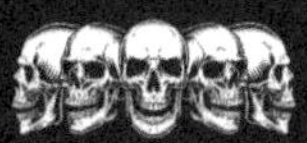

Scarlett is still hanging over my shoulder by the time I get to the room. The door is already unlocked, waiting for us. Swinging it open I make a beeline for the bed, throwing Scarlett down on the sheets. I groan at the sight of her.

"Goddamn *mi estrella,* I have never been good at control but I am holding onto every bit of it I possess right now."

Scarlett quirks her head, "Who ever said you have to have control, Sonny?"

Her words ignite something inside of me. I close the distance between us, crawling onto the bed and lying on top of her. She opens her legs so our bodies are able to fit together just like they are made to.

"If there weren't a good two hundred people here tonight, I would have done a Kanye and been on that stage quicker than you could say 'Beyonce had one of the best videos of all time.'"

Scarlett laughs and a part of me warms inside. After seeing way too many frowns in my direction over the last few days, it feels good to finally have a bit of her happiness back, even though I know I don't deserve it and I never will. It doesn't stop the absolute craving I have for even a shred of her.

I have more than made my piece with having to share her with my friends. If anything, I prefer the idea of having to share her. Knowing that there are four (if Dawson pulls his head out of his ass) other guys that are willing to love and protect my girl just as much as I am, gives me some kind of piece of mind. Especially in the line of work we are in.

I have no delusions that Scarlett isn't going to get hurt. Danger is quite literally in the job description. But, unlike my dickhead best friend, I have no intentions of sending Scarlett back to Australia. If I could glue us together and keep her with me forever, I would.

"Well then, Kanye, I suggest you show me exactly what you would have done if you had stormed that stage. Because right now, all I see is that you have stage fright."

Scarlett's chuckle at my expense further ignites the fire inside of me. She's baiting me but I'm already hook, line and sinker.

I chuckle, grabbing my phone from my pocket and setting it up in one of the phone stands already in the room exactly for this reason. I hit the facetime call button, before turning around and walking back towards my girl.

Scarlett gives me a questioning look.

"Just showing you I have absolutely no issue with stage fright or performance anxiety for that matter. If anything, this might be a good lesson for those boys, as long as I have a willing student?" I tease her with a quirk of my brow.

But just like I knew she would, my girl meets me head on, "Yes, Sir. I can't promise I will be a good girl for you though. You may need to teach me a lesson in how to behave."

I chuckle as I slowly undo my belt, pulling it out roughly and looping it, ready for Scarlett's wrists.

She offers her hands up to me with zero hesitation, just like I hoped she would.

I tighten the belt cuffs around her hands before pushing them above her head.

"Lesson one, don't move," I growl into her ear, smiling with triumph at the whimper that escapes her.

As I sit back I take in my girl. It didn't take much effort at all to get her worked up this much. Her chest rises and falls in quick succession. Her nipples are pebbled hard underneath the scraps of lace and leather that cover them. From this close, I can see the rosy colour peeking through the small holes. She was teasing us the entire time. Giving us pieces of her and luring us into her deadly trap.

The thong covering her pussy is already damp. I'm not sure whether it was from that dance or me but I take it as a win.

Glancing back at my phone, I can see each of the guys have already answered.

"Lesson number two, you will use a safe word if and when you need it. I'm happy for you to push your limits. We will use the stop light system. Green means you are good, yellow means slow down and red means stop. Do you understand?"

Scarlett nods enthusiastically but it's not enough.

"Words, Scarlett."

"Yes, sir," she whispers, causing a smile to break on my face. She's a quick learner.

With one hand I pull my shirt off over my head, throwing it behind me. My jeans follow suit. I leave my boxers on, giving Scar a sneak peek into just how she makes me feel. I crouch down at the end of the bed, grabbing her ankles and pull her down to me. A squeal slips from her mouth at the sudden movement.

I unclip the suspenders from where they are attached at her stockings before reaching behind her back and unzipping the garter. I don't bother removing the stockings or her heels. I grab her hands pulling her up to sit as I work out how to get her out of the bra. Slipping my knife out of my pocket of my jeans, Scarlett's breath hitches as I bring it up between her tits, slicing through the offending leather and lace.

"Shelly is going to kill you." Scar breaths heavily as she watches as I flick the knife back into itself.

I chuckle, "It'll be worth it."

I lean up, sucking one of Scarlett's nipples into my mouth. She makes a mewling sound and I feel her hands grip my head. My teeth bite down on her nipple, causing her to yelp in pain.

"Already forgot lesson one?" I growl. Her eyes widen as she

remembers my rules.

A sinister smile spreads over my lips, "Hands and knees now. I want that ass up in the air."

Scarlett rushes to do as she is told. I turn and walk over to the phone, speaking low enough that she won't hear me, "Room five. Our girl needs someone to keep that filthy mouth full and those wandering hands busy."

I pay my phone no mind as I walk back over to my girl. She looks so perfect presenting for me. Her ass is rounded perfectly and my hand tingles with want to slap it, knowing I would leave a perfect handprint.

Slowly I slide my hands up her thighs and over the bulbs of her ass.

Tucking one of my fingers under her thong, I run my finger down until I come to the soaked part of lace. Pulling back as far as I can, I let it go, smiling as it slaps her pussy and elicits a yelp.

"Your actions have consequences, *mi corazón*. Next time you move those hands, I won't be as forgiving."

"Yes sir," she whimpers, nodding her head against the bed.

I hear an urgent knock at the door, walking over I unlock the door knowing it will be at least one of the guys. My offer was way too tempting for them to give up.

To my surprise, Nicky, Dacre, Pike and Dawson all walk in the room, eyes widening at the position Scarlett is currently in. Their eyes heat as they give me a questioning look.

"Welcome boys," I chuckle. I watch as Scarlett stiffens and turns her head towards the door. Her eyes heat as she spots the four newcomers. I can already see ideas rolling through her head. Fantasies that I'm sure she hasn't even thought of yet. But I plan on making every single one of them come true for her tonight.

I need to give this to her. I need to show her just how good we are for her. Dawson is a questionable add on at this point but I know Nicky, Dacre, Pike and myself need her.

Living without her these past few months has felt empty. Like a gap I could have filled entirely with loving her. Devoting my life to her.

Tonight, I plan on showing her just how serious I am about her. Tomorrow, I will get down on my knees and beg for forgiveness.

Pike locks the door behind him as they walk inside. Dacre walks straight over to Scarlett and runs a hand over her face, tucking a few loose strands of hair behind her ear.

"Hey, Star. Is it okay if we are in here?" he asks.

Scarlett nods and mutters a quiet "Yes, sweet boy."

I humph, unable to hide the tinge of jealousy I feel at the nickname Scarlett has given Dacre. I make it my personal mission then to encourage her to call me *papi.* I swear hearing the word come out of her mouth sent me into orbit and I still haven't been able to recover even after all this time.

"Dacre, I think our girl needs something to fill that mouth of hers," I chuckle, walking over and caressing her ass.

Dacre's eyes widen at my words. I know that Dacre's only ever been with Scarlett that once. It's a big step for him but I know that he needs this with her. She needs this just as much. He looks down at Scar who smiles and nods her head which seems to give him confidence.

Scarlett looks back at me while Dacre is removing his shirt, "May I move my hands please, Sir?"

I smirk at her obedience, "I have another idea of something you can do with your hands."

Her eyebrows raise in question. I snake my hand around her waist, lifting her torso so she is kneeling on the bed. Her back curves to my front and I can't help but pepper kisses along her throat as I loosen the belt cuffs from her wrist. The belt drops to the bed in front of her but none of us pay it any mind.

I turn my head, nodding for Nicky and Pike to come over. After years of working alongside each other and being able to read each other's cues, they already know what I have in mind.

They instantly lose their clothes, throwing them carelessly as they stalk towards the bed. Nicky takes up the left side, Pike takes the right and Dacre moves to the middle of the bed. His cock is already in his hand, slowly pumping it in anticipation. I glance back at Dawson who has taken a seat in the corner of the room. Scarlett turns her head at the same time, tensing as she sees him.

"I can kick him out if you want, Scarlett. You say the word and he's gone."

She shakes her head, "No, he can watch. Let him see what he misses out on," she snides before turning back towards Dacre.

Falling back to her hands, she crawls up the bed, swinging her hips as she goes.

I groan, taking in the sight of her. Innocent, she is not. Dawson isn't wrong in his declaration that she is a vixen. Or Eve sent straight from the Garden of Eden to lure us into temptation.

Dacre releases his cock just as Scarlett reaches him. Dipping her tongue out, she licks from his balls right to the tip of his cock before bringing it into her mouth and sucking him down, gagging as she gets a few inches from the end. Dacre throws his head back as she slowly retreats, letting his cock pop from her mouth. Spit strings from Dacre's dick to Scarlett's mouth eventually breaking as she looks up at him.

"Fuck me dead, Scar," Dacre moans, his eyes heating.

"Hmm, I don't know about fucking you dead, but I can certainly make you forget your name," she quips making us all chuckle.

I crawl up onto the bed grabbing hold of Scarlett's hips and bringing her back into my crotch.

"That's our job tonight, *princesa.*"

Grabbing the sides of her thong, I pull, ripping the fabric from her body. She gasps as her head flicks back to me. She opens her mouth just about to cuss me out but I cut her off, turning her head and shoving her back down onto Dacre's dick, filling her mouth and stopping her from mouthing off any further. Her disobedience is cute but I need her obedience right now.

They both groan as Scarlett gets distracted and starts sucking Dacre like she's got a point to prove.

I pull my cock out of my boxes and slap it against her dripping cunt. I slowly tease around her opening, sliding in the tip before pulling back out. Scarlett moans in anticipation, desperate for me to slam home. I plan on doing just that but I can't help but tease the little cock tease herself. She has made me hard all night and I plan on making her feel the pain I've felt.

Nicky and Pike slowly crawl closer to Scarlett so they are kneeling on either side of Dacre. Scarlett must get the hint as she wraps a hand each around both of their dicks and slowly starts pumping, pulling moans and curses from their mouths.

After teasing Scarlett a little longer, I know that if I keep going the way I am, I'll end up busting a nut on her ass and, while that thought is tempting, I need to feel her cum around my cock first.

I breach the entrance of her pussy slowly teasing the tip inside before thrusting all the way to the hilt. The sudden jolt causes Scarlett's to take all of Dacre down her throat, making her violently gag. I chuckle as she comes up for air.

"Fuck you, Sonny," she attempts to growl but it lacks heat as she pants trying to catch her breath.

I bring my hand back, slapping the delicate flesh of her ass from where I'm pounding her from behind. She yelps but it soon turns to a moan as I rub my hand over it, helping to ease the sting.

"I suggest you put that dick back in your mouth *mami*," I chuckle, "or don't. Your ass would look perfect all bruised up."

Scarlett moans and I know she isn't completely opposed to the idea. I bank it for another day. I know I need to work her up to impact play.

I fuck in and out of her pussy like I'm trying to win a marathon. Nothing has ever felt as good as she does right now. Her tight wet heat squeezes my cock and I know she's just about to go over the edge but I can feel she needs more. I feel a hand snake around the front of her body. I turn, surprised to see Dawson crouched on the bed as he bends down to where Scarlett is taking Dacre's length into her mouth.

"Come for us, Scarlett. Come around Sonny's cock." he whispers in her ear.

Scarlett moans and with two more strokes, her channel becomes impossibly tight, squeezing my cock as her orgasm overcomes her. I shout as I follow her, the most intense orgasm of my life taking me over.

I hear Dacre, Pike and Nicky all follow along, cursing as pleasure takes its hold.

I slowly come back to myself, looking down at where Scarlett is resting her head in Dacre's lap as he plays with her hair. Nicky and Pike are both grabbing cloths from the bedside tables and cleaning themselves and where their cum is roped over Scarlett's hands.

I slowly pull out of Scarlett, she gasps at the loss of me.

I can't help but stare as I watch my cum run out of her pussy, slowly dripping onto the sheets under her.

"That's going to be my new wallpaper," I say, reaching over to find my phone and snapping a photo before she can move.

BOARDING P
NAME: SCARLETT SMIT
FROM:
TIME:
CLAS
SEAT:
President

chapter
THIRTY-FOUR

scarlett

Unescapable heat is the first thing to wake me. That and I feel like I'm being weighed down to the bed by a ton of bricks.

I blink my eyes open, startling when I don't recognise the room I'm in. I turn my head to the side, coming face to face with Pike. His blonde hair is messy yet he still radiates the perfection I've come to adore from him. His arm is wrapped around my waist with his hand squeezing my breast.

There's a serene look on his face, still deep in slumber. I feel another body wrapped around my back and attempt to turn my head. Nicky's body completely curves to mine. I feel the hard rod of his cock nestled between my ass cheeks.

It's only then that I realise the three of us are all naked. The only thing overing us is a thin sheet someone must have thrown over us.

I attempt to wiggle my legs, feeling they are too weighed down but two arms hold them tighter to their body.

I look down seeing that Dacre has my legs completely embraced and from the feel of the grip he has on them, it doesn't feel like he intends on letting them go anytime soon. From the look on his face, I don't intend on disturbing him either, even though my bladder is screaming at me.

I see another hand wrapped around Pike. Slowly pulling myself up onto my elbow, I find a sleeping and completely naked Sonny wrapped around him.

A chuckle slips from my lips and I can't help but wish for my phone to capture the moment. Not only does the image warm my heart, it also brings filthy ideas to the forefront of my mind. Ideas I know the boys might not be interested in partaking in; not yet at least.

I know Grace would support my ideas. That dirty bitch loves a good sword crossing scene.

I take another look around the room, knowing there was one more person in here last night.

Dawson is lounged over one of the chairs in the corner of the room. Compared to us on the bed, he is fully clothed. His leather jacket and his boots are the only things he seemed to remove.

Watching him sleep, I'm able to really take him in for the first time in months. I had already burnt his image into my mind from torturing myself with the photos we took together, but it's different seeing them in the flesh. The quality is clearer and more perfect.

While Dawson has always been a grumpy cat, the stress is starting to show on his face. Frown lines sit deep on his forehead even while he is asleep but it's the most relaxed I've seen him since I arrived. Like even still during slumber, his worries plague him.

He feels like such an enigma.

Why did he come into the room with the other guys last

night when he has been so adamant about making me leave?

Why do I still catch him looking at me from across the room, glaring at me like I'm a puzzle for him to solve?

And why the fuck is he such an asshole when not a single one of us in this room or this organisation alone can change what my future holds? He has known since we were little that this was my role. Was he the same way when we were younger?

My internal monologue of questioning must be loud enough to rouse Dawson as his eyes slowly start to blink awake. I watch as he takes in the room around him.

He sits up, rubbing his eyes before running a hand through his hair.

He pauses for a moment and I watch as he slowly starts to remember the night before. His head shoots up and his gaze immediately connects with mine.

I brace myself for the ire that I have become used to when it comes to Dawson. It seems to shock my system worse when he gives me a small smile. It slowly widens as he takes in the bed situation. I hear him chuckle as he spots Sonny entwined with Pike.

He takes his phone out of his pocket, pulling up the camera app. I hear the shutter go off as he captures the two of them. Before he takes another snap, I make a silly face, making him snigger as I hear the shutter go off again.

He tucks his phone away, before walking over to the bed. He looks down on me and must take pity on me as he slowly starts prying Dacre's arms off my legs and instead wrapping the limbs around a pillow. I start shifting Nicky's arms around me, halting when he groans and rolls over. I sigh a breath of relief.

Two down, one to go.

Pike is a little more tricky. Dawson hands me another

pillow so I slide it in-between my body and his arms.

I wiggle myself up into a sitting position. Dawson reaches out for me and I take his help as he lifts me out of the tangle of limbs, not wanting to wake anyone else up.

Dawson sets me down on my feet but doesn't let me go far.

"Morning," he whispers quietly enough for only me to hear.

"Morning," I reply in a similar tone.

It takes a moment for Dawson to realise that I'm naked and he's fully clothed as his eyes roam my body, widening as he sees me.

He takes a step back and looks around the room trying to find something amongst the chaos of the boys stripping off in their haste to get to me. Eventually he gives up, stripping off his own shirt and pulling it over my head.

I'm left stunned for a moment. Not only at the fact that Dawson quite literally gave me the shirt off his back, but the eye candy he's freely giving me so early in the morning.

Dawson may be a dick but he's a fucking sexy dick.

"Do you want to go talk?" Dawson asks, keeping his voice low. I look up from his chest and see the vulnerability in his face. It shocks me enough that I don't question or hesitate in saying yes.

He grabs my hand, silently opening and closing the door before leading me down the hallway to the dressing room.

Pinks' is completely empty this early in the morning, so I know we are the only ones here.

I give Dawson a questioning look before he shrugs, "I thought you might want to wear pants for the conversation we are about to have."

I chuckle, nodding as I go and grab the spare change of clothes I packed for after my performance. I pull my panties and jeans on but leave the shirt Dawson gave me. If he thinks

I plan on giving it back to him, he is sorely mistaken. You can't give a girl a *Bring Me the Horizon* band tee and expect her to give it back.

I slip on my sneakers and run a quick brush through my hair, taming the knots. After the night we had, there are plenty of them.

"Are you decent?" Dawson calls out. I give him a muffled yes through the hair tie in my mouth.

Sliding the curtain across, Dawson walks in, smiling as he sees the shirt still on me.

He takes the brush from my hand from where I'm aggressively brushing as well as the band from my mouth.

"Let me do it," he mumbles. I nod as he slowly starts pulling the brush through my hair.

He's gentle as he slowly starts untangling the knots. A gentleness that I didn't think Dawson could ever possess. Once the knots are combed out, he parts my hair and slowly begins to braid it.

"Where did you learn to do this?" I ask.

Dawson's smiles but it's a sad one. My heart clenches as he stays silent for a while. He twists my hair right until the end before tying it off with the hair tie.

"Before you were taken from us, I used to braid your hair all the time. You refused to let anyone but me do it. Even your Mum wasn't an exception to the demand," he chuckles as he looks at me through the mirror, "You always said that I was gentle, and you liked the way I did it. Every day I would spend ages sitting with you, brushing your hair before braiding it."

I stare at Dawson in shock, "You did?"

He nods, smiling, "It was always my favourite time of the day. The smile you would give me once I was done always made it worth it." He looks back down at my hair, reaching up and playing with the ends, "I didn't realise how much those moments meant to me until now." Dawson trials off and I stay quiet, allowing him to collect his thoughts.

Eventually he looks back up at me and by the look on his face, I know this needs to be said face to face. I turn around, facing Dawson properly.

"The day you were taken was the worst day of my life. I couldn't eat or sleep properly for months after," he sighs, "It was the same for all of us. It was empty with you gone. But each day we held onto hope that our dads and the rest of the 'Birds would find you."

A lone tear drips down his face and I catch it with my thumb. He hangs his head as he continues.

"When your dad came back, we were all at your house with our mums waiting. I knew from the look on their faces that it wasn't good news." Another tear falls from Dawson's eye and my heart breaks for him.

He looks up at me, tears silently falling from his eyes, "They didn't have to say anything. I just knew that you were gone." He takes a deep breath, "That day repeats in my head over and over again." He grabs my head in his hands as he steps into me, "That's why I keep asking you to leave. To go home. I need you safe, Scarlett. The thought of you being in any kind of danger is unbearable to me."

I feel the truth in every single word Dawson speaks. I feel the heartbreak in his tone as he pleads with me. While I hear what he is saying and can sympathise with him to some degree, he also needs to understand where I'm coming from.

"I hear you loud and clear Dawson, I really do. But this is my home. It's always been my home. I feel like this is exactly where I am meant to be. Even though parts of this life terrify me and at times I put on a brave face, I need to do this.

"There are women out there who need me. Children out

there that are living through what I somehow survived. I feel like this is my calling. Not being some barista in some beach side town in Australia, but being a figure in this organisation and saving lives," I plead with Dawson, begging him to understand me. I don't know why I need his approval or support of me being here but I do. I've craved it from the moment he snubbed me when I first returned.

I see the fear written all over his face, the same emotion that has been haunting him all this time, "But what if something happens and you get hurt again? I can't live through that. I don't think any of us can handle losing you again. And there's a risk of that being here."

I nod my head agreeing with him, "I know that. Trust me I do. I've been warned relentlessly by Mum, Dad and Rhodes. I see just how serious it is just based on the training we do. But I need you to put some faith in me," I say gripping Dawson's hands,

"I'm not an eight-year-old child. I'm not entirely defenceless. And with the five of you standing at my back, I know that I can do this." I pause as I look deep into Dawson's eyes, "Have faith in me."

Dawson remains silent for a moment as he assesses me. It feels like he's dissecting me. Inspecting every single facet of me.

Eventually he nods, "I'll try. But I swear to God if you get injured again, I'm locking you up and bubble wrapping you."

We both laugh, breaking the tension in the room. Dawson's hands drop from my face but he grabs my waist, like he's not quite ready to let go of me yet.

I point a finger at him, remembering myself and just how much of an asshole he's been, "This doesn't mean that things are okay between us. You have a fuck load of grovelling to do and I don't plan on letting you off easy. You've been a fucking cunt."

Dawson winces, "Shit, that's not even the friend kind of cunt I've heard you call people before either."

I raise my eyebrow and he lifts his hands in surrender, "I know. I have been a cunt. But I promise to ease up. I don't expect anything between us."

I nod in agreement, "Friends?" I say as I hold a hand out. I still internally wince at the word. Being friends with Dawson doesn't seem achievable but it's better than being at war with him.

"Friends," he nods as he puts his hand in mine and shakes.

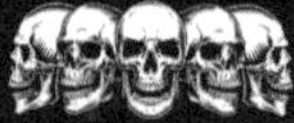

Eventually we both let go of each other. I round up all of the shit I've spread around the dressing room, looking around to make sure I've got everything. Knowing me, I will have forgotten something for sure. Dawson grabs my bag off me as we walk out of the dressing room and back down to the room where the boys are still asleep.

They've moved since Dawson and I left. Pike and Sonny are still spooning but now Dacre is holding Nicky's legs, having ditched the pillow.

Dawson snorts as we walk in, pulling his phone back out again to grab a couple of snaps of the moved positions.

"You need to send me all of those photos," I giggle as I walk over towards Dacre.

"Already done," Dawson says as he puts my bag down in the corner.

I run my fingers through Dacre's hair, giggling as he smiles and snuggles his face further into Nicky's legs who makes a groaning sound before trying to dislodge Dacre's hold.

Dacre frowns before opening his eyes. His face brightens when he sees me in front of him but quickly morphs into confusion as he looks at the legs he's cuddling then back to me.

He groans as he lets go of Nicky, "Was I cuddling Nicky's legs all night?"

I giggle as Dacre pulls me into his lap once he sits up. A thin sheet is the only thing between me and his morning wood but he doesn't acknowledge it and neither do I. He buries his head into my hair, hiding himself from reality.

Nicky eventually sits up too smiling when he sees me wrapped in Dacre's arms,

"Morning, baby girl."

"Morning, Nicky."

Our low conversation seems to rouse Pike, who looks down at the arms wrapped around his waist. He groans before rolling out of Sonny's embrace and pushing the sleeping man out of bed.

He hits the floor with a loud thunk.

"What the fuck," he slurs as he pops up over the side of the bed rubbing his eyes before looking at all of us confused.

"The fuck is, I'm not your little spoon, Sonny," Pike growls as he launches himself off the bed, finding his boxers and jeans before pulling them back on.

Sonny just shrugs as he pulls himself back up onto the bed, "Not my fault you are cuddly, Pikey boy."

Pike grunts as he pulls his shirt on over his head, "The next time I feel your cock anywhere near me without Scarlett between us, I'm going to fucking remove it."

Sonny must hear the violence in Pike's tone as he surrenders, holding his hands up. "It's all illchay, bro."

I snort, shaking my head at Sonny. He looks over at me as that cheeky smile of his returns, "Like that one *mi alma?*"

"Sonny, for the love of my vagina, don't you dare go all eshay on me."

Dawson, Nicky, Dacre and Pike all look confused and like we are speaking a different language as their gazes dart between us. Really, we are. The eshay culture is ripe through the younger Aussies. Something I'm more than glad to leave back where it belongs.

Sonny just laughs at me. If I know that cheeky little bastard as much as I think I do, it won't be the last I hear of him embracing the lifestyle.

I hop out of Dacre's lap and allow him to get up and get dressed. It takes the guys all a moment to find their clothes from where they are scattered throughout the room.

I sit on the bed watching as they pull their clothes back on and one hundred percent embrace the delicious eye candy.

It's still unbelievable to me that the five of them are interested in me. That the instant connection we formed in Australia hasn't fizzled out. If anything, the heat has turned up a notch. Even with the issues between Dawson and I, there is still a spark there.

Once they are all dressed, they turn towards me. No one has to say anything, they all know what today means.

Today is Saturday. Explanation day.

If it was left to the guys to describe, from the looks of their faces, it would seem it's more like doomsday.

BOARDING PASS
NAME: SCARLETT SMITH
FROM:
TIME:
CLASS:
SEAT:
President

chapter
THIRTY-FIVE

dacre

Dread fills me as I look down at Scarlett. I knew that this day was coming. I had been trying to psych myself up for it since she came back.

We all know that she needs, and deserves, an explanation. But now that we are here, nothing that I feel like I can say will be enough to justify what we did to her.

The way we broke her heart, ghosted her with no explanation after promising we would never leave and doing just that. Bringing her worst fears alive. Putting her through months of heartache all for nothing in the end.

Little did we know just how entwined our fates were.

Would we have done anything different if we knew that it was our Scarlett all along?

Would we have dragged her back here with us? Would we have kept quiet and protected her from a distance?

There's so many what if's. So many things that we could have done differently.

All we can do now is try and explain ourselves to get Scarlett to see how we were feeling in the moment and why we chose to do what we did.

Pulling up one of the seats surrounding the pole in the corner of the room, I take a seat, facing Scarlett before taking a deep breath.

Each of the guys take a seat around the bed, any earlier banter between us dissipated. There's a thick tension in the room.

My throat feels tight as I try to clear it. It's obvious the guys have volunteered me to be the sacrificial lamb.

I put my elbows on my knees leaning forward as I hang my head for a moment. Taking in another breath I finally look up to Scarlett.

"Our plans for our relationship didn't change with you the entire flight back to LA. The entire time we spoke about our plans. We already were looking at flights for you to come over to us."

I chuckle, the boys echoing me as we are thrown back into memories from the past.

My smile drops quickly, "Everything changed the moment the plane hit the tarmac. It was utter chaos."

Nicky nods, "The last time we saw the club in this much chaos was when you were taken."

Scarlett frowns as she looks at the expressions on our faces.

"One of the raid teams went out on a mission. They were expecting to intercept a shipment of women bound for one of the trafficking rings. But it wasn't women they found."

The feeling I felt that day when we got home floods over me again. My stomach clenches around nothing and I'm thankful we decided to have this conversation before we ate anything.

I swallow down bile as I look directly at Scarlett, "It was a shipment of children."

Scarlett straightens, her hands slap over her mouth. Her eyes are filled with horror.

I nod, pushing through the sick feeling in my stomach, "We all knew what these rings were capable of. But this wasn't one known for trafficking children. It was always women who were fleeing violent home lives or women living off the street.

"We have been searching for years for the rings that were dealing with children. There was always word on the street about them but we could never infiltrate them. We were always blocked."

Dawson grunts, "It seemed to be a new road block each time we tried but we always attempted to stay on the trail."

Pike agrees with Dawson, nodding as he adds, "Saving any human life is important but there is something about protecting children from these monsters that hits closer to home."

Scarlett nods as her hands drop from her mouth, "So what happened with the children? Are they okay? Do they have good families to go back home to?"

I smile at her questions even though the situation is dark. I knew she was meant for this life and her concern for the lives we saved proves that.

I nod, "They are all okay now. We were able to return the majority of the children back to their families who were thoroughly vetted before we did so."

"No way were we going to send them back to situations that would see them ending right back where we found them," Sonny curls his lip.

"What about the other kids?" Scar asks in a low voice.

I give her a sad smile, "Unfortunately we couldn't return them back to their families. Some of them were sold and some of them came from abusive households."

She sucks in a breath but I continue, "A couple of the older couples in the club took in the kids that couldn't go back to their families. They are helping them get back on the right track. They are enrolled in school and are seeing a therapist. They are okay." I try to reassure her as best as I can.

Scarlett sighs in relief and I along with her; her shoulders dropping as she sinks back into the bed.

"For weeks we were so caught up in sorting out club business and the stress that those situations brought that we completely neglected you and I'm sorry for that."

I trail off as Pike interrupts, "We are all sorry for that. It's a piss poor excuse and we know that but at the time we were at such a loss," Pike sighs before looking up at Scarlett, "I don't feel like anything I say is going to make what we did any better, but you have to know just how badly seeing those kids fucked with us. The first thing I thought when I saw them walk out of the van into the clubhouse was you," Pike chokes out the last few words and a tear rolls down his cheek.

I turn to Scarlett and see the tears are already rolling down her face.

I take a deep breath threatening my own tears at bay, "It brought back a lot of shit we tried to push down." My voice is sombre as I push through.

"We knew we couldn't lose another person we loved. Losing you the first time destroyed me. Destroyed us." I look around at the guys who all nod in agreement.

"We decided that the best course of action was just to stop all communication with you. We already hadn't replied to your messages or returned your calls so we thought that it would just be easier." I deflate.

Hearing the words again, the vow we said all those months ago in order to protect our girl just seems so fucking pointless now. I'm not afraid to admit how ridiculous it was. Ghosting someone that lived on the other side of the world just to protect them?

If I could smack me from nine months ago in the mouth, I would.

Scarlett narrows her eyes at us, "And you all thought that would be the best course of action? Ghost me with no explanation?"

I wince and so do the guys. She's right.

"I'm sorry, Scarlett. Nothing we can do or say will make any of this better. We fucked up. It's something that we are going to have to make up to you every day for the rest of our lives. If you will have us," Nicky says as he walks over and kneels in front of Scarlett. He takes her hands in his and holds them tight.

"My feelings for you haven't changed. You have consumed my every waking thought these past months. From morning to tonight. I am completely at your whim."

Scarlett remains speechless as she looks at Nicky with her eyes wide. A mixture of emotions run across her face as she looks at him.

Longing, hope, love but I can also see anxiety. The fear that we are going to hurt her again. I don't blame her for being weary of us. We did it to her once before. But this time it's different.

"How can I trust you again? How can I give myself to you and trust you with my heart? You all broke me. My heart has been in pieces for months," she says in a quiet voice and my own heart breaks seeing the raw emotion on her face.

"All we can ask of you is to just give us a chance. If you have to keep your walls up around us that's okay," I say as I walk towards her and kneel beside Nicky, trying to reassure her in any way that I can.

"What you say goes, Scar. No matter what we are yours. You want us to walk on hot coals for you, we will. You can us to tattoo your name on us, we fucking will," I declare.

Her eyes widen at my words. Little does she know though that she is already tatted on me. Not her name exactly but the tattoo that takes up my back is dedicated to her.

My Star.

My girl.

The woman who will one day be my wife. The mother of my children.

BOARDING P
NAME: SCARLETT SMIT
FROM:
TIME:
CLAS
SEAT:
President

I have to take a few deep breaths as I take in the dedication Nicky and Dacre are showing me. I look at them in disbelief. Seeing them on their knees before me, laying their feelings out bare for me in the way they are doesn't feel real. I feel like it's a dream that I am going to wake up from.

But from the look on their faces, it's real. They want me. They love me and they are actually here to stay.

Pike walks over and bends down beside Dacre. His hand snakes up my leg, squeezing the top of my calf, "What you say goes, Princess. You determine how fast or slow this whole thing goes."

Sonny walks over kneeling down beside them, "*Mi hermosa diso,* I knew from the moment I met you again, you were the person I would kneel before you for the rest of my life. I am yours, and I hope one day I can call you mine."

I can't help but smile. I want what he wants too, what they all clearly want. But I can't help all of the what if's that filter in. The doubts that still linger.

I look up to my last guy. If I can call him that.

Dawson stands back from the rest of the boys almost hesitantly. I can see it written on his face as well. But a piece of me knits back together as he takes a step forward.

He doesn't need to say anything but he does utter one word, "Yours."

It feels final then. Like the band is back together or some other ridiculous rendition of a reunion.

But pain still holds strong in my chest. I can't just let go of that hurt. The heartbreak that ruled my life for months. Because their words are just that, words. They are empty right now and, until they have action behind them, I refuse to let my walls down and let them back in again completely.

"I'm still so fucking mad at all of you. You broke my heart."

Each of the boys nod, Dawson grimaces.

"You are going to have to show me that your words aren't just empty. I expect you five to grovel."

Sonny smirks, "Oh baby, you know I have no issues being on my knees for you."

We erupt into laughter as Sonny stands up and pulls me into his arms. "I'll do anything to prove my words to you, *mi amor.*"

His voice is quiet in my ear. I nod my head against his chest. Sonny's arms wrap around me tight, squeezing like he's trying to keep me here. To tether me to him.

He eventually drops his arms from around me, letting me take a step back.

Dacre is the next one to step in, pulling me in tight to him. "I love you, Scarlett."

I nod again into his chest.

He lets me go and Pike pulls me into his arms. He doesn't say anything, but he doesn't need to. I can feel it in his embrace. In the way his arms tense around me.

He lets me go, caressing my face as we pull back.

Dawson steps into me next. I'm surprised when he pulls me into his arms as well. He doesn't say anything either but it kind of feels like an extension of our earlier conversation. It feels as though maybe his declaration of us just being friends isn't his intention at all. That his feelings are more in tune with the guys and how they feel about me.

I don't hate it, but it feels unexpected.

With Dawson, it feels like a rollercoaster. One minute he is all in, the next he wants me to disappear. At this point, I'm not even sure he even knows what he wants.

He lets me go and I'm immediately pulled into Nicky's arms and spun around. I hold around his neck tight, giggling as he helps relieve the tension.

I needed it. Something to slice the doom and gloom feeling in the room. He eventually sets me down, holding me a second longer so I can gain my footing.

"What are your plans for the rest of the day, baby girl?" Nicky questions.

"Ah, training with Wyatt I think," I say, grabbing my phone out of my back pocket from where I stored it earlier. My eyes widen as I see the time and the messages from Wyatt asking where I am.

"Fuck," I yell, looking around trying to find my bag, "Fuck, Fuck, Fuck."

"What?" Dacre asks, worried as he looks down at my phone.

"I'm half an hour late. Fuck!" I grab my bag but pause, "Can one of you guys take me to the clubhouse?"

Dawson immediately nods, grabbing his jacket and throwing it on, "I'll take you."

I nod before turning and smiling at the guys, "I'll talk to

you all later?"

I hightail it out of the room without getting a proper answer. My first training session with Wyatt and I'm already late.

D awson doesn't hesitate as he swings his leg over his Ducati as we rush out into the carpark. The bike roars to life and if I wasn't in such a rush, I would take time to appreciate it a little bit more.

I swing my leg over the back of the bike, threading my hands around his waist. His chest is naked still so I can feel the way his skin prickles as my hands graze over his stomach. He takes off, making me tighten his arms around his waist. I feel the vibrations of his chuckle as he takes off out of the car park.

It only takes a few minutes before we are pulling up in front of the clubhouse. I throw myself off the bike but pause, leaning down and kissing Dawson's cheek.

"Thanks, Daws."

His cheeks heat as I turn around and run towards the building. I only hear the roar of Dawson's bike taking off once I get inside the building.

I rush towards the training room, a few of the older guy's eyes widening as I rush past them. I smack the doors, throwing my bag off to the side as I take the last couple of steps towards the range.

Opening the door, I see Wyatt leaning against the wall with his phone in his hands, starling when he sees me barge my way in.

"I'm so sorry, Wyatt. I got caught up with the guys and my phone was on silent."

He smiles as I pant, trying to catch my breath. "It's okay, Scar. We aren't in any rush."

I breathe out a sigh, thankful for his understanding in my tardiness.

"Okay, where do we start?" I ask, clapping my hands together.

Wyatt walks over to a table, grabbing a pair of earmuffs off a table and handing them to me.

"First, we are going to start with loading and unloading a gun. You need to know your way around a gun before you can shoot it."

I nod in agreement. Makes perfect sense to me.

Wyatt runs me through loading and unloading the handgun. I nod along with his teachings, playing close attention to his movements. I ask a few questions along the way. Wyatt is a good teacher. He's patient and doesn't make me feel like a complete idiot.

When it's my turn to load the gun, I fumble a little bit. The gun in my hand feels strange. I don't expect it to be as light as it is for something so powerful.

Once I've got it loaded, Wyatt asks me to unload it. I don't find it as difficult to unload which I take as a win. Sighing a breath of relief at the approving nod Wyatt gives me.

"Good job, Scar," He smiles, "Now, I want you to reload the gun but this time you are going to actually shoot it."

My eyes widen and he laughs, "Don't stress. I will be right here with you. But from what I've seen so far, you will have no issues. This is only a .22 so it doesn't have any kick. It's a really good starter gun."

I nod as I pick it back up and reload it. Wyatt hands me a

clip and shows me how to load a few bullets in before telling me to load the rest. They are a bit fidgety and we laugh as I struggle to get the first few in.

"I did the same thing the first few times I had to load clips. Mr Green made me sit in here and load and unload until I didn't fumble anymore."

I pause, looking up at Wyatt with a suspicious look. If this guy thinks I'll be sitting in here loading and unloading clips, he's got another thing coming.

He shakes his head, "Don't worry, I'm not that insane. But I do recommend coming down here as much as you can and practising loading, unloading and shooting. We have another range that Dacre will most likely take you where we handle the bigger guns. It's good to practise real life scenarios where we may end up in a gun fight and you need to access your weapon quickly to take down the enemy."

"Shit," I choke, "all of this is so far from my life back in Australia. It's hard to believe this is reality and not some kind of joke."

Wyatt chuckles as he leans against the booth of the range he has me set up in. "I sometimes feel like that too. But after your first mission out, it all very quickly becomes real. The things that we see, the things we have to do aren't for the faint hearted…" He trails off and I see the demons come to life in his eyes. I put my hand on his arm, squeezing and letting him know I'm here. He looks up, giving me a small smile as he puts his hand over mine.

"It's worth it though."

I nod, agreeing with him. Even though I haven't been exposed to the carnage yet, I know it will be.

"I think you are going to shake things up here for us, Scarlett."

I scoff, dropping my hand from his arm, "You say that like

it's a bad thing, Wyatt."

He shakes his head, "Not at all. Your Dad was the first person to make big changes around here. But under your ruling, I know that you are going to make your own. I can't wait to see what you can do."

His smile is earnest and I know just from the look he's giving me, Wyatt's got my back and I know I'll have his if and when he needs me.

"Come on, let's get you shooting targets."

Wyatt helps direct me to the target, pointing out where the safety is and asking me to flick it on and off a couple of times; enough that I'm comfortable with it. He helps position me, legs spread and braced, elbows up and my grip tight on the gun.

"Take a breath and find your mark," he says quietly in my ear. I close one of my eyes, lining up my sights on the black circle in the centre of the target.

"When you are ready, pull the trigger and let that breath you are holding out."

I move my hand to the trigger confident with myself and pull. The bang from the gun is muffled thanks to the ear muffs and I smile at myself. From this distance we can't see where I hit but I don't care. I shot the gun. I did it.

"Good job, Scar. Cock it again and let off another. If you feel confident, keep going until the clip is empty."

I feel Wyatt step away from my back. Just like before, I line up my sights directly on the black dot, suck in a breath before pulling the trigger and letting my breath go as I do.

After another shot, I feel like I go into some kind of trance. Line up my shot, breath in, trigger, breath out, reload. I repeat it over and over again until the clip is empty. I drop the clip out, putting it on the table and making sure the gun is safe before turning around and removing my ear muffs.

Wyatt is holding his phone up, smiling. I assume he's still recording so I give him a dramatic bow which he laughs at, before putting his phone back in his pocket.

"You're a natural, Scar. Let's see how well you did." Wyatt starts wheeling in the target and I clench my teeth, scrunching up my nose and preparing for the worst. What I don't expect to see is a hole completely blown through the middle of the target.

"Fuck off," I mutter, "Fuck off, there's no way I did that." I stare at the target in shock.

Wyatt chuckles and I turn to look at him, "What did I say, you're a natural. Those boys have no idea just who you are, do they?"

I laugh, "That's exactly what I plan on proving to them. I'm not some meek little princess."

Wyatt looks at me with pride as he nods. A sly look then comes over his face as he looks me up and down.

"What?" I say rolling my eyes.

"What's going on with you lot anyway? It's obvious you have Dacre, Nicky, Sonny and Pike all wrapped around your finger." I snort at hearing it out loud but Wyatt continues,

"Then there's whatever the fuck that mess is with Dawson." He waves his hands around as if describing the mess that it is, "I know you guys used to be good friends when you were younger but it seems like you spent some time together when they went on vacation."

I nod, taking a breath before I fill Wyatt in on the entire story. The facts of what I know from before, my accident which I'm sure he already knows and then when we met that night at the beach. I try not to get choked up as I explain them leaving and the months that follow. I take a breath expecting to see pity in Wyatt's eyes but instead I see fury.

"Those motherfuckers. How dare they treat you like that! And what a piss poor explanation. I know the exact situation they were talking about and, while I can sympathise with them in not wanting to see someone they care about hurt again," he shakes his head as he tries to find the words.

"I hope you plan on putting them through hell," he finally says, raising his eyebrow.

An ominous grin turns the corners of my mouth, "Oh I plan to, and I have a really good plan that semi includes you, if you are up for it?"

Wyatt laughs, nodding his head, "I think I know exactly where this is going, and I am already so down with the plan."

I hold up a hand, "But this doesn't mean that you and I are going to be a thing. I know we've been flirting a bit but," I shake my head and give him an apologetic look, unable to hide a grimace.

He laughs, "Don't worry, even if you didn't already have your hands full with five guys, I still wouldn't be interested."

I tilt my head, confused as I try to work out the meaning of his words. It eventually comes to me, my eyes widening as he nods, giving me a small smile.

"Yeah, I'm gay." He winces as he rubs a hand through his hair. "Actually, you are the only person that knows."

My mouth drops, "Oh, Wy. Thank you for trusting me."

He nods but I can see the anxiety on his face. I walk towards him wrapping my arms around him. He holds me tight in return. I eventually pull away from him but grab his hands.

"Why haven't you ever told anyone?"

He shakes his head, "I don't want them to look at me differently or think that I'm hitting on them when he are hanging out or whatever."

"Not even Rhodes? He's your best friend. He would never make you feel that way."

Wyatt blushes, turning his head slightly and I instantly connect the dots.

"Oh, you and Rhodes," I say, my brows wiggling.

"Please don't say anything." He squeezes my hands tighter, pleading with me, "I don't think he sees me like that, and I don't want him seeing me in a different light if he doesn't feel the same way."

I nod, "Your secret is safe with me, Wy."

He nods and sighs a breath of relief, "It's just so hard. He never asks Jethro to join in when he is with another girl, he always asks me. Of course, I say yes because well…" he trails off and I nod, even though I feel ill talking about my brother's sex life. But Wyatt is trusting me with this, and I refuse to be a little bitch about it.

"Sometimes I'll catch him looking at me during the act and I'm not blind. I can see the desire in his eyes when he looks at me. But he will then shake his head and go back to fucking whoever it is."

It's my turn to squeeze Wyatts hands in mine. "It sounds like he may be a bit confused too. Let me do a little bit of digging…" Panic fills Wyatt's eyes, "Don't worry, I won't even allude to anything involving you. You are helping me out with making the guys jealous so if I can help you out with Rhodes I will." I smile at him, "I also kind of love the idea of having you as a brother-in-law."

Wyatt laughs as he pulls me into his chest, "Thank you, Scarlett. You have no idea what this means to me. Just having you here to talk to. You may already be well on your way to best friend territory."

"Oh, those are fighting words, Wy. Don't let Noah hear you say that. He would be on the next plane over."

Wyatt raises his eyebrow.

"Gay?" he questions, and I laugh.

"Oh no, that boy is as straight as a pole unfortunately."

We both laugh as I start loading another clip and Wyatt hangs up another target sheet.

BOARDING P
NAME: SCARLETT SMIT
FROM:
TIME:
CLAS
SEAT:
President

chapter
THIRTY-SEVEN

scarlett

Monday seems to come quicker than it normally does. Due to the earlier change in the week my training sessions with Wyatt and Sonny were swapped.

What I didn't expect was to be woken up on what I thought was going to be the day I finally got to sleep in. Yet, Sonny's tongue had other ideas.

I can't say it was the worst thing in the world being woken up to an earth-shattering orgasm. It certainly made our training session running through the clubs laws and policies much more tolerable.

It was also different seeing the club version of Sonny. It was like once he crawled out from under my blankets as I caught my breath, it was all business from then on out.

I sigh as I read the text from Rhodes reminding me that we have training again this afternoon. By the stupid emojis that follow, I know he's not going to take it easy on me. A part of me appreciates it but the other half would gladly punch his annoying ass face in.

I walk in the kitchen to find both Mum and Dad sitting at the table eating breakfast.

"Morning," I mumble as I fix myself a cup of coffee, needing the fix like the addict I am.

"Morning, how did you sleep?" Mum asks, taking a sip of her own coffee.

I groan, "Ugh, like shit. I feel like my brain is being filled with information and I can't quite keep up."

My father hops up from the table, placing his plate and mug in the sink, "I know this period is hard for you Scar, but we need to prepare you. Things are starting to ramp up around here and I want you prepared for what's to come."

I nod, understanding, "I know. I'm trying and I really am."

He smiles, "The boys have all given me really good reports back from your training sessions."

I raise my eyebrow at him.

"They've been reporting back to me about your progress. Don't worry, there's nothing sinister going on. I just want to keep tabs on your training. Make sure that the men I have organised to stand by your side are the right fit. I don't want you taking over and not having the backing of people that are on your side." He shakes his head as the president comes to the forefront for a moment, "I won't throw you to the wolves."

I smile up at him and nod, "Thanks, Dad."

It feels strange to call him Dad but what else am I meant to call the man in front of me? Calling him Ren just seems wrong. Because no matter how I feel in regards to my situation, they made a choice that they thought was best for me at that moment. How can I condemn them for protecting me? Parents don't always get everything right but at least they tried. From moment one, I have seen nothing but love from the man. These past weeks he has done nothing but try to atone for his mistakes, taking the load off Mum completely and allowing himself to take the blame. It's admirable.

He calms down enough that he smiles in return, "It doesn't feel real hearing you say that to me again."

Mum interrupts us and I'm thankful as I feel tears start to well in my eyes, "Before we are all reduced to tears, your father and I have a little surprise for you." She grabs my hand and drags me towards the garage.

"Your father and I didn't want to have to make you rely on your brother or one of the other boys to get you around so we thought that this might suffice for now."

My eyes widen as I stumble towards the bike sitting in the empty spot in the garage. A Yamaha YZ450F sits in all of its glory. My mouth drops as I run a hand over the fresh wrap.

"We got it completely blacked out for you. The blue stood out way too much but I think the silver detailing around the branding gives it that bit of hit it needed."

I nod, vaguely listening to Dad as he talks about the bike.

"Do you like it?" Mum asks, a hopeful sound in her voice. A similar one to the one she had when she brought me my jeep.

"I fucking love it!" I squeal as I jump into my father's arms. He lets me go and I rush over to Mum and engulf her in a tight hug. "Thank you so much!"

"We knew that you have had your eyes on a new bike for a long time. Those old bangers you used to have did the job but this one will really keep you on your toes." Dad boasts and I can instantly see where I get my love for bikes from.

It is certainly hereditary.

Mum walks over, interrupting our discussion and trusts a black helmet into my hands.

"Don't forget your helmet," she smiles before handing me

my bag I must have dropped in my excitement.

"Have a good day at school," Dad says, grinning as I slide my helmet on and throw my leg over the bike.

"Please be safe on that thing," Mum says, a worried look on her face, the same one she wears everytime I go for a ride. I give her a nod and a thumbs up. She doesn't seem convinced, especially not as I start the bike, a small squeal escaping my lips as it roars to life. I kick up the stand and give a few revs of the bike before taking off down the driveway, barely slowing the bike for the front gates to open.

I gun it down the street, laughing to myself at the feeling of being on the back of a bike again. The only thing missing is sand under my tires and I would feel at home again.

Homesickness clenches my stomach. While I have been surprisingly happy here, there is never anywhere like home and Australia will always be that for me, home.

I pull into the school parking lot and immediately all eyes are on me. I smile beneath my helmet, pulling up next to the guy's bikes. Rhodes, Wyatt and Jethro are standing with my guys as well.

Rhodes walks over to me smiling as I pull off my helmet and set it on the handlebars.

"It's no Harley but it'll do," he laughs.

"Don't go trying to throw a showdown, Rhodes. You don't want to lose to your big sister do you?"

He shakes his head as I swing off my new bike, quickly fixing my skirt.

I turn, surprised as I see Dacre walking over from where he and the guys just pulled up on their bikes.

"Damn, Star. That bike is insane!"

I smile as he kneels down, checking it over and I can't help but smile. Arms snake around my middle and I giggle as a chin rests on my shoulder.

"The rider is pretty insane too," Pike whispers in my ear before kissing me on the cheek. "Morning, Princess."

"Morning, Pike." I turn my head before capturing his lips in my own. Before pulling away from him, my teeth lightly graze his lip, biting down for a moment before I let it go.

His eyes darken as he licks over the small drop of blood left behind, "Don't throw down a challenge with me either, sweetheart. You know I don't care where we are. I'll have you bent over that bike with my cock jammed deep in your pussy before you know it."

My thighs clench and my panties dampen. I bite my lip as I turn to Pike fully. "I don't think I'd be opposed to that, not one bit."

Pike groans, grabbing my ass in his hands.

"Yuck, get a fucking room you two," Rhodes says, knocking Pike out of my hold who glares daggers at him. "I don't feel like seeing my sister being mauled by one of her boyfriends this early in the morning." He grunts as he turns to look at me.

"Please keep that in mind when you have one of your followers with their tongue down your throat," I say, aiming him with a knowing smirk.

Jethro and Wyatt both laugh as Wyatt swings an arm around Rhodes' neck, "She does have a point bro."

Rhodes snorts, "Don't deny it, you love it."

I see the panic in Wyatt's eyes as he turns to me, pleading with me.

"You are both disgusting," I groan, banging my hip into my brothers.

grunt as I nearly fall off my bike. I knew Rhodes was going to be a tough teacher but he really put me through my paces this afternoon.

I grip my aching calves as I hear laughter from behind me.

"Fuck you, Rhodes."

"I told you I wasn't going to take it easy on you." He reminds me and I groan, feeling the bruises that are slowly starting to form on my body from his beat down.

"And I appreciate that but damn, you could have eased up a little bit."

Rhodes comes up beside me, allowing me to throw and arm around his shoulder, helping me to limp my way inside.

"The enemy won't go easy on you, Scar. I know I was brutal but you need to see how it will really be. They won't care that you're female."

I sigh, knowing he's right.

"I know. I'll be ready for it when the time comes," I say as we get inside. I drop my arm from his shoulder and brace myself on the wall instead.

"You will be," Rhodes says with a strange look on his face. It kind of looks like a mixture of worry and something else but in my beat up state, the thought of trying to examine emotions feels way too intense. A headache is already setting in and I don't need to add to it by overthinking. A sport I am all too familiar with.

I push myself away from the wall, wincing as something in my hip twinges, "If you need me, I will be face down in a bath of epsom salts."

Rhodes chuckles, "Please don't drown. I kind of like having you on the right side of living."

"Maybe next time don't beat me to a pulp and I won't be threatened with the grim reaper so soon," I snide, earning me a sullen look.

"Not funny, Scarlett," Rhodes grunts and he turns, storming away to sulk. I chuckle at my joke, but wince as I take a step. What did I say about payback again?

BOARDING P
NAME: SCARLETT SMIT
FROM:
TIME:
CLA
SEAT:
President

chapter
THIRTY-EIGHT

scarlett

I feel like the only reprieve I get for the next month is the measly eight hours sleep a night my body craves.

Training is ruthless. I knew it was going to be. I had mentally prepared for it. But physically? Not one bit. I have aches in places I didn't know could ache. seem to spot a new bruise each time I get into the shower. Epsom salt baths have become my new best friend.

Sonny offered a relaxation massage which ended in him trying to use his dick as the device which I promptly told him to go fuck himself.

But I force myself through the trainings. Sparring with Rhodes, Dawson, Nicky and Jethro. The latter who has seemed to warm up to me, even if it is only slightly.

Memorising policies, procedures, accounts and a range of businesses that I'm slowly starting to understand.

And slowly becoming more and more confident in weapons.

Wyatt and Dacre have been the most patient teachers. It's

either that they aren't willing to correct me or it's that they see the potential in me. The fact that it feels like a second nature to me now and that I only really need them when it comes to asking certain questions about calibres and when I can step up to the next size gives me that confidence that maybe it is just me getting that good.

What I didn't expect was the hours after my training with the guys where Dad would pull me into his office and show me the daily operations and the organisation that goes into setting up the ground teams that go into the rings. Ensuring the running of our more legitimate businesses, something Rafe and Valen run the majority of. There's also the not so legitimate businesses which Butch runs. Something Dad leaves entirely up to him, only checking in when he needs to. I nod my head taking note of each directive.

I find myself regularly rubbing my temples to relieve aches and popping an obscene amount of pain medication.

All of the club training sees me falling slightly behind in my school work but I can't find the will to care. It currently feels like attending school is just all for show. Some kind of façade to put on for the civilians in Rydell so they don't expect anything sinister is going on underneath it all.

I know they aren't that stupid though.

Just by the looks some of the kids at school give me know where I stand versus where they do. They give us a kind of respect in the hallways. Never ones to start any drama.

No, the dramatics are saved for Coco and her bandwagon of club whores; a name I despised at first but at this point, I couldn't care less.

It's clear that she's pissed off that Dawson has pushed her to the side.

If I had a dollar for every time she has called me a greedy slut these past weeks, I'd be able to buy myself a new bike.

I don't let her words affect me. Instead, I let them roll off me like the utter bullshit it is. There's no point in letting her piss me off. I've got enough to worry about than some desperate groupie trying to fuck with my head.

Dawson and I know where we stand. While he has faded to the back a little bit, still unsure with everything, he's no longer hurling insults or telling me to leave.

Instead, I savour the moments he graces me with little smirks of his. Slight touches during sparring sessions that leave me hot and heavy when he finally calls time.

But not once has he acted on any of the touches.

He's not oblivious to the way he affects me either.

But he seems insistent on teasing me. So, I have been feeding it right back to him. Scrunch bum bike shorts and crop top bras have been my best friend during our training sessions.

Wyatt gave me a confused look when he joined Dacre and I for our training session on Wednesday, but I just winked at him.

It seemed Dawson isn't the only one not touching me at the moment.

Since Sonny's wake up call and my heated kiss with Pike in the parking lot, it's been teasing but limited touches.

I've had to put my satisfyer on charge daily. I swear the poor thing is going to have to be replaced at this rate if one of those motherfuckers doesn't hurry up and fuck me.

Pike messages me and reschedules our training session for Saturday so both him and Sonny can sit down and go through some documents with me.

I don't mind though. Not only do I get reprieve for one

day but I finally get to hear the guys play.

Memories of Dawson singing while we were on our way to the airport still ring in my ears and the anticipation at hearing them all together has me giddy.

"Girl, you need to slow down. Pinks' isn't going anywhere and you are giving me anxiety with how fast you are pressing that blender into your face. I don't think your poor body could take any more of a beating." Brandy looks at me horrified as I pull the sponge away from my face.

"Yeah, but her pussy still can," Maxie mumbles. I choke on my own spit as Rippy, Jen, Maxie and Brandy all descend into laughter.

"Your poor kitty must be sore having to deal with those five boys," Jen says.

I roll my eyes as I finish blending my foundation before adding some contour, "my kitty hasn't had any beatings in over a week and she is hungry for some man meat."

I can't help but laugh at her honesty, having come to love it as we have all gotten to know each other more.

But in all seriousness, these boys need to get their shit together. We all giggle as we finish our make-up, and throw compliments as we talk through outfits.

"You can never go wrong with a little black dress," Brandy hands me a sequined number she brought over.

I hold it up and nod immediately, knowing it's exactly what I'm going to wear. Brandy, Jen and Rippy are already dressed, sitting on the bed waiting for both Maxie and I who have been having a wardrobe crisis. Maxie finally settled on a tight fitted white mini dress with cut outs at her ribs showing off her torso tattoos.

Maxie throws her bra off without a care in the world.

"Damn girl, you have your nipples pierced?" I say in surprise, seeing the bars glistening in the light.

She turns to me fully, popping out her chest slightly to show them off. "Yeah, we all got them done. Kind of like our own little initiation into Pinks'." A cheeky smile is aimed my way and I can already tell the direction of her thoughts.

"It's time for you to join the club," Rippy smiles, nudging Brandy who smiles and pulls a kit out of her bag.

I look at Brandy in horror, "Are you qualified to do that?"

She waves me off as she starts setting her supplies up, wiping down everything with an alcoholic wipe. A needle is pulled out of a plastic wrap.

"Come on babes, titties out and let Mumma get started," Brandy says as Jen pulls out a seat for me.

"I swear if you disfigure my body Brandy, I will murder you."

"Don't worry, I've done this heaps of times. I've got my certificate and everything," she says as I'm forced to sit down in the chair. I look over at Maxie who has pulled her dress on and nods at me.

"She did mine and I can promise you, she's a pro."

I nod my head as I take my bra off, leaving me only in a small thong.

Brandy grabs an alcohol wipe and thoroughly cleans down my nipples. It feels weird having someone other than the boys touching me but with the threat of a needle, I can't think of much else.

Once Brandy is done prepping me, she puts dots where she wants the piercing to go before using a clamp to hold my nipple in place. I curse as I grip the arms of the chair.

"You'll be okay. Just take a deep breath and on the count of three I'll do it." Brandy reassures me as she kneels down. Her gloved hands grab my nipple as she lines up the needle with the dot she drew on me.

"Okay ready. One…"

"AH FUCK! You said 'on three', you bitch!" I yell at the pain in my nipple. I knew nipple piercings would hurt but I didn't expect the tugging sensation. I don't know what hurt more. The initial sting or that pulling feeling as the needle pushed through my flesh.

I feel another pulling sensation and I grit my teeth.

"There, all done. Time for the next one."

"Yeah nah, that's not happening," I shake my head as I stand up, grabbing my dress and pulling it on. I lift the dress up over my tits and hiss at the sharp pain of the fabric against the fresh piercing.

"Fucking hell," I grit my teeth as I slowly fix my dress to my body. Cursing myself for now being resigned to wear something so tight.

"Aw toughen up, Australia." Rippy slaps my shoulder, "You are one of us now. Officially one of Pinks' Ladies."

I can't help but grin as the girls cheer around me, hooting and celebrating, helping me to feel just that little bit more at home.

***

Pinks' is almost shoulder to shoulder when we walk in. It seems to be the hang out place for the entire club even though the clubhouse has a pretty decent bar. Rippy leads us through the crowd before getting frustrated and pulling me to the front.

"Make way for the baby Pres!" she yells at the top of her voice. It seems to do the trick though as the crowd makes way enough for us to find Rhodes, Wyatt and Jethro.

The three of them are sitting at one of the couches surrounding the main stage where one of the girls is currently spinning on the pole.

I pull out a fifty from in between my tits, being careful of my new piercing. I walk up to the stage, waving the note at her. She gracefully slides down the pole before crawling to me. Her bra is already off so I slide my hands down her naked body, tucking the note into the garter around her thigh. She kisses me on the lips making me chuckle.

"Thanks, Scar baby."

"No worries at all, Pix. You look incredible up there."

I met Pix during one of the many late-night rehearsals leading up to my initiation a few weeks ago. If it wasn't for her, I would have looked like a complete novice on the pole.

I hear a grunt and turn to see my five guys staring at Pix and I. Backing away from the stage slowly, I give them a little wave before walking over to the couch where the girls are already sitting with my brother.

Wyatts eyes brighten when he sees me, "Fucking hell, Scar. You look incredible."

"Thanks baby," I giggle, kissing his cheek. I squeal as Wyatt pulls me into his lap, turning to look at him as he gives me a kiss on the shoulder. I turn my head, giving a small quirk of my brow at his boldness. His eyes flick to the right and as discreetly as I can, I follow their direction.

A girl I didn't see on my way over is currently grinding on my brother in the middle of the club. I turn up my nose at the sight.

"Yuck, Rhodes." I yell over the music, kicking his leg to get my attention. He pauses his make out session to look over at me. "It's family night, get her the fuck out."

Rhodes turns to the girl who is now frowning at me.

"You heard her, off you go," he says, pushing the girl off his lap.

"Fucking whore," the girl mutters as she turns her back. I stiffen instantly, pulling myself off Wyatt's lap and grabbing the girl's shoulder and spinning her around.

"I suggest you watch who the fuck you are talking to, pet. You wouldn't want to piss off the wrong whore in this club," I sneer, keeping my voice low as I get right in her face.

She rolls her eyes, seemingly oblivious to the danger staring her down. "You already have Wyatt. There's no need to be greedy and demand Rhodes to."

I gag, "Yuck cunt. Rhodes is my brother you toad."

Her face drops completely as the dots start connecting in her mind.

"Scarlett, I… I… I didn't… I…" she stutters and I shake my head.

"Be a good little groupie and go fetch us a round of drinks will you," I say in the sweetest voice I can muster.

She immediately turns tail and pushes her way towards the bar.

I turn back just as the entire group erupts into laughter.

"Holy shit, did you see her face?" Jen laughs, smacking her leg.

"Now that's more like it, Australia," Rippy says, holding up her hand for me to high five. I do so, chuckling.

"She just needed to be taught a lesson," I shrug as I sit back down in Wyatt's lap who is still laughing.

"I knew there was a bad bitch down inside of you. Just didn't know it took a nipple piercing to bring her out of her cage," Maxie chuckles as she grabs a drink off the table and throws it back.

Rhodes looks at me in shock, "Don't tell me you did," he pleads. I wince in response, and he shakes his head.

"I think I need to go bleach my fucking brain. That and five fucking tequila shots."

He says, launching up out of his seat, Jethro following close behind.

It doesn't take long before the lights darken and hoots and hollers of the crowd deafen us. The strum of the guitar sounds out over the speakers and the girls scream as the stage lights up. My mouth drops as I take in my guys.

Dawson stands front and centre holding a microphone and its stand, a small smile on his lips as he looks out over the crowd.

Pike, Nicky and Sonny all stand behind Dawson holding their respective guitars.

My eyes find Dacre and I bite my lip. Sitting behind his drum set, his eyes are already on me. His shirt has its sleeves completely cut off, showing off his muscles as they tense getting ready for the song to start. Sonny walks behind a piano and the intro music of *Heathens by Twenty One Pilots* sounds out over the speakers.

I smile as I stand up, grabbing Wyatt and Brandy's hand and lead us straight to the dance floor.

I spend the entire song dancing and singing along to the lyrics, laughing at the ridiculous dance moves we pull out.

This song couldn't be any more appropriate for us.

I feel free as I jump around with my new friends. Once the song fades out, we yell and cheer for the boys.

One song fades into the other as Brandy, Maxie, Jen, Wyatt and I make the dance floor ours. We spin around, jumping, screaming the lyrics of the songs at each other.

I can't hold my laughter in as Wyatt pulls out an air guitar during one of the guitar solos. He does quite an impressive impersonation I must say.

We clap as the song ends before turning towards the stage.

"I hope you don't mind if we get a little bit hot in here with this next one," Dawson says into the microphone, making all the girls scream. My core clenches at the innuendo in his voice as he looks right at me.

Nicky steps up to the front of the stage, plucking the strings of the guitar. It takes me a moment to catch onto what song they are going to play but when I do, I smile before backing up into a hard body. I already know it's Wyatt just by the feel of his hands.

"She said "He's so sweet, I wanna lick the wrapper." Dawson sings low into the microphone.

I grind back into Wyatt's body, running my hands up my body.

We jump around during the chorus but slow it down during the verses, grinding our bodies together. Wyatt grips my waist tight, bringing his face close to mine.

"Those boys are going to fucking murder me."

I turn my back on Wyatt, still moving my body as I look up at each of the boys. Dawson looks ready to storm off the stage, rage fuelling his body. Pike, Nicky and Sonny are standing stock still watching me as they play but it's impossible for them to hide the heat that escapes through the rage. I chuckle to myself as the song starts to fade.

"Won't you get on your knees?" Dawson whispers into the microphone. I hold his eye, winking at the exact moment he sings the last word.

He stiffens as his eyes heat.

The entire club cheers and claps as their set ends. I turn whispering to the girls that I need to pee. They nod their heads as they head back to the couch. I grab Wyatt before he leaves, kissing his cheek.

"Thank you," I whisper in his ear.

He chuckles, "You better visit my grave site every day. I expect fresh flowers."

BOARDING PASS
NAME: SCARLETT SMITH
FROM:
TIME:
CLASS:
SEAT:
President

chapter
THIRTY-NINE

My eyes didn't leave Scarlett once during our entire set. Not only because of how delectable she looked as she swayed to our music but because my eyes couldn't leave each place that cunt, Wyatt, held her.

I've never felt such intense, burning jealousy like that before. I know she said she was going to put us through our paces, but I didn't expect this.

Seeing Scarlett with Dacre, Sonny, Nicky and Dawson doesn't bother me. I don't get jealous. It's more of a FOMO kind of feeling. But seeing the way she danced and laughed with him set me on a whole other level of feeling.

She is fucking mine.

Once the final note rings out on my guitar, I throw it into the stand and march down the stairs to find my girl.

The crowd is thick and tries to pull me in different directions. It seems like every soul in this goddamn room wants a piece of me but the only one that can get that is

Scarlett. And I still can't find her.

I push through the bodies until I get to the couch I first saw her sitting at while we were setting up. Rippy, Brandy, Jen and Maxie are all sitting around chatting but pause when they see me.

"Scarlett." Is all I say. My fury won't allow me anything else.

Brandy smiles as she points towards the back of the room. "She said she was going to the bathroom."

I turn around and push my way back through the crowd. The bodies must realise I mean business as they slowly start parting for me, allowing for clear passage to the bathrooms.

The door to the female bathroom swings open and Scarlett walks out laughing at something one of the dancers, Pix I think, says to her. My eyes lock in on where Pix's hand caresses Scarlett's shoulder. The way Scarlett's head throws back as she laughs again, and the way Pix looks down at her in awe.

Yeah, no. This isn't fucking happening. Not today, Satan.

I return my brisk pace, making a beeline in their direction. The girls pause as I take my final step in front of them blocking them from going any further.

"Pix," I growl, looking at the woman who now has her arm around my girl.

"Pike," she returns, her voice low and sultry but it doesn't affect me. Nor has it ever.

"She's mine, Pix."

Pix just laughs as she twirls a strand of Scarlett's blonde hair around her finger. Scarlett chuckles as she looks in between us both.

"I don't see a ring on her finger, Pike."

I chuckle as I cross my arms over my chest, "It wont stay like that for long."

Both Scarlett and Pix are stunned at my words which gives me an opening to steal my girl back from the vultures who keep trying to take her from me.

I grab her arm, pulling her into my chest. Her body instantly moulds to mine, just like it always does whenever I hold her close. I bend down bringing my mouth close to her ear, sniggering as I feel her shiver under my touch.

"You think you can spend all night teasing me with another guy and expect me not to react?" My chuckle is low, eliciting another shiver from her.

"That's not how this game works Princess. You are mine. No other man apart from the five of us is allowed to touch you. Do you understand?"

Scarlett nods but I shake my head.

"Words, Princess."

"Yes Pike, I understand."

"Good girl," I mutter as I slowly move her around to face me. I tilt her chin up as I smile down with her. It's not the kind smile she was expecting.

The Pike that kneels at her every will is gone.

The face she is greeted with is fuelled by malice.

"But you've been a bad girl tonight. Do you know what bad girls get, Scarlett?"

She shakes her head and whispers, "No."

"They get punished."

I bend down, throwing Scarlett over my shoulder. I chuckle as she squeals. Her punches to my back and ass fuel the need inside me to see her punished.

I turn back to Pix as Scarlett keeps up her ire, doing her best to dislodge herself from my hold.

"Good seeing you, Pix."

I turn down hallway after hallway, finally coming to the back of Pinks', a place I know not many people frequent, especially not when they are as busy as they are tonight. I place Scarlett down and immediately push her up against the wall.

"Keep fighting me, Scarlett. It'll only make your punishment that more delicious."

Scarlett sneers at me as she crosses her arms over her chest.

I throw my head back and laugh, "Ah so we've decided to be a brat tonight have we?"

She sticks her tongue out at me in answer.

"On your knees now."

She shakes her head.

I slam my hand into the wall beside her, delight filling my chest as she flinches.

"You want to stick that tongue out at me, I suggest you get down on your knees and put it to good use."

Scarlett's eyes heat but I still see the defiant little brat holding strong. I press a hand down on her head and push down so she is forced to her knees. She eventually understands that I won't relent, eventually falling the rest of the way.

She sits on her heels in front of me, looking up with those beautiful blue eyes of hers that have captured my soul.

"See, what a good girl. You look so fucking pretty on your knees in front of me. I wonder just what you will look like with my cock down your throat as you choke on it."

The heat in Scarlett's eyes flare as she looks down, coming face to face with my cock that's painfully trapped behind my zipper.

Like the desperate little slut I know she is deep down, she unclips my belt, letting the ends hang open as she slowly unclips the button of my jeans and pulls down my fly.

She's slow to pull out my cock but the relief I feel is immense as she finally releases it.

She doesn't waste a moment longer, taking pity on me as

she licks up the underside of my cock.

I groan as she travels back up, taking her time tasting each inch before she takes me fully into her mouth as deep as she can before gagging around me. She pulls back slowly, saliva covering my cock before she sucks me down again.

Just like I thought, she looks like a goddess. Even though she is the one on her knees, she still holds all the cards.

I feel my orgasm start to build up as she fastens up her speed.

Just as I'm about to cum, the sound of a gun firing jolts me.

Scarlett's lips pop off my dick as we both look in the direction of the noise.

POP.

Another shot goes off and I quickly tuck my cock back into my boxers, buttoning my jeans in haste.

"Fuck, fuck," I say, grabbing the 9mm tucked in the back of my jeans.

Scarlett stands up, grabbing my shirt.

"Pike, what's going on?"

I shake my head as I check to make sure my gun is loaded, turning off the safety as I point it towards the empty hallway.

"Do you have your gun on you?" I ask, turning my head for a moment as I look at her. She shakes her head no, eyes wide as she curses.

"My thoughts exactly. Stay behind me. If I tell you to run Scarlett, you get the fuck out of here do you understand."

She starts shaking her head, "No, there's no way I'm leaving you."

"I need you to listen to me on this one occasion, Princess. Please." I beg her, gripping the side of her face in my hand, my eyes pleading with her. While I love her defiance and ability to push back at us, I can't have it in this situation. Not when I don't know what we are about to walk into.

She eventually nods. Even though I prefer her words, the nod is enough for now.

I pull her behind me, making her grip the back of my shirt as we slowly make our way back to the main room of the club. The hallways are all completely empty but the closer we get to the main room, the louder the yelling gets from whoever decided to fuck around and find out.

I push one of the doors leading back into the room open slightly. Ren, Grant, Butch, Rafe, Rick and Valen all stand in a defensive line, guns pointed at five men in cuts. It's hard to see them properly through the small gap in the door so I instead look around the room trying to find the boys.

Rhodes, Jethro and Wyatt are kneeling behind a table turned on its side, weapons drawn over the top.

Dacre and Sonny are crouched half behind the side of the stage with their weapons drawn too. A body lies beneath them and I watch as Dacre tries to stop one of the prospects from bleeding out. From the pool of blood underneath him, it doesn't look like he's going to make it.

Dawson and Nicky are crouched not too far from them, covering for two half naked girls currently clinging to each other.

I watch as they talk amongst themselves for a moment. Nicky looks up right in my direction. His eyes are wide as he mouths, *'Scarlett.'*

I nod and watch as he sighs a breath of relief, confirming to Dawson who looks at me and nods.

"Clinton, it was a mistake for you to turn up here tonight." Ren's voice a deep rumble as he addresses one of the men in front of him.

The man laughs and I try to adjust myself to try and catch a glimpse of him but startle when a hand lands on my shoulder, moving up to squeeze my neck tight.

I slowly move the gun into Scarlett's hand as the person leans down behind me.

"What do we have here? Two little peeping Toms?" He sounds deranged as he chuckles, before he kicks the door in causing every single gun, not trained on the men in front of our fathers, to turn to us.

"Look what I found, boss. A pretty little sparrow and its protector."

Fuck.

BOARDING P.
NAME: SCARLETT SMIT
FROM:
TIME:
CLAS
SEAT:
President

chapter
FORTY

scarlett

I jump as the hand lands on my shoulder. I should have known not to turn my back on an empty hallway, but like the dumb girl in a horror movie, I did. Now the villain is right behind us and has both Pike and I are completely at his mercy. We are fucked.

I move the gun Pike handed me in between my legs praying that I can keep it wedged between my thighs.

I don't let myself focus on the way the gun rubs against my already worked up core. These assholes better have a good excuse for their interruption. Lady blue balls certainly weren't what I had in mind when Pike pulled me down that empty hallway.

A lump sits in my throat as I take in the scene around me. I spot Dawson and Nicky protecting two of the girls who are holding each other and weeping quietly. I see the fear in their eyes and anger boils inside of me. Knowing bits of what some of these girls have been through has me gritting my teeth.

They were promised freedom when we saved them. Protection. Not this chicken shit bullshit.

I stumble as we are brought to the centre of the stand off.

I lock eyes with Dad.

He's putting a damn good bravado of being cool, calm and collected but his eyes betray him.

I give him a slight nod to let him know that I'm okay, even if there is a small part of me that is freaking out. What I've learnt these past weeks in my training goes through my head like a rerun.

Locate your exits. Done.

Does the enemy have weapons? Yes. A fuck ton of them based on the ones I can see.

How many of them are there? Six including the Jack Sparrow wannabe that shoves us into position before walking around us and chuckling. He's really rolling with the pirate core aesthetic, sporting an eye patch over his left eye. It does sweet fuck all to hide the rest of the scaring on his hideous face. All he's missing is a wooden leg and a parrot on his shoulder. But judging by the limp he has, maybe he does have a wooden leg after all.

I try to hide a snort but fail, gritting my teeth as the five men turn to look at me.

"Got something to say girl?"

I jolt as I take in the man in front of me. I try to keep surprise off my face but I know I fail.

The carbon copy of Dad stands opposite him. My gaze darts between the two men.

There's no way.

"I can see you see the family resemblance between your President and I," he chuckles before pausing, holding up a finger, "or should I say your false president. A poser if you will. A man sitting on a stolen throne."

Dad snorts, "My position has always been mine Clinton, you and I both know that. Father even dismissed your attempts to claim it from me."

Clinton grunts, "That old bastard always saw something in you. I imagine he would be rolling in his grave if he knew just how far the Thunderbirds have fallen from his time."

Dad chuckles, "Fallen is certainly an interesting word to describe the current state of my club, Clinton." A menacing look comes over his face as he tips his head to the side. "We've certainly been making things difficult for you haven't we? Seen a drop in sales recently?"

Clinton clicks his tongue, "You have been pesky that's for sure, brother. But there are many things even the great Ren Crux still doesn't know."

"Oh, do share Clinton. It's not like you to not boast about your crimes," Dad says, spreading his arms wide, like he's giving him the floor.

My uncle takes a step forward and I stiffen as each gun trains in on him tighter. He just chuckles seemingly unfazed by it all. Maybe he is. There's a gleam in his eye. A psychotic one that tells me he doesn't have a conscience anymore.

"You have a traitor in your club," Clinton's smile widens as Dad and the guy's fathers each stiffen. I feel Pike harden beside me and I will myself not to clutch onto him like I'm desperate to.

Clinton slowly starts to laugh, the sound echoed by his minions that stand behind him.

"That's exactly how I know that my darling niece wasn't killed that fateful day." My spine snaps straight as Pike immediately tries moving me behind his back in an attempt to protect me. I catch Rhodes out of the corner of my eye standing, as he slowly makes his way over to the group. His weapon remains tight on our uncle.

Clinton's eyes light up as he spots Rhodes, "Ah, nephew. It truly is a family reunion.

"Tell me boy, how do you feel about your once presumed dead sister taking back the role that has been yours these past however many years?"

Rhodes chuckles, shaking his head as he comes to stand next to Pike and I.

"Good try, Clinton. You think that I'm threatened by my sister taking back what is rightfully hers? I'm not like you. It's an honour to stand by my sister's side."

My heart soars at Rhodes' declaration. I'm not going to lie in saying that I didn't have worries that he held resentment towards me for coming back and taking what he has worked so hard towards. I turn to look at him and find his eyes already on me. He gives me a small nod, one I return.

He's got my back and I've got his. Just like we always should have.

"Fool!" Clinton's voice booms as he looks at the both of us in disgust. "You have ruined your son, Ren! Filling his head with the ideology that women are good for anything more than the hole between their legs."

"Don't forget the other two holes, boss." One of Clinton's lackey's shouts, causing the six men to holler.

I curl my lip in disgust. Forcing myself out of Pike's grip, I grab the gun still wedged between my thighs pulling it out and aiming it right at Clinton.

"See that's where you have fallen short in your belief on the values of a woman. Not only are we fucking incredible in bed, we can also spot a man with an ego large enough to compensate for his small cock."

I hear a few of our men snort and I can't keep the satisfaction off my face as the expression on Clinton's drops.

I take a few steps towards the centre of the stand off,

ignoring the curses and mutters from behind me.

"See Uncle Clint, women are so much stronger than men will ever be. It would be wise if you took a few lessons from your betters," I smile maliciously.

Clinton chuckles, "You have such vicious words for a meek little thing, niece. It reminds me of those few days you spent with me all those years ago."

I stiffen but keep my gun trained on him. It takes all of my strength not to shake under his glare as his eyes look over my body. My stomach curls at the look in his eyes, at the way he looks at me and not in a way an uncle should ever look at their niece.

"You've certainly grown into a beautiful young woman. When you are mine again, I'll have to make sure I keep that mouth full."

The room erupts in curses and shouts but I don't move a single muscle as I keep the centre of Clinton's chest locked in my sight. I know it would all be over with the pull of the trigger.

It doesn't take a genius to connect the dots to know that this is the man that stole my life from me. The man who broke up my family. Who stole my memories. Who broke my boys.

Not again.

My finger slips down to the trigger but Clinton catches the movement.

"Ah ah, darling niece. I wouldn't do that if I was you." He shakes his head, clicking his tongue. Patronising me like a young child.

"Give me one reason not to put a bullet in your skull right now. You took everything from me. It's only fair that I do the same to you," I say as I run my finger over the side of the trigger.

Clinton laughs, "Not when a bullet is already destined for your boy."

My gaze snaps to one of the guys behind Clinton, his gun aimed at Pike.

It feels like my entire world slows down as my hands drop, the gun that was once in my hand falling to the ground. I watch as the man's finger caresses the trigger, shouting as dread overcomes me.

Just as he pulls the trigger, I jump in front of Pike just as the second bullet fires, screaming as I feel both bits of lead tear into my flesh.

All I feel is pain.

The world around me buzzes as I slowly start falling to the ground. More gun shots and yelling sound off around me but I can't give it the attention.

All I feel is the two wounds as pain travels through my body.

Arms capture me before I hit the ground. They cradle me to their chest as I'm slowly brought to the ground. I scream as I feel pressure on my thigh.

"Scarlett, baby. Please stop squirming, I need to stop the bleeding." A voice breaks through the ringing but I can't place it.

"Star. Star. No. No. Not again." A voice panics as I hear a body dropping down beside me. A hand tries to grip the one hand not against the body holding me but pain shoots up my arm, making me scream out.

"Fuck, she took two bullets." One of the voices yells.

Someone else applies pressure to the bullet hole in my arm and I cry out again.

"Fucking cunt," I yell as my world slowly comes back into focus.

Sonny is leaning over me, his face drained of colour but he

attempts to smile as I look back at him. "There's my girl. You stay awake for us okay, *mi alma.*"

I grit my teeth as the pressure on my leg gets tighter, "Fuck you, Sonny."

He chuckles darkly, "That's it baby, keep swearing at me." He looks down at my body, his face blanching as he looks at someone in front of me. "Have any of you *bastardos* called the fucking doc yet?"

Someone mutters beside me but I don't hear what they are saying as my hearing and vision start to buzz again.

"Fuck! She is losing way too much blood!"

"Scarlett." A quiet voice begs from above me, I groan as I blink a few times, willing my vision to clear again.

Dacre has taken Sonny's spot as he looks down at me.

"Hey, sweet boy," I moan as another shockwave of pain travels through my body.

"Star, you keep your eyes open and focused on me okay?" he pleads with me. I try to nod but the movement causes me to cry out again.

"It's okay, baby. You just stay still. Let Dawson and Nicky staunch that bleeding until the doctor gets here okay."

"Okay," I whisper.

I hear the boys sigh in relief as I stop struggling and allow them to hold pressure to the bullet holes.

Tears stream down Dacre's face as he looks down at my body.

"Sweet boy," I mumble, immediately getting his attention. He looks down at me and one of his tears drops to my face, mixing with the tears streaming down my own.

"I love you, Dacre."

He smiles, choking as more tears fall from his face.

"Of course, you would say those words in a moment like this," he chuckles through the tears.

"I had to tell you," I whisper, feeling the once unbearable pain slowly being numbed.

A cool calmness washes over me as I smile at him before looking at the man who is holding me.

Pike.

"I love you too, Pike." He immediately starts shaking his head no.

"No, don't you fucking dare Princess. I know what you are thinking and I refuse," he chokes, shaking his head, "Our time isn't over yet. We only just got you back and I'm not losing you."

I smile at him, before turning my head to Nicky, Dawson and Sonny who are standing over me.

Three matching ghost white faces look down at me. Panic filled in each set of eyes.

"I love you three so fucking much."

Dawson shakes his head as he pushes tighter to my wound. I wish I could say I can feel the pain but all I feel is pressure. A loan tear rolls down his cheek.

"Don't you dare go trying to utter a goodbye to us right now, Vixen. You aren't done torturing us. I know you are desperate to see me on my knees before you and we can't do that if you give up right now," he says as another tear rolls down his cheek. "Don't you dare give up." He demands of me and I hold onto his words just as everything starts to go hazy around me.

How could I not confess my deepest feelings for them? They have haunted me for almost a year now. They've been stored away until the time was right. Right now is as good a time as any.

Delirium takes over as I continue muttering confessions. I don't even know if I even make sense right now. Each word seems to slur even more. I think one of the figures hovering over me said to keep my attention on them but I can't remember.

I think I can hear shouts and cursing around me, my body jolting and the pressure on my arm lessening for a moment as the body holding me stands and begins to run. Or I think it does.

I grunt as the body launches us into what I can assume is a car.

"Go, fucking drive!" are the last words I hear as everything slowly fades out of existence and black encases my world.

AMERICA 100
AMERICA 100
TES OF AMERICA
WE TRUST
President

NEED MORE?

*Keep reading for a special bonus alternate scene
from Clinton's POV*

alternate POV

clinton

The smell of blood, piss and shit turns my nose even as I look down at the naked redhead. Her form is crouched in the corner of her cage. She trembles under my gaze, terrified of what I might do to her.

Good.

Bitches belong on their knees.

They should know their place. Men are superior after all.

I think back to when I had my little bitch of a niece and just how pretty she broke under my hand.

I don't know what the fuck my brother was thinking making her heir to his fucking circus he runs.

He had a perfectly good boy right there that was more than capable to take her place. Who cares if it wasn't him that was born first.

I'm still convinced the hospital that they were born at got it all wrong.

That young man is a Crux man after all.

Knowing that I will never have to deal with that little

skank ever again still sends an exhilarating feeling through my bones.

Knowing that my brother lost something he cared about even deeper makes it all that much better.

I kick the cage with my boot making the whore scramble back into the wire. I'm sure the metal has started to cut into her skin by now.

How dare that motherfucker ruin what my father built. We had the power right in our hands. Yet as per usual with Ren motherfucking Crux, he had to go and be the 'better' person.

It was always about doing the right thing with him. Even my father couldn't stand his above board bullshit.

He liked the dark and depraved just like I do.

It feels better cumming when the person you are fucking is terrified. Their screams make the orgasm that much better.

Add a little bit of blood to the mixture and it's better than the best drug money can buy.

Unable to hold myself back anymore, I pull the sobbing bitch from her cage. Her cries become louder and it does nothing but make my dick even harder. It sends a thrill through my body knowing that she is going to fight me.

She's new, not yet broken like some of the bitches we keep around. They still have their uses after all.

For some of my men, a hole is a hole. It's just a bonus that they have three.

I keep a firm grip on her hair, dragging her behind me as I make my way down the hallway lined with cages. I made them to resemble dog kennels.

Seems ironic that all bitches are caged the same way.

Turning a corner, I hasten my steps as anticipation thrums through me. Flinging open the door to my office, I throw the whimpering bitch to the ground.

Her form rolls until she hits the coffee table with force. She screams in pain. I feel my cock pulse at the sound.

Walking over to my bar-cart, I pour myself two fingers of whisky. Taking the first sip, I revel the burn in my throat.

Turning around, I chuckle as I watch the little cunt crawl towards the door. It's cute that she thinks she has the ability to escape my clutches.

She will die by my hands.

They all will after a while.

But I want to see her break first. I want to watch the way the fight leaves her eyes. When she has no hope left. When any thoughts she had of some knight in shining armor coming to save her finally dissipates from my mind.

When she turns into a mindless zombie.

Walking over to her, I yank her hair, delighted when she screams for me to stop.

"Please! Please let me go! I'll give you whatever you want. I promise you'll never have to see me again. I won't go to the authorities."

I tisk, "Beg all you want. You aren't leaving."

Her cries intensify as I throw her in front of my chair. I take a seat so she is crumbled right in front of me.

"Please, I have a family. They will be wondering where I am."

That really makes me laugh this time.

"Oh, you stupid girl. Your family has long forgotten about you by now. You are nothing but a dirty little whore. Why would they want you tarnishing their name?"

She finally looks up at me and holds my eye contact.

I watch as the fire among her cracking eyes slowly starts to light.

"You mother …"

I don't let her finish her sentence. Instead, I slap her across the face, delighted when she cries out.

"That's enough out of you. You are here to service me. Undo my button."

She looks back up at me, the fear back firmly in her eyes. She begins shaking her head again which earns her yet another slap, this time with a bit more force.

"Undo. My. Button. Whore." My words are said through gritted teeth. I love the defiance and I love the fight, but fuck if it doesn't get me angry when they don't want to bend.

"No …"

"NOW!"

Her hands reach up and fumble with the button of my trousers. It takes her a ridiculously long time just to get it undone.

She looks up at me once she is done as she waits for my next instructions.

"Pull my cock out and choke on it."

She gulps as she looks at me for a moment. There's a hint of hesitation before she nods.

Her full body shakes as she pulls my cock from its confines. The hard length snaps out, almost hitting her in the face.

Precum beads at the tip in anticipation.

Her hand holds me loosely as she gives me a tug.

Tisking her again, I thrust my cock up into her hand.

"Tighten your grip and use that mouth. I told you to fucking choke on me, not whatever bullshit you think that is."

She lets out a breath before her lips wrap their way around my tip. I groan as she sucks me all the way into her mouth. As she comes back up, her teeth scrape along my cock.

Sucking in a sharp breath, I slap her again.

"Stupid fucking whore! If your teeth scrape me again I will blow your brains out and fuck your dead cunt!"

Her whimpers turn into cries as she puts me back into her

mouth again. Her eye is already black from my hand and begins to swell as she continues to suck me further.

I grip her hair beyond the point of pain, feeling my dick jump in the whore's mouth as she screams around me.

I push her down, my dick working its way into her throat.

She chokes and gags around me, the feeling making my eyes roll into the back of my head.

My pace fastens as I force her head onto my cock.

Unable to hold back any longer, I push her head back down as spurt after spurt of cum jets down her throat.

After I'm fully sated, I throw her off me. I chuckle as I watch her continue to dry reach, barely able to suck in a breath after denying her for so long.

I tuck myself back into my pants. Walking over to a cage I keep in the corner of the room, I open the door and hold my arm out.

"In you go, dog. I have no more use for you tonight."

She doesn't bother acknowledging me, instead shakingly crawling over on her hands and knees. Once fully in the cage, she collapses in on herself.

I smile down at her, "I think you aren't going to take long to break. Shit, you are already halfway there."

I spit on her, snorting when her body jolts.

I'm sitting at my desk completing some paperwork when one of the lower members comes barging into my office. He is breathless as he rests his hands on his knees.

Instantly my temper flares, "What the fuck do you think your doing barging into my office without knocking?!"

I shoot up from my desk, causing both the lower Scorpion to jolt up right and the bitch in the cage to shriek. I don't bother paying the latter any attention. My focus stays purely on the man in front of me.

"I'm so sorry, Sir. Normally I wouldn't have barged in here like this but some of the guys have apprehended a man at the front gate wearing a Thunderbirds jacket."

My eyebrows instantly shoot up to my hairline. What the fuck do my brother's little punks want?

I nod my head, coming around my desk before ensuring my glock is still firmly in the back of my pants.

"Take me to him," I direct the Scorpion.

We walk through the compound, passing other members who nod at me, giving me the respect I deserve. I don't bother giving them even a hint of a greeting. They know their place.

After my brother took over The Thunderbirds he immediately began changing rules.

No more skin trade. Women were to be 'respected'. That the rules for their initiation were to be changed. Instead of being sexed in like was the tradition since the beginning of the MC, they were to do some stupid fucking strip dance.

A strip dance? I could have watched that shit for free.

If men are to go on missions and be jumped in, so should the women. After all, all these goodie two shoes want is equality.

Yet, Ren shut me down. As per usual.

Some of the other guys and I finally had enough.

Friend went against friend. Brother against brother as I got my revenge in the form of blood for what was ripped out from underneath me.

The last I knew, Ren believed I was dead until I stole his

daughter. It was a bit of a shock for him knowing that I was still alive.

Going out on my own and starting The Scorpions was my fuck you to my brother. Starting a club where men like me could be accepted. To earn money our way. To enjoy the depravity of life just like we were meant to.

The Scorpion leads me into one of the back rooms. Just like I expected of my men, the visitor is completely surrounded.

My eyebrows raise as I take in the man in front of me.

I can't help the chuckle that escapes past my lips.

"Out of all the people I expected to see in this room, you were the last person that came to my mind."

The visitor just shrugs their shoulders at me. Their posture reads nonchalant but I know better. It's just a mask. I wouldn't expect any different to come out of a man from under my brother's reign.

"I didn't think I would ever be here either, but I have information I think you would be interested to know."

I roll my eyes. These men always think they have something that I want. Information on drug imports, when missions are going to take place; it's always something.

Not once has there been information that I generally care about.

Yet every time, I listen. Normally these situations end with a bullet to the head.

But who knows. Today might just surprise me.

"Do tell. Make it worth what little time I have for you."

My voice is stern as I stare him down.

His eyes squint slightly, like he is trying to assess me. After a moment he raises his eyebrows before tilting his head.

"Scarlett's alive."

My laugh would put even the most sinister man to shame. The men around me laugh too.

My little whore of a niece, alive? What the fuck does this clown take me for? A fucking *fool*?

"Nice try. Come back when you have better information."

I go to turn but he stops me.

"I have proof."

I snap back towards the visitor, strutting towards him until I am right in his face.

"Do you think I am stupid? I beat that little bitch for days. Her life was worth nothing when you useless Thunderbirds pulled her from my cages."

Spit hits his face but he doesn't back down. I would be impressed if I wasn't so fucking irate.

He holds up his phone, nodding towards the device.

"Need anymore proof than this?"

My eyes widen in disbelief. Right there in front of me is my niece, only ten years older. Just like my mother, she is beautiful. But unlike her, she isn't six foot fucking under.

I snatch the phone from his hands as I zoom in on her face. She doesn't seem to realize the photo is being taken. Her smile is carefree as she looks at what looks like another one of the Thunderbirds senior members' sons. Figures she would be back in their clutches.

I grit my teeth, clicking my tongue as I squeeze the phone, the device cracking under my hold.

I throw the phone, unable to control my anger. A roar escapes me as rage all but consumes me.

It shouldn't surprise me that Ren was a sneaky little fuck and was able to hide his daughter for this long.

I don't focus on the way the men around me flinch away from my outburst. I guess they are just lucky that right now, my anger isn't aimed at them.

Looking back to the Thunderbirds scum in front of me, I pull my anger back in.

"Why are you giving me this information?"

He just shrugs his shoulders, "We both want the same thing. A man in power."

I scoff, "And what? You think you are the man for the job?"

He shrugs his shoulders yet again, the movement beginning to piss me off even further.

"I just don't want to see *her* in that position. She doesn't deserve it. She didn't work for it. I want her gone."

I snort, *me and you both.*

"This changes everything," I mutter to myself. Turning around, I begin to pace the room. I run over scenario after scenario in my head.

I can't let my brother win. His ideology of equal rights is bullshit and I refuse to have anything with a pussy between its legs in power.

I turn back to the man.

"She needs to die. This time for good." My word is final, as per usual and to my delight, the Thunderbird nods.

"Agreed."

An idea comes to my head at that moment.

"This time I think I want to have a bit more fun with her though. She's a beautiful girl now," A devilish smile comes over my features, "I bet her screams would be even more delicious as I ram my cock into her."

The men around me all hoot which only helps to completely eradicate the anger I felt earlier.

Excitement now fills the spot.

The possibilities are endless. She won't be as easy to break this time around.

Now, the little bitch is actually going to be useful for something.

I turn around and look at my men, giving my visitor my back.

"Who wants to go on a hunt, boys?"

The Scorpions all jeer around me, their cheers filling the space of the room.

I turn back around, "You are mine now, Bird."

He nods sealing both his and Scarlett's fate.

You are mine, little sparrow.

BOARDING P
NAME: SCARLETT SMIT
FROM:
TIME:
CLAS
SEAT:
President

ACKNOWLEDGMENTS

Wow, I can't believe I am here again, writing another one of these.

This life is insane.

Firstly, I have to give a big thank you to my readers and ARC readers. If it wasn't for every single one of you, I don't know if I would have had the push to write as quickly as I did. Seeing your reviews and messages (mainly those that involve me being yelled at) truly meant so much to me. I also apologise for another cliffhanger… or do I? (Laughs in evil author) Please apologise to your therapists for me. I will also be accepting voice notes at this time for you to vent your frustrations and undoubtedly share how much you despised that ending.

To Shannon. I couldn't have done this without you, again. You have given me so much confidence not only in myself as a human but as an author. From not only helping me when I am in the pits but celebrating alongside me in my wins. We are quite literally on opposite sides of the country, but you never fail to be there for me. I love and appreciate you so much.

To my betas, Pyro, Layna, Heather and Chanel. Thank you, thank you, thank you. Your words of encouragement have given me life. I have gone into this process with so much confidence from you guys and I will be forever thankful for each of you.

BOARDING P
NAME: SCARLETT SMIT
FROM:
TIME:
CLAS
SEAT:
President

ACKNOWLEDGMENTS

continued

To my editor, Callie. I cannot describe how thankful I am for you. Not only for loving this book so much but for coming along for this journey with me. I appreciate you! Your comments and words of encouragement have meant the absolute world.

To Jess and Dani, I love you both so much. Our nights on discord chatting and laughing are my absolute favourite. You are the best hype girls and I'm so thankful to call you both friends. And Jess, your love for Dazza is everything! You deserve the award for number one fan!

To my husband, Ryan. Thank you for standing by my side while I pursue this crazy dream of mine. You are the ultimate book boyfriend. The grumpy to my sunshine.

To my kids, I love you both so much. All of this is for you. I hope when you are both forty and I finally let you read this, you will be proud of me.

Now onto the next book that will no doubt have you sobbing into the bottom of a bottle of wine.

about
ALEXCIS

Alexcis Morris lives in a remote town in central Queensland, Australia. Having grown up around the region, she now resides on a farm with her husband, two daughters, 2 dogs and a bird named Errol.

She published her first novella in April 2024, after becoming inspired from a quote from the movie, Grease.

If you don't find Alexcis in her writing cave coming up with her next heartbreaking cliffhanger, you will find her either nose deep in her current read, camping or four-wheel driving. Wherever she is, some sort of adventure follows.

Follow her on:

♪ @alexcismorrisauthor

◎ @alexcismorrisauhtor

President
AMERICA 100
AMERICA 100
TES OF AMERICA
WE TRUST

GREASED

THE THUNDERBIRDS SERIES

BOARDING PASS
NAME: SCARLETT SMITH
FROM:
TIME:
CLASS:
SEAT:
President